Redemption Cove

Redemption Cove

David Calder

Thank you for reading my work. My books can be obtained either through my website, David Calder Books, or online book retailers.

This is fiction. Names, characters, places, and incidents are either products of my imagination or are used fictitiously. Resemblance to actual persons, living or dead, businesses, companies, events or locales is entirely coincidental.

"He who lives in harmony with himself lives in harmony with the universe."
  — Marcus Aurelius - The Philosopher Emperor - 121-180 CE

For Immensely, out of a contingent life.

ONE

Canadian Northern Woods
Summer 2018

I gasped in a breath, ready to scream out in anger and frustration as my last act on earth. A giant hand cut it off. A deep voice said, "Shhhhhh be quiet. Let go the handgun."

I turned my head. Stared in amazement at my benefactor. He freed my mouth and said, "Where are you hurt?"

"Buckshot. My right leg ah... ow!"

He probed. "You've cut an artery. Have to stop the bleeding. Gimme your shirt."

I lifted my arms feebly. He wrenched it off over my head.

"You're lucky I heard shots," he said as he shredded the shirt like paper. He tied a strip that cut into the flesh just above my wounded knee. "SITREP. How many?" he demanded.

"Two," I gasped out. "They split up."

He was swiveling his head, weighing up options.

The leg numbed, clearing my head. Our options seemed few. The other side of the stream was brightly lit. We'd be framed in the sunlight and easy targets. I'd never make it up the gravel road. The quagmire downstream was out of the question.

The big man dragged me a few yards behind the bole of a tree. I slumped where I could peer around it. He quietly slid back the action and eased a round into the handgun. "This thing accurate?"

"Used to be."

"We wait."

TWO

N.E. 20th Street, Bellevue, Washington
The previous December 21st

As I pushed out through the front entrance of Andy's tavern, I was flat disgusted. The Broncos had powered to a Thursday Night Football 41-33 win on the strength of Brock Osweiler's arm. He'd been up and down so much all season; I'd had a hundred bucks on the Colts, but only made half of that back on the pool table. At least my beloved Seahawks were still in the playoff race. Just.

I hollered back, "Sor-ry," at the woman whose foot I'd stumbled over and the man whose drink I'd spilled lurching to the door, got a steady stance on the sidewalk and worked at getting my keys out of my slacks.

Damn things went in there easy enough.

Then I noticed an inch or more of sneaky snow around my shoes. Unbelievable. Streets had been clean when I went in. This was 'rain-town,' dammit. Though that's mainly an exaggeration to discourage the other half of California from moving north.

The keys came out. I pushed off in the direction of my V8 Explorer parked at the curb, and with some adjustments, arrived at the driver's door. Looked up and down the street. The air had a bite and the sodium-vapor street-lamps hovered above the parked cars like great yellow snow-globes. No cops anyway.

I got the windshield swept clear, pulled out into the already quite-pronounced ruts, and headed for the 520 and the floating bridge. As the big Ford bounced across the hollow where 148th crossed 20th, Overlake Mall was just a looming mass in the whiteout.

I was wishing it was a couple of hours ago. She'd have been out showing a house. I'da been home free. I was putting off thinking about the fight I had coming, though it was going to be bad, that was for damn certain.

I fed 'Greetings from Asbury Park' into the CD slot and cranked the volume. Bruce and I were belting out the Go-Kart Mozart number when the rear end of a crabbed-out Sound Transit bus bulged out of the murk.

I wrenched the steering wheel. Too much.

My truck slid sideways onto the wrong side of the road, spraying snow from skidding wheels, still doing better than the speed limit.

A Toyota 4X4, all blunt nose and chrome grille, was suddenly right there. Aimed at my door.

The driver's window exploded into my face. The impact thumped me sideways.

There was the sweet smell of talcum powder and a sense of bones breaking low down on my left side. No pain. Just a body slam and a sickening sense of my body losing its structure.

It's funny what the mind does. I remembered I'd just got new tires.

In the instant before everything went blank, I knew I was in a whole new level of trouble.

THREE

Sisters of the Cross Hospital, Bellevue, Washington
December 25th

Life came and went over the next few days. It'd be light for one brief period amid a bustle of drip changing and vital sign checking, then dark the next time I woke.

On the afternoon of the day I finally became fully conscious, a broad-faced, sandy-haired man a little younger than me - which made him mid-thirties - arrived at my bedside. A Formica badge on his white coat said he was, 'Doctor Jens Jorgensen - Consulting Surgeon.' He gave his best clinical smile.

"Mister Adams. How you feeling?"

I gave a nod that jarred every nerve. Earlier a nurse had touched my scabby face while adjusting an oxygen tube and that had hurt too. "Just some minor glass cuts," she'd said. "You'll be fine."

I feel anything but.

Jorgenson said, "We've kept you sedated to reduce post-surgical shock. Are you able to talk do you think?"

When I didn't speak, he unclipped a pen from a clipboard. "Good let's do that then."

He tilted his head whenever he asked a question. It irritated the hell out of me.

"Do you know what day it is?" Tilt. "Can you pinpoint the pain?" Tilt. "Can you move your left foot?" Tilt. It was a goddamn wonder Doctor Jens bloody Jorgensen didn't break his neck.

I gave one-word answers. He made short notes. When he'd hung up the clipboard he said, "Mister Adams. Can I call you ah, Benjamin?"

People make that mistake with my name all the time. I don't correct them anymore. "Ben."

"Ah Ben. Well there's the, ah... proverbial good news and bad."

I tensed myself and discovered I shouldn't do that either.

He said, "You've had a lot of surgery but you've come through it well considering. Your left femur was badly broken. We inserted..."

"We?"

"The hospital here."

He was oblivious to how dehumanizing that was.

"We put in a rod. There are screws coming out of your thigh muscle. We'll make adjustments later to get the contour and length right. You should be just fine there." He paused and frowned. "Ah your hip however, ah pelvis really, is another matter."

Ice water pooled in my stomach.

"The bone around your femur socket was pretty much a scrambled-up jigsaw puzzle. We did the best we could."

I craned anxiously down the bed.

He pushed me gently back down. "You have a body cast, Ben. And a catheter and colostomy bag. It'll be awhile before you can tolerate, ah, any strain down there."

Oh wonderful. Can't even take a crap.

"But I should be okay, right?"

He drew a long deep breath. "Well yes. Should be. But the hip joint is a painful area. Ultimately, it's up to you. What you can tolerate. How hard you're prepared to push yourself."

"And... if I can't?"

He made a face and a little sideways motion with his head.

The ice water flooded my chest.

He steepled his fingers. Tapped the tips on his chin. "Ben there's something else.

I'm already in shit up to my armpits. What more can there be?

"Well ah, I don't know you, your personal situation, but ah your blood tests on admission registered well over the alcohol limit."

I looked away.

"Also ah, we got your details from your wallet." He motioned toward a shelf by the bed.

Can they do that? I suppose they can do anything.

"Eileen Adams, we assumed that's your wife? She hasn't returned our calls, but I believe there's a parcel for you at the nurses' station."

My left hand curled reflexively around the gold band that represented so many broken promises. It cut into my flesh. A lonely hopelessness I hadn't felt before, even at home when I was a kid, overcame me.

"Perhaps you could use a counselor," Jorgensen was saying. "I can leave you a few names." He seemed to make a decision. "There is one other bit of help I can give you."

I can use all I can get.

"Bellevue PD's requested a toxicology report. As your doctor for now I'm going to refuse to release it. No one else was injured in the crash. I suggest you simply refuse to speak to them. Hopefully it will end there."

"Thank you."

"Well then, I'd better get on with my rounds. I'll pop by in a few days to see how you're doing. You're in good hands." He headed jauntily for the nurses' station, but turned.

"Oh, and Merry Christmas," he said brightly.

Speak for yourself.

The quiz session exhausted me. I alternately dozed fitfully and fretted about Eileen's parcel. It was a bad sign. Things had been a bit more strained than usual recently, but were they that bad?

Eileen and I had just sort of... happened. We met at the big software company on the east side of Bellevue when I was project-lead on the new desktop, and she was temping while finished her finance degree at U Dub. Total opposites. Me the awkward geek introvert, she friendly and kind with that great ability to turn every event into a party. But somehow it worked.

We were working the Las Vegas Comdex show together in '96, and maybe it was that euphoric sense we were changing the world. I don't know. We bought a license just as the courthouse was closing and found a chapel that provided witnesses.

Mike and Tracey came along quickly while times were good. They were hardly toddlers, before our arguments became shouting matches. She'd go sulk in the bedroom. I'd take off to a bar. When the kids left for colleges just this past fall, we had nothing left in common. That had to be it.

Stop kidding yourself man. There's been only one track on that stuck record for years. Her yelling about your drinking and lying, and you defending the indefensible.

I'd sure have some making up to do after this little performance.

God I could use a beer!

FOUR

Sisters of the Cross Hospital
December 27th

Days rolled by. No Eileen. Whatever was in that nagging parcel couldn't be good. I'd almost plucked up the courage to ask for it, when a very welcome visitor walked into the ward.

Russell Langwell. Mid-30s ex-Californian surfer, slightly spreading waistline, tousled blond hair receding at the temples. We'd joined MagnaTECH as coders around the same time, three or so years earlier. Now he was development director, my boss, and my friend. He and Jill had seen me in the depths and I'd slept off many a bender on their couch. I'd always been able to count on Russ. I was damn glad to see him.

He wore what passed for a uniform in the Seattle software industry. Jeans, loafers, a pinstriped poplin dress shirt unbuttoned at the collar, and in a nod to the day's weather, a windbreaker shiny-wet at the shoulders.

"Ben," he said, hooking the jacket on the end of the bed. "How you doing man, how you feeling?"

"About how I look, Russ. Good to see you."

"Yeah yeah. I tried to get in sooner, but things are nuts with being short-handed."

Guilt infused me. "Jeez I'm sorry Russ. Look I'll be back on board in a month or so."

"Don't worry about it man."

He looked away, too quickly, midway through the platitude. Made a production out of pulling around a chair. When our eyes

7

met again, his trademark grin seemed strained.

"Yeah well, main thing is you got to get yourself healthy. If there's anything Jill and I can do, uh... personally, you only have to ask, you know that."

My bull-shit detector screeched.

It couldn't be. Not Russ.

He noticed and squirmed. "Aw man I suck at this. I'm sorry Ben. You're being canned."

"What?"

"Yeah, what with the drinking and the DUI..."

"I don't have a DUI."

"Glad to hear it, man. Just Eileen said..."

"Eileen? How the hell..."

"I called her..."

"You called my wife and not me?

He looked chagrined while my eyes bored into him.

"Russell you can't do this!"

"I'm sorry man I got no choice. Word from up top."

"But I'm entitled to notice, severance..."

"They won't do it. They figure they got enough for cause, with your lateness, the booze-breath. Your way over your leave allowance, and now this, but..."

But? But what! Their damn market-leading financial program is practically all my work. How can they do this?

A white rage came. "You fuckers!"

Russell jolted back. "Hey, hey I'm trying to get to the good part, just wait..."

"You asshole! You use me up and now you have your damn software upgrade you crap on me like this? When I've got nothing?"

Russell stood, face flaming, and jabbed a finger for emphasis. "Wait a minute. We didn't put you in here. You did this to yourself you drunken ass. You need to listen..."

"Just get the fuck out. Get..." I completely ran out of air.

A nurse rushed up to Russ. "Sir, sir, you can't do this. We have patients..."

"You're an ungrateful jerk, Ben. Now if you'll just damn well listen..."

I gasped out, "Get the fuck out. Just..." White spots shimmered in my vision.

Russell's arms flew wide. "Ah fuck what's the use!" The nurse had him firmly by the elbow, pulling him away. He grabbed the windbreaker. "I'm going! I'm going!" echoed around the ward.

My midsection was hell-fire. A nurse put an oxygen mask over my face. Another did something at my drip. The pain of a million raw nerve endings eased away into nothingness.

When I awoke that evening, I gritted my teeth and punched the call button. The parcel turned out to be a bulky manila envelope sealed with a lot of tape. I had a nurse slit open the flap end. A sheaf of papers, a few other loose items, and a typed letter tumbled out on the bed-cover.

> Ben;
> I'm sorry you're hurt. When the hospital called I wasn't surprised, just hollow. They've left messages so I know you came through surgery okay. This will hurt too, and I'm sorry for that as well, but it's necessary.
> For a long time I've tried to keep something of us together, but I've been fooling myself. You're empty and there's nothing of you to care for any longer. I'm done with you staggering in night after night, held together only by your damn job. I don't know if there's treatment for what you have. I hope so.
> I've had the legal papers for awhile, thinking things through. This has just brought things to a head. I'm moving to Denver to be nearer the children. I've told them what's going on. They don't hate you. Like me, they just don't know you anymore.
> I've listed the townhouse. I'll box up your things and get a storage unit at that U-Haul place down on 34th. Please sign the papers. Don't make this harder than it has to be. The offer's fair and we had something once. You were a better person once. I hope you find that again.
> Goodbye.

The loose stuff was my American and Canadian passports, handgun carry-permit, and some check and bank books. There were bank and 401K and IRA statements and the truck pink slip. Also a set of divorce papers with one of those impressive legal letterheads in antique script.

I went right to the settlement part. Eileen wanted her BMW, most of the money in our bank accounts, and the townhouse in Magnolia. She'd pay all the bills and the kids' tuition from then on. There'd be no alimony.

I'd get my five-year-old V8 Explorer—meaning it was probably salvageable—plus $25,000 on top of the few grand in my personal bank account. Also my 401K and IRA accounts, small as they were, and the MagnaTECH stock options that had been part of my salary package. Russell obviously hadn't told her I'd been fired and they were worthless. On the other hand, she'd be lucky to clear fifty-grand from the townhouse after paying off the home equity loan.

She was right. It was fair. But fair or not, I still felt like trash someone had kicked down a back alley. I lay back with an arm over my eyes to shut out the light and hide the tears and asked myself over and over.

How did everything go so fucking wrong?

The next day a ringing telephone woke me. It seemed maybe noon. The sky beyond the windows was a startling blue. The ward was otherwise quiet except for an orderly, dishing meals from a trolley. The telephone stopped and started again. A nurse came and handed me a handset from a bedside phone I hadn't known was there.

"Dad?" The voice was female and distant.

"Tracey?"

"Yeah dad, it's me."

"Are you here? Home?"

"No, I'm in Breckenridge. Mom called the dorm in Boulder and they found me. There's no mobile reception up here."

"Oh."

Tracey is into saving the planet in a big way, and had chosen U Colorado at Boulder as much for its Environmental Science program, as to escape the tension at home. She said something garbled by static.

"What?"

"I said Merry Christmas."

"Thanks sweetheart"

"I'm sorry I couldn't call sooner."

I've been here five days. She couldn't make one damn phone-call?

"It's okay, little one. Merry Christmas to you too."

"Dad don't call me that! I'm not little anymore!"

After the awkward silence I asked, "Have you heard from Mike?"

"I think he's in Amsterdam with friends. You can probably get him through Syracuse University. They have a dorm there."

"Did mom tell you...?"

"Yeah she did. Hey, I gotta go. It's getting late and we want to hit the slopes again."

"I…"

"Yeah yeah. I hope you are fine dad, I really do, it's just…"

"Well, have a great time there."

"Thanks. Bye."

I held onto the receiver for a few more moments, then dropped in on the bed.

The same night, I had the nurse bring me a pen, signed over the townhouse and initialed all the banking authorities, and asked her to have someone mail them for me.

There's no point in holding her hostage.

The divorce papers went back in the envelope. I needed time to adjust.

FIVE

Sisters of the Cross Hospital
January

So everything was peachy, except my wife had left me, my son and I weren't speaking, and my daughter and I had nothing to say to each other. I'd lost my home, my family, my job. Maybe even the use of my legs. Yeah well sometimes self-pity's all you got, you know?

My days had settled into a monotony. I felt I was watching my life in a tableau rather than actually living it. Around me were people disfigured or with life-threatening injuries - in more pain than I could imagine - yet the misery barely touched me. I was numb with my own loss and sorrow.

Then early on New Year's morning I woke to a beeping alarm. Down the ward a nurse ran to a bedside yelling, "Crash trolley! Could we have the crash trolley down here please?" I heard someone counting compressions, and several times, "Clear!" followed by a thud. Then it all trailed away to whispers, before a precise time was spoken out loud, and curtains were pulled around the bed.

That had been a young man, husband to a young wife, father to a curly-haired toddler. He'd been on his way home from a drugstore swinging a carrier bag of baby formula, when a car careered up on the crosswalk. New Years' Eve he'd been holding his baby and laughing with his wife. I'd envied their happiness with each other, their youth and, especially, their future.

As I lay hating myself, with the sky growing incandescent

outside, something shifted in my head. I vowed with all my heart to leave the booze alone and straighten up my act. And no matter what it took, I would I learn to walk again.

Not just that. I will run.

The body-cast came off around the middle of January. Every movement hurt, my legs were terribly wasted and the left one had developed a stubborn contrariness when I tried to move it.

"Nerve confusion," said Doctor Jorgenson. "Just keep working on it."

Easy for him.

"No, this is good Ben," he said. "The pain tells us the sciatic nerve is fine."

"If it's that good a thing, Doc," I said, icy beads running down my temples and ribcage, "You try it some time."

I rediscovered reading. They had a library cart like in the old prison movies. The shuffling librarian even looked like an old lifer. The last novel I remembered engrossing me had been Mario Puzo's 'The Godfather.' His 'The Last Don' hooked me too. Maybe I'm a closet gangster. Anything would beat a failed husband and father and an unemployed drunk.

I also watched a lot of PBS. Cooking shows, since cooking is an enduring love. And sports. I cheered myself hoarse as NFL miracle-man Nick Foles outclassed Tom Brady and led the underdog Eagles to a stunning 41-33 victory over the Patriots.

Then in the middle of after-game celebrations. Doctor Jorgensen brought a couple of business-suited colleagues to my evening bedside. They so polite you'd have thought they were touting for business, which they were in a way.

One said, "Mr. Adams, as you may know, Sisters of the Cross, is a surgical teaching hospital. Extended ah, rehabilitation isn't something we do here."

"Is this about cost, payment...?"

"Oh no, there's absolutely no problem there. We'd like to transfer you to our Issaquah campus to continue helping you get well."

"Uh well, okay."

So, come Monday morning I was parked downstairs in a wheelchair in a waiting room, with my worldly possessions on my knee in a paper bag smaller than an airline carry-on, waiting for a shuttle bus.

I was also wondering what was different, until I realized I hadn't seen, or even thought about, my mobile phone since the accident.

The previous me would have been tapping on it all day long.
Maybe change WAS possible.

The Issaquah Plateau is in the Cascades foothills, east of Bellevue-Redmond, overlooking gorgeous Lake Sammamish. A toney suburb, where a grid of Douglas Fir-overhung lanes are flanked by the beyond-impressive homes of some of Seattle's legion of tech zillionaires. The Pines Rehabilitation Facility, smack in the heart of that, is a collection of red-brick bungalows in a half circle around a small lake. The rehabilitation part centers on an aircraft hangar-sized gymnasium. Administration operates out of a U-shaped and ivy-clad, red brick building that encloses a glass-roofed atrium the size on average back yard.

On sight it crossed my mind again who was paying for all this. But they'd said my Insurance was good, though I couldn't remember paying a single premium, and that was good enough for me.

My bungalow had a motorized bed and a wall-mounted flat-screen TV in the main room, a nook for coffee making, and a separate bathroom and shower. Except for the waist height handrail circling the walls, it might have been a 4-star hotel suite.

A very brisk and efficient nurse evaluated me, which in addition to the expected medical stuff, involved a lot of painful pushing, pulling and prodding. Later, after a room-served dinner that wasn't half bad, I lay on my high-tech bed remembering the young man in the trauma ward and the promise I'd made myself.

I will walk. I will make a life worth living again.

Despite my bravado, it was hard to shake the feeling I was a lost soul.

Next morning at the Pines dawned brightly, scented pleasantly by the smell of wetland and fir needles. Somewhere a woodpecker rap-rap-rapped for its breakfast. Nuthatches yanked in the tree beside my picture window. Squirrels foraged boldly along the edges of the landscaped pathways.

Breakfast arrived accompanied with a little plastic cup of pre-emptive painkillers. The person bringing it told me someone would be along to collect me around nine. Expecting interrogation, I gritted myself in full resistance mode, but instead of a burly orderly, it was an attractive African-American woman, 30s, impeccably groomed in a simple cream dress, navy heels that accentuated her shapely legs, and a navy jacket with an unimpressive number of medical badges.

She greeted me breezily. "Good morning Mr. Adams. May I call you Ben?"

Knock yourself out.

"How about we take a stroll?"

Roll.

"Don't I have treatment this morning?"

She laughed throatily. "Oh hush. Your jailhouse tan could use some rays."

I'm naturally dark. Eastern European genes. But right then I was rather pallid, after seven weeks indoors.

The Pines had wheelchairs the way a country club has carts. They almost needed traffic lights. The woman helped me into one and we headed along a path toward the lake shore. Once in motion she said gaily, "So tell me about you!"

"What's to tell?" I kept my voice nonchalant. "I had an accident. Now I'm here."

"Car accident."

She knows more than she's letting on.

"That's right."

At the junction of paths by the shore was a bench seat. She arranged the wheelchair beside one end and sat, radiating professional concern. She reminded me of actress-singer Diahann Carroll. A wisp of fine black hair had escaped her French knot and trailed behind one of her elegant teardrop earrings. A diamond encrusted with amethysts, which threw off slivers of light with every movement of her head. They didn't seem like standard nursing accoutrements.

Looking at me with a discomforting directness, she asked, "Why did you have your accident Ben?"

"You mean 'how' right? And what's it matter now?"

"No. I meant why. And everything matters. We treat the whole person here."

"If you don't mind, I'd rather..."

"Save it for the therapists? You have. I'm Doctor Nadine Lawler, Director of Rehabilitation Services. I've read your file, but there are a few gaps."

I fidgeted with the wheelchair's armrest.

"It says you were driving too fast in snow. That's odd considering. I'd have thought you'd know better. Seattle isn't Vancouver, but snow is still snow."

The inside knowledge surprised me. "How do you know...?"

"As I said, we treat the whole person. It's my business to know."

The lake was lovely and deeper than I'd expected. Two swans, swimming parallel to the beach, veered away before they got too close.

I can identify with that.

"It also says you were drunk, though there's no blood level recorded. Are you an alcoholic, Ben?"

"I haven't had a drink in weeks."

Not even a twitch of a smile.

"Is that what you think about? Getting out of here and drinking yourself leg-less?"

It's more than crossed my mind.

"I'm asking because this treatment will be very difficult. Your body has to relearn things it no longer knows how to do. That's painful. I'm not going to kid you."

The implication that I didn't have the guts touched a nerve.

"Look Doctor is this helpful for you? Because it sure as hell isn't for me! I thought I was here for physical rehab! And who are you to judge me, anyway?"

She smiled a slow smile. "You're fighting back. That's good. Hold on to that. It's your sense of who you are."

I was too angry to accept the olive branch, which didn't hang in the air long, anyway.

"Good. Shall we get started?"

Knock yourself out.

SIX

The Pines Rehabilitation Facility, Issaquah, Washington
February 6th

I was delivered into the clutches of an athletic-looking Englishman named Kim McKay, and his slim red-headed assistant with 'Brenda' on her badge. They pushed me deeper into a cavernous and state-of-the-art equipped gymnasium.

We stopped at an equipment cluster that was parts crane, trapeze, treadmill, and Isoflex machine, with free weights and a set of gymnastic parallel bars thrown in. They fitted me into a harness studded with sensors and I began my rehab regime.

The machine ingeniously neutralized my weight and for the first time since the crash I could exercise my legs with relative ease. But nothing could have prepared me for the mass of fire that that grew in intensity inside my lower torso. Still, we persevered as long as I could take it, which initially wasn't much time at all.

This became my life, five days a week, two sessions a day, despite numerous setbacks due to twists and strain as well as a high degree of frustration at what seemed to me to be snail's-pace progress.

After about three weeks of this, I had my first session in treating the rest of me, which the good doctor had alluded to that first day down by the lake.

An orderly collected me as usual on a Monday morning, but instead of the gym, he wheeled me along a winding path to the administration building. I was left alone in a spacious cedar-lined office, gazing out through an expanse of glass into the garden. A young blue jay hopped and pecked at the edge of a path.

Doctor Lawler walked in smiling and carrying two frothy coffees. She put one in front of me and went to her seat behind a redwood desk which wouldn't have looked out of place in the Oval Office.

I was definitely not in the mood to be badgered and stared hard out through the glass. The jay had caught an earthworm and was straining backwards, trying to work the length of it out of the ground without breaking it in half.

The doctor asked a question and I looked back at her. That same strand of hair was loose behind her ear again. I imagined it was in the book of shrink tricks under 'How to Seem Approachable.' I tried to be cordial.

"No, I haven't been back to Vancouver for years."

"Tell me about that."

"What's to say? I left right after college and I've been here ever since."

"A hundred twenty miles and you haven't been back, even for a weekend?"

I tried to keep the irritation out of my shrug. *Why can't she just stick to how my workouts are going?*

"And your family?"

"Sister in Toronto. Brother up north. In the family house, I think." *Why did I tell her that? I give an inch she'd going to take a mile.*

"Are you close?"

"Not very. Not at all really. Why is...?"

She did some tension-diffusing things with her hands and then folded them disarmingly under her chin. I wasn't buying a bit of it.

"Then tell me your interests. C'mon. What do you like doing?"

"Cooking. TV sports. Work."

"Outdoors stuff?"

"Not too much."

She looked down at some notes and I thought I'd won the exchange. My attention swung back to the blue jay. He'd won the battle with the worm, but now the foraging squirrel had gotten too close. The bird flared into flight, beak working silently.

That's double-glazing for you.

"Why did your wife leave you Ben?" Doctor Lawler said.

I could feel my cheeks burning. "Are you married Nadine?"

"Yes."

"Long?"

"Ten years or so."

"Kids?"

"No."

"Hubbie can't get it up?"

Her face flared scarlet. Her lips went thin. I pressed.

"When did you two last do it, Nadine?" I elongated the name into a sneer like Louis Gossett, Jr. in 'An Officer and a Gentleman.' "And where do you get a qualification in nosiness anyway?"

"Boston University, four years of Medical School, a Cervical Surgery internship, then eight years in Psychiatry. Where did you get the qualification in being an ass?"

"Crappy childhood. Simon Fraser U computer science. School of hard knocks," I fired back.

I waited for the snappy retort, instead she said quietly, "My husband and I have a truly wonderful relationship thank you very much, and I lost a child. At six. In an auto accident in our driveway. June thirteen two years ago."

I had never felt so ashamed in my life.

"So how about you cut out the horse shit,' she said, 'I'm trying to help you here."

"I can take care of myself."

She leaned forward, forearms on the desk. "No sir, I don't think you can. And this isn't about me. I'm not the one fighting for whatever it is you call a life, you are. I'm not the one who needs every bit of help he can get. You are. I'm not the one in a medical facility who thinks not a single soul in the world gives a rat's. Okay, so I was fishing for a reaction and I got one. What say we call it even and get past it?"

I made a slight motion with my head. She sat back. After a few seconds she said, "Tell me about the bad childhood. Or was that a wisecrack too?"

"I don't know that it's worth dredging up."

She waited. I gave in.

"Okay. Immigrant parents, Russian."

"Adams?"

"Adamov. My mother said they got out of Moscow on papers for Israel in the 60s. Except only my father was Jewish, so they picked Canada instead. I guess Adams was more acceptable with the cold war and all. And it's Ben-yah-min with a 'y'."

"Poor?"

"Not at all. My father had a precious metals business. We were quite well-off, I think. Nice house in a good part of West Van. Money wasn't a problem."

"Then what was?"

"Booze and violence."

"So, not a happy household?"

"Hell-hole. A kid has no defense except maybe curl up in a ball and wait until it's over."

"Was he always that way?"

"Seems that way now."

"He's gone I assume?"

"Both of them. Cirrhosis with my father. Mother had TB when she was a little kid, emphysema later. I'd probably have gone back for her funeral but I didn't know about it for months."

She nodded and the sadness in her eyes looked genuine. "Can you think of anything good he gave you?'

I shrugged.

"Anything at all?"

"Chess maybe?"

"Oh?"

"He learned in the old country under a grand master. Started teaching me when I was about six or seven. By the time I hit ten, I was winning adult tournaments. But... well let's just say by the time I got to sixteen I was too busy just surviving."

"Do you still play?"

"Not in a long time."

"I'm sorry."

In the silence that followed, I remembered a nagging question. "Doctor?"

"Please call me Nadine."

"Okay. Nadine who's paying for all this?"

"It's covered under the COBRA provision of your work medical insurance I believe."

"But I'm not employed anymore."

"That's what COBRA's for. You get to keep your insurance and make the payments yourself."

"But I've made no payments."

She held up a palm. "The business side's not my forte, Ben. You'll have to ask administration." Before I could respond, she threw me a curve. "Ben, what does getting out of here, actually look like to you? In your head I mean."

"I uh... don't know."

The blue jay was back. There was no sign of the squirrel.

"No seriously Ben. No job. Nowhere to live. What will you do?"

"I have absolutely no idea."

SEVEN

The Pines
February

Nadine Lawler's last question plagued me.

What exactly would I do? Where could I go? Was there anything I was good at that didn't destroy me? Or the people around me?

I was a good software coder. I knew that much. Organized. Innovative. Meticulous. But that life had helped ruin my marriage, along with any real connection with my kids. And for all that success, who did I have in the way of friends, apart from Russell? And look what had happened there!

How else could I make a living? The cash in the bank wouldn't last long. There was no doubt I had to change the way I lived. Or more accurately, actually live, rather than just exist as before. And I couldn't do that without being fit and well. It gave me a goal. I set about achieving it with a bloody-minded determination.

By the end of February, I wanted out of the wheelchair. I could get around my bungalow perfectly well with the help of the railings inside the little bungalow. But when I asked for crutches, they said it was too soon. Not to rush it.

Next time I was at the gym I asked Brenda to help me over to a set of parallel bars. Balancing only, I squatted, and then forced myself upright with my legs. Then I did it again. The pain was breath-taking, but it got me what I wanted. The next morning an orderly helped me across the quad on my new crutches. It was the last time I needed that kind of help.

My new mobility opened the floodgates of recovery for me. The emphasis of the therapy program changed right away from strength exercises to mobility skills. Within ten days I was down to one crutch, and it wasn't long after that before I could cope with just a cane.

I'd have to keep working at it, but that was the moment I knew I was well on the road to recovery.

Baseball season, a minor passion, started in early April,

I tried to catch as many televised Seattle Mariners games as I could. The last Wednesday afternoon in April I was sprawled on my bed watching the rubber game of a three-game set against the White Sox in Chicago. King Felix Hernandez was on the mound with the score 2-1 M's after the third, when Nadine Lawler appeared in my doorway.

She was holding some paperwork and looked serious, but couldn't resist one of her ice-breaking wisecracks. "Is this the secret plan for the rest of your life? Watching sports?"

I laughed. "No. Just baseball."

"Well you'll need to find another place to do that I'm afraid."

She offered me a business letter. Before I'd scanned it, she said, "I'm sorry Ben. That's from your insurance company. Your way past your regular cover. They are pulling the plug at month-end."

I killed the TV. "That's Sunday!"

"Don't panic. We don't dump people on the street. You're good for a few more days yet. But I wanted you to know right away, so you can think about what you'll do."

That damn question again.

What indeed? I had no home. No job. No wife or family, or any friends for that matter. Most everything I owned was in a lockup in Magnolia. I hadn't even opened a single piece of mail since Eileen's parcel. Just hadn't had the heart for it."

"No seriously. What do you think you'll do?"

"I might go up north for awhile." That surprised me, coming right out of left field.

She beamed. "That might be good. How will you get there?"

"I think, uh, I have a truck somewhere."

"Your insurance will know about that. We can follow up if you like."

"Please."

I caught the last out of the ninth. Though Hernandez was far from the fire-breathing dragon of old, he at least beat the Sox comfortably, 4-3. I wondered if my prospects were as promising.

By the next mid-afternoon, the Pines' front office had tracked down my truck at Upshaw's Body & Paint, 'Your One Stop Shop,' in the Midlakes district east of the 405. I paid the cabdriver with the last twenty in my wallet and limped inside.

When I asked for whoever was in charge, a young Hispanic man sanding down a fender, yelled out back, "Jerry! Someone to see ya!"

This was a gray-haired, pear shaped man with a considerable double chin, who cheered up considerably when I told him why I was there.

"Oh yeah yeah. Be good to get that outta here. Been a long time."

When he backed the Explorer out for inspection, I was amazed how good it looked, considering how hurt I'd been. The body and paintwork were like new. Even the inside was immaculate.

"I remember when it came in," he said, pulling a wipe rag from the back of his overalls and dealing with a tiny grease mark by the mirror. "Soft panel stuff mostly. Frame's tough in these things. Henry still builds them good."

"So can I...?"

"Sure thing. Just the co-pay and you're good to go."

"Sorry?"

"Your part of the repairs? $750?"

"Oh right." I felt for my wallet.

"No credit cards and only certified checks,' he added. "Seven ee-leven next door has an ATM but."

I was punching in the maximum, $1000, when I thought I'd better check the balance first and cancelled. A moment later, I was staring at a printout that said I had $566,000 and change in the account.

Impossible!

I counted the zeros. No mistake. I studied the card. Right account.

Must be a bank screw-up. Or escrow money from the townhouse maybe? No that'd be way less unless the real estate market has taken off while I'd been out of circulation. Has to be the bank. I've read about a few of these SNAFUs on the net. Sheesh.

I decided to worry about it later and went back to pay Jerry.

"She'll be good as new," he said as I pulled my walking stick in after me and tested my ability to use the pedals.

Thank God it's not a stick-shift.

Heading east in a drizzle, the Explorer felt safe and solid. My hip also seemed to be working fine. My concern about the looming long drive north abated.

Then I braked hard at a light and my mobile phone solved a mystery by tumbling out from under the seat. I plugged it in to charge. Just past Redmond it beeped and told me I had 58 messages. I pulled over and thumbed through a few, then hit 'Delete All.'

What the hell difference could any of them possibly make now?

I nosed back into traffic and headed on toward the cloud-wreathed plateau.

EIGHT

The Pines
April 26th

Back in my bungalow, I sat on the bed with my legs up and began sorting through the mail I'd accumulated and never opened.

Seeing bank statements reminded me to make a call about the bogus balance. But why not dream awhile longer? Eileen and I had always been, I guess, comfortable, but that kind of screw-you money had always been just a fantasy.

I recognized Mike and Tracey's handwriting on a couple of envelopes. Another had what looked like Russell's untidy scrawl. Twisting the knife, I assumed.

I was opening the first kid's envelope when Nadine's voice from the doorway said, "Find what you're looking for?"

"Just starting."

"I saw you drive in." She took a step inside and leaned against the door-jamb. "Do you have some time?"

"Sure. Come on in. Can I get you a coffee?"

She shook her head. Sat down and crossed those shapely legs, said, "You know we have maybe 80 patients pass through here each year?"

"That's a lot."

She nodded. "We have a good reputation. About half are spinal victims. Know what's the number one cause of spinal trauma?"

I shook my head.

"Motorcycles. We get dozens of bike victims here."

She wasn't there about motorbikes. I didn't respond, just

25

listened.

"Know what it's like to tell a guy in a back-frame who's wondering why he can't feel his feet, he'll never walk again?"

"Awful I imagine."

"Worse than that. They're usually kids in the rage of youth and they're drinking and partying, and you have to tell them it's all gone. They won't even be able to wipe their own ass."

I kept my body language very quiet.

"So. you know what you treasure? The ones who get truly well. Some recover physically, but stay mental cripples. Others get well head-wise and never get out of a wheelchair." She paused, then asked quietly, "Which one will you be Ben?"

"I can walk. I think I'm over the physical hump. And I want to get my life back now."

"What about your mental hump?"

"That's Greek to me."

"No, it's not."

"Sorry?"

"You are heading out of here to go... where? You talk about getting your life back. What life is that exactly?"

"I'll find a place, get a job."

"I'm sorry but you don't have a clue. How the hell will you survive, let alone thrive, back in the world that put you here?"

"What's it to you?"

"I care about you as a person. I think in some ways you're a savant. Enormously good at certain things, I'm sure, but with no sense of belonging, and hollow because your life isn't grounded in anything."

"Are you suggesting I get religion?"

She shook her head emphatically. "My experience is that religion gets you or it's just a different kind of crutch. That's not what I mean. You need to heal your life Ben."

"And just how do I do that? You seem to be the expert!"

Nadine uncrossed and crossed her legs again, forehead furrowed.

"You'll need to find that out for yourself. You were happy once, and then you became unhappy. Everything you learned after that was about surviving. Being a functioning drunk was part of it. But if you don't go back and find the place where you first became broken, and heal that Ben, you'll end up in exactly the same state again."

"They say you can't ever go back."

"That's bullshit. Except for the body aging, life is actually timeless. It's our perception of us that changes. We cubbyhole ourselves."

She leaned forward, emphasizing with her hands. "You've been escaping for a long time. Your father was a brute and all you had to defend yourself with was your smarts. I bet you were a whiz in college, right?"

"I had a scholarship, had to maintain it."

"Then you came down here as soon as you got your diploma?"

I shrugged. "They were hiring."

"From then on, what are your best memories?"

"I was too busy going from place to place for memories."

"Child to adult, student to grownup, Canadian to American resident, those sorts of places?"

I'd never quite thought of it that way, but she was right. "And up the ladder in my job."

"What was different about here, the U.S. from there? What stands out?"

"The sheer pace. When I arrived in Redmond, it was like grabbing the door handle of a passing bus and just flying along horizontally. If you couldn't keep up, their attitude was they hired the wrong guy."

"But they hadn't, had they?"

I smiled despite myself. "No, they hired the right guy."

"You thought you'd found yourself, didn't you? The real you?"

"Sure."

She shook her head. "You hadn't. You'd found the perfect escape. Just become a brand-new person in a brand-new place, but with all your baggage still unresolved."

She leaned forward in the chair, elbows on knees. "You can't avoid the past forever. Sooner or later you have to confront it. Kill the bogeyman."

This was making mesmerizing sense.

"Can't you see you've never grieved for what you lost? Just buried yourself in being smart and respected? It's not too late. You can still go back and fix it."

"Sorry?"

"Ben if you leave here and find a bar, get hammered, you'll lose an opportunity few people ever get. To get off the merry-go-round and truly start over. Most people trapped in the past never get that chance."

"I don't understand."

"You understand perfectly, you just don't know it yet."

She got up and extended her hand. I took it.

"Ben, any more words will only muddle things. If you've heard me, I wish you well on your journey."

As she turned toward the doorway, that strand of hair came loose again and brushed her cheek.

I stared out across the compound for a long time, as shadows grew long and melted together into thick dusk. It was like she'd left a vacuum where she'd sat. Finally, I turned back, clicked on the bedside lamp, and went back to opening mail.

Mike had aced his first semester of dental school and was already filling fake teeth. Some Dutch girl was on the scene and he was saving hard to go back to Amsterdam. Tracey loved Boulder and had a boyfriend at the Ravencrest Bible School in some place called Estes Park. I smiled at that. She always was the spiritual one. Then I realized from the postmarks that they'd been written only days apart. I could hear Eileen nagging, "Have you written your father?" Better than nothing, I supposed.

The January joint bank statement showed Eileen withdrawing her life from mine, moving around some money, rearranging some automatic payments. Expected. Then the February statement froze me.

There was a huge deposit labeled 'MagnaTECH Merger Disbursement Account.' I hurriedly riffled and found a letter with the same heading on the front. Read it with shaking hands. Thirty thousand of the share options I'd believed lost, had been cashed in for me at $22.50 a share.

Wow. The takeover sure pushed up the price.

Reason given was the takeover of MagnaTECH by a software behemoth from back east. If you do your own taxes, you'll know the name. Stock options have a cost. The strike price, they call it. After deducting that, an average of $1.75 a share, as well as Washington State capital gains tax of 15%, the amount deposited was $529,125.

The money wasn't a mistake

I dug through the dresser drawers for the divorce papers and checked the deal. The money was all mine.

With quivering fingers, I tore open the letter from Russell. It was dated the same day as the deposit.

You're a dumb ungrateful bastard Ben. Telling you about the merger was more than my life was worth. Now it's done and you'll realize why we fired you. Having our lead developer up on a DUI at the exact moment of the final negotiations was unthinkable. I put my ass on the line to rescue your stock options regardless. Why couldn't you trust me?

Dr Lawler won't let me see you because of how things were at Christmas, but now the deal is settled I want to set things straight.

Man, I hope you'll take this from a friend. If you do nothing else, you have to get off the booze. You've been a drunk as long as I've known you. It's amazing how well you've held it together, but you need to stop.

Find another way to make a living if you have to. You're the best coder I know but there's more to life than that. You have money now. You can go anywhere.

You know where to find me. You've got some ground to make up, but we'll deal with that then.

It was completely dark outside. A soothing, woodland-scented breeze wafted in the open door and caressed my face. A calm settled over me, accompanied by a yearning for... I wasn't sure what. Somewhere to belong, maybe.

One thing I did know. My life had just lost all its limitations except the ones in my head.

NINE

Seattle
April 30th

I drove up the long, curved driveway and away from the Pines the following Monday morning, amid one of those sharp squalls that keep Puget Sound's forests green and mossy.

Skirting Lake Sammamish and merging on to I-90 westbound, I was reminded how awful is Seattle traffic, but how spectacular her landscape. Columns of taillights stretched into the distance, but the squall had vanished, the jagged Olympic Mountains soared on the horizon across the sound, and snowcapped Mount Rainier hulked in the southern sky.

Exiting on Madison, I arched over the Battery Street tunnel and down into Magnolia on the lower west side. A Remax 'SOLD' sign jutted from our front lawn on Crockett. A new Dodge van with temporary Idaho tags sat in the driveway. It jolted me briefly, then I was glad for her.

The U-Haul lot was down by the shipping canal, where the air smelled strongly of diesel and seaweed. While a young staffer with a spiky haircut found the paperwork and key, I watched a Japanese container ship inched its way into the Crittenden Locks. A couple of sea lions played chicken with the screws, hoping maybe they'd churn up a hapless steelhead.

The lift-door storage unit was stacked tidily with brown cardboard boxes taped shut and labeled in Eileen's neat hand. I borrowed a box-knife and cherry-picked as much as the Explorer could hold. I consolidated some clothes down into a couple of boxes, then filled two more with computer stuff including a laptop, peripherals including a big monitor, and an internet phone. I crammed in a couple of sleeping bags in case I wound up living out of the truck and squeezed small stuff and toiletries into gaps. I agonized over my German stainless-steel cookware and utensils, but there wasn't the room and they could be replaced.

Lastly, I dug until I found my 9mm Smith and Wesson model 32 semi-auto, along with cleaning gear, a box of full jacketed ammunition and a couple of spare clips. I couldn't legally abandon it, so I stuffed everything in a rear side compartment that closed up as part of the interior body trim, thinking I'd figure out what to do with it along the journey.

Eileen had paid six months in advance. I put another six on a credit card before I headed north.

You never know.

As I cruised north past Green Lake, I realized I was driving on an Alaska Way that didn't actually go to Alaska, the lake wasn't really green, and I didn't even know if I was Canadian or American anymore.

Well aren't I just the poster boy for rootlessness?

Again, that intense yearning for a place to belong hit me. With such force this time, my eyes smarted.

At Mount Vernon the spring Tulip Festival was in full swing and glorious fields of red, orange, and purple separated by yellow dividers of daffodils, stretched for miles on both sides of the I5. Eileen and I had visited once, when our relationship was young and promising. I'd seldom been outside the city since and to be in the midst of such natural beauty took my breath away.

Passing the off-ramp for Anacortes and the ferry terminal for the San Juan Islands, I was flooded with memories of an afternoon drinking jugs of Redhook so cold chips of ice glinted in the amber depths, taking money at pool, off the crew of a crab boat. I could taste that beer again, and the urge to take the turnoff whitened my knuckles on the steering wheel. Then I recalled I'd spent that same night passed out in the car while Eileen had the cops out hunting for me.

It had always been that way. The pleasure of that first drink, then more and more trying to maintain it. Then creeping stupidity, followed, inevitably, by sickness and uselessness. I couldn't just have a single drink and leave it at that. A chasm opened and I accepted every invitation.

I'd thought of joining a 12-step group, but couldn't face the

31

admission of weakness. I heard an echo from Eileen's letter at the hospital. 'You're empty Ben. There's nothing left of you to care for any longer.'

Am I? Can I change? God I barely miss her! Did we really have so little?

I turned on XM Country just as George Strait sang the first words of 'Troubadour.' I watched the road and let the music swell up around me.

Canada, or at least the built-up area near the Peace Arch on the U.S side of the border, appeared out of the coastal haze at around noon. Traffic backed up and began creeping forward a few feet at a time. A big camper in front of me finally moved through, and I held out my Canadian passport to a large unsmiling immigration agent in a badged-up gray uniform.

He watched me from the corner of his eye while he punched the numbers into a terminal. Then in a gravelly voice asked, "Anything to declare?"

The pistol. Jesus.

"No."

The backs of my hands prickled.

What was I thinking? Handguns are illegal here. I had some vague idea hours ago about throwing it off a bridge and flat forgot. Why do I even have the thing?

Because I could. It was one of those American freedoms I was so attracted to after staid, colonial Canada. I'd gone along to the range in Bothell with a workmate and learned that green card holders could get a carry permit. The gun had been good value second-hand, and I suppose I got fairly good with it before the novelty wore off.

"Heading home eh?"

"Uh no, visiting, I'm Seattle based."

I gave the address in Magnolia. To heck with the facts. If he opened the storage compartment in the back I was screwed anyway. He checked that on his screen and then walked a couple of paces down the side of the truck. "What's in the boxes sir?"

"Just personal stuff, clothes."

That didn't sit well. He expected clothes to be in luggage. All he had to do was wave a hand toward the secondary inspection building and a dog and handler would be there in seconds. His hand stayed down. "Will you open the back please sir?"

I'm screwed.

I popped the back hatch with the remote on the key-ring and in the side-mirror saw him lean in. There was rustling, the sound of cardboard on cardboard, and then something opening. I felt sick. Then the back came down and I heard boot steps approach. I stared straight ahead.

Fuck.

"Your spare looks flat, sir. You should have that looked at."

He's looked in the spare wheel compartment under the back floor. Unbelievable!

"Oh right. It just came out of the shop. They must have missed that. Thanks."

He handed me my passport. "Welcome home, sir. You have a good one."

TEN

East Vancouver, British Columbia
April 30th

The haze thickened, the deeper I became enmeshed in the southern Vancouver sprawl, though the sky was bright, with thin cloud along the western horizon. The dash-display said 66 outside, a BC heat-wave for the last day of April.

I had no plan. Just a vague idea where I wanted to be later in the day.

I was putting-that-off, and since Dr. Lawler had said I should try to find where I had become broken, I wanted to explore every possibility. I drove across town to Burnaby and took a turn up the hill at the sign for Simon Frazer University. I circled the ring-road until I found a parking spot in the lot next to the Human Sciences building and overlooking the Academic Quad.

Classes were switching. The students seemed younger than I remembered and moved quicker. Memories blossomed. Parking my rusted out brown Honda on the ring road. Walking between classes in the snow. Studying in the Quad gardens on warm spring afternoons like this one. None seemed likely antecedents for my kind of angst.

There was a café where the used bookshop used to be. I needed their bathroom. And coffee anyway.

Getting out of the truck was a struggle. I leaned against the door until a flare of pain settled, before pushing off on my stick.

Inside the décor was chrome and plastic. A pleasant smell of roasted beans, burgeoned.

Bathroomed, I studied the menu, which was big on triples with skim. The cashier was an attractive woman, around 30, wearing an oversized SFU sweatshirt. After brining me a regular plain large coffee to go, with milk not creamer, she flashed me the peace sign.

"Two toonies."

"Sorry?"

"Just testing ya. You don't look like a regular student. That's four bucks."

Oh the coins. Right.

She pointed at the stick. "Skiing accident?"

"No ah, car. You take American?" I showed her a fifty.

"Oh no sorry I can't change that. Tell you what. Say that you're looking to maybe enroll, and the coffee's free. We're part of the student union."

"Maybe post grad?"

The smile became a chuckle. "There ya go."

The interaction felt good. Warm. The first conversation I'd had in months that hadn't started with, how's the hip today?' The coffee was very good.

"So are ya looking...?"

"I was here once."

"Ah a graduate? You get a refill then. What year?"

"After Y2K. Computer science."

"Oh yeah, I'm taking a couple of classes there this semester. I'm Carol. Pleased to meet ya."

"Ben."

"Has it changed much? This is my first year back after, well... I got a kiddy and she's old enough now. I like it a lot."

"It's the same but not the same."

Two Asian kids pulled her attention away. A line was forming behind them. The spell was broken. Whatever Doctor Lawler said I should find, it wasn't here. Nor was the sense of belonging I'd hoped for. This was not my place anymore. My stick tapped sharply on the parquet as I struggled away.

The quad now bustled. My attention was drawn to a pushing and shoving match going on near a fold-out table stacked with literature. Hand-lettered signs leaned against the table legs. One read: Support the Elsipogtog and Mi'kmaq Bands. Another: NO FRACKING UNDER FIRST NATIONS LAND.

It's always something. Back in my time it was tuition hikes or nuclear.

A small woman with flowing black hair was using a clipboard with some kind of petition on it to separate a weedy native-Canadian youth with his black hair cut Prince Valiant style, from a stocky white guy in a football letter jacket. The ball player's face was almost as red as his carrot top. His freckles stood out like liver spots. "Be cool! Be cool!" she was saying.

As I skirted the melee, the red-haired guy snarled, "Stupid injun!" I shook my head sadly.

At the truck, I broke the rules about no medication while driving. Then at the foot of the hill took Burnaby Parkway toward West Van. And a lot of bad memories.

Kitsilano, which kids called Kits, is that once-stately part of West Vancouver sandwiched between Tatlow Park and the westerly suburb of Burrard, which we called Buzzard. I lived my childhood and bore my bruises along its streets, invariably with a chess set under my arm as I stomped through its frozen puddles.

On West Broadway I almost overshot, but hung a not-very-safe turn on to McDonald and slowed down to gaze at houses I'd once known well. Many had been replaced by bargain-basement apartment blocks. The survivors were much the worse for wear. I made the familiar turn onto Wilkins and drew up outside my childhood 'residence.' I can't say it was ever a home.

Back then it was a lustrous cream, two-storied Victorian. This was the paint-peeled version. Broad cracked-concrete steps led up to a wide front porch flanked by balcony-columns. Half the upstairs balcony railing was missing, and the rest had gaps like rotted-away teeth. Sun-bleached heavy drapes obscured the front lounge, but the front and back doors were ajar. Through at the back, part of a slope-sided water delivery truck was visible.

Back then, I'm sure it seemed an elegant house where maids dusted and scrubbed, gardeners kept lawns and landscaped gardens immaculate, and genteel folks lived cultured lives. Except I lived in it and I never knew when the drunken bastard would rampage through the place raving in Russian, striking things that would break and scatter. I scattered, but I didn't break. I distanced myself and lived like a seagull on a wave-swept rock, rising above every breaker and settling again, alert for the next one.

That distance I created made me invulnerable. The same distance, I was coming to realize, was my curse.

Why am I even here at this derelict place?

I got out and labored up the cracked front steps. The door-pillar still wore the screw-marks where the *mezuzah* had been fixed. A flickering blue light glowed behind the drapes and a fast-moving sports commentary droned.

"Hello in the house!"

Chair legs scraped. A paunchy man in a grimy tee shirt and age-shiny red track pants shambled into view. One hand swept hack his straggly salt and pepper hair, showing his bloated face mottled with three-day stubble. I found myself staring at an apparition of who I might yet become.

I said, "Hello Yuri."

His bloodshot eyes squinted, then he leered. "Well looky here eh? The fuck you want?" If he noticed the stick and limp, he ignored them, but looked furtively around, then said, "You better come in then, eh."

A Canucks hockey game played on a small color TV perched on a coffee table. Yuri lumbered past it and dragged the drapes apart. Dust motes swirled like tiny golden stars. Slumping down into a tattered lazy-boy, he said "You wannabeer?" as he reached into down into a half empty two-four of Molson screw tops.

I shook my head.

"Suit yourself. Well, have a sit then. May as well be brotherly eh?"

The couch stank of sour food and stale hops.

"So what brings you here banged up and all?"

"I wanted to see the house so I drove by."

Yuri said truculently, "Mine. My house now!" He pulled on his beer and belched. "Whatcha do with the leg."

"Car accident."

He drained the bottle, let it clink on the hardwood floor, and got another. "Slumming are ya eh? Didn't bring the posh wife I see."

"We're apart."

"Are you now? Thought you'd visit the trash up here then eh?"

I sat very still.

"Yeah ya little prick. Got shot of us didn'ya?"

"Yuri, I didn't come to fight."

"Just as well. You're a fuckin' cripple now and I'd kick your ass."

I pulled the stick closer, glad it was in my strong-hand, and calculated the distance to the door.

"Nah," he said, subsiding. He belched. "Nah s'not worth it."

I tried a neutral subject. "Your wife, she's ah..."

"That bitch," he said with a lot of phlegm, "Her and her damn protecsh... protection order. Said I hit her. I tell ya eh? I hit she'd know about it. Little push is all it was, little push."

His arm swung down and thudded on the beer box. The sound

surprised him and he looked down blankly.

I levered myself cautiously upright. "Yuri, I got to go. You take care of yourself man."

He waved an arm elaborately. "Wait wait, I got sumpum."

He lurched to the fireplace which had mail stacked on it. I went quickly to the porch while his back was turned. He followed and thrust a thick envelope into my hand.

"Here. I'da burned it but the lawyers'd only find ya sooner or later eh, so ya might as well have it. I dunno if it's even there anymore."

Making a dismissive motion at nothing in particular, he tottered robotically back inside. The door creaked and slammed.

ELEVEN

I tipped the contents of the envelope from Yuri onto the truck's passenger seat. A collection of items forwarded by some law firm. Family photos, the '94 BC Junior Open Chess winner's certificate, minor things. Also, a certified copy of my mother's will; barely two pages, including signatures.

Scanning past the 'whereby' parts to the bequests section, I found my name and the words 'Cabin on surrounding land...' I went back and read slowly, '... totaling 11.7 acres at Lake Kaldekut, Regional District of Stokely-Wa'anedot.'

Memories welled from a deep recess I'd long bricked off like an abandoned mine shaft. I'd been 11 or 12. We'd traveled a long way in a white station wagon, to a lake, with a cabin on a stony beach with a jetty. And a marsh.

Timid little Natalya had hung back when Yuri and I found animal tracks, convinced that the large ones were moose. We wouldn't have known a moose from an elephant. We'd swum and fished, even caught some, though more through persistence than expertise. Every day had been a wondrous adventure.

That was what? 26, 27 years ago?

The will had an impressive letterhead with a crest and the words, 'Frobisher and Wilson, Conveyancing and Probate Lawyers since 1921.' It was five or six years old. But stapled to the front page was a business card from a place called Lakes District Real Estate, 'Specialists in Lakefront Property Sales and Management' with an address in Laketown, BC V0J 1E0, Canada.

I could call, but why would they remember a years-old will of an almost penniless Russian widow?

I'd have to go look for myself.

While paying for gas at a Husky station back on the Cornwall Avenue corner, I bought a Rand McNally of the Province, and went back to the truck to study it.

Laketown was on the Yellowhead Highway, AKA Route 16, about 140 miles west of the rail-head city of Prince George. The anywhere-to-anywhere matrix said that was about 1000 kilometers north, 600-something miles.

There didn't seem anything distinctive about the place, except for a lot of First Nations reserves in and around it. Perhaps it was a logging town. I remembered the kerfuffle at the Frazer U quad. Maybe mining. Kaldekut Lake was a good-sized irregular blue mass a few miles south of the town.

Memories of that summer welled up again. My father had been preoccupied, either staying in the cabin or roaming about by himself. For a short, precious while we'd been free of his menacing oversight.

Then as if she were right beside me, I heard Nadine Lawler say, "Find the place where you are broken, and heal that Ben." I finally understood.

I'd been looking for something or someone to take this burden off me, for the booze to blot it out or some person to understand and agree how awful it was, and that it wasn't my fault and I'd every right to feel sorry for myself. Except nothing and no-one ever would.

Nadine wasn't saying undo it. She meant accept it, that it happened and I survived and it was in the past now and unchangeable. Leave it behind and open my mind and heart so that anything was possible. An absolute certainty possessed me that those endless possibilities lay far to the north.

I stopped one more time; at a strip mall with a mailbox. I signed the divorce papers against my thigh, including my agreement to the settlement, added probably too many stamps from a convenience store, and dropped the envelope through the slot. It landed with a thunk of finality.

Then I made the left turn on to the Stanley Park Causeway, toward the Lions Gate Bridge, the Sea to Sky, and wild places beyond.

At a little before nine on Wednesday morning, I rounded a curve, coasted down a decline, and saw a sign in a graveled parking area that said, "Welcome to Laketown."

I pulled over and got the map book out again, for bearings. Laketown was no metropolis, just a smear of civilization along the north shore of a small bar-bell shaped lake. 'Popn. 2732' it said in minuscule print. Nor was 'Lake' town a misnomer. Lake Bouclier lay just to the northwest, Lake Kaldekut to the south and yet another, very large, named Beauchamp a little further south again.

Around the next bend were traffic lights, with a major road joining from my left. The near left corner hosted a small shopping center with a grocery outlet. In the hillside opposite was an Irish-style pub-restaurant called McGee's with a banner advertising an All U Can Eat dinner night.

As I sight-saw another half-mile, there seemed to be every type of commerce a resident could want. A DIY store, a couple of places selling hunting and fishing equipment, an inn and several restaurants, and an internet café. Also, an interesting-looking deli called Otto's with Tyrolean posters in the windows. On a prominent corner was a garish video-rental, I guessed for those cozy snowed-in times.

Civic pride was also rampant. Lamp stands were a freshly painted green, and sidewalks trimmed a cheerful yellow. Baskets of spring impatiens; joyful splashes of blue, red, pink, and purple, decorated building-eaves. Foot and street traffic were surprisingly brisk. I guess I'd expected somewhere sleepier.

I ate at a lumberjack-themed café, then pulled out the business car and backtracked until I discovered Lakes District Realty back where I came in. A single storied, beige building trimmed in deep blue, with a black wrought-iron grille like a busy picket fence across the upper frontage. The windows were plastered over on the inside with bios and photographs of properties, apart from a small plastic 'OPEN' sign. A bell jangled when I opened the door.

A counter spanned the width of the place, on which a 'Help Yourself' sign was propped against a steaming coffee machine with a nest of styrene cups and a jug of milk.

My kind of place.

Back of that, at the keyboard of a Macintosh, was an attractive woman in probably her late 40s. Casual but classy dress. Stylish brunette pageboy. A welcoming smile. I told her my name and a little of why I was there.

She put out her hand. "Marjorie Campbell, but please call me Marge. Everyone does." Then she went thoughtful.

"Do you think we might manage the place? Adams, right? I'll have a look." She turned back to the computer and searched without finding anything. "Perhaps it's old. We have some paper records as well. I'll check. Do have coffee though. It's fresh."

The tall shelving behind her was packed with brown manila files. I poured coffee while she checked the 'A' section.

She came back frowning. "No Adams, sorry. Could it be under someone else?"

"I'm really not sure.'

"Do you at least know where it is?"

"On Kaldekut Lake."

I could tell that was a real surprise. "Really? Kaldekut is on the Lodgepine People's reserve. There are very few legacy places around there."

"Legacy?"

"Well, before '92 there were a few leases but most are gone now. Let me look by the area." She came back a handful of folders she laid on the counter. "I've got a Winston, O'Connor, Demetriev..."

My mother's maiden name.

"That's it."

"Oh. It's right on the water. And the last tenant, nice man, in the computer business I think, just vacated. It doesn't say if John's done a maintenance check yet. Ah, here he is."

A fit-looking, 50-ish, mustachioed man in Dockers, check shirt, and a baseball cap with a Caterpillar tractor logo, came through from the back and placed a briefcase on the counter. His grin was cheerful and open, and I warmed to the guy right away.

Marge said, "How was fishing honey?" To me she added, "It's just opening. John goes every chance he can."

"Fine dear fine. Lot of good-size kokanee around." He noticed the folders. "Can I help?"

"Ben was asking about that place at the far end of Lake Kaldekut. The one that's just come empty."

"Ahhhhh I was there yesterday. Needs a couple things, tap in the kitchen's dripping, little stuff." He appraised me. "You looking at renting?"

"No uh..."

"John, Ben is the owner."

"That so?" His grip was as solid as the rest of the man. "God we've had it on our books for... well as long as we've had this place. I thought it was corporately held or something." There was a slight burr to his accent, and not just the standard Canadian 'a boat' for 'about'. I guessed Scottish.

"Ben, do you have like uh, proof of ownership or anything?"

I showed him the will and pointed out the 'nee Demetriev' part of the legalese and the section after my name. He grunted a few times as he read it, exchanged a little side glance with Marge, then said, "Well, you'll want to have a look."

He took down a set of keys from a board and fanned them. "This is the chain at the bottom of the road. This one's the back door. The sliding-doors have a bit of wood in the channel when you want to go out on the deck."

I took them and hesitated.

"Yes?"

"Can you, ah, give me some directions?"

"You've never been there?"

"Not since I was a kid."

"Ah well, now. Well." He found a palm sized item with bank logo on it which unfolded cleverly into a map. Laid it flat and drew a line back to the highway at those traffic lights. "It's about 22 K's."

Maybe fourteen miles.

"About... here," he said, holding the pen tip on the map, "Watch for a road on your left. Then it's probably another 10 K's. About the last half is gravel."

"Okay."

"You'll see a green road maintenance shed on the left next to a pile of sand. Your driveway's right opposite. Can't miss it."

"I'm sure I'll find it. What's it like? I mean it's been a long time."

The two of them exchanged glances. I prepared for some major disappointment.

John said, "Let us know what you think eh?"

"I will."

TWELVE

Lake Kaldekut, British Columbia
May 2nd

The side road was easy to find. When I hit the gravel part, I slowed until the chatter underneath became a low rumble.

The road ran due east by the truck's compass, along a ridge paralleling the south shore of the lake, which was huge and glassy and blue. Runoff had carved arroyos down from the roadside, through tall trees, which became gravel-fans bulging out from the shoreline.

The driveway, as he'd called it, was yet more gravel edged with yellow clay, graded out of the near downslope of a narrow, wooded stream-valley. Sunbeams angled through the canopy, creating intricate patterns on the road and the needle-covered forest floor. After perhaps 150 yards the road widened into a turnout at a shallow ford. A chain, slung between two rusty steel posts and secured with a padlock, barred the far bank.

I found the right key and let the chain drop. Continued another 50 yards between tree-trunks towards a glint of open water. When the trees parted I braked hard, skidding slightly on damp grass. The scene through the windshield was bewitching.

I'd nosed out onto a sweet-grassy verge that sloped away gradually maybe 75 yards, to a stony beach. Left-to-right the open area was perhaps 200 yards. Where trees and lake met to my left was a swampy area fringed with Tule reeds. Straight ahead a jetty jutted out from the beach. To the right of the jetty and back a few yards, was a large clapboard cabin, and some smaller structures.

It was skin-tinglingly familiar. But also, not at all. This couldn't be what I remember from childhood. It was all too new.

The jetty had been professionally built over pontoons moored between tall timber pilings. Beyond that was an arm of the lake, maybe 300 yards wide, bounded on the far side by a headland.

The cabin had been recently re-sided and the shake-shingle roof looked brand-new. A wooden deck hardly weathered, extended out on the water-ward side. The waist high railing had a gap above wooden steps. There was even some outdoor furniture.

Most incongruously of all, on the peak of the roof was full sized satellite dish, the kind used on city buildings for high-speed data.

This must have cost a fortune!

Agitated waterfowl noises made me look back along the beach. A mixed flock, resting on the beach, had stood up. Mostly mallards, but some white-headed ducks I didn't recognize, as well as a pair of Canada geese. The group decided I was trouble, skittered out into the water and swam away toward the marsh. Beyond them a single grebe, with its long graceful neck and pearly throat, dived and as quickly came up with a fish.

The Explorer undulated on its springs as I eased across the verge and nosed up to the cabin. Hoar frost lingering in the shade crunched when I stepped down.

The other structures were a well-stocked woodshed with a splitting-axe stuck in a block, and a smaller tin-roofed shelter protecting some bulky object covered by a tarpaulin. I lifted one corner to find a John Deere snowmobile waited for the next winter. It was old, with a well-patched seat, but the tracks showed recent use, and the cans of oil and gas beside it sloshed when I bumped them with my foot.

Another oddity was a 40-gallon oil drum chained to the back of the woodshed. It had a lever-latched lid. The contents reeked when I popped the latch for an instant.

Compost? I don't see a garden.

I tried the back-door key. It turned, and the door opened.

This is the right place. Does this all really belong to me?

A light switch didn't work, so I headed toward a glow leaking in under some drapes. I immediately stumbled because the lake end of the cabin was stepped down from the rear. The jarring hurt my leg, but not too much.

The place smelled of mouse-bait. Behind the drapes were the sliding-doors. I remembered the piece of wood, then slid them open on a spectacular view of distant mountains. A clean breeze cut into the room.

The lounge area had a wooden three-piece lounge suite with futon bases and some brown throw rugs. Beside a modern pot-bellied stove on a hearth was fire-starting paraphernalia, including a cardboard box of newspapers. The single bedroom had a double bed and mattress and a closet with some empty wire-hangers. The walls were cedar and strikingly bare.

Left of the back door was a nook with a table and two chairs, then the kitchen. It was spacious with dual sinks, a four-burner gas oven and grill, and a small microwave. The refrigerator looked new. Right of that, the bathroom was cluttered with a small washer and drier, but had a shower stall and on-demand gas water heating.

The floor of a walk-in pantry had a recessed lift ring. Beneath were wooden steps down to a basement with the bulky shapes of the equipment for running the place. I'd need the facilities working soon, or I'd be sitting in the dark, so looked around for anything helpful.

In a drawer with a collection of fliers for various businesses in town and restaurant menus; one advertising gen-u-wine southern soul food of all things, was a laminated sheet with steps for waking up the utilities. They seemed straightforward enough. I lifted the hatch again and went downstairs.

The basement was only under the raised rear part of the cabin. The walls were plywood, held in place by upright slats. The long side facing the main part of the cabin looked older than the rest. Perhaps the ground was more stable there.

The cheat-sheet said to check the gauge on a large propane tank. It read nearly full so I wouldn't need to top off for awhile. When I turned the main valve, nothing exploded.

I must have been doing something right.

The hydro feed came into an electrical board above a gasoline powered Honda backup generator. There was also an un-interruptible power supply unit of the kind used in computer network rooms.

Overkill I'd have thought.

I pushed the green buttons on the panel. An overhead bulb came on and a bench freezer I hadn't noticed started humming. Just so I knew how, I fired up the emergency generator, then shut it off quickly before it deafened me. The final thing downstairs was the electric water pump, which thumped persistently until the pressure tank filled.

Back upstairs I had electric lights and the fridge interior light was on. Last on the list were the pilot lights in the stove and gas water heater. When I tried a tap, there was a welcome hiss from the gas unit and clean hot water flowed.

In the better-light I noticed a small electrical panel down at skirting level in the lounge and took a closer look. There was a socket for TV or video, and an internet jack point.

Marge said the tenant was in the computer industry. Perhaps he was telecommuting.

Not having eaten since my breakfast tour of the town, I checked around. The fridge was bare except for a bowl of baking soda. The cupboards had a fair range of pots, pans and cutlery but nothing edible. Then I looked up and saw a plastic grocery bag on a ceiling hook away from the mice. A useful stash of dry food items like powdered milk, coffee, tea, rice, soup, flour and the like.

Thank you, John!

The trip downstairs had aggravated my hip, so I took some painkillers and started bringing the contents of the truck inside.

When looking for a place to hang coats, I discovered a trove of outdoor equipment in a cupboard by the back door. Snowshoes, a snow shovel, tire chains, a heating blanket for a vehicle engine. Also, waterproof boots, and overshoes that were much too small for me. Fishing rods and a box of tackle. They reminded me of the success Yuri and I'd had from the old jetty so long ago.

When I set the box of computer stuff down in the lounge, the geek in me looked forward to making it all work. At least that was in my skill-set, even if nothing else was.

I agonized over the handgun. I should still have gotten rid of it, but it was unlikely to get me in any more trouble, so I stowed it at the back of the shelf in the bedroom closet.

Then I made a hot drink from instant coffee and dried milk, and sat at the table in the breakfast nook, nursing it in both hands, feeling pleased.

A week ago, I couldn't have imagined this. Now I have... a home?

Then I started writing down a shopping list. It looked like I needed everything. There wasn't even a bar of soap in the place.

THIRTEEN

Lake Kaldekut
May 2nd

Two pages of shopping list later, my thoughts went back to fishing.

I was a complete rookie, but I could learn. I dragged the tackle-box and rod-and-reel out of the cupboard and studied them. The reel was a simple cross-winding type and the line seemed new and strong enough. Tying on something red and zigzag shaped with front and rear triple hooks, I went out to the jetty to try my luck.

First cast, the lure went 10 feet, and I spent the next five minutes untangling an overrun on the reel. Eventually, I figured out how to clamp my thumb on the line when the lure hit the water. My style was far from pretty, but I could get the lure out maybe 20 yards.

I tried fast-retrieving, and the lure skipped on the surface. I did it slower the next time, and something grabbed the lure in the depths. My heart raced but whatever it was let go just as quickly. I cursed and kept trying.

The air was very cool and the orange sun almost at the horizon, when the rod next jerked in my hands. Whatever it was, was strong; the line burned my thumb. I prayed it wouldn't tangle and cranked as fast as I could to take up the slack.

The fish broke surface, slung-jawed and silver. Probably four pounds or more. Tearing the calm water to foam. Fish had just meant food before, but this visceral battle held meaning. I was desperate not to lose it. After several lengthy runs, it weakened and started to come in. With no net I had to lead it along the jetty to the beach and drag it, flopping and heaving, up on the stones. I hobbled down and swept it away from the water with my good leg, dropped the rod and punched the air in triumph.

There was just me. No performance. No politics. No one to impress. I'd taken food from the wild with my two hands. I felt a satisfaction more profound than ever before.

As a bonus, there was the fish to enjoy. In good times when Eileen and I entertained, Salmon Amandine was a favorite entrée. I doubted there were almonds in the bag in the kitchen. And definitely no butter. But there was tomorrow. And the town had a deli.

I gutted the fish with a small knife from the tackle box, cut off the head and washed the body with clean water, then admired the result with a glow in my chest and a broad smile on my face. But it was becoming deep dusk. I took the fish in one hand and the tackle in the other and headed for the cabin.

I'd taken about two steps when a deep 'whuff' sounded behind me. I turned in surprise. And froze. An enormous black-bear stood where I'd cleaned the fish. So near, I could see the intelligent eyes and the lines of its face even in the gloom.

They say don't panic. Don't run.

The bear's nose twitched.

It's the smell of the fish. It doesn't want me.

The bear nuzzled the ground and came back up with the head and guts of the fish, then reared away toward the forest. Bears run like horses, a sort of bounding gallop. It disappeared into the gap where the driveway exited the forest.

A loon called from out on the water, breaking the spell. It had turned bitterly cold. I picked up everything I'd dropped and walked towards the hulk of the cabin.

I still had challenges. Like getting a fire going in the stove. And conjuring up hot food out of that cache.

Driving away from the cabin next morning, I watched anxiously for movement along the forest-line. I left the chain down at the ford in case I had to get back to safety quickly. But all was still and quiet, and bear-less. I still accelerated the Explorer a little too aggressively up the hill, wheels surging in the loose gravel.

I skipped the grocery store on the corner of the highway. I needed to get the big-ticket items first. Besides, I had almost no Canadian money until I found a bank.

The hardware store, a big red barn of a place, had a Visa

symbol on the glass by the entrance. In their furniture department, I found kit-sets to make up a computer desk and four-drawer dresser with a mirror. From their house-wares I took one of just about everything non-edible you need for a household. At checkout, I asked if I could pick it all up at the delivery dock. They noticed the walking stick and were happy to help.

On the way out, I noticed a sign for sporting goods. A tall, fit looking man in his late twenties, in a camouflage hunting jacket and Ducks Unlimited hat, was finishing up a sale. I admired the rack of hunting rifles, wondering if I'd need one for the bear, until the customer left. The camo-guy greeted me cheerfully, and I explained my situation.

"Lake Kaldekut's good fishing," he said, "what you can get to anyways. Better at the far end 'o course but that's a Nations' reserve."

"What's the far end compared to where?"

He drew me a map on the back of a specials-sheet. My place was about as easterly as you could get from the public boat ramp.

"Since you're living there, it must be open fishing. Char in the deep might go 15 kilos but around the shore it'll be kokanee, that's our landlocked salmon, and some rainbows."

I described the fish I'd caught.

"Jack kokanee. Terrific eating. About this big you're saying? That's a good one!"

"Umm, what I don't have is a license."

He grinned. "We won't lock you up for one illegal fish, long as you don't make a habit." He pulled a thin flat book in front of me and dropped a pen on it. "Let's call you a resident. Usually needs a utility bill or something but you're good. $36 for the year to next April."

As I wrote I realized I didn't know my address, let alone the postal code. I put down the 'The Cove, Lake Kaldekut.'

As I pocketed the paperwork I asked, "Can you help me with some hooks and that kind of thing?"

"Mr. ah..." he said, trying to read the carbon copy.

"Ben. Ben Adams."

"Judd McCauley. Sports Goods Manager. Sure, I can. Over here."

I bought a variety of lures in different colors, and some spare hooks and swivels.

"Those'll cover most conditions over your way Ben," he said. "Remember the fish are closer to the top mornings and evenings.

Middle of the day you need to fish deep."

As he put it all in a bag he said, "Anytime you need fishing tips or anything, you drop in, hear?"

"That would be great Judd."

"Come any time. I'll be around."

Well that was small-town-friendly.

FOURTEEN

Laketown
May 3rd

Better than the grocery store, there was an open-case wholesale-outlet a few hundred yards closer to town. SUVs and 4X4 pickups crowded the parking lot, some with rust damage under the wheel-guards from salted roads.

I trolleyed the aisles, working systematically down my food list. Many of my fellow customers were native Canadian, the men in work clothes and boots and with hair sometimes in a ponytail. Youth among them were generally in jeans, tee-shirts and high tops. Women wore skirts, western boots, and cotton tops, often with intricate beadwork around the neckline.

It wouldn't be practical to skip into town every time I was short of something, so I went heavy on canned, dried, and frozen food; anything I could throw in the oven and have ready to eat within a half-hour. Last of all I added a whole frozen fillet of beef. A cabin-warming treat for one.

Approaching checkout, I noticed a tall, dark-clothed man with a short military-style haircut, with his back to me examining automotive items. When a couple passed by, the woman almost curtsied and her partner genuflected with his head. Obviously, someone important. The man turned. A Nations' person, maybe 30, with massive shoulders above a linebacker's tapered physique, and high cheekbones that looked carved from granite. He moved a few yards to another aisle, on the balls of his feet like a wild animal that might leap in any direction at any instant.

A group crowding an aisle parted deferentially and I lost him. He would not be easy to forget.

All trucked up, I remembered promising to stop by and see the Campbells. I had questions anyway.

John was leaning on the counter. He broke open a big grin and shook my hand. "Well here you are. Marge, Ben's here."

"I'll be out in a while," she called from the back. "Hi Ben."

John said, "How do you like the place? Lovely spot huh? Few lovelier."

"No, I imagine not. It's, well terrific. Thanks. You give good directions."

He chuckled. "We try to please."

"Actually I'm going to stay a while."

"Oh you are? I'd better take this down then." He ducked under the counter and removed a bio from the window.

"I have a few questions if you have the time."

"Shoot."

"Do you know who installed the satellite dish? I need whatever goes with it to get on-line."

"I recall Kerry over at Hume's Electronics talking about that. They're down the road on the right. By the alley. Said the tenant needed it for tele... something."

"Teleconferencing?"

"That's the one. Said it had to work just like the city."

"Thanks. I'll go by and see him. Now how do I come to have a snowmobile?"

"Oh, that old thing? I forget who left it. It runs good though, I think. Least it did a couple months back. If you're around after summer I'll give you some pointers on driving it."

"Sounds great thanks. So... where do we stand with money John? The maintenance-bill on the place must have been huge with the deck and the dish."

"Oh no. Your tenant was there a couple of years and he paid for all that himself. We owe you money I'm sure, less a small termination fee. I'll work it out and let you know, fair?"

"Fair. Could you also recommend a bank?"

"I'd say, uh, Vancouver National right across the street's good as any. It's who we're with. Jim Hanrahan, the manager, is on the district council. They're quite supportive of the local businesses."

"Great! I'll give them a shot."

He saw me hesitating. "Something else?"

"Ah no. Well, I was going to ask about, uh, bears."

He grinned wider. "Don't tell me..."

"Yeah. A big black one paid me a visit. Came up behind me when I was cleaning a fish. Scared the bejesus out of me."

He laughed heartily and slapped the counter. "Did he now?"

"What do I do about it?"

"Do?" He chuckled. "Ben you don't do anything about bears except show them a lot of respect." I started to question that, but he gestured with his palm up. "Let me give you a rundown. First-off he's hungry and a hungry bear is an unpredictable bear."

"He?"

"Yeah it'll be a boy. A girl she'd have cubs this late in the spring."

"Oh right."

"But hungry or not, if you're sensible he's nothing to worry about okay?"

"Okay." I knew I sounded more convinced than I felt.

Marge emerged, greeting me warmly and bringing fresh coffee for the counter set-up. As I sipped, she asked, "What's the topic here?"

"Bears."

"Ah those damn pests. Did John tell you one practically lived in our crab apple tree last summer? Swam the lake every day to get to it."

"They come right into town?"

"We're down on the lake a wee way out, but yeah."

"Anyway" John said, "They have incredible senses. He smelled that fish and came looking lickety-split. Place like yours is a larder for him. Back of that little swamp there, there's wild cabbage and ling root. He'll live on that and any fish he can steal from you until the berries come on. In say a month."

"What berries?"

Marge said, "Uh huckleberries, dogwood, little bit of salmonberry along that stream. We'll have wild blueberries soon as well, but the bears have to fight us folks for those."

"And he won't leave for anything?"

"Only to get laid."

"John!" Marge said, though she was grinning.

"Oh, hush dear. When the urge comes probably the middle of June, he'll look for a lady friend. Till then he won't be far away. If you see him just ignore him, go about your business, calm like. He'll live and let live."

"Gee thanks for the reassurance. I think."

We all laughed and he slapped my arm. "Watch your garbage

though. We have a town law did you know? Spring-to-fall it has to be locked up or buried deep until collected. Big fines."

The drum by the woodshed. Of course.

"Umm are there that many bears around?"

"Oh God yes! Tweedsmuir? The big national park south of here? Got more black and grizzly bears than anywhere in Alaska. On Prince Rupert Island? You can see a half dozen blacks and cinnamons any time you like at the town landfill. Oh yeah we got bears."

"There are grizzlies too?"

"We get the occasional one, but they're travelers. Your grizzly's a meat-eater and he's always hunting. They like the big river valleys and the high slopes where the big game lives. They'll travel 20 kilometers a day."

"Oh." The thought was scary, but exciting and interesting too.

He caught my tone. "Don't be disappointed. A big grizzly's an animal you don't want around. Matter of fact, there was one seen a week or two back near the road-kill dump. You don't want to meet him. Trust me on this."

Well they do call it the wild north.

"Thanks John. Now I'd better head off and see about this banking. I appreciate the coffee Marge. You folks are great."

"You're always welcome Ben. Good to see you getting settled."

FIFTEEN

Laketown
May 3rd

I name-dropped the Campbells and mentioned bank accounts, at the teller-cage at Vancouver National Bank, which brought James Hanrahan out to meet me. I instantly remembered Aristophanes' observation that a politician crawls around under every rock.

A jowly, obsequious, late-50s man, in a three-piece suit with a yellow tie and matching handkerchief in the breast pocket, he wrapped my hand in both of his and said, "It's always good to meet new folks in town. We're here to help with all your business needs."

"I don't have too many business-needs right now, sir."

"Jim."

"Jim. But I do have some banking stuff I need taken care of."

"That's what we do!"

Wow what a surprise.

"Let's go in my office."

If the bank was more modern than I expected, his office was outright opulent. He saw me notice. "You were expecting maybe a small-time operation managing people's savings accounts?"

"Well... not this."

He attempted to dazzle me with his best smile. "This community is more affluent than you might think first-up. The mills and mines do very well, and we have a lot of snowbirds."

"Snowbirds?" I could only think of the song.

"Ah, it's a play on sunbird. It means the reverse of those folks

56

who head south in their RVs come winter, to Arizona, Florida."

"Oh."

"Lot of folks like the cold too. Lot of retired business people. You'd be surprised."

"I never thought about that. You think folks want the endless summer."

"The biggest part of our municipal costs is snowplowing, keeping their driveways clear. If folks can't shop our businesses," he made an expressive wave with his hand, "Well..."

"I see. What I need is a local account and checks and an ATM card."

"Who're you with now?"

"Seattle First."

"Ah you're American? I wasn't sure."

"No I'm Canadian. Actually dual."

"Alright. no problem there. Are you a property owner?"

"I just inherited a place here on Lake Kaldekut."

He looked quickly at me. "You're sure it's Kaldekut?"

"Yes, why do you ask?"

"Oh nothing. That's in our district."

"No really. Why?"

"Well there's so little private land out there it's a surprise. The frontage on the main road is private or district, but there're only a few other places and I thought I knew them all."

"I'm way east of there about six miles."

"Really? And you just inherited the place?"

"Is there something wrong with that?" I didn't mean it to come out so harsh but I just disliked the guy.

"Ben, I don't mean to be ah, nosey but do you have a... deed or something?"

"I actually have it in a will. I haven't tracked the registered deed down yet."

"I realize you're not asking for a loan but do you mind if I see it?"

I reluctantly brought it out and he read it carefully, pursing his lips a couple of times. When done, he sat back and laced his fingers.

"Know anything about aboriginal title in BC? McKenna-McBride? In particular the McEachern Supreme Court decision of '91 and the one in '97, 'Delgamuukw-BC?'"

"Not a thing. I didn't follow politics back then."

"Okay. Back in the 70s through 80s there was a property boom here. Lakeside places were all the flavor and back then all the reserve land, the First Nations land, was considered controlled by the districts in trust."

"So?"

"During the boom there were some waterfront leases offered in places that were, well, gray area as to the title. And a lot of city folks bought them, including some out where you are. Those leases were advertised as 'perpetual,' automatically renewable at no cost every thirty years. You with me?"

"Okay."

"Anyway the Nations' folks claimed they owned their lands outright. In '91 a group of chiefs, some from around here, including Chief George of the Lodgepine people, tested that in Federal Supreme Court."

I have a bad feeling about this.

"Oh?"

"Yes. And they lost."

I relaxed back in my chair.

"But they tried again in '97 and won."

A prickly feeling rippled through me. "How do you think that affects me?"

He wants to string it out, the pompous prick.

"The important part is what happened between those decisions. I don't know how your mother came by your place, maybe she was an original owner."

"I doubt it. I think my father acquired it somehow, and it just passed to my mother. But it happened, I'm sure she was the right and proper owner, and now I am. It says so in that will."

"Okay, but just hear me out. When the decision came down in '97, the one in their favor, the Nations nullified anything done by the districts without their permission. Sales, leases and renewals, even had a few roads moved."

"But the will says it's mine and that was probated in '08." I found the part. "See it says 'cabin and eleven-something acres' right there."

"No. It doesn't."

"What?"

"It says 'on.'"

"Huh?" I looked again and saw the word.

"It says 'on surrounding land.' That's usually shorthand for leasehold. You may find you own the cabin just fine, but it's sitting on a canceled lease."

I must have looked sick. His political instincts overrode his arrogance; he tried to make nice.

"But we're speculating here. It could as easily mean the boundary has never been confirmed. There are some homesteads in the district. Perhaps yours is one. Maybe this just needs clarifying with the Nation concerned. They're part of the local Native Development Corporation. Have an office down a few blocks in the big wooden building. Someone there should be able to clear it up for you." He straightened, ingratiating smile back in place. "Now your banking needs. How can we help?"

He called in one of the tellers to do the work. I opened a checking account. I didn't want the stock option money tied up in certificates-of-deposit so put it in an interest-bearing call account except for around $20,000 for the checking account. The checks and a debit card would take about a week.

Hanrahan shook my hand as he saw me out, but I wasn't paying attention.

All I could think of was losing the cabin.

SIXTEEN

Laketown
May 3rd

Not wanting to pester the Campbells again, I walked to the central Visitors' Center to ask directions to the District Council offices. They turned out to be one-and-the-same.

Those offices were at the rear, and big and open-plan, with a mezzanine balcony and meeting rooms circling the interior. At the help-counter I was served by a slim, serious woman with glasses and teeth slightly too big for her smile. She said, "I'm sorry I can't look up the deed for you. But I can take an enquiry if you'll fill out a form."

"You don't keep records here?"

"We do, but not that far back."

"The 90s is a long time?"

"I'm sorry those were, ah, destroyed. We have to get the information from the land title offices in Vancouver."

"Destroyed?"

"Yes, our original offices burned down and we lost all our early records."

"Come again?"

"Yes. It's very unfortunate. But we were starting to computerize at the time and some information had already been registered with BC Land Title and Survey, so we can at least ask."

I filled out a form with as much as I knew. "When did the offices burn down?"

"Sorry? Oh in '91."

I wondered why that date sounded significant as I walked to my next port of call.

Hume's Electronics had a buzzer on their front door, and like the restaurant I'd been in the first day, a mud-room for shaking off snow before hanging coats. Inside under glaring fluorescent tube lighting was a hodgepodge of boxes and loose parts on front-to-back shelving. The walls had posters for different generations of PC manufacture.

A girl in secondary-school uniform told me Kerry was out on a call, and would I please come back in half an hour?

Fine. Otto's delicatessen was directly across the street. And where better to pass the time?

Entering Otto's, the delectable smell of smoked sausage and rich cheese, garlic pepper, fennel and bay, in fact the whole pot-pourri of aromas; enveloped me. It was how home should smell. Gourmet heaven.

The place sparkled and the insides of the windows were brightly decorated with two-sided posters of European scenes and brands. It was also very well stocked, with an island and shelves stacked with exotic canned and packaged food, hanging clusters of meats, strings of garlic, and a giant wall display of spice containers.

They were in the lunch trade. A stainless cabinet had a range of delicious looking sandwiches, each with a toothpick-garnish. A woman in her late 20s or early 30s, it was hard to tell with her back to me, was filling a special order. She turned and smiled. And transfixed me.

She was full figured, in a white apron over what appeared to be a hand sewn, unusually plain pale-blue dress. Her un-made-up face was gorgeous and lightly freckled, framed by honey-blond hair in a pageboy. Her top lip turned up slightly. The smile was pure sunshine.

I realized I was staring when she tilted her head in playful amusement. Blushing, I turned toward the spice rack, held my walking stick like a fashion accessory, and stood up as straight as I could.

The customer left, and I saw Ms. Stunning approach in my corner vision. Her dress hem extended demurely below the knee. She moved with sinuous grace. "Can I help?"

"I was, ummm, looking for something for a beef recipe, or maybe to go with fish."

"That's a difficult combination. Which is the main course?"

"The beef."

"You like to do French or Italian?"

"Ummm..."

"The French use a lot of thyme and garlic. Italian is more around basil and oregano. Tuscan is, anyway. You sound American?"

"Uh yes. Actually I was thinking of Chateaubriand."

"Oh sure. You'll have to get by with dried rosemary but we have some fresh tarragon and garlic in our herb chiller."

"Oh you cook?"

How stupid is that?

"My aunt loved Elisabeth David's provincial recipes, but I lean Italian now. If you'd like to go that way, we have ah... oregano over here, and fresh basil in the chiller."

"You sell a lot of that?"

Damn it Ben!

She chuckled. A throaty little expression of happiness.

Maybe she likes me too. No way. Stuff like that doesn't happen.

"Oh, we have our customers. Narrow strip of the population though. Moose steaks on the grill with beer are more the local specialty. Though with a little Cajun and a good beating with a baseball bat, moose can be pretty good."

The corners of her eyes crinkled with humor. I wanted to hug her. Before I could think of a witty response, a woman-patron came into the shop.

"Excuse me. Please don't go away."

What did she mean by that?

She chatted gaily with the customer who was choosing sandwiches. I picked out some indispensable flavorings, including some Himalayan pink rock salt, all in clever containers with little grinders for lids. Took a half-gallon can of extra virgin from the center island and some twist-wrapped fresh herbs from the chiller. As an afterthought, I went back to the spice rack for some lemon pepper for the fish.

She came back to me. Close enough I could smell fresh soap. I leaned in to get more of it. She said, "You were saying you didn't expect to find a place like this?"

"Yes it's great!"

"Thank you. I've recently come home and I'm really enjoying it."

"Your father is Otto?"

"Oh gee I'm sorry. Yes, and I'm Libby. Libby Mueller."

I seized the excuse to take her hand. It was soft and warm, but strong too. A glow spread up my arm. "I'm Ben."

She laughed heartily. It set the crinkles dancing.

"What's funny?"

"You look like a Ben."

I laughed too. "What the heck does a Ben look like?"

"I don't know. Interesting? Thoughtful? Someone with character?"

Not terms I could have imagined about myself even a week ago.

Self-consciousness flickered into her expression. I wished it away, but it didn't go. She took the items out of my hands. "Here let me take care of these. Looks like... $63.75."

I better get out of here before I make a complete jackass of myself.

She gave me the bag and a printed receipt.

"It's nice to meet you Libby."

"It's short for Liberty. My mother... well maybe another time."

"I hope so."

It was good that I had to turn my back to cross the street. It hid my cheesy grin.

I must be more love starved than I thought.

I walked toward Hume's about internet access for the cabin.

SEVENTEEN

Laketown
May 3rd

The buzzer on the door of the electronics shop made its annoying sound again, and brought a lean kid in his early 20s, with a wide face, flared ears and sandy hair, to the front counter.

"I'm Kerry junior. My dad's back at the house if that's who you want."

"No, that'd be you I think. John Campbell said you did some work at a cabin I have."

"Probably, if it was computer stuff. Where exactly?"

I told him and he frowned. "Yeah, I updated that system just recently." He looked miffed when he added, "There's still a bill on that last work."

"John hasn't paid you?"

I had the Campbells down as salt-of-the-earth folks who wouldn't stiff anybody.

"Oh no, the work was direct for that Adrian guy who lives there. He promised me a check but it hasn't shown up. I've even been out to see him a couple times, but he's never there."

"I'm sorry but Adrian's not around anymore. How much is the tab?"

It was $800.63 for a dish upgrade, amplifier, and labor. I guessed this place didn't make much money. A bad debt like that would kick a big hole in the bottom line. Besides, I needed him.

"How about I take care of this since it's my property?"

He cheered up considerably. "Would you? Be a big help!"

"What do you take?"

"I can run a card."

"Okay but I need some other stuff as well.'

Before we'd exchanged three more sentences, I knew he was the real deal, a true geek, one of those kids who almost thought in binary. Like me at the same age.

He explained the new dish was absolutely state-of-science. The tenant was using it for high-speed, two-way streaming video, on a 50-inch screen-and-camera arrangement. Adrian had said he was in sales, Kerry thought probably, for an information technology company, since he knew his ones and zeros almost as well as us.

I picked out a satellite-enabled DSL modem and a hub to connect everything together, and he arranged an account with a satellite service provider, and a regular phone number so I could use the internet phone just like a land-line. The DSL box was about five times the cost of one that worked with a regular phone line, but I didn't quibble. I was newly rich after all.

On the way-out Kerry promised he'd swing by and set it all up for me if I ran into problems, but I was barely listening. I was thinking about the abrupt departure of Adrian the tenant. I'd decided to ask John about that the next time I saw him.

Turning south at the corner on my way home, I noticed blotches in the sky. They'd become black rain clouds on a strong westerly by the time I reached the unsealed road. Coming out of the trees in sight of the cabin, the cove was in the grip of a torrential rainstorm.

While lighting the stove I learned something else about my mystery tenant. He followed the money markets in a big way. A few papers were local, but most were national financial rags: The Wall Street Journal, New York Financial Times and Boston Financial News among others. All addressed to Mr. A. Reeman, Poste Restante, Laketown Post Office. He was fast becoming a very interesting character.

The chill gone from the cabin, I got out the salmon I'd caught, basted it with Italian dressing and lemon pepper, and baked it in aluminum foil. Divine with crusty French bread.

Then I crawled under the sleeping bags, having totally forgotten to get bedding, and lay enjoying the sound of rain pelting down.

My last thoughts were of a beautiful woman smiling at me across a room.

In the morning a magical stillness had settled over the cove. I opened the sliding-doors and drank it all in. The land and trees and water, even the rocks, seemed to exude their own light. The lake mirrored the forest and bluff and sky so perfectly I felt as if I was cradled in the center. I felt... embraced.

I wandered on along the beach with my morning coffee, where the waterfowl were back midway between the jetty and the reeds. They fled, honking and quacking.

Where the tall reeds rose, some large cloven-hoofed animal had come down to drink in the dawn. The tracks were big and round and the water still cloudy where it had stepped. I was instantly a kid again, seeing the same tracks with Yuri.

Hoping for a glimpse, I went to where it had pushed out through the fringe, and walked in a couple of yards. Inside was very cool and the pine trunks slim and close together. By my feet I saw a shiny black object, symmetrical but rounded at one end and dished at the other. I reached to pick it up and stopped. Eased my hand back.

It was the beak of a nesting goose. Then the rest of the bird took form around it. The beady motionless eyes, feathers of the head and graceful neck. She watched me fearlessly, perfectly sheltered in the thick fork of a fallen branch.

I backed out into the open. Glimpsing nature in the process of renewal made me feel even more a part of this place. Grinning delightedly, I turned back toward the cabin and left her in peace.

Over more coffee, I pondered about how to speed up my recovery to full-health. I'd be lying if I said meeting Libby wasn't heavily influencing that train of thought.

I've always considered my ability to focus-intently on things as a strength, though I'm sure Eileen and others would disagree. It had won me numerous chess tournaments, but could also make me seem cool and distant, which was certainly at the root of my issues with my children. But I couldn't change that overnight, so I used it on myself the way I once used it to debug faulty computer code.

Stiff and sore each morning, I also tired quickly if I overdid things, but otherwise functioned fairly well. The main outward indicator was a persistent limp that worsened with pain. Straddling a line in the floor, I tried walking along it without allowing my left foot to scoop outward. The strained posture triggered a deep ache in my lower left side.

I was sure I limped because my body was used to me favoring that side. I decided not to pick up my walking stick again unless absolutely necessary, and make it just as much of a habit to walk normally.

I'd also need some kind of regular exercise regime. Yoga came to mind, but that was mainly about sitting-in-place. I needed something that emphasized activity. I could probably find something on the net once I got my computer system working, which reminded me I had other things to do.

A couple of hours later after some false starts, I had the kit-set furniture together. The fake wood finish looked chintzier than in the store, but with the dresser in the bedroom, I felt more settled just putting away socks and shirts and sweats. The computer desk went against the wall to the left of the doors by the electronics jack-plugs. I immediately added a bendy desk light and an ergonomic chair to my mental shopping list.

Among the computer equipment from Seattle was a docking station for the laptop that enabled an external screen, keyboard, and mouse. The laptop was completely dead, but came back to life after a few minutes on wall power. Setting up the satellite modem was as simple as installing the software and entering the account details. I could browse the internet within minutes. Plugging in the internet phone gave me a weird feeling of disconnectedness. I'd no-one to call and no-one from my past life knew where I was, or cared, I was sure. I shook off that hollow feeling by making a very late lunch.

Back at the desk, I checked whether my Skyway West internet accounts were still active. My ID and password direct to the server failed, not surprising since the account had been owned by MagnaTECH, but through some IT-Admin-oversight the web-mail login still worked. Soon I was browsing through 2,754 emails.

The ones from Mike and Tracey were duplicates of the letters they'd sent. Most others were newsletters or approaches from headhunters. A part of me wanted to read some of them, be back in that zone where I got my self-worth from how well I could type characters into a screen and group them to produce some company's payroll or financial report. Instead, I deleted everything and signed out.

Then I brought up an internet search window and thought for a minute about which of life's mysteries I wanted to solve most.

Adrian the tenant, for a start. That situation didn't add up. He'd made a sizable investment in this place. Then just packed up and left? Perhaps it was all on some company tab. Then why leave a bill unpaid? I did a half-hearted search on 'Adrian Reeman

Executive Sales BC,' and got thousands of results, but nothing useful. I'd really have to discuss it with John Campbell.

Then there was the cabin title. Hanrahan simply had to be wrong.

The lawyers who probated the will must have cleared that up, but I needed rock-solid proof. I searched on 'Land Title BC' and found the Land Title and Survey Authority of British Columbia (LTSA) website. A map showed I was in their Prince Rupert region. That office was in Westminster, Vancouver, hours 9 - 5, Monday to Friday. It was past that, so I'd have to wait if I wanted to talk to someone.

The same search had also found numerous pages on native title, which Hanrahan had mentioned.

I read through those for the next hour or so. By the time I finished, the glow in the room had a pink hue as sunset tinted the sky. But I thought I understood the basic problem with Canadian aboriginal relations: a well-justified distrust. The First Nations had been tricked, bull-shitted, bullied and generally screwed over for a century-and-a-half, and had every right to be pissed off about it.

However, the cove was my number-one concern. I switched back to the LTSA site, but learned nothing more.

I put on the lights and heated a TV dinner that actually wasn't bad. Then rather than sit up by the fire, went to bed intending to give the matter some deep thought.

EIGHTEEN

Laketown
May 7th

I'd been pushing my hip hard, so I spent Friday and the weekend being kind to myself. But by Monday morning I had a plan, and other business to conduct, anyway. I saddled up my steel steed and headed for town, deliberately sans walking stick.

I found John Campbell standing at his front counter opening mail, looking like he'd just come in off the lake; which he had. After I'd admired several good-sized trout he had in a cooler, I responded to his initial greeting with, "Everything's great and no more bear problems so far, but ah... I was wondering about that guy who rented my place."

"Adrian Reeman?"

"Yes, seems odd to me. He spent a ton of money making himself at home and setting up a remote office Kerry Hume says was as good as anywhere. Then he stuck Kerry with a bill and simply quit town. Did he tell you why?"

"Nope. I rarely spoke to him the whole time he was here. Didn't even see him leave."

"How did he pay you?"

"He was there over two years. He gave us a year in advance and then a check about every three months."

"He didn't give you any notice?"

"That's a weird thing. He just left a note one day. It said he didn't need the place anymore. Didn't even ask for his security deposit back. Lot on his mind, I guess."

"You'd have thought he'd remember that."

"Then next time I checked, few days before you arrived, place was empty."

"And he didn't give you a forwarding address?"

John shook his head.

I wasn't sure exactly why this bothered me so much, it just did. "Do you still have the note?"

"I'm sure I do as proof of termination. Let me check." He fished in a file-box and found a white, folded, handwritten-note. It was scrawly, like perhaps it was written standing up with the paper against something.

John came out a second time with a lease, just a standard four-page form signed at the bottom of each. The signatures were neater but still kind of floral. No additional information there. I supposed, strange or not, Reeman's disappearance would have to remain a mystery.

"Thanks anyway John. Oh, about money, did you say I have some coming?"

"Sure. Let me go print a statement."

He was soon back with a printout and a chagrined look. "Gee I'm sorry. I thought there was an arrangement for this. It's a lot." He showed me a balance sheet with a number of large deposits, a few smaller debits, and a balance of over $18,000.

"Wow that much. How does this work?"

"We take 15 percent off the top. Rest goes to an owners' account. We pay the property taxes, and any maintenance. What's left gets sent wherever the owner wants it."

"That was the arrangement you meant?"

"Yes but the onward payment was canceled years ago, so the money has just accumulated. I'm sorry we didn't pick that up."

I had complete faith in John. After probate the lawyers would have left that to me to sort out. "It's really not a problem John. Just thanks for all your help."

"I appreciate that. How do you want to handle the money?"

"The bank is sorting out some accounts for me. I'll bring you a number so you can deposit it if that works."

"Sure thing."

I really wanted to see Libby, but if I went in there and she acted like I was just another customer, it would spoil some good feelings and I wasn't ready to give them up yet. Instead, I got in the Explorer and headed toward my real destination in town.

A BC Heritage Trust historic plaque beside the entrance of the building that housed the Lakes District Native Development Corporation, said it was the largest wooden structure in the area. Being a hospital back in the 19th century explained the shape of it, a two-storied 'U' with the wings stretching back from the front offices in the bottom part.

Beyond the standard airlock-entrance were gleaming floors and tasteful cream and pastel décor. In a large waiting lounge with coffee tables and couches, a small dark girl sat rocking a very young baby in a stroller. Two teenage native Canadians, one very tall, wearing what Satellites called grunge gear, leaned against an enormous fireplace looking bored.

Behind a reception counter a large woman with gray streaked hair pulled back behind her head, eyed me suspiciously. Her body language said either very bad day or intruders weren't welcome.

I love old buildings. I stood and looked around like it was the Sistine Chapel. The rooms off the corridor beyond reception had no doors. I glimpsed beaded decorations on the walls within.

"Can I HELP you."

"Oh sorry. I'm interested in First Nations' reserves. Actually reserve boundaries."

"Any particular Nation?"

"Lodgepine?"

"Yes, they're part of us. We have some maps."

"That would be great. Thanks."

"You'll need to leave ID."

I produced my U.S. drivers' license, reminding me of yet another thing I had to do. She logged it on a sheet. Then led me to one of the door-less rooms that had a lot of cabinets with thin but wide drawers. She traced down with her hand and pulled one out to display a large laminated topographical map. Then walked back out to reception without another word.

You have a great day too ma'am.

The Nations' name for Lake Kaldekut was Tling'wa. The Lodgepine reserve was in pale pink and the name for that was We'tutahe. It covered most of the area between Kaldekut and Beauchamp Lake to the south, and extended along the eastern shore to, as far as I could tell, right where the cabin was.

I pored over the fine lines to see if my place was in or out but it was impossible.

When I returned to reception, a small woman was walking away from it. Ms. Sweetness and Light still took her good time, but finally looked up and said, "Yes?"

"I'd like to talk to some..."

71

She cut me off by calling out, "Oh Charles, Charles?" to someone behind me.

I turned. and it was the big man from the wholesale-club, in jeans, cowboy boots, and a white tee shirt that bulged at the biceps. He was on the broad-and-beautiful wooden staircase that led upstairs.

The woman said, "Your father would like to see you." He nodded and continued upward, surprisingly quiet for someone in boot-heels. She turned her attention back at me.

"I'd like to talk to someone please about leasehold land on a reserve."

"We have very little of that. You mean on We'tutahe land? I'm not sure there's any at all."

"Could I speak to someone please?"

She fidgeted a moment, then picked up a phone and dialed. After a short exchange she said, "Mrs. Robitaille isn't available until tomorrow afternoon. Does one pee-em suit you?"

"She's the only person who can answer a question?"

"She's the Executive Director and the only one authorized to handle land inquiries."

"Then one o'clock tomorrow will be fine. Thanks."

The woman handed me back my license and nodded curtly.

Don't let the doorknob whack you in the ass on the way out.

The reserved parking spaces in front had been empty when I went in. Now there was a smoky-blue Chevy double-cab pickup, with Ontario plates and fat tires, in one of them. A sticker in the back window was for the Town of Petawawa, Ontario, 'Home of CSOR.' Another had the shield of the Canadian Military, and CSOR spelled out as 'Canadian Special Operations Regiment.'

Well howdy doody. Charles is an ex snake-eater.

Which explained the spectacular physique and obvious physical skills.

All very interesting. But I needed evidence to back up my claim to the cabin and land. I headed home to keep working on that.

NINETEEN

Lake Kaldekut
May 7th

The moment I got inside the cabin, I looked up a number on-line, then picked up the internet phone. The woman who answered at the LTSA in Westminster said her name was Maggie. She had a smoker's voice with a hint of whiskey in it. I explained my problem.

"We usually need more information than that to confirm a title hun. You're getting this off a will? You realize you'll need proof of relationship to get anything in writing, don't you? Let me have your mother's name again."

There was no title on file in either of the family names. The record mustn't have made it to the land office. Bitter news.

"Can you at least tell me who owns the land at a specific location?"

"If you can tell me the exact GPS numbers, I might be able to find it in our geographical information system."

I knew how to do that. "Hold on a minute please ma'am."

I brought up Google Earth and typed in 'Lake Kaldekut BC.' When the globe image stopped revolving and the red marker popped up, I hovered the mouse pointer where the cabin was and read her the coordinates.

"That's on the boundary of a First Nations' reserve."

"Okay, but can you tell me if it's inside or outside?"

"It could be either. 160.45? That IS the boundary."

"If it's outside who'd own it?"

"Either the Lakes District Council if it's incorporated, or it would be homestead land if it's not."

"And if it's inside the reserve?"

"Then it's a matter for the Nation concerned. Anything else hun?"

"No. Thanks for your help."

"You're welcome hun. Thanks for callin'."

I felt even more uncertain than before.

To cheer myself up, I started work on a proper meal. Cooking is more than just a passion with me, and apart from the fish, it'd been awhile. I'd planned this as a celebratory dinner. Commiserative would have to do.

I put a handful of baby Idaho potatoes, along with an egg, into a pot to boil. Then sliced the beef fillet I'd left out to thaw into three thick pieces, rubbed them with olive oil, and laid them in a triangle in a baking dish. On top went a good sprinkling of seasoned-salt and dried ground rosemary. Fresh-chopped would have been even better but you couldn't have everything. To make sure the beef broiled rather than baked, I made a tent over the top with tinfoil and put the dish under the grill on 425 degrees.

I was in my element, prodding and turning and flavor-tweaking, with a huge grin on my face.

When the egg had boiled firm enough, I mashed it in a small bowl with mustard, oil, salt, and lemon-pepper, for my own version of Caesar dressing without anchovies, which I hate. That went out on the table along with some torn salad-greens for the side. By then the potatoes were just tender, and the Chateaubriand perfect; brown on the outside but delicate pink inside. While it rested, I made some garlic-butter and brushed the beef with it, then served myself a succulent piece surrounded by potatoes and garnished with sweet basil.

Once a glass of New Zealand Sauvignon Blanc was mandatory; I've never been big on red wine with anything except desperation. Now I happily drank juice and the combination of flavors was indescribably good.

Nursing that glow of satisfaction, my problems at bay for at least a brief while, I brought in some items I'd remembered to stop for at the DIY.

I assembled the computer-chair and got the bendy light positioned, then browsed the news sites. I felt removed from the world in a good way, and the only item of interest was my Mariners were 19-13 but still trailing the surging Angels, and the Astros, in the American League West.

Wow the Astros? With their lineup? They gotta be cheating somehow.

But it could have been worse. I could have inherited a penthouse in New York and had to endure the Yankees year after year.

I was about to tear up a local newspaper for the stove, when I found the front page interesting. Skipping the fire, I made up the bed with new sheets, duvet and pillows, and climbed in with a bunch of papers to get a perspective on the town.

The Laketown Bugle was a 12-page broadsheet. The copies I had spanned a number of months. Headlines included a downtown trash-can arsonist, a logging-truck taking out a bridge and closing Route 16 for days, and the Lake Beauchamp ferry hitting a wharf after a steering failure. Editorials were humorous and prodded away variously at the damage to the main street from heavy trucks, mischief by high-school youths after school-hours, and council lethargy. A well-written column by an RCMP Staff Sergeant named Scott McKinnon chronicled local crime, mostly the petty issues around drugs and alcohol that I imagined plagued many small towns.

Ultimately, there was only one major insight. I learned what the little metal sockets down on the curbing in the main street were for. Navigation flags. An April edition gave the snowfall totals for the past winter; seven feet plus, with a front-page picture of snowmobiles parked like cars.

Something to look forward to.

My curiosity about what was hanging on the walls at the Native-Development-Corporation offices was assuaged the next afternoon when I turned up for my 1:00 p.m. appointment with Mrs. Robitaille. There was no-one behind the counter. I walked down the hallway for a closer look.

They were beaded artworks. Women's blouses, tee-shirts, and denim jackets with beautiful patterns expanding out from the neckline in intricate whorls, lines and block patterns of turquoise, green, red, and black. Each bead a brightly polished jewel, from pea size down to as-fine as a pinhead. An information sheet said they were hand-made from semi-precious stones from the shores of local lakes, and bead-work was an art form going back to Hudson-Bay-Company days. The price tags were in the hundreds of dollars.

I was about to look farther down the hall when the very small woman I'd noticed during my first visit appeared at my elbow. "Mr.

Adams?"

"Yes."

"I'm Nancy Robitaille. Coral said you have a land question."

"Yes. If I may."

"Unless it's brief let's go in my office."

That was down in the other wing where we sat and she looked at me expectantly. For want of a better way, I put it how Jim Hanrahan raised it. "I have inherited some land on Lake Kaldekut and I'm trying to find out if it's freehold or leasehold."

"Ah." She made that little twitch people do when something important pops up and they don't want to acknowledge it. "Most of that shore is reserved, of course. The boat ramp belongs to the district council, but the remainder has reverted to the owners."

"Reverted?"

"Yes. There was a landmark court case that returned possession to our people. Any leases issued or renewed by the council before then were nullified."

"Okay."

"So I don't think I can help you."

"Then can you please tell me who can?"

She had very dark eyes that narrowed when she frowned. "Mr. Adams, we're a corporation set up to support the people of our Nations. We're not an information service for settlers or squatters."

I felt a flush under my collar. "That's good because I'm neither of those. I'm simply trying to confirm my legal situation."

"I can tell you this. Tling'wa and its shores are our historic land, and the Supreme Court of Canada has confirmed our rights over it. If you are squatting there you will be required to leave."

"Excuse me a moment. All I'm asking is to know where I stand with my property."

"Stand? You don't stand. You sit. You sit your settler ass on our land. And you want to come here and weasel information out of us, fishing for ways to keep it there."

"I'm sorry. That wasn't my intention. I've come to you for information because I'm new around here."

"Well I'm sorry too. We are not. Our people have lived on these lands, currently on what our settler government has let us keep out of the goodness of its heart, for thousands of years. And settlers like you have been trying to cheat us out of it for hundreds of years. We're tired of it."

Our eyes stayed locked a few seconds. Then she let out a big breath, flicked her hands apart and back together.

"Mr. Adams you may actually be a decent man. You may not

even mean any harm. You're just one of a long line of settler bull-shitters. Maybe you just don't know any better. But you need to understand that we do not allow settlement on our land."

"I don't know if I'm on your land. That's why I'm here. Can't you just tell me where the boundary is?"

Her face turned stony again. "Our ancestors made their land markers with a forked stick here and there, a hawk feather held down by a rock or a lightning-struck stump. We claim that land by native title. If you want to establish a settler's boundary you will need to do it in a courtroom."

"I may just do that."

"Then good day to you Mr. Adams."

TWENTY

Laketown
May 8th

When I left Nancy Robitaille's office, my spirits were shattered. My gift from the heavens had just been yanked away from me like a toy in a cruel game.

I wanted to give in to despair and feel sorry for myself. Go home and walk on the beach one last time, to remind myself what I was losing, before they chased me off the place. But I couldn't. I had no place else to go. I drove to the realty office instead.

No one was around, so I ducked under the counter and walked out back. It was starting to rain and John was in a courtyard under the hood of a red and cream F150 pickup.

"Jack of all trades, huh?"

"Yeah damn thing's got a miss. I'm throwing in a new set of plugs. How're you doing?"

"I've been better."

He looked up at the drizzle and cussed. Put the wrench down on the fender and wiped his fingers with a rag. "Anything I can do?"

"I could really use your phone. Be some long distance."

"That's okay. I can always take it off what we owe you. Go right ahead."

I got the phone number and witnesses' names off the will and called the probate law firm. No, Mr. Hughes wasn't with them anymore.

"Mr. Frobisher then? Or Mr. Wilson?"

"One moment please."

James Wilson had a big voice, the kind that might carry in a courtroom. "A will you say?"

"Yes, but my inquiry isn't directly about that."

"Let me find it anyway for background. It won't take but a minute. It's all on-line." After a pause punctuated by a few "mm's," he said, "Fairly straightforward. Simple probate. Bit of an issue tracing beneficiaries."

"Sorry about that."

I asked if they investigated the property title. No, it was a basic witness and distribution situation. They simply passed on what my mother told them to record. "Would you be prepared to represent me in a title case?"

"Not really our type of case. Is the other party in the city?"

"No. Up in central BC, Laketown. It's actually a First Nation."

"Then unfortunately no."

"If it's a matter of cost, I can put up a good retainer."

There was hesitation while he framed his answer. "Cases involving First Nations tend to be extremely contentious. We prefer to stay uninvolved. I'm sorry. You could try the Law Society for a recommendation." He gave me a number and ended the call.

I massaged my forehead, wondering if I wanted to go through some referral agency to get representation. It seemed like throwing a dart at a list on a wall. Then Marge came in the back door with a leather purse over one arm and a paper grocery sack cradled in the other. "Hi there. John thinks I should cheer you up."

"Thanks. I could use it."

"Let me put this stuff away first."

I mulled over my options, sure of only one thing, I wasn't giving up. When she was back and John had joined us, Marge said, "Come on then, spill the news."

"It's complicated. I'm going to need a lawyer."

Marge said, "Have you done something?"

"No. It's the cabin. There's a question about the land."

"I thought you received it in the will."

"The cabin yes, but there's a possibility it might be on Lodgepine land. The boundary isn't clear. I've spoken to them but can't get a straight answer."

Both were quiet for a few seconds until Marge said carefully, "You're saying you want to sue the Nations to confirm your title?"

"Basically, yes."

"Have you any idea what a big deal that would be around here?"

"No. Why?"

John shrugged. Marge frowned at him before she replied. "Ben you'll have figured John isn't really a local. We met in San Francisco when I was traveling after college. However, I am, and I remember how it was in the 90s."

"What are you saying?"

"We had a lot of protests, even a riot."

"Huh? Who was doing that?"

"The young people from the reserves. We had marches, the whole thing."

"But that's ancient history now, surely."

"It is and it isn't. We do have reasonable harmony since it was all sorted out in court, and Laketown's a different place now as well. There's tourism, retirees. Mining has grown. But not a huge amount of that has benefited the Nations. The tensions are more papered over than resolved. Logging is still a point of contention. Along with the pine-beetle damage, the Nations still see land they consider theirs being stripped."

"Okay."

"And mark my words. Folks here do not want it dredged up again. If you go to court with the Nations, people won't like it."

John said, "Marge, do you want him just to walk away from his own place?"

She sighed. "I suppose not. I guess you have to do what you have to do. Just so you know how it will be."

I sighed heavily too. "I guess I do. But first I have to find a lawyer."

John rubbed the back of his neck a few times like he had a crick. "There's always Hal."

Marge spluttered. "And he's darn fool enough to do it too!"

"Hal?"

"Hal Pritchard," Marge said, "He's got an office in town."

"You don't sound too encouraging."

"Oh, he's an excellent lawyer. He's just... different is all."

"Okay, but does it make him a bad choice?"

Marge said, "Oh I'm not saying that. He was with some big firm back east before moving here when he married Jessica. Jessica Summers, the Mayor's daughter."

"Do you think he'll help me?"

"Why don't you ask him yourself?"

They told me how I could do that.

TWENTY-ONE

Laketown
May 8th

The office of Harold R. Pritchard, Attorney at Law, was above a medical clinic in a small block of business units just the other side of downtown.

Several mothers and their cherubic jet haired children watched me through a rain-streaked doctor's waiting room window as I climbed the outside stairs. There was no one in reception. I called out. "Hello?"

A man my age with swept back, longish brown hair, emerged from a room in back. He was in slacks and a pale yellow-striped sports-shirt. More strikingly, he was so tall he had to stoop to get through the doorway. He peered at me over a set of thin framed reading glasses he held against the bridge of his nose with one forefinger. "Yes?"

"Harold Pritchard?"

"Hal. I don't like Harold."

"Hal. Okay. I'm looking for a lawyer."

"You found one. Any particular reason?"

"Ahhhhh…"

I guess he realized how brusque he was being. "I'm sorry. Connie's off with a sick child. Come on back and tell me how I can help."

Framed certificates adorned the walls of his inner sanctum, including a law degree from McGill University in Montreal, a Canadian bar-certificate, and one that said he'd been an academic

All-Canadian. On a sideboard was a stand-up picture of an attractive woman and two young girls. Another showed him in a red basketball uniform dunking a ball, which fit with his tallness. He pointed at a couch. I sat down and introduced myself.

"You aren't local, are you?"

"Well yes and no."

"The yes part?"

"I have a cabin out on Lake Kaldekut."

"A snowbird then?"

"No. Look. Can I tell you why I'm here and see where it goes from there?"

He interrupted only once more, to get a yellow pad and take prodigious notes. At times he made half an 'uh-huh' sound, just the 'uh' part. Occasionally he spiked the ball-point on the pad. Several times I wondered if throwing a dart at a list might have been preferable, but in the end, I got it all out the best I could.

"Let me see," he said. "You own a cabin but can't prove you own the land it sits on. It's possible the land belongs to the Lodgepine Nation, but no-one can or will say for sure. You want to use the courts to prove ownership, or failing that, your right to residence under some form of lease. More or less it?"

"More or less."

He tossed the pen on to the desktop. "I'm tempted to say you've got to be kidding man, but I can see you're serious, so I'm going to take it slow and see where it gets us, eh?"

"Okay."

"First off this is 21st century Canada. We can be a silly country and over time we've done some mean and stupid things. One of them was the way we treated the Nations. There's three ways you can take over a place. European, Australian, and North American. The Europeans enslaved people. Shipped and sold them. The American south didn't invent slavery. They just exploited a good deal handed them by the Brits."

"Okay."

"Then there's the Australian way. They didn't screw around. They exterminated anything non-white they could find. Plain and simple. Probably went with the class of settler they brought in."

"Is this going somewhere?"

"Yes it is. Then there's the North American way and I say that because it's been similar both sides of the 49th parallel. You lie. You cheat. You push the people, our Nations, their tribes, into smaller and smaller spaces and make them dependent on you. They complain and it looks like it might stick? You change the rules."

"Mr. Pritchard, I didn't come here for a history lesson."

"Hal. Maybe not, but you have a legal problem and I know a little bit about the law so hear me out okay?"

I eased back onto the couch.

"Okay. So time passes and the clock ticks over into last century. And eventually the Nations win the right to self-determination, sort of. And let me tell you, if you take a walk through the halls of justice in this country, or past a legislature, provincial or federal, the smell of the middle-class guilt that resulted in that will knock you down."

"Really?"

"Uh huh. And if you think there's equal justice in this country or maybe any other, then you also believe in Santa Claus. There is only the way the river flows or the wind blows. And the wind here does not blow in your favor. It blows for the Nations."

"I see."

"Therefore, trying to prove title to a piece of land that might be on a Nations' reserve may be an expensive and hopeless exercise."

"I'm sorry I wasted your time."

He sighed. Wrinkled his nose a couple of times. "I didn't say that. It might be fun to try."

"Sorry?"

"In the end this is still a country of laws. One law for everyone."

"But against all the odds?"

"What's life without challenges?"

"You said expensive."

"Worst case scenario yeah. Mucho dinero."

"And if I still wanted to try?"

"What the hell? I'd be in like Flynn. Give me a dollar."

"A what?"

"A dollar. A loonie. Are you penniless? You must have one."

I found a coin and handed it over. He broke out an enormous grin. "I saw that in a movie once and always wanted to do it." He tossed the coin and snatched it back out of the air. "Okay now I represent you. First of all, there might be an easy solution."

"What's that?"

"A document search might clear it all up."

"I told you, I tried that."

"You had someone look for a registered title. I'm talking about the original survey docs. Those should be in Victoria at the archives."

I knew that was the provincial capital, out on Vancouver Island. It made sense. "Okay."

"Another thing is, I know Nancy Robitaille. She's a smart cookie and a bulldog for her people. You can expect her to file against you."

"File?"

"Trespass. You'll need a court ruling against that, just to buy us the time to look into this properly."

Holy hell.

"Just be prepared. No biggie. We can handle it."

"When can you start?"

"I already have. I need a good retainer though."

"Sure."

"Say $6,000 plus expenses? $10,000 to start? I'll need it today."

"I can do that."

The rain had strengthened, and jabbed at the back of my neck all the way down the street to the bank. The place was quiet except for Helen Reddy on the muzak.

"...living in a world of make-believe, yeah, maybe."

A teller flashed her best customer-service smile, but it froze when I told her my name and why I was there. She gave me a terse, "Excuse me please," and disappeared around the corner toward Jim Hanrahan's office. In less than a minute she was back with something in her hand that didn't look like a checkbook.

"I'm sorry sir, we're not able to help you with the accounts you requested."

"I beg your pardon?"

She handed me what she was holding, a one-page letter. "I'm sorry, but I'm only authorized to give you this."

When my mouth worked again, I said, "Can I please speak to the manager?"

"I'm sorry. Mr. Hanrahan's not available. That's all I can tell you."

A woman behind me in line was giving me an ugly stare. Embarrassed, I stepped away from the counter and looked over at Hanrahan's office door, which was closed. Then I looked down at what she'd given me.

It wasn't easy to get the gist right away, and the rain was now teeming outside, so I found a corner to lean in near the door and read more carefully. With increasing horror.

I was just finishing when there was a touch on my arm. I looked up into the eyes of a bearded, corpulent man roughly my age. Wet raincoat. Soggy hat.

"Mr. Ben Adams?"

"Yes?"

The man piston'd out his arm and pressed a document to my chest. Reflexively, I lifted a hand and held it there.

He said, "You've been served. Have a nice rest of your day."

TWENTY-TWO

Laketown
May 8th

"But I'm not in the U.S., dammit!"

Hal had finished reading the bank letter, and the subpoena served on me by the U.S. Justice Department. He shrugged. "You're an American citizen. The important thing, is you have to do what the subpoena says. Fraud is an enormous deal. Go down to Seattle and talk to them."

"How did they even find me?"

"That's obvious. When Vancouver National put in a request to your bank in Seattle for the money." He mimed the jaws of a trap snapping closed.

"Dammit I haven't done anything! How can they freeze my bank account?"

"We're talking about the U.S. government here. They can do whatever they please."

I moved my head dumbly from side to side.

Hal said, "Listen I believe you. Just the fact you were in hospital when the company was sold, backs that up." He handed me back the paperwork. "Just showing up and answering their questions might clear it all up."

"Okay but 1:00 p.m. on the 11th? That's Friday! That's less than three days away."

"You still gotta do it. Making the effort shows willingness to cooperate."

"Should you be there?"

"No. If you lawyer up right away they'll assume you're guilty. Just go down there and tell the truth and clear it up if you can. If that doesn't work, we'll think of something else."

"Okay."

"What about my retainer in the meantime?"

"Give me another half-hour."

The 'CLOSED' sign was up at the realty office, but I pounded and John's face peered out. When I'd explained he said, "It's too late for the bank. What exactly do you need?"

"I'm broke and I need the money you owe me from the rental account. Can you cut me a check for the lawyer's fees?"

"I'll have to make it out to you personally for our tax records. You can countersign it over."

"Also I'll need another one for myself. Lawyer's is $10,000. Could you make the other one $5,000? There's more than that in the account."

"Better yet. I can make it three grand and find you $2,000 in cash out of the safe if that helps."

"Very much. Thanks."

Then I had a totally unrelated thought. "Also, can I borrow the rental file? That box you had?"

He ran me off copies instead.

Forty-five hours later I was sitting in an interview room in the offices of the U.S. Attorney, Western District of Washington, 2nd floor, corner of 5th and Union in Downtown Seattle.

I was actually staring into a battleship-gray day, at high-rises and a monorail track glinting wetly in a drizzle, remembering how I'd gotten there.

I'd taken the inland route south this time, having travelled up through Squamish, Whistler and the Curry Pass last time, much of which was still winter-treacherous. This trip had been a whole other kind of education. The mountain pine-beetle Marge had mentioned, long kept in check by bitter winters, had woken with global warming and ravaged millions of acres. Tracey would have been heartbroken. After a night at a motel south of Fraser Canyon, I'd got up and driven more hours to catch the 10:45 a.m. Alaska Airlines shuttle from Vancouver International to Tacoma. During the cab ride up I-5, I'd chewed over how to handle this, but really had no clue.

Just as I was wondering if the monorail still ran, a serious looking man in his mid-40s entered the room. Styled brown hair, triangular face, wide forehead and narrow chin, thin and straight nose. He was in a well-cut charcoal suit, pale blue shirt and purple tie. Trailing him was a well-dressed blond in her twenties. They had legal pads and the woman a digital voice-recorder. They sat across the long table from me and the man looked me over very deliberately before asking, "Do you know why you're here?"

"Only that it's something about an investigation into stock fraud."

"Correct. I'm required to inform you you're under no coercion here except what's in the subpoena, which is to present yourself so we can ask some questions."

"You don't consider freezing my bank account coercion?"

"We find we get more cooperation with a stick and a smile, than just a smile."

I wasn't about to have a pissing session with the U.S. government so didn't react.

The blond women turned on the recorder, and the guy dipped his head and said very precisely, "Assistant District Attorney Jason Stoneman commencing an interview at one nineteen pee-em May fourteen with..." He looked at me. "Would you please state your full name and address for the record?"

"Benyamin Ilyich Adams. Laketown, British Columbia, Canada."

"No street?"

"No."

"Are you an American citizen, Mr. Adams?'

"Naturalized."

"Do you understand your rights against self-incrimination under the Fifth Amendment? You have to be here, but you don't have to answer the questions. If you do, anything you say may be used in a court of law against you."

"I understand that."

"You can also have a lawyer present. If necessary at our expense."

"I've nothing to hide."

He chuckled mirthlessly. "Okee-doke. Do you wish to make a statement about anything before we start?"

"No."

"Alright. When did you join MagnaTECH?"

"August 2014."

"What was your position there?"

"Senior Developer and later Lead Developer."

"What was your salary?"

"$110,000 to start. About $125,000 when I left."

"Not bad money."

"Maybe."

"Any other inducements?"

"Yes 15,000 stock options to begin with, 5,000 more for every year I stayed."

"How did those work?"

"I'm sure you know all that."

"What's important here is what you understand. Not what we know. Okay? So how did the stock options work?"

"The first ones were to vest after five years. The rest progressively. Each block had a different strike price."

"Vest? Strike price?"

"'Vesting' let me buy that number of shares at a discount, or 'strike' price, and then sell them at the market value and keep the difference."

"And what was the strike price?"

"The first block, the 15,000, were at $0.75 each. The later ones had different prices. I think the average was around $1.75."

"And when could you do that?"

"The first ones after five years, then the others annually after that."

"And did you vest them?"

"They were vested for me."

"But it hasn't been five years."

"There was also a clause that they would all vest if the company was sold."

He wrote something before taking a different tack. "Do you know a Mr. Russell Langwell?"

"Sure. He was my supervisor."

"How about Peter Prendergast? Richard Cotton? James Burton?"

"Prendergast was the Company president. Cotton and Burton were our sales and marketing VPs. They joined much later than me."

"How about a Graham Caldwell?"

"Sure I knew him. He was the head of finance and one of the founders along with Prendergast."

"Did you have any conversations with Peter Prendergast about stocks?"

"He was there when I interviewed. Some lady from HR explained my package, but he and I didn't talk about them specifically."

"How about later?"

"I wasn't in the habit of talking with the company president about anything."

"How about those other people? Did you ever have discussions with them about strike prices?"

"No. That stuff came from HR. It wasn't a real chatty place. You kept that stuff to yourself."

"Never?"

"No."

He wrote some more then looked at me intently. "Please think carefully before you answer. Did you participate in any discussions about stock options around the time the company was sold on January 3rd of this year?"

"I've already told you no. Anyway I was in a hospital."

His eyebrows spiked. "Illness?"

"Car accident."

"How about when you returned to work?"

"I never did. I was terminated while in hospital."

He had become very specific with his words, like they had to be exactly right. "Did you have any other discussions at any time about stock options related to the buyout of MagnaTECH?"

"Again, I've already said no. The first I heard about it was a letter I received awhile later."

"Do you have anything else to say?"

"Just one question. What gives you the right to freeze my bank account?"

His look was steely. "The law, Mr. Adams. Manipulation of stock options is a very serious matter. It calls into question our entire equities industry."

"What does that have to do with me?"

"You'll have to figure that out for yourself."

He said into the recorder, "Interview concluded at one-forty-three pee-em," and we all went out to the lobby. He didn't offer to shake my hand. In fact, hadn't smiled once.

I asked, "How long is this likely to go on for?"

"That's out of my hands. We'll be in touch."

I didn't think he meant it as a friendly promise.

Within two hours, I was back on a plane out of the states. In three and a half, I was in my truck driving east out of Vancouver. The Ford gulped up the miles and I did the same to caffeine at 24-hour truck-stops. I made it back to Laketown in a little over twelve hours.

When I reached the edge of town, I detoured to leave Hal a

note. Laketown's main street slept quietly in the pre-dawn darkness. Otto's deli seemed particularly lifeless, which made me feel very lonely. The feeling lingered all the way to the cabin where I stumbled in and fell into the dreamless sleep of the exhausted.

TWENTY-THREE

Lake Kaldekut
May 12th

Eileen used to say when I concentrated on something, I was like a dog with a bone. She didn't mean it admiringly. I suppose I am kind of a thorough thinker.

I woke sometime after noon in just that frame of mind. Determined to make progress, somehow, someway, on my problems and mysteries. This damn thing with the cabin ownership, in particular, was going to eat at me constantly until resolved.

Munching an energy bar, I brought John's box of photocopies out to the table on the deck. The setting immediately lifted my mood. Beyond the sapphire-smooth lake, the distant Howson Mountain Range reared spectacularly up into an unusual, streaky sky.

The oldest copies were on top. The first was a property management agreement with a company called Evergreen Realty, signed by my father, Ilya Adams, and one Howard Laidlaw. The arrangement was just as John had said, though the percentage had gone up some over the years. Nothing helpful jumped out.

I dug further and found a recent property tax bill. The amount wasn't much. I supposed because the cabin didn't use any council facilities. If I'd hoped something like that would point me at some source of property information, I was disappointed. It referred only to a 'cabin on Lake Kaldekut,' care of John and Marge. From the numerous maintenance bills and rental receipts, I did learn that

Evergreen had become Laketown Realty eight years ago, and the cabin had always been rented out, usually year to year.

Which all added up to a big fat nothing as far as proving ownership went. Another dry well.

I was wondering what to read next when I heard a vehicle arrive. I saw the top of Hal's head walk past the kitchen window and hollered him out to the deck.

"I got your note," he said, easing his long frame into one of my barely adequate deck-chairs. "Nice view."

"Yeah it is pretty. Thanks for coming out."

"No problem. They give you a hard time?"

"They made me feel like chopped liver, but I was expecting that. Seems they're questioning some of the management's stock options."

Hal spread his hands. "I'm not big on the stock market. In what way? And why?"

"Because options are where the big money is in software, Hal. Less so now, since the law came in that you have to pay tax the moment your shares vest, even if you don't cash them in. But still, if you join a start-up and it makes it big, so do you."

"Really?"

"Oh sure. Say a company invents a killer app or, like MagnaTECH, gets a big share of a market and then gets bought out. The guys in early with the lowest priced options make a fortune. The late joiners though, after the company is already going places, much less."

"Soooooooo, if you get control of the company, there's a big temptation to backdate your own stock options? Claim maybe you gave some early advice?"

"You got it!"

"Don't options have to be registered somewhere?"

"Probably, but seems that can be fudged."

"Oh? Did the ADA suggest who might have done that?"

"Yeah he mentioned some names. There weren't that many of us."

Hal said, "Wait. Let me write those down, exact spelling if you can."

Sipping coffee later he said, "We're entitled to their evidence so I'm going to request these people's files. Since you were in hospital, maybe we can convince them you're in the clear, and get the hold lifted."

"You think so?"

"We can try. You can bet though, that this is one big fishing exercise. That's how big law enforcement works. They don't try to make individual cases. They cast a net over everything and make the fish prove their innocence." He put away his notebook.

"Okay! That's our next step."

Then he turned serious. "I really came out to tell you the Nations' filed against you."

My reaction made Hal nod in sympathy. "Yeah not a good thing. Sorry."

Well, I WAS warned.

"How bad is it?"

"They're asking for a trespass-order to remove you and anything man-made from this site."

"How long till the hearing?"

"Probably 60 days. Circuit judge only hears civil cases here once a month. It's unlikely the Nations can get it on the next month's card, but the following one for sure."

"Does it change anything?"

"Not really. You might want to think about the ongoing costs, though."

"The $10,000 won't cover this?"

"You're good for now. It's the other side of this hearing I'm talking about."

"But if we win this we're fine, right? I mean that's as good as a title, surely? The judge would be saying I'm not on a reserve."

"More likely it's just the beginning."

Hal climbed into his Lexus SUV and headed it away toward the trees.

I wasn't ready to give up on John and Marge's records. It was getting late in the day, and though I expected John would be out fishing, but I found their office number and tried them anyway. John answered, jovial as usual, until I mentioned fishing.

"Hell no! It's gonna blow up like a bitch. Can't you see that from where you are?"

Outside was tranquil with the same almost artistically streaky sky. The breeze may have kicked up a notch, but the day was still heavenly.

"No. It's nice here."

"See that wild sky? That's a roaring westerly up high. Brings the banshee wind. When it cools later, that'll drop down on us like you wouldn't believe. Short but sharp. Better shutter your windows and park your truck in a lee tonight."

It still seemed serene with no chance of change. "Okay thanks."

"What can I do for you?"

"Uh you know the copies you made? I can't find anything to support the original agreement."

"The agreement's not there?"

"The agreement's there, but nothing to go with it. It's signed by someone called Howard Laidlaw."

"S'right. Marge's dad. We took the place over from him when he retired."

"Oh. Well I was hoping for a purchase receipt or something."

"Now there's a thought. We always ask for proof of ownership. Howard should have done that as well."

A smidgen of hope.

"Oh okay. Can you think of any other place he might have kept something like that?"

"I'm sorry no. Let me ask Marge to be sure. She's right here hold on."

After some rustling and voice noises without words, Marge said, "Hi Ben. Everything we have would be there. I tell you what though, my dad might remember. Has a mind like a filing cabinet that man. He's knocking 80, but he still has all his marbles. Maybe even gained a few."

"Could I ask him?"

"We were just talking about that. Would you like to come to a family supper? Tuesday night?"

"Okay."

"Great. Stop by here, say around five pee-em? You can follow us home so you don't get lost."

"I'll do that and thanks for the invite."

"You're welcome and don't forget to close your shutters tonight. It's going to be a bad one. See you Tuesday."

Progress!

It was almost 4:00 p.m. and I realized I hadn't really eaten in three days. I browned some frozen chicken drumsticks in olive oil, salt, and garlic pepper, along with some diced onions and mushrooms, then poured a can of soup over the top and let the result simmer in the pan while I tidied up around the place.

After the quite-a-bit-better than satiating, dinner, I walking out back to put the scraps in the drum. And stopped in mid-stride. The sky had turned a malevolent black. White-caps seethed on the wide water beyond the headland. Raindrops slapped at me and a giant gust rocked me back on my heels.

Running to the deck, I flipped the table and chairs upside down before I had missiles coming through the door-glass. I fought the outside shutters closed, then got further soaked moving the Explorer where the cabin would shelter it from most of nature's anger.

Back inside, photocopies whirled in a vortex until I pulled the door shut behind me. I toweled off while watching from the un-shuttered window in the kitchen, as the tips of the tall pines lashed like the tails of vicious animals. Soon the noise climbed to something between a roar and a shriek, and the same trees were almost invisible through the downpour.

I banked the fire and tried to browse the internet, but reception was so bad I was wasting my time. Instead, I lay under the bed-cover and listened to it howl, occasionally feeling a shudder as a gust wrenched at the underneath of the deck.

TWENTY-FOUR

Lake Kaldekut
May 13th

On blinking awake Sunday morning, the world was as silent as if all the sound had been washed from it. I stretched and rolled over.

Then I thought of my father. Why on earth would he own a place like this?

First-off, he was a city dweller. Born and lived until he was 27 years-old, my mother had said, within 20 blocks of the Kremlin, Lubyanka, and Lenin's Tomb. They used to skate on Gorky Park, for God's sake. Why would he buy a place in the woods 600 miles from the nearest big city? Also, he was careful with money. If he'd wanted a property investment, there was an inner-city boom while I was growing up. He'd have known many of the realty folks in West Van from temple. Nope. There was no sane reason he'd decide to invest up here. Yesterday's clothes littered the bedroom floor. Dockers' pants and a sloppy sweat top. His standard apparel was a dark suit and fedora hat, often with a long black overcoat. My father choosing to live in the woods? Not in a million years, unless there was some very important reason. We visited here once as a family for maybe a week and a half. Then suddenly this place no longer existed? Why? Thinking about that was painful. My emotions distorted the memory. But I knew for certain this place was wrong for my father. And there was something I wasn't grasping.

But I let it go and got up and dressed, wincing as I pulled on sweatpants. It was a particularly bad morning for hip pain.

Doubtless the mad scramble when the storm hit. But I couldn't keep popping pills every time I was sore. I needed to overcome it some other way.

I had been trying to follow something called *Kami no Michi* (The Way.) A set of Japanese exercises I'd found on the net. Once again Libby Mueller was central in all this. Call it testosterone, deprivation, or just a hope that she felt the same connection. But when I saw her again, I wanted to be a complete man, not a cripple.

The exercises were helping, but I risked getting plateaued; learning to live with my limitations when what I really wanted was not to have any. I decided, right there, to work harder. Push through the pain. Then I limped to the kitchen and made scrambled eggs on whole wheat toast.

Happily fed, I went outside to see the storm's aftermath, and it was breath-taking. Areas of the verge where there'd been hardy grass, were scoured down to stony earth. Along the forest-edge, entire branches had been stripped of needles from thrashing against each other. And there was a new feature in the cove. A giant log, with a mass of gnarled roots, had been shoved ashore. It was too big to move, so I'd have to get used to it. I was grateful it missed the jetty.

I wondered how the nesting goose had fared. The marsh reeds were ragged and the resident waterfowl nowhere to be seen, but high above the lake I could see v-shaped skeins of the goose's relatives, disturbed by the gale perhaps and streaming toward northern breeding grounds. I decided not to increase her stress by checking on her.

If it's nice out later I'll put that extra work into exercising while getting some sun.

And true to my vow, mid-afternoon found me midway out on the jetty, leaning into my first exercise. The routines were founded in *Shintoism*, so were both physical and spiritual, but I'd been skipping the spiritual part. The starting place was to find a point of balance in the awkward stance I had, then adjust my posture until it was normal, and hold that. It hurt, but I knew that would ease and the sun felt great on my face.

I had my back against one of the tall jetty pilings, shifting my weight on and off my left leg, when the first of the waterfowl returned. A pair of buffleheads, beautiful creatures, distinctive from each other by the drake's white head, and from other ducks by their fast wing beat. They splashed down by the marsh. I smiled as they flapped playfully in circles, glad to be home.

Re-focusing on my exercises, I changed positions and reached back with my good leg. Into nothing. I toppled backwards and into the water. The cold was breath-taking. I spluttered and cursing myself for losing track of where my feet were. Then I realized my predicament.

The nearest piling was only an arm's-length. I reached it easily. But the wood was slimy and I couldn't grip. The attempt pushed me away like a squeezed orange-pip. I fought my way back in close and grasped the edge of the decking, but my hand slipped off that too. Worsening things, there was a current; I was drifting away from the beach. And beginning to feel weak. Even if I grasped hold, I doubted I'd have the strength to climb out. My best option was to kick and dog-paddle to shore before hypothermia set in.

The pain in my side and fierce cold became too much before I'd made ten yards. Teeth chattering, I knew I wouldn't make it ten more. Fervently hoping it was shallow enough already, I took a breath and went under. When one foot brushed slippery stones, the bright surface was still inches above my face

Kicking off shore-ward. I slowly made it back to the surface. Snatched a breath before sinking again. The bottom was nearer this time; my head barely under the surface. But my sweats were waterlogged. I couldn't rise again. My lungs burned.

I'm going to die.

The water came alive around me. Fabric brushed my arm. A hand grasped my wrist. I was being pulled through the water. My knee scraped the bottom and my head came up for air. I choked and coughed, then collapsed face down on dry stones.

A hand slapped my back several times. I heaved up bile and water. Tried to roll over. A hand held my head down. "No no stay there! Let the water out!"

A woman's voice, husky and familiar. There was a wet denim-clad thigh inches from my face. I twisted to see more; the hand held me firmly. "In a minute. Get your breath! My heavens what were you doing?"

"Drowning?"

"No kidding. Oh Lord!"

I tried again to roll on my side and she let me.

It was Libby Mueller.

TWENTY-FIVE

Lake Kaldekut
May 13th

"Can you walk?"

I made optimistic noises. When she got me upright everything still seemed to function. The sopping sweats were hanging off me. Her long denim dress was scuffed and soaked, and what was once an attractive cashmere top looked ruined.

Breath back, I said, "I'm so sorry about your clothes."

"I've got others in the truck. Can you make it inside?

"I think so."

She'd arrived in a powder-blue Honda CR-V, that was slewed sideways with the driver's door wide open. While she headed for it, I made efforts toward the cabin, driven as much by embarrassment about how I might have left the place.

I threw my wet things in the washer, and myself hard with a towel to restore some circulation. Suddenly felt embarrassed by the state of the cabin, a string of drying underwear and threw those in also. At least I was clean-shaven. I gave the sink a lightning wipe on the way to the bedroom to dress. When I came back out, she was in the bathroom changing.

"Yeah I'm fine. Be out in a minute."

"Would you like a hot drink?"

"Tea if you have it."

I hate the stuff but remembered some in the original cache. I was heating water on the gas-stove when Libby emerged in an old paint-spattered cotton sweat-suit. The pants had a fray at the knee, and she was dabbing her hair with a towel, hopefully a clean one. She was a total mess and breathtakingly lovely.

"Where can I put these?" She held up her wet stuff.

"Ah just toss them in the shower." That earned me a giggle, the most delightful sound the place may have ever heard.

"Men! I tell ya!. How about a plastic bag or something? I'm dripping here!"

Clothes disposed of, Libby said, "Water's boiling Tarzan."

"Oh sorry." I rushed to turn it off. "I don't feel much like Tarzan."

"Johnny Weissmuller. He was a swimmer too. It's in the ballpark. I have no idea what I'm saying. Let me do that."

Libby took the couch, the glow back in her cheeks. I eased into one of the chairs. She sipped some tea. I tried my coffee, then said the first thing that came to mind. "Why are you here?"

"You weren't coming to see me. You didn't leave me much choice!"

"How d'you even find me?"

"This is Laketown. Everybody knows everything."

The implications broadened my grin until my face hurt. "I'm sorry."

"You don't look it, but it's okay. One of us had to do something." She sipped, watching me impishly over the rim.

"I wanted to."

"Then why didn't you?"

I started to make an excuse but cut off the words. Lying would spoil something magical. "I was afraid, I guess."

"Of me? I'm a picture!" She swept her free arm wide, then plucked at the frayed knee. "Helping my friend Joan out last weekend. Lucky I had them."

"I'm really sorry about your clothes."

She laughed. "I'm not! Heck of an icebreaker!"

I bathed in that for a few seconds. Then she said, "You have gorgeous green eyes. They go with your color."

"My mother was very blond."

"But you're dark."

"My father's side."

She said, "They're lovely eyes. I've thought about them a lot." Her face said that slipped out. She covered up with her cup a moment.

"Oh, you have?"

She sipped slowly. "That day. I wanted to follow you."

"You did?"

She said, "Oh heck, that makes me sound like a stalker, I

mean, I wanted to follow you across the street when you went to Hume's. I couldn't leave the shop anyway, but I went out to the curb. You didn't turn around."

"Why?"

"That day, didn't you feel anything?"

She felt it too!

"Yes."

"Well I did. I... you did?"

I told the plain truth. "It felt like my future had appeared before me."

Her eyes grew very large and I wanted to stretch across and kiss her. Then they glistened with happiness. "I remember. I could hardly..." She passed a finger under one eye and drops spilled. "If you are teasing me!"

"I'm not."

"But I don't know anything, except you live in the woods and like to cook. And you can't swim."

"I don't think that matters right now. Maybe later, but I think our hearts have touched, and that's what's important."

She smiled and sniffed.

"I'm sorry I was stupid. Forgive me."

"I do, I do."

She laughed and a couple of teardrops flew off. I wanted to capture that sound. Play it back forever.

She said, "Look at me! I'm not exactly out of a magazine, am I? I have an ass for one thing!"

"Yes you do. And what an ass it is!"

"You big meanie!" She mimed punching me on the arm.

"No. You're perfect."

"I'm far from that."

"Don't you think I should decide for myself?"

She went to speak and stopped. Her face was stricken. "I don't even know if you're married. Please say you're not!"

"I'm... I was. Technically still am. We've been apart awhile."

"Me too!"

"You are or were?"

"I was. In Calgary. It ended last year. I came home to get over it. You have kids?"

"Uh huh but they're grown. At colleges in Colorado. You?"

"No."

"That's probably not the worst thing if the relationship was bad."

"I didn't think so at the time," she said wistfully, "But you're probably right."

Unable to stand the physical distance any longer, I reached out and caressed her arm. She tensed and I pulled back. It hurt.

She said gently, "I want that too, but this is so crazy. Right now I'm afraid it's a dream. If I wake up and we've ruined it, I won't know what to do."

"Getting to know each other would help."

"Yes it would, but I'd like more tea first."

We talked, sharing journeys, hopes and hurts, at times crying for each other and ourselves, at others laughing till we ached.

The subject of my hip came up. I didn't hide anything, but didn't emphasize my drinking problem either. The only topic she seemed to skirt around was her ex-husband. Understandable.

During a relaxed pause, I got up and made food. Veal strips with a quickly put-together bacon-and-shallot sauce, and a salad. I watched the enjoyment spread over Libby's face at the first bite. We lit the fire and sat watching the light from the glass porthole dance on each other's faces. I wished it would never end. But as dusk settled, she said. "I have to go?"

"Oh, why?"

"Well our church has a special service tonight, and I promised my dad I'd be there. It's in an hour and I have to change in town."

I'm sure I pouted.

"I don't really want to go."

"From what you've said, you have to. When can I see you again?"

"How about a date?"

I laughed at the quaint word but she was serious. "Okay. When?"

"Wednesday night? McGee's all-you-can-eat-night is really good. Pick me up from the shop about six?"

"Yes ma'am."

"Brat!"

Parting was a comedy of false starts. She started her truck, got out again and pecked me on the cheek. Put the lights on, then got out again. I put my palm against her warm cheek and she nuzzled it.

"Drive safe."

"Stay out of the water!"

"Brat!"

Her laughter faded. The jeep's taillights flickered away among the trees and went out.

TWENTY-SIX

Lake Kaldekut
May 14th

On my second day of really knowing Libby I took the first of what would become regular walks in the forest around the cove, just the gentle low part, trying to give myself some endurance. Also to think about what she had told me by the fire.

Religion obviously had very different importance levels in our lives. She'd said she was Mennonite. I had no clue what that was, and for once had resisted the urge to look it up on the net. I didn't think that would give me the nuances of what it meant to her.

Me? I didn't know what I was. My father's parents had been Hasidic; I'd seen pictures. But my mother's folks were Russian Orthodox, and since Judaism passed down matrilineally that sort of left me nowhere.

Growing up, the word 'Jew' had shared the black horror-hole that was my father. When still trying to please, or at least appease the bastard, I had attended temple, but only ritually. Not that I wasn't spiritual, just that organized religion seemed so contrived.

It turned out I wasn't in a contemplative mood after all. I kept hearing Libby's wonderful laugh and seeing those lush lips and the way she filled out that paint stained top. What her faith meant for us we'd have to deal with as we went along.

Rounding a bend, I almost walked into a porcupine on a trail. The size of a medium dog, it swelled dramatically as it flared its quills like a bird fluffing its feathers, making a noise like a sack of beads being shaken. Then moved away unhurriedly with a comically rolling gait, uphill and out of sight among the tree trunks.

Crossing the verge toward the cabin, I pulled up at the delightful sight of the mother goose and her new brood in the shallow water by the marsh.

The young ones weren't tiny. She'd obviously been keeping them under cover until their growing need for food had overcome her fear of danger. And mischievous little things they were, cavorting around and heading off on little forays into their wondrous new world. Giving the mother all she could handle keeping them close to the marsh and safety.

I wondered what might prey on a goose in these parts. A marten or a mink? She could surely fight those off. There were plenty of falcons and ospreys about, but the first were too small, and the second mostly fish-eaters I thought. Would an eagle risk swooping in to attack this close to the cabin?

Whatever her fears it seemed to me they weren't at much risk.

Late on Tuesday morning I called Hal's office number hoping for progress.

After a few rings it cut over to a mobile. There was a lot of background noise when he answered. I said, "Hi Hal. Are you driving? I can call back."

"Nope. I'm flying!"

"What?"

The connection distorted for a few seconds, but I made out him saying, "… plane going to Victoria." It seemed odd that he was even answering the phone. Maybe the little local carriers didn't mind that up here. Then a background voice said something in clipped phrases. Hal said, "Wait a second." When he came back he said, "Sorry about that. Any news your end?"

"I talked to John Campbell again and I might have a lead. I'll know something Wednesday."

He said, "Good. I'll be out on the island until Thursday I expect."

When he mentioned where he was staying, I was glad it wasn't at Victoria's landmark Empress Hotel. In my new financial-straits, I needed the expense money to last awhile. He ended with, "Talk to you when I get back," as the signal died.

Right after that I tidied myself up and went into town to complete some chores before dinner at the Campbell's. Passing Otto's, the desire to see Libby was almost irresistible, but I didn't want to spoil the anticipation for either of us.

The Canadian Merchant Bank seemed as good as any. I

opened an account with John's $3000, and they promised me checks with my own name on them and an ATM card, within a few days. I held onto the last of the cash in my wallet till then.

A BC driver's license was even simpler, just some forms at an insurance office, standing up for a photo, and they made it up for me on the spot. I got fresh plates for the truck too while I was about it.

Then I looked for a library.

The visitors' center directed me to a brown concrete building with a wrought iron sign above a brightly lit entrance foyer, a block back from the main street at the head of an alley opposite the development corporation's offices. It served the local high school and junior college as well as the public. A lot of children's art displays with a First Nations theme adorned the walls

The lady librarian was a large cheerful woman. She took my new license as proof of local residence despite the less than specific address. I became member 3902. It was good to have a local identity at last.

I picked out several novels by Robert B. Parker; I remembered his Spenser character. He seemed to have moved into westerns. And several more of the Stone Barrington books by Stuart Woods that I'd enjoyed in the hospital. Their cooking section had a half-dozen illustrated Italian-recipe books. I borrowed them all.

TWENTY-SEVEN

Laketown
May 14th

At the realty office a little after five, Marge thanked me for some flowers I'd brought, and said John had gone fishing.

My mood plummeted. I'd been counting on meeting her father. "We're not having supper?"

"Certainly we are. He should be at home by now. He likes to have some fish to show my dad when they come over." She mimed bafflement. "Don't ask. It's one of those hunter-gatherer thingys."

I followed Marge's dark-gray Volvo SUV a few zigzags south of the main street to a cul-de-sac at the end of a ridge. She motioned me to put the Explorer next to a parked small Cadillac. We went on down a steep concrete driveway.

The house at the bottom was timber-clad and opulent, on a sprawling lakeside lot, flanked by others like it. Lawns studded with blossoming fruit-trees. A smokehouse down by the water. A gazebo over an outdoor spa-pool.

A white fiberglass fishing-boat, the trailer hitched to John's pickup, occupied the center space of a three-vehicle garage. Fishing gear littered the shiny gray-painted floor.

Marge looked to the heavens martyredly as we passed the mess, shucked off shoes and followed, "We're in here's," through into a huge lounge. A floor-to-ceiling glass wall overlooked the picturesque lake. The other walls displayed stunning C.M. Russell, outdoor and wildlife paintings.

A man in cream slacks and a polo shirt, the image of how Clark Gable might have looked if he'd lived that far into his 70s, relaxed in a La-Z-Boy chair. An elegant white-haired woman in a blue dress and pearls shared a leather couch with John. He introduced them as Howard and Lucy. Their handshakes were firm and welcoming.

John had a short glass with pale-amber contents, probably scotch on the rocks. Howard's was likely a jack and coke. There was a twist in Lucy's clear glass, perhaps a G & T. I let myself have the moment. The alcohol hitting the back of my throat. First one of the day. Ice and fire. The glow building from the inside out.

"Drink Ben?"

"Just a club soda, please."

"Another for you, Dad?"

"Just one more. Lucy'll be calling me a lush."

Leaving John and Howard joking back and forth about fishing, obviously good friends, Marge led me through to the kitchen of my dreams. Pale green marble counters. Twin butcher-block islands. Brushed steel appliances. Cream walls and three bright Rockwell prints adding just the right touch. From the divine aroma, supper was already under-way.

"Can I do anything?

Marge said, "No, it's under control I think."

She donned oven mitts. Cracked the oven door. A bouquet of smoky meat, rosemary, thyme and more than a touch of garlic, set my taste buds salivating.

"Smells amazing."

"Well thank you, Ben." Marge said, "Slow baked short ribs. One of dad's favorites. I'll make stroganoff sauce if I can remember how."

"May I?"

Her eyebrows elevated. "Sure. Please!" She showed me where to find things, then went to find a vase for the flowers.

I diced some shiitake mushrooms and spring onions and browned them in a little butter. Stirred in a cup of sour cream, a good splash of Worcester, and an even better one of brandy from the bar. I was playing with the flavor with pinches of this and that, ready for the juices from the ribs, when Marge came and tried a little on a spoon.

"Out-of-this-world, Ben. How did you learn to do that?"

"Just an interest. It's easy with a kitchen like this."

"Don't lose the interest. The world of food lovers needs you!"

While Marge was getting ready to serve, John showed me through the house which he'd built himself. It radiated their sense of taste and his craftsmanship, and showcased beautiful wood grains, some with a gorgeous blue stain he said appeared in aged beetle-killed timber.

On the wall of the staircase to the second story, was the huge hide of a white bear and a smaller one of a black wolf. And like something by Georgia O'Keefe, shelves displaying the fanged skulls of predators he'd taken, in order of size from coyote up to the big bears. I gained a whole new respect for John as both a craftsman and outdoorsman.

It was too cool for the patio so we ate in the chandelier lit dining room. Baked potatoes and steamed green vegetables complemented the succulent ribs. My sauce was a big hit. If anyone noticed I didn't touch the wine John brought up from his cellar, they didn't comment. Desert was a quite wonderful cheesecake Lucy had made.

Back in the lounge over digestifs for them and coffee for me, Howard-quite a raconteur with what seemed an encyclopedic memory, entertained us with a history of the district.

Laketown was on the original telegraph trail, also the site of a fur trading post, before becoming a logging and mining center, and then a service and tourism town.

He told of booms and busts, occasionally seeking Lucy's agreement. The realty company had been a second career for Howard after bossing his own logging outfit. He'd begun by selling pieces of land he'd logged, before branching into property management, and later selling out to Marge and John to retire. By appearances around me, it had all been very successful.

His storytelling skills were at their best describing the town's biggest unsolved crime: the robbery of a gold-shipment passing south from Wright Creek in April '85, at the site of the corner shopping center.

Three gunmen had held up the lightly guarded shipment in a snowstorm and after a brief shootout, transferred the strongbox to a pickup truck and vanished into the maze of logging back roads. No one knew how they got away. Howard had all of us on the edges of our seats.

Eventually he said to me in his rich sonorous voice, "John tells me you're in that place at the far end of Lake Kaldekut,"

I nodded.

"Beautiful place."

"Thank you."

"He says you have some questions about it."

"I do."

"Was originally a developer's show-cabin. Some bunch out of Smithers had the council in their pocket and thought they could pre-sell enough of them to fund a tract. Then the local situation flared up, and they faded away. Did a real impressive job there though. What in particular do you want to know?"

"Do you remember how you came to manage it?"

He cogitated briefly. "Would have been August of '93. Late that summer anyways. I remember the year because it was a warm one, the lakes thawed real early. Feller came to see me. City feller. Asked me to manage it for him. I remember he wanted it in his wife's name."

That's the year we came here. He must have put the place up for management before we left.

"That was my father."

"Do tell now? Come to think of it he looked a bit like you."

"You remember him that well?"

"Oh shoot yes. Never forget a face. He was a fine-looking feller like you if you don't mind me saying so. Same hair, kind of up a little at the sides there. What's that... a widow's peak?"

I laughed uncomfortably. Compliments have always been a problem for me.

"Smartly dressed feller too. Wore a suit with a waistcoat. Had a good hat."

"And that was it?"

"Yes he signed an agreement and I guess skedaddled back to the city. John will have the paperwork."

"He does. But wouldn't you also have gotten some kind of ownership paperwork? He could have been anyone."

"Probably not. Why would I? The place was either on a leased parcel of Chief George's land, or district land, and the district council would have known about that. I could have checked any time."

"Chief George?"

"Yes he's still the Grand Chief of the Nations Development Corp. Though I hear his son Charles is making a move up."

I sloughed off the distracting extra-information. "My problem is I can't prove I'm not on the Lodgepine Nation's land and they've filed a trespass case against me."

He whistled. "That's a tough one. What are you going to do?"

"I'm going to fight it."

His voice was slower, deeper, when he replied. "Has, ah John mentioned..."

"Yes I have," said John, "but he's determined and I agree with him. A man should stand his ground if he believes he's right."

Howard looked grave. "The local folks won't like it. The Nations keep this place alive during the slow, cold times. They boycott your business; you better hang it up until the tourists come back in the spring. And '91s not that long ago. No one wants a repeat of that."

"Ninety-one?"

"The riots! Big court case set it off. Supposedly about the Nations' right to hunt and fish any time they pleased, but everyone knew it was about land ownership. Anyway, they lost the case and the news was on the radio early afternoon. Kids at the high school broke a few windows. School called the Mounties, and they had the kids in a classroom. Their families came down and there was a set-to. It spread to the street and before you knew it, they had a crowd and decided to march on the district offices, which were," he coughed and fanned his hand in front of his face, "just across the road from the office."

"Where the bank is now?"

"Uh huh. Anyway, by this time the Mounties were on the way from Smithers, and Vanderhoof but before they arrived, the folks in the street set the place alight. Burned for two days. Right down to ash."

"Must have been difficult for you being just across the road."

"You bet. Heat peeled the paint right off our place and melted the lead on the roof. Had to move all our files out the back door and pile them in the back of a truck in case it went up. We made it through though."

"What happened afterward?"

He snorted. "Hardly a damn thing. RCMP moved everyone off the streets. Most had already gone back to the reserves. No charges laid. We re-painted and re-roofed. Few years later they went back to court and that time they won."

Lucy said, "Howard, you know we should be..."

"Yes dear." He put a big hand fondly on her knee. "She doesn't like me to get excited. Probably right. I hope that was helpful, Ben," he said as Marge moved away to get their coats and John went to fetch the Cadillac.

"Very much. Thank you,"

"Any time. Good luck to you."

I sure hope so.

TWENTY-EIGHT

Laketown
May 15th

On Tuesday evening at six I was outside Otto's in my best slacks, shirt, and sports coat. Libby came out a side door, smiling mischievously and looking gorgeous; in a mid-length washed-denim skirt, a matching jacket over a crimson blouse, ankle-boots, and carrying an elegant blue-fabric purse with a silver-edged flap.

I said, "Wow!" and made it in time to get her passenger's door.

She said, "Going my way?"

"You look wonderful. Sure am."

"Thank you."

She'd added some light makeup around her eyes, which sparkled. As the truck cab filled with her perfume, she said, "Not gonna throw me in any lakes, are you?"

"Not planning on it."

"Be a big improvement."

"You're not going to let me live that down, are you?"

"Might take a while."

She leaned quickly up and kissed me. I leaned in and we lingered a moment. She ended it by chuckling so our lips bobbled. "I wanted to get that out of the way so I wouldn't be thinking about it all night."

"I'm glad. Any chance of seconds?"

"I'm gonna to let you think about THAT all night."

"Brat! Well, which way ma'am?"

"Back thataway. McGee's at the highway junction."

McGee's' was frontier style with saloon-style tables and fabric-backed period-chairs. A male trio, dressed for outdoor work and holding frosty beers, nodded to us from stools at a bar table. No one was eating yet.

A waitress took us to a table where Libby sat before I could pull the chair out, but I got her jacket. She adjusted a little, a delicious shimmy, put her bag down at her chair leg and said, "So how's your week been?"

When I got to the part about dinner with the Campbell-clan and Howard's story of the riots she said, "I was just a kid then, but I know it cast a pall over the whole town."

"Literally."

She laughed. "I suppose yeah. School was closed. We had hordes of Mounties patrolling afterward but the Nations' people stayed on their land. It gradually settled down."

"That's what Marge's dad said."

"Not completely though. The Nations' kids had a leader, a chief's son, and they'd all hang-out together on breaks. I had one friend from the Nations, Margaret Nine Trees, but even she found it hard to be... just a normal girlfriend, I guess."

"You said leader?"

"Prince Charles."

"The Nations have Kings and Queens and Earls?"

"Nooooo," she laughed," Well not really."

"Why the title then?"

Another waitress came. Libby knew her and they chatted while I admired the trophy heads along the walls, including a big elk, and to add humor, a Jackalope; a mythical creature of the old west with deer horns on a jackrabbit's head. A blackboard said 'Live Music Fridays and Saturdays till Late', alongside a couple of amplifiers and a microphone stand. Behind the bar was all mirror-glass except for a bull moose head, with, predictably, a lead-glass Moosehead beer sign hanging crookedly from its antlers. There had to be at least an inch of ice on the chrome housing of the draft beer handles. I licked my lips.

Libby said, "Trust me," and ordered the all you can eat seafood special, times two. Then she asked for a strawberry daiquiri. I ordered a tall orange juice. I saw her look.

It's going to come out sometime. Just I'd rather not tonight.

When I prompted her about the 'Prince,' she said, "Well back when the Hudson Bay Company controlled all this land..."

"That's way back."

"Mid 1800s I think. There were as many French as English and Scots here. I guess the HBC needed supporters among the Nations. One of their biggest was the High Chief Niawata from right here in Laketown. The HBC arranged an award from the Queen of England and the chief was so impressed he vowed to name his sons after English royalty and it's carried down from there. The son of the current chief is Prince Charles. Makes sense now?"

"That's a great story. What's he like?"

"Charlie? Very impressive. He's a war hero too."

"Really?"

"Uh huh. Was a Major, I think. Got some medal or other in Afghanistan."

"I didn't know Canada was even in Afghanistan."

"Well the paper said he was there with some special unit and rescued some people under fire. The details were hush hush though."

"What was he like in school?"

"A big sport-star. Lacrosse is huge here. I think the Nations invented it. Charlie was team captain every year."

"But personally?"

Libby wrinkled her nose. "He's very polite. But it's like being near a wild tiger or lion. Beautiful, but at any moment... you know?"

Food arrived and ended the conversation for awhile. Bowls of broiled shrimp with several types of dip. Golden fried flaky fish. Split Alaska crab legs with a butter sauce. Light, crisp fries on the side. I tried a piece of fish first. Libby grinned at my murmur of enjoyment.

"Halibut," she said. "From the sound off Prince Rupert. Bertrand Latour, the owner, gets it fresh off the boats. The whole town comes here on Wednesdays."

And the place was filling up. Libby smiled at one or two diners as they passed. She pointed out the Mayor, a rotund, glad-handing guy who worked the room before sitting down with a couple of other men Libby said were councilors. Hanrahan wasn't among them. At one point, a big man in a white chef's outfit, who I gathered was Bertrand, waved at Libby before going back through the swinging-doors to the kitchen. "He's my biggest customer."

We had seconds of the halibut and a couple of extra crab legs each. The crowd thinned again until it was just us and a few stragglers. A phrase Libby had used on Sunday afternoon came back to me. "What exactly is a 'Jack Mennonite'?"

She grinned wryly. "I guess it's a term around rebellion."

"Rebelling against what?"

"We're not like the Amish as I told you."

That had been my first thought, of families in summer bonnets and long dresses, in horse-drawn buggies on back roads in places like Pennsylvania. "Sounds sort of disparaging," I said.

She made a face. "Yes, that's an aspect of it. It's a close community and most never leave it. When someone won't live the pure life, like me, those that do can be judgmental. Even cruel."

"Oh."

She nodded. "You have to understand it's as much a lifestyle choice. Modest dress. No makeup or jewelry." She plucked a strand of hair. "This should be longer and braided. What makes it tougher is my father is also the pastor here."

Her having to leave so abruptly that first evening dropped into place. "That must be hard."

"I think it's much harder for him. When I don't conform, it's like an advertisement of failure. But we're taught to love our parents and our parents to love us, and he knows I need the job. So we accommodate. I try to be respectful. I don't rub it in their faces. But I'm 30 years old and I'm not going to live like a nun."

She shifted her silverware into alignment for something to do with her hands, and added, "The worst thing is the divorce. We can't even talk about that."

"I'm sorry. That must be very difficult."

"It is but I love my father no matter what, or who, he disapproves of."

There was nothing I could say to that. Her daiquiri made a noise when she put the straw to her mouth. I looked around for the waitress who was in regular clothes now and helping the barman turn chairs upside down. I paid the check and helped Libby with her chair. When she stood up with her purse; I kissed her cheek. "We'll work it out." The words brought back a wan smile.

Inside the truck, she sat with her knees together a moment before blurting out, "I can't stay with you tonight."

I'd had no expectation, but the rejection still hurt.

"I'm just getting used to this and it wouldn't work with the shop. I have a big stock delivery first thing."

"It's alright."

"But I can come Friday if you like. Come and stay."

My heart leapt. I said, "Okay," kind of carefully, and we kissed. Gently then urgently, then tenderly again.

Outside her father's house, a steep-roofed 'A' frame, on a side street parallel to town and a few blocks up a hill, she kissed me quickly a last time and slipped out of the truck before I could make more of it. I watched while she went up a cobblestone pathway, until the front door closed and a light came on, before I driving slowly away.

I made it all of two blocks before my emotional roller-coaster finally stopped at the top. I punched the air and hollered, "Yes!"

TWENTY-NINE

Lake Kaldekut
May 17th

It was already past the middle of May, and spring at the cove was ripening into summer. The air smelled of wildflowers and murmured with insects. The forest seemed more achingly green each time I looked at it, and the storm-battered shoreline was fast renewing. Anticipation of the coming weekend with Libby had added such a glow to my life, it was a pleasure just to be around the cabin.

I had someone.

In the light of that fact, the previously mountainous challenges of proving ownership and persuading the Feds of my innocence dwindled to simple struggles to be fought and won. I settled in to relaxing and enjoying my surroundings.

On Thursday morning, nearing the end of my morning walk, I again saw the mother and her four goslings emerging from the shelter of the reeds. They were growing fast. No longer just mischievous balls of fluff, though not yet fluff-free, they'd become handsome hyperactive creatures with jet-black legs and beaks. I was happy for the company.

Later, after exercising into a sweat, I dragged the couch out on the sunny deck to sprawl out and read more about Virgil Cole and Everett Hitch in the old west. They, Stone Barrington and Dino Bacchetti in New York City, had become regular companions.

However; it seemed this would be a thinking day. I once believed my fanatical work ethic was my greatest strength. In reality, it had been slavish devotion to the mindless daily-ritual of seeking respect in the eyes of strangers I didn't care two bits about. How could I have been so obliviously shallow? That I might make a fortune from it, if I won the battle with the feds, didn't excuse anything.

Also, as excuses went, there probably wasn't one for how I'd treated Russell. Except perhaps I was off my head. How could I have exploded at him like that? Even after my behavior, he'd taken care of the hospital bills and had the class to write a gracious letter. The advice in it still resonated. I'd indeed been a dumb bastard, and I did have to find another way to make a living. If I ever got the chance, I would man-up and make it right with him. But regardless of how things worked out, I would never go back to the life I had left.

A movement drew my attention to the beach. The geese had travelled unusually far from the marsh and were coming ashore between me and the stranded log. The young ones immediately slumped down in a group, tired from keeping up with mom.

I looked for my place in the book, but squawks of fright made me glance up again. A solidly built animal, dark-brown and hump-shouldered like a bear but smaller, perhaps 40 pounds of sharp-teethed predator, had sprung from behind the roots of the log.

Wolverine.

It reached the birds and slashed out a talon-tipped paw, flinging the mother goose away in a burst of feathers. Then it rounded on the petrified goslings, face a snarling mask. It snatched with its jaws at one, then another. Each time was a crunch of teeth through flesh and bone. The remaining two fluttered away terrified in different directions. The wolverine hunted down the first and killed it with one snap. The second headed directly toward me, wing stubs flailing. The beast closed the distance at amazing speed, but the bird veered, and the gnashing jaws caught mainly feathers.

I was on my feet screaming.

Instead of finishing the job, the wolverine froze, then backed away, uncertain, before deciding I wasn't an imminent threat. It methodically gathered its kill by the necks and trotted unhurriedly away, as if the birds were weightless, around the log and away across the verge, leaving only a few drifting white tufts.

The survivor remained on its belly, head up, waiting for the end. When I went down the steps from the deck, it tried to struggle away, but I caught it easily. Less than a pound in weight, I could feel wet-warm blood on its side and a pounding heart.

My immediate thought was to put it out of its misery, but some impulse stopped me. I carried it to the kitchen and put it gently down on the table top. It moved one leg feebly in a swimming motion and weaved its head a couple of times, then lay still, watching me.

I found two bleeding slashes just back of the right wing-root, but the wounds hadn't penetrated the body cavity. Just the same it was a wild thing in pain and I shouldn't let it suffer. Yet I wavered.

Why not give it a chance? It might die of shock anyway, but why not?

I retrieved a cardboard box from the woodshed, lined the bottom with newspaper and softly lay the bird down in it. Eileen had been allergic to everything alive or dead, so I'd never had an animal in my care; not a cat or a dog or a parrot. But common sense said that any creature in shock needed quiet and lots of fluids. I put a bowl of water in the box, and that in the corner of the kitchen by the pantry with a dishtowel over the top, and left it to the quiet part.

Sunset splashed the sky with reds, oranges and crimsons Van Gogh never dreamed of. I closed my book, and the sliding-doors against the chill, and made a quite decent parsley, chives, basil, and tarragon omelet.

I checked one more time before heading off to bed. The injured gosling was hunched in one corner, eyes watchful, but the water level in the bowl had lowered. I stroked its back, which was warm and the heartbeat slow and steady.

Only time would tell.

If it makes it through the night, I'll have to learn what they eat.

THIRTY

Lake Kaldekut
May 18th

Friday morning, I went immediately to the kitchen to check on Bird (the name I'd decided to give it since I had no idea if it was a boy or a girl.) It cheeped when I lifted the cloth. So far, so good. It had done its part by lasting the night. I logged on to the internet to do mine.

One website suggested chick feed. Not terribly helpful since I hadn't a clue what that was, but I imagined it was some kind of mashed grain. I found a box of cereal, crushed some in a bowl, and added milk. When I put it in the box, Bird showed no interest. I went to make coffee. Within a minute I heard pecking on the bowl.

Progress.

The rest of the day, other than reading, I cleaned the cabin until I was sure it wouldn't disgrace me. With more hope than confidence, I even changed the sheets. At one point I called Hal's office. He should have been back in town, but there was no reply and it didn't transfer to his mobile.

Disappointing.

I also thought more about the two nagging mysteries, why my father bought this place and the strange case of Adrian Reeman.

My father was an impenetrable wall. It seemed everything in that space was distorted. I couldn't let go of it, but couldn't think dispassionately either. Perhaps that would change now I was on a path to healing. As for Mr. Reeman, it was bizarre he should spend all that money and then walk away, but I couldn't for the life of me imagine why.

By five-thirty I'd showered and shaved and had a cheery fire going. I didn't expect Libby until around seven-thirty, but what I had planned for supper would take awhile, so I made a start.

I like to give my pasta sauce time to boil down and the flavors plenty of time to mingle, so I got that going first, then started on the dough. Absent a rolling pin, I pressed it out with a plate, folding it until the consistency was right. I was cutting out the last of the circles with a big coffee cup when I heard a vehicle; it couldn't be her. It wasn't even six-thirty.

But it was. She was in slacks and a different colored cashmere sweater, her hair fluffed out a little at the sides, framing her beautifully formed face perfectly. I was in sweats and a stained apron with flour down the front.

Two for two in debonair impressions.

"God I wasn't expecting you for another hour."

"Oh, should I come back?"

"Don't even think about it! You look wonderful!"

She said, "Well thank you kind sir!"

I took a bulky bag off her shoulder, leaving her with a plastic carry bag with the tops of two wine bottles sticking out the top. She said, "Let me guess. You're making dinner." I tried to brush a smear off my front, but the flour on my hands just made it worse.

"You're a genius. Yes, just a little something."

She beamed brightly and held up the wine bottles, a South African Zinfandel and a New Zealand White Sauvignon. "Will you join me?"

There it is.

"Ahh no actually I don't drink."

"Not at all?"

I imagine I shuffled a little, watching her face. "Not at all."

"Does that have something to do with your hip?"

"Yes sort of. It's complicated."

She shrugged. "Okay. I'll take one though."

The Kiwi white had a screw top. I poured some into a water tumbler. She sipped, observing me over the rim.

"I'm sorry," I said, turning back to the pasta. "I thought this would be in the oven when you got here."

"Can I watch? I love to see a man at work."

"Sure."

It's almost impossible to screw up ravioli filling. Along with ground beef, I portioned spices into a deep oven-pan by the palm-full. She was right by my elbow when I started adding chopped garlic. "Sure you want to be this close? It smells!"

"Yes it does. It smells terrific!"

My kind of lady.

With the last tasty-filled *mezzelune* folded and crimped, I layered them between leaves of bright green spinach in a deep baking dish. Splashed each with some sauce and a good sprinkling of Italian seasoning as I went. Finally poured on the rest and topped off with some Parmesan.

"Forty-five minutes should do it," I said as I closed up the oven and doffed the apron.

She toasted me. Then she noticed the covered box. "Oh a kitten?"

"Let me show you."

Bird looked up at us calmly with bright black eyes.

"Oh! Is it hurt?"

"A little bit. I rescued it from a wolverine."

Libby said, "Wow!"

"Yeah killed the rest of the family right in front of me."

She lifted Bird and held it against her. It squirting droppings on her sweater. She laughed loudly, which made it struggle.

"Let me," I said. While she washed off the gunk from her top, I changed the box and settled the little creature down again.

We watched the sunset and she sipped wine until the food was done, then I got plates and utensils and served us each a portion.

"I thought it was a man's heart," Libby said between steaming forkfuls.

"Huh?"

"I thought food was the way to a man's heart. You're sure winning mine."

"It's an equal opportunity household. Eat or I'll steal yours!"

"Just try buster," she said, jabbing at me with the fork.

While I cleaned up Libby took her bag into the bedroom, then I topped off her glass and we settled in the lounge by the flickering fire She said, "I never knew a guy who didn't have a TV. I swear!"

"The laptop's got a decoder. I can probably find some public broadcasting. There might even be a war movie on DVD somewhere."

She did a little rabbitty thing with her nose and pulled me close. "I don't think so. We'll just have to entertain ourselves." When we parted for breath she said, "Umm do you have anything?"

"Oh my God no!"

"It's okay. I do."

In the bedroom, she slipped off her top and tossed it toward her bag. I took off mine so I was bare-chested when I unsnapped the catch and her bra fell away. On the bed she nestled into me like it was the perfect place to be, and my body certainly agreed. My mouth found her breasts, and I teased each swelling nipple until her breathing was ragged. Then I tensed a little and Libby said, "What is it?"

"I ahh... don't think I can."

"What?" Her hand brushed my stomach, then moved lower, stroking. "This tells me you're wrong."

"It's not that, it's my hip. I can't put any weight on it."

Libby caressed me until I writhed, then said huskily, "I know a position that will work." Her breasts glided silkily down my chest.

She was right. It worked wonderfully.

THIRTY-ONE

Lake Kaldekut
May 19th

A red dawn glowed through the window when I awoke, and 'red sky at morning, sailor take warning,' played in my mind like a bad jingle. Libby stirred beside me and said, "Good morning you!"

"Good morning you too."

"Oooo garlic morning breath," she said, and vaulted out from under the covers.

So much for my masculine charm.

I checked on Bird, which was doing fine on its breakfast-food diet, then made eggs for us. When we'd eaten, Libby tilted her head the way a woman does when getting-her-way matters, and she asked how my hip felt.

"It's not bad, why?"

"I'd like to go walking with you this morning. Climb and explore."

The climb part was a concern. But tomorrow could be a complete-rest day. She'd already said she couldn't stay that night.

"I'm ahh... sure."

We halted on an outcrop and absorbed the view awhile. The lake was steely under an evenly gray sky, but we could see far beyond the cove's enclosing headland to where the mountains dissolved into haze. Moving on, we reached more level and sparsely wooded ground. The breeze was in our faces and we seemed invisible to the wildlife. Woodpeckers rapped among the canopy.

Several times, perfectly camouflaged ptarmigan erupted at our feet and clattered short distances before vanishing again. A deep-brown pine-marten let us get close before scampering down off its perch. A brace of golden-eagles circling lazily on the updrafts. We wandered happily. I thought often about what I'd missed as a city-boy.

At the edge of a swale, Libby pointed. Three exaggeratedly eared mule deer were quartering across an open area, picking at anything green. A buck with a mass of antlers trailing tassels of velvet, and two dainty does. They were oblivious, and we watched them out of sight before plunking down on the carpet of fir-needles to rest before turning back. After a while Libby said, "It's unusual you don't drink."

"Is it?"

"Heck yes. Every guy here thinks he's a big tough logger or a cowboy or something. It's a badge-of-brotherhood that they drink like fish. Or is that fishes? But you don't."

"I stopped."

"Got tired of it?"

I said, "You could say that," and hesitated. Libby arched her eyebrows and gazed at me calmly.

"I was a drunk."

She plucked at some coarse grass stalks, which made little snapping sounds as they broke. "I'd have thought creating computer-software needed a lot of concentration."

"Not really. Once you've grasped it, you can do a lot of it on cruise control. It's mostly being systematic. And careful, I guess. In front of a computer, anyway."

"They say alcoholism is a disease..."

"I didn't say I was an alcoholic. I said I was a drunk."

"Isn't that semantics?"

"No. Not in my book anyway. Alcoholics feel a compulsion, I think. I simply wanted to, but I'm too controlling to let something like that own me."

She reacted sharply. "That's an awful word to use about yourself!"

Struck a nerve there.

"I'm sorry. That came out wrong. I've been in therapy and sometimes I think out loud and kind of clumsily. I'm really sorry."

A few moments passed before her face softened. "Did the therapy help you understand why you drank?"

"I think so."

"You only think so?"

"No, I know so. Since I was a little kid, there's been something broken in my life and I've spent a lot of years just holding the edges together. Drinking shut out some of the pain."

"You were drunk when you had your accident?"

I nodded. "I'm amazed it didn't happen way sooner."

Libby said, "Is this going to be a problem for us? For our…" She stopped at the crossroads.

"I don't know. I used to hide in it. From things being too bad, I guess. Or being too good and they wouldn't last. Anyway I'm getting better. I don't want it the same way anymore. And no, I don't think it's a problem for us. That's if you want me. But I can't promise. Not yet anyway."

She put her palm in the hollow where my jaw and throat joined. I leaned into it. She said, "We both have pain my sweet. And pasts."

I pulled her to me and clothes flew, and there weren't any more words unless you counted her unintelligible sounds against my chest, or my groans. We held each other for a long time in the afterglow, as our hearts slowed and moisture on our bodies cooled and dried.

We said very little on our way down to the cove. No words could add anything to how we felt.

The red dawn had not lied. Sunday morning arrived gray-brown and threatening. I put on a Kathmandu jacket and went out to see what to expect.

The big water beyond the cove raged and the northerly wind carried a thin, stinging sleet. Winter clearly planned a bitter parting encore. I closed the shutters, stacked some more split wood against the cabin, and carried a double-armful inside to bank up the fire.

Bird was waiting excitedly, wings-stubs waggling. Its box was a mess. It would soon need more living space than a three by two-foot cardboard box, which raised a dilemma.

Even in good weather, I couldn't just put it outside. It would be a meal for something, and very quickly. But could we possibly co-exist indoors?

Why not? If a parrot can be house-trained, why not a young goose? Surely the only difference is size?

I barricaded off the kitchen area with pieces of decking from the woodshed. Then lay down newspaper and several water-bowls and let Bird loose in the enclosure. It began poking in every corner and crevice. I went to browse the net, but came back and checking on it regularly.

As expected, it relieved itself frequently. I was counting on it being a creature-of-habit. Sure enough, it went most often in one corner near the back door. I cleared away the rest of the paper and kept an eye on it. If it strayed too far; I'd nudge it in the right direction. Good habits might take time to entrench, but after a couple more hours I thought it had the idea. I made up another box with an opening so it could come and go.

Then I checked the weather again, which had deteriorated significantly. The wind might have dropped, but the temperature was borderline freezing, and the sleet had become a rattling hail.

Back in the warm cabin I remembered to call Hal, Sunday afternoon or not. His office phone clicked over to his mobile and he answered with, "Sorry Ben, I'm at the lake battening down. I see your number here. Can you give me a few minutes to get squared away?"

I wondered if he had a yacht or a powerboat, but either way he called back within 15 minutes. It was the first time the phone had made a sound since I'd moved in and, for a second or two didn't recognize it. It crossed my mind just how far removed I was from when phones rang around me all day long.

"The document search was a complete bust Ben, I'm sorry. I was really hoping there'd be something."

"Me too," I said dejectedly.

"I was also wrong about the Nations not getting their case on the court docket for at least a month."

"Oh shit."

"Can't disagree with that. It's down for two weeks from Wednesday. That's June 6th. And they're going all out on counsel. Their lead guy is a heavy-hitter from Ottawa. We'll have our hands full."

My disappointment and trepidation hung in the air.

He said, "Yeah, sorry it's not better news."

"You did your best, Hal."

"Let's catch up right before the hearing. Talk to you then."

At the last of the light, the wind died away to nothing. A snowstorm like brownish cotton-wool descended. I watched from the kitchen window as the first fluffy flakes drifted down and shattered on the stony ground.

I was reasonably well prepared if it stuck around awhile. Low on fresh food and vegetables maybe, but there were ample frozen, so scurvy wasn't a serious danger. Plenty of dry food as well, including frozen bread. Powdered milk-and cereal too, so Bird wouldn't starve either. I ate the last of the ravioli, banked the fire for the night, added one of the zipped-open sleeping-bags to the bed, and turned in.

In the morning as I crossed the barricade into the kitchen, I about stepped on Bird, out of its box and waiting. I looked around to see what mess there was. Apart from one splash, it was all on the patch of paper. Grinning, I reached down and gave it a pet.

This might just work out.

The snow continued, with perpetual motion along the edge of the forest, as boughs released their burdens and flicked back up, before starting to bend again. I was enjoying it. Growing up in West Van, snow was something you dressed for and put up with. A couple of decades in Seattle had turned it into entertainment.

Around noon on the second day I ventured outside and found it powdery and dry to walk on, with a distinctive crunch underfoot. I could bury my hand with fingers out straight, in the accumulation on the Explorer' hood. The satellite-dish on the roof was half buried, which wouldn't help the internet reception any. But by nightfall it was easing, and by 8:30 p.m. stars dimpled the rapidly broadening areas of clear sky. Around 10:00 p.m. the northern lights rose on the horizon; smoky purple, green, and orange streamers that swirled and writhed across the ionosphere. I fell asleep to the mesmerizing flicker of it against the bedroom wall.

And the next day I went snowmobiling.

THIRTY-TWO

Lake Kaldekut
May 24th

The day was blinding-white, and the snow calf-deep, as I crunched out to the snowmobile shelter, in a hooded-parka, a cap with flaps over my ears, and carrying a snow-shovel in one mitten. The only other sounds were plop-plopping from under the trees, and drip-dripping from the cabin eaves.

A simpler form of transportation, than the 80s-vintage snowmobile, would have been hard to find. There was an on-off gas valve, manual engine-choke, a retracting starter-rope like an old lawn-mower and a twist-throttle like a motorcycle. A foot lever engaged the tracks forward and reverse. The clutch gripped when you accelerated and released at idle. The four-stroke engine had a stick to check the oil level. I added a half-quart. The fuel-tank under the many-times repaired tip-up seat was nearly full. I set the choke to maximum and pulled the rope. It coughed after a few pulls, then fired to smoky-life. I backed off the choke and let it idle while I dug it out.

When I tried it around the verge, its skis dogged-down if I turned too slowly, otherwise it was easy to handle. I felt like a pro after only a couple of circuits.

This is a hoot!

Then I aimed it at the gap in the trees, to go up the main road and see when I might be able to get out in the truck. A drift cushioned me over the ford.

Then a couple of bends up the road and off to my right was a square-ish black mass. I paid it little attention until it moved. My mind screamed '*Black bear*!' I backed off the throttle. The snowmobile dug in and almost threw me over the handlebars. I'd need to watch that.

But it was a bull moose, its lower legs hidden and its head in some bushes. I expected it to crash away in a shower of flung snow. Instead, it simply lifted its head and stared at me, chewing. A young animal, because the palms of the antlers were small, but still probably the size of a small horse.

The high-revving engine hadn't bothered it; perhaps that's why so many of the silly things get killed on the roads, but it didn't like it that I'd stopped. The beast made a lunging movement with its shoulders, climbed a bank and walked off slowly through the trees. Despite my frozen face I smiled watching it go.

After all these years!

At the side-road, I looked left and right. Ungraded snow extended into the distance in both directions. But something had traveled along the road before me. The surface had holes in it, like a giant on stilts had walked past. And so recently I could see scatters where snow had kicked up behind.

Curious, I got down and walked closer. The holes were oval and large. I squatted and put both hands, palms flat, in the bottom of one. There was room to spare. Then I made out one large pad and a half-circle of smaller ones. At the leading edge, slashes had cut cleanly down through the snow. The hair arose on the back of my neck. They were bear tracks. Grizzly bear tracks.

The thrill I felt when John Campbell had said they were around, vanished. Now I was shaking. I was afraid to look up, but I did. First left from where the animal had come. Then right where the tracks continued another 50 yards or so before making a right into the trees. All around was desolate.

A grizzly! Less than a half-mile from the cove! Maybe less than a half-hour ago!

I'd suddenly become clumsy and inept. It took six or seven changes of direction before I was headed back down the access track. And then I almost ran off the side on the first bend. Eventually I rumbled across the open verge and parked the machine in its shelter. Sat on it a minute settling my breathing and thinking about what John had said

Grizzlies are travelers. Perhaps they travel that road all the time. It's miles away by now, surely.

Just the same, I double-checked the garbage drum was sealed tight before going inside.

You never the heck know.

John Campbell was skeptical the following afternoon when I finally made it into town to tell him.

"A grizzly bear? I believe you saw what you saw Ben, but they don't like to travel in the deep snow if they can avoid it. A really hungry one might, but it's been a good spring and there's plenty of food around. Are you sure the snow hadn't melted and made the tracks bigger?"

"I'm not kidding John. They were fresh. I could put my hands down flat in one. I even saw pads and claw marks."

"Okay, but it flies in the face of experience. Sure one was seen in April at the road-kill dump, but it would have been right out of hibernation, and I told you they range. Two in as many months would be real unusual."

"I saw the tracks John."

He shrugged and put a friendly hand on my arm. "Okay I'll let Jack know."

"Jack?"

"Jacques DeLeon. Local fish and wildlife officer. He also runs the dump."

"What's that for?"

"We have a pack of gray wolves northwest of town."

He saw my look. "Don't worry about them. Unless you're keeping sheep or young calves, they're no problem. Anyway, the road kill dump is part of their feeding program. We take all the moose that gets killed on the roads along with the odd deer, and the wolves clean up the carcasses."

I struggled with the image a second or two.

John slapped me heartily on the shoulder. "Just a fact of life my friend. We don't have wildlife, it has us!"

"Thanks a lot."

But the real downturn in my day happened after I sloshed my way along to Otto's.

A warm front had lifted the temperature into the high 50s. The snow was disappearing as fast as it came. Run-off from the roofs of businesses, had the gutters along Laketown's main street overflowing.

There was a Collins B-1 school bus parked outside, except it was gray instead of yellow, and had 'Mennonite Community - Bouclier Lake Parish' on the side. A number of kids, all dressed primly, the girls' hair braided, milled inside. Libby was supervising.

I resisted hugging her, which was hard. Except embarrassing her would have been worse.

The severity of the storm had surprised everyone, socking in southwestern BC, and Washington State as far south as Olympia. The kids had been on a Victoria Day long-weekend camp, and had only just been able to make the eight-mile trip home.

Victoria Day? I'm so out of touch.

Then Libby said she'd wished we had talked sooner. Her father had asked her to go to a church-conclave with him, down in Coquitlam east of Vancouver, for the next two weeks. She thought some dedicated time might heal some rifts. An aunt was going to run the store.

I was deeply disappointed, particularly since it meant she wouldn't around for the court hearing, but our relationship was strong and getting stronger, and absence makes, as they say. We promised to talk on the phone often, I clung to a hand-hold as long as possible, and left her there on the slushy sidewalk knowing I'd ache for her every day.

On the way out of town, I shopped as well as called in at Hal's office. He'd nothing new except he'd filed a demand with U.S. Justice, through a Seattle compatriot, that they show just-cause. "Not holding my breath, but at least it's in their half of the court, Ben."

I needed low four-wheel drive to cross the ford, with a big pile of library books on the passenger's seat to keep Bird and me company until the court case.

THIRTY-THREE

Laketown
June 6th

I arrived at the courthouse on Ballentyne Street for the trespass hearing, 20 minutes before the one o'clock hour.

It was a tall stone building, with a high-pitched slate roof. There were colored lead-glass windows either side of iron-bound double-doors, and foot-worn stone steps. You'd have thought it had been a church, but a historical-buildings plaque with a diagram said it was a jail back in 1862. The larger legal complex included the modern buildings both sides. Enclosed walkways connected all three. One so judges could enter with dignity when it rained, the other for bringing prisoners for judging and sentencing. I doubted their dignity was a big factor.

Hal was carrying a briefcase and a thick manila folder. He motioned, and I followed, to a small room in the administration area. The folder looked impressive, but the couple of things in it added up to very little, when it came to proving ownership of the cove.

I said, "Why the crowd?"

I'd had to wend through groups of people, most of them Nations' folks. Some had children clinging close. A couple of men smoked furiously off to one side. Clusters of older people talked animatedly. No one paid me any overt attention, but I sensed the groups draw tighter when they saw me.

Hal said, "You're kidding me, right? This is political gunpowder. Don't you get that yet?"

"But why? It's just a little plot of land on a lake."

"Not to them. The Nations can't afford to lose. It would call their whole reserve system into question. Force them to prove boundaries everywhere."

"One little piece of lakefront?

"Ben I'm going to assume you're being obtuse here. Look. I'll do my best but you should expect this won't be the end of it. And it's likely to get more difficult and much more expensive."

"Then we'll just have to get my damn money back from U.S. Justice."

"I'll keep trying to do that Ben."

As he gathered his things I asked, "What if we don't get past this first hearing?"

Hal said, "In about 60 days you'll need to hire yourself a barge. Or put a match to the place."

The court was bigger inside than it had appeared. The judge's bench wore the flags of BC and Canada on either side. There was one table for clerks and bailiffs, and two more for the opposing parties, either side of a center aisle. We were last on the docket.

The cases before us were a debt dispute and some mining issue requiring a court order. The public gallery was packed. You could bet they weren't there about money owed or mining. We sat in the back and waited to be called.

Judge Cornell, a gray-haired man with a lined face, wore a black robe with a forked white collar, over a charcoal worsted suit. He looked tired. Circuit Judge. I could imagine that.

Tired or not, he cleared the cases before ours quickly. We took places at the left-hand table, me on the aisle. Nancy Robitaille and a large pudgy-faced man with very thick fingers, wearing a very good suit, took the other. A slim, studious young companion scribbled down notes every time Nancy and the big man conversed.

The clerk gave a brief summary of why we were there, and at the end of it, the judge cocked down his glasses and said, "And what says the plaintiff?"

The big man rose, and in a high voice, said I was on the We'tutahe-Nation land and they wanted me to take everything man-made I had and depart. Of course, he used a lot more words than that, including that the Nations were the backbone of the country, everyone else was an honored guest, and it was the Nations' prerogative to decide the boundaries of their lands. A couple of times the studious man delivering documents to us, and the clerk who gave them to the judge. Copies of court judgments. Each time Hal shook his head like it wasn't a problem.

Following the big man's diatribe, the judge wrote for a moment or two longer before turning to us. "And the respondent says?"

Hal stood and gave out paperwork too, copies of the will and an affidavit from John Campbell, but the clerk came to him, and I simply passed the copies for the Nations' folks across the aisle.

Hal mentioned how a daisy-chain of good faith removed any deceitful intent. I saw the judge nod slowly during his note taking. Perhaps a point on the board for us. I saw from Nancy Robitaille's exasperated body language she thought so too. Hal wrapped up by saying that everything we possessed pointed to my having every right to be at the cove. He didn't dwell on how thin that 'everything' was.

After a few more moments of writing, Judge Cornell asked was there anything else. The big man started to reiterate some previous point and after a few sentences the judge held up a hand. "Mr. Longfellow, I'm well aware of your reputation in aboriginal rights, but we're not arguing an aboriginal rights case here today. We're hearing a simple case of trespass. And I have yet to see any clear evidence that Mr. Adams is trespassing on your client's land."

Longfellow choked a little and shuffled his paperwork but didn't sit.

"Do you have anything more concrete in that area to show me, Mr. Longfellow?"

"Ah no Your Honour. The boundary records in question appear to have been lost. We're here today to state our customary rights as confirmed in the case of..."

"Mr. Longfellow, this is not a customary rights case either. Now please do you have anything else to add?"

Longfellow said, "No, Your Honour," and subsided.

Judge Cornell's gaze traveled to us, and he frowned. "Mr. Pritchard I must say I'm not used to seeing you associated with this type of case. Nonetheless, have you anything additional to say or provide on behalf of your client?"

Hal stood quickly and said, "Your Honour we await your learned decision."

The judge said, "We will take a 30-minute recess," and the gallery burst into activity and conversation.

We stayed well clear of the crowd. Hal couldn't stand still. The faces I could see were mostly impassive, though a few gave resentful glances. The depth of the Nation's emotion hadn't touched me before. Now I realized, with sadness, I had become a symbol of something hateful.

Then people began going back inside like a pool of water draining. We took our seats again. Nancy and her team were somber. The judge put his hands together before him and looked down at his notes a moment before speaking.

"I have considered this matter at length. More than would seem called for on the surface of it, but all present know there are issues of gravity underlying this matter, which touch on the complex relationships within our society. I wish I could resolve this today. I wish there were clear evidence that would allow me to make a firm decision. I also wish the boundaries that divide our society, both physically and socially, were so clear cut that right was obvious in every instance. However, that is to wish for the moon."

He drank water.

"Neither party has proven their case. This leaves only two possible solutions. Either the parties resolve their differences through negotiation outside the court system, or that this case be decided by a higher court."

He drew his notes together in front of him.

"Therefore. I rule that this matter, in the absence of such resolution, be referred to the Supreme Court of British Columbia for a decision on whether Mr. Adams is in fact, to use Mr. Longfellow's term, 'squatting' on First Nation land and should be removed. I also rule that Mr. Adams may stay where he is until a final decision is rendered, but may not make any changes or improvements of any kind to the property. Court is adjourned."

I looked across at Nancy Robitaille. Her head moved slightly side to side as she mouthed, "Don't even think about it."

THIRTY-FOUR

Laketown
June 6th

Hal's office manager, Connie, a middle-aged, efficient-seeming woman, read my mood and showed me through into his office without attempting chit-chat. He was leaning back in his office-chair saying a lot of "uh huh's" into his desk phone.

It was a very nice chair, with deep-buttoned leather upholstery. Pivoted as he moved. Probably had up and down and recliner controls too. When I went back to doing something at a computer, now I was getting thrown out of my damn home, and was poverty-stricken thanks to U.S. Justice, I thought I'd get one just fucking like it.

Hal hung up the phone after a minute or two and said, "Whoa whoa calm down. It's not as bad as all that."

"You think?"

"That was a friend of mine at the Supreme Court in Smithers. That's the nearest one. I've already spoken to Nancy Robitaille and they're not going to budge."

"Yeah, I got that message in the courtroom."

"So we're working on getting your case moved."

"Why's that?"

"You saw the crowd. You can bet there were reporters there too. You'll be in all the national papers. 'Little guy takes the First Nations to court for a piece of their land.' We can't possibly try this locally. We'd get flayed from both sides in the press, Nations' advocates on one side and everyone afraid of the backlash if you

137

win on the other. No sir!"

"Why does this all have to be so damn hard? All I want is to live in my cabin and be left alone. Not a lot to ask."

"C'mon it's not that simple and you damn well know it. Like it or not, you're a threat to all the Nations' reserves in BC. Potentially, all of Canada."

"It's that simple for me! Hell I'm not even need to own the damn land! I'll be happy to lease it if I have to, damn it!"

Hal sighed. Took off his glasses and pinched the bridge of his nose a few seconds. "Well there's no point in being so sour. At least you get probably a year's grace, no matter what happens. Enjoy that!"

"A year?"

"That's about how long it'll take to get on the calendar in Victoria. I'm filing a brief to have the case moved there as we speak."

I hope I'd recovered a little graciousness when I said, "Okay. What's the downside?"

"Cost as I've told you. I just can't do it pro-bono. We're gonna have to clear things up with U.S. Justice and get your money released."

Something from the courtroom came back to me. "What was that the judge said about not expecting to see you?"

Hal grimaced. "Cornell only knows me from divorce cases and some conveyancing. It's what I did in Toronto before I met Jessica and came here. He's just not used to seeing me argue points of law."

"Hal, have you ever done a big court case?"

"A few big divorces and one or two big property disputes, yeah."

"Anything criminal?"

"No, you have to be a Barrister to do that and this isn't a criminal case, anyway."

"Then have you ever represented anyone in the Supreme Court?"

"Not a one. Look, you came to me. So will you stick with me, or do you want to look for someone more experienced?"

We locked eyes a few moments. His gaze was steady.

"Okay. I'll stick with you."

"I'll get right onto the U.S. people, try to move something along there, and let you know how it goes."

On the way home, as I rounded the first bend down my access road, I glimpsed movement to the left in the trees. I focused.

Ravens flapping among the tree trunks. *Unusual.*

The birds themselves weren't unusual. I saw ravens all the time. Just never under the firs. I pulled up and got out of the truck to see what the attraction was.

Jumping the stream which was back down to a trickle, I climbed a bank and walked maybe 20 yards through the trees, startling more ravens clustered on the ground in the process. They flew cawing through the boughs and out of sight, leaving behind a scattering of objects. As I got closer, the objects became the desiccated remains of a moose, just tatters. From the skull and small antlers, it looked like the same one I saw from the snowmobile.

I walked another step and stopped cold. The massive rear leg bones were splintered.

An hour and a half later I was standing beside the kill again, with John Campbell and a very compact, extremely fit-looking man in his mid-40s, with salt-and-pepper hair mostly obscured by a red plaid cap with ear flaps. Both he and John were wearing fluorescent hunting vests and had rifles. John held his, a wood stocked Remington with a telescopic sight, in the ready position.

The small man was Jacques DeLeon. He had a BC Fish and Wildlife badge on his vest, and the rifle over his shoulder had a plastic stock and a scope and was close enough I could see the caliber engraved on the action. .338 Winchester Magnum.

So much for grizzly bears always passing through.

DeLeon said, "He's a big feller I tell you that. Has to be to take even a small bull like this in the open. They'll do it in the deep snow, sure, but they're chicken-hearted really. Prefer an advantage."

He circled to view the crunched-up bones and torn strips of hide from a different angle, sniffed a couple of times, and nudged the skull so it rocked over on one antler. Then walked a few feet and scattered a stack of droppings with the same boot. "Ten days give or take?"

I nodded. I hadn't told him when I saw the tracks. Unless John had told him, he knew his stuff. I didn't think John had.

DeLeon stepped back, weighing things up.

"Yeah quite big. So was the one by the dump. Could be the same beast's stuck around." He looked at John, turned to me. "Thanks Mr. Adams. We'll keep an eye out."

Suddenly my year's grace in the cabin didn't seem so graceful.

THIRTY-FIVE

Lake Kaldekut
June 9th

"It's really grown!" Libby said.

"Yes," I said, "And its great company."

Libby had returned from Coquitlam and came out to the cabin on Saturday evening, and it was Bird's feeding time.

Oddly enough, its affection for me, which extended to sometimes laying its head on my lap while I was reading, to get a pet and a treat; didn't include her. It would let her pick it up without struggling, but when she put it down, it would bolt for shelter. Giving me what I swear on a human would have been a glare of disapproval.

The weather had warmed delightfully since the court hearing. It still wasn't margaritas-on-the-beach weather but good enough for short sleeves, so we sat at the table out on the deck and ate finger food; a big Italian salad with homemade pita bread and dips. We didn't talk about bears or the court case. The first might have spoiled the mood, and I was still thinking through the implications of the second. Instead, we went to bed and made long slow love between crisp clean sheets, with the loon out on the lake at its most mournful under a full moon, and I was in heaven.

Then the damn alarm went off. It was one of those combo things like the one above the bed in Seattle, with a reading light on top, a radio not quite on the station, and set too loud so it made an ugly sound when it burst into life.

I didn't have an alarm.

I sat upright. There was a glare through the drapes by the deck. The racket was coming from the forest side of the cabin. Somewhere very close.

Libby stirred. I put a hand on her shoulder to reassure her, then pulled on pants and a shirt.

When I slid open the doors, the noise doubled. Playing something that wasn't exactly music and not quite rap, but with a lot of distorted bass.

Two vehicles were in the open, lights blazing, facing the cabin. The nearest was 20 yards or so. It was bulky with square headlights, doors open, vertical lines on the grill. Maybe an older-model Jeep Cherokee. The other was pickup-shaped with round headlights, 10 yards farther back and to the left. Between the two were silhouettes of five men. Slim. Objects in their hands. One turned his head. I saw the outline of a braid down his back.

A high-pitched voice hollered, "Get off our fucking land honky!" There was a blur of movement and I caught the shape of a beer bottle before it shattered against the cabin-wall to my left.

They're drunk. Bad situation.

A different voice said, "We see you; you prick. Get the fuck off our land!" There was no point in responding.

From inside Libby asked urgently, "Who are they? What do they want?"

"Stay inside sweetheart. Just drunks."

A figure reached into the back seat of the Jeep, and he took form for a moment in the glow of the inside light. Black hair. Plaid patterned shirt. When he stepped back, there was a half-gallon plastic bottle in his hands. "Yeah you fucking settler," another voice shouted from farther away. "Get off our place or we'll burn you out!"

I dove in through the drapes and ran to the closet. Found the Smith & Wesson. Groped for a clip and whacked it home with my palm, racked the slide.

"Ben what are you doing?" Libby's eyes were huge in the half light. She was staring at my hands.

As I brushed by her, I whispered, "They've got a Molotov cocktail and are trying to set fire to the place. I have to keep them away. Stay back."

They weren't any closer. Yet. I went quickly to the railing next to the steps and got my hands in the position I learned at the range. Arms straight, fingers of my left hand locked around the butt of the pistol in my right. "I don't know who you are but you better back off. I'm armed!"

The first voice said, "Get off our land you honky asshole. This is our place. Go back where you came from." A chorus agreed.

"Don't come any closer. Just get in your vehicles and leave."

There were a few indistinct words and I saw another missile coming. Pushing my arms out to the right where the lake was, I punched off a round. No gentle squeeze. Just smacked the trigger and felt the recoil heave my arms back. It wasn't as loud as I expected.

It acted like a starting gun. The silhouettes scattered. Two headed for the distant vehicle. Three toward me. One reached the driver's side of the Jeep and leapt in. Another got in the front passenger's door. The back-seat man stumbled, veered out a bit, still with the container in his hand.

Their faces were in the light by then. Maybe not enough to pick them out of a line-up, just the parts of a face that leave an impression. High foreheads. Black hair combed or pulled straight back. One had a frizz. Thin faces. Thin noses. Bright, excited eyes.

The one trailing swung his right arm back as if to sidearm the container at the cabin. I brought my arms back in front at the same instant my left foot slipped and went down into the step-well. My finger was still on the trigger and the handgun fired. The round struck the roof of the Jeep at a shallow angle. Sparks flared as it glanced off into the darkness.

The swerving kid dived head first into the back seat of the Jeep. The driver had it in reverse, but the wheels were spinning. They gripped, and it roared backward. The pickup had already turned and was headed for the trees. The Jeep kept going backward, weaving a lot for a good ten yards, then swung quickly and followed.

My hands prickled with adrenaline and my chest heaved. I pulled back the slide of the handgun and set the action-lock. Heard the clunk of the ejected round on the decking. Climbed down the steps into the wash of the lounge lights Libby had turned on and picked up the plastic bottle. There was some kind of cola-colored slush in the bottom. It stank of rum. Shards of glass reflected twinkles of moonlight at the base of the cabin wall.

I sat on the lower step and put the handgun on the deck. A moment later, I heard Libby's steps and felt her settle behind me. I said, "I completely overreacted."

"You thought you were protecting this place."

"Is any place worth killing someone for? It's pure luck I didn't. They were just kids."

"You didn't know."

"I did really. I could see that much."

After a pause she said sadly, "It's done now. Come inside. You're getting cold."

"In a little while."

After a few minutes morose reflection, I policed up the fired-brass and the ejected round off the deck and broke down the Smith and Wesson into parts so it wouldn't be as intimidating if Libby saw it again. Put everything back on the shelf in the closet. I'd figure out what to do with it when my head was clearer. Libby's reaction was my immediate concern.

I needn't have worried about her seeing the handgun. She was lying on her side facing the wall. She didn't respond when I put a hand on her shoulder. I let it fall away, then lay on my back staring at the dim ceiling, listening to the nervous twittering of the loon.

How the hell am I going to get out of this mess?

Libby went back to Laketown after a breakfast we barely picked at. We hugged perfunctorily at the steps. There was something defeated about her shoulders as she trudged to her Honda and left.

The gun was a fine piece of machinery and I didn't really want to dump it. Instead, I cleaned and heavily oiled the parts and reassembled it. Triple-grocery-bagged everything gun-related, after blowing in the bags first to make sure they were airtight, and sealed up the bundle with duct tape.

Then I took a shovel and walked through the trees to the chain barrier by the stream and buried it next to the right-hand post.

You just never know.

THIRTY-SIX

Lake Kaldekut
June 10th

I tried to nap awhile when I got back from the ford, but it didn't take. Instead, I lay there thinking, or rather worrying. Uselessly.

When I'd had enough of that, I decided to take my mind off things by doing what had often worked in the past: working with food. It was the end of spring garlic season, and I had strings of it I'd planned to process and freeze. Being up to the elbows in a big bowl of garlic may not be everyone's idea of fun, but I enjoy it, though it's best done when no-one else is around. I got a couple of pounds of butter out to soften, then broke up the cloves from three big strings into my biggest bowl, and began shucking off the shells.

Bird came and rubbed itself against my leg, perhaps to find out why I was moping and get fussed over, but didn't like the smell, so it went in its box and preened. More pinfeathers were showing. Kids sure grew up fast.

When the cloves were out of their casings, I bruised and diced them. Bagged some of it in olive oil to freeze, and added the soft butter to the rest along with Italian seasoning, black pepper and paprika; and hand mixed it, wrist-deep in the reeking mass. Divided it into rolls wrapped in cling-wrap, then put the fruits of my labor in the downstairs freezer. Last of all, I poured some oil-of-cloves over my hands and rubbed it all over my arms to kill the smell. An old farmers'-almanac trick.

When I was idle again the vague sense of dread returned. It

144

proved prescient, because as I was sitting on a deck-chair in the watery sun of a dull early afternoon, trying to get things into perspective, a white Chevy Tahoe with red and blue RCMP markings; eased out of the trees and drove slowly across the verge.

The truck stopped in the middle. An officer in a lemon-squeezer hat got out. Brought out the hand piece of a radio and talked into it awhile, then adjusted the hat and walked towards the cabin.

Two things were obvious. He had company nearby because those kinds of radios have a short range. And he was armed, with the protecting strap over the holster undone.

I stood up and put my hands on the railing where he could see them. He kept walking until he was about five yards away. I said, "Good afternoon officer."

He acknowledged me with a head dip and a touch of his hat brim. "Good afternoon sir. How are you?"

No red jacket and blue pants with yellow stripes tucked into polished calf boots for this guy. He was in green military camo. Probably a SWAT uniform. He was an impressive man, and it wasn't just the uniform. Of a similar age to me, he had brown hair clipped real close on the sides, thick neck muscles, a wide mouth and a square jaw. Also outweighed my 175 by 30 pounds, much of it on his shoulders. The stripes on the right one said Staff Sergeant. For all that he seemed genial enough, with a friendly smile.

He studied the fresh marks on the cabin wall, then took two steps to the right. Picked up a shard of green glass with half a label attached, that I'd missed, and said, "Looks like you've had a party."

I didn't say anything.

"Mr. Adams, right? I'm Staff Sergeant McKinnon and I'd like to talk to you about a complaint we've received."

I waved him up on the deck and he climbed the steps cautiously. When we were sitting, he took a notebook with a leather cover from a thigh pocket and opened it to some notes. "Sir, we had a man turn up at our station this morning with his son. A mister..." He consulted the notebook. "Aaron Elkpath and his son Joseph. With a vehicle the boy's been driving. They allege he was shot at here last night." When I didn't speak, he added, "We're giving it some credence because the vehicle has gunshot damage."

"Okay."

"Big bullet scar along the roof."

"Maybe someone was target shooting, and a round went astray."

He considered this a moment, watching me intently. "Doesn't look like it. Could happen, sure, but that'd be rifle fire. This looks like a low-velocity round because it didn't penetrate. Also was copper-clad like something from a handgun. Maybe nine-millimeter. Plus it was fired from above. Suggests it was deliberate."

"Sorry Officer. I can't help you there."

"They say it happened here."

"Do they say how?"

"Well, these are Nations' people now. Lodgepine. The kid says he was out with a few friends on their reserve and they were attacked. Unprovoked."

"What time do they say?"

"Early morning some time. Kid wasn't too clear on that. His father did most of the talking."

"That all seems reasonable to you officer?"

He moved his jaw side to side a couple of times. "It's a free country and I guess they can look around their land 24/7 if they like."

"I suppose."

He nodded a little bit and said, "Tell you what. There's a way to clear this right up."

"Okay."

"If you'll let us have a real good look around inside without having to go into town and get a search warrant, it would show some good faith don't you think?"

"I have no problem with that."

"And you let us do a field GSR test."

"What's that?"

"It tests your hands for gunshot residue. Tells us whether you've fired a gun in the last 24 hours or so. If you haven't, we're going to say we're sorry we troubled you."

The pool of ice water formed in my chest and trickled out to my fingertips. But backing out would be the same as admitting guilt. I'd have to let them go ahead, and challenge it later.

"Okay. Sure."

"You mind standing up again at the railing?"

He kept his eye on me all the way to his truck, got on the radio again, and within three minutes another Tahoe parked by the cabin. Three more Mounties got out, including a younger guy with a suitcase, maybe a trainee. McKinnon met them, and they all came up on the deck.

For the next 45 minutes, I stood out there while they searched the cabin. They weren't destructive, but I'd say by the time they finished, every space had been looked in and every object lifted, turned, and put back. One officer always watched me while the others worked. They also searched downstairs, and in the Explorer. And I'm sure they didn't miss the woodshed and snowmobile shelter either. If they disturbed Bird, I didn't hear any squawks or see goose-down fly.

Toward the end of it the younger guy, who I'd since gathered was a field technician, sat down with me and opened the case. He brought up a device like an oversized portable-microscope with a battery-pack on the side. A sticker said, 'Adkins Corporation. Lead-Barium Analyzer'

Then he took out a roll of double-sided tape and a thing like a rubber stamp with a curved bottom. Put a strip of tape on the stamp and started working over my hands and wrists. Rocking back and forth, changing the tape often until he had a row of them tacked by the corners to the edge of the table. Then he slipped one under the lens of the machine and started examining.

Eventually he looked at McKinnon and said, "The gentleman is clean Sergeant." He closed up the kit, and everyone except McKinnon walked back to their vehicle.

McKinnon looked at me quizzically for a few moments then said, "Well, shoot. Really sorry to take up your time, sir. Just a kid trying to get out of wrecking the family truck, I guess."

"That must be it."

"Has to be. You take care now, Mr. Adams."

I sat on the steps and watched them leave in convoy. Then slumped over with relief.

THIRTY-SEVEN

Laketown
June 11th

Hal said, "This is getting out-of-control Ben."

"I know and I'm sorry."

"What the hell were you thinking?" he snapped back

I knew it was rhetorical and didn't answer.

He glared at me while fiddling with a pen on his desk. Then added, a few dozen decibels quieter, "This is the same shit that got this town in trouble before. How the hell will we hold up our heads in court if you're gonna take potshots at people?"

"That's unfair. It was an accident."

"At the very least, it was incredibly reckless. You need your head read."

"I'm sorry."

He did the pinching thing with his nose. Rubbed his eyes. Put his glasses back on and got up. "We'll have to get back on the front foot. And there's only one way to do that."

We pulled into the parking lot at the Development Corporation offices a few minutes later. The vehicles in the reserved parking spaces included the blue Chevy double-cab with the stickers in the back window. Hal knew where he was going. The door was open. He poked his head in.

Nancy Robitaille looked up and frowned. "Mr. Pritchard, I don't believe we arranged a meeting."

"Just like Mr. Adams here didn't invite any guests to his cabin the night before last."

She looked at him a long moment, then at me and back at Hal, then lifted her arm off the desk, palm up, and dropped it again. "Why don't you take a seat?"

She held down an intercom button and a tinny voice said, "Yes Nancy?"

"Coral, would you ask Charles to come down to my office please? Thank you." She glanced at me and said, "Mr. Adams I can't say it's a pleasure to see you again."

I opened my mouth to respond, but Hal dug me in the ribs. He shook his head very slightly.

Okay. I'll see what happens.

In a minute or so I heard footfalls, and the hulking figure of Prince Charles filled the doorway. All in black. Boots, jeans, and a roll-neck sweater with fabric patches over the shoulders.

Nancy said, "Charles would you join us please? These gentlemen have come about something falls in your area." To us, "Charles handles security for us."

Oh terrific. Now we're both going to get thrown out. This is going great.

Charles nodded and lowered himself into the only other chair in the office, at right angles to us, face blank.

Nancy focused on Hal; hands clasped together on her desktop. "What exactly have you come about Mr. Pritchard?"

"I want your people to stop harassing my client."

Her eyebrows arched, and she put her head at a slight angle. "And who says they're doing that?"

Hal said, "I do."

Charles shifted in his chair. Nancy sighed. "You don't really know what goes on here, do you?"

Hal said, "I have a very good idea what's going on. I don't want any more intimidation of my client at his place of residence, where if you'll remember, he's protected by force of law until the issues between us are resolved."

Nancy said very carefully, "If, and I say if, such a thing happened, I can assure you that this organization, and no-one here, had anything to do with it."

"And how are we supposed to know that? They threw bottles at Ben's house! Threatened to burn it down!"

Nancy said icily, "I also understand there's an allegation of gunshots in response. If you're suggesting some of our young people may have gotten carried away and let their legitimate outrage at his intrusion on their lands get the better of them, I don't think you are in a position to claim the high ground. I'm told it's a miracle your client isn't in jail for assault with a deadly weapon."

The very small woman and the very tall lawyer locked eyes a few more long seconds. Charles stirred in his seat again, face still blank.

Nancy sighed. "Let me show you something." She nodded to Charles, who stood up so she could get out from behind her desk. "Follow me please."

Part way back along the corridor, she opened a side door. We stepped through into a warehouse-area full of racks of food. Canned. Bagged. In bulk, on pallets. And household items, including a stack of pink diapers. A curtain-side truck was backed into a loading dock and a small forklift was operating.

It's a food bank.

Nancy said in a conversational voice, "Over 70% of the Nations' families in this district rely on us for some portion of their subsistence needs. Charles would you mind bringing around your truck?"

Hal and I got in the back, Nancy in the front, and Charles drove across the main street, past the end of the road where the library was, and kept going. Past regular suburban houses with steep roofs and tended lawns. When they thinned out, we climbed a hill and on the other side were more structures. But not family homes this time.

They were trailer homes, permanently on piles. Uniformly gray. Four to a row divided by a lane. There was a little trellis halfway along each indicating separation into two units, each with a single door above a couple of steps, and a thin chimney pipe from a stove. There was a big pile of coal dumped in the open beyond, and though it was warm, some chimneys had smoke rising, so I guessed they cooked on them too. Beneath each unit was a wide vertical polythene pipe for plumbing. Also clutters of rubbish. Mostly beer cans.

Gee-zus.

Charles pulled to the side of the road where we could see down one of the lanes. A couple of kids were playing. One a very young girl in a stained cream dress with something like matted leopard-fur around the collar. She stared at me with sad eyes.

I was reminded of a concentration camp except that a few vehicles, rusty old pickups mostly, some obviously not in running condition, were parked under lean-to's. It was a sight sure to instantly depress.

"This is how many of our people live," Nancy said to neither of us in particular. "The government got a bulk deal on these trailers. The unemployment rate for Nations in Canada is about 19-percent. Ours is about 30. Most who do have jobs, work at the saw-mill in Quilton, for not much better than minimum wage. The rest get by on welfare and what we can do for them."

Charles drove slowly along as Nancy continued. "The best thing we can do for these kids is get them out of here as soon as they can leave school. We have outreaches in Smithers and Prince George where there's work. We place as many as we can, the employable ones. The rest, well..." She flared her palms and put them back together again.

Hal and I looked at each other. He shook his head.

Nancy said, "There's a German social scientist called Max Weber, who once said that when a society sets up goals for itself, and then systematically denies a sector of that society any hope of achieving those goals, it must expect a significant level of aberrant behavior. It's my belief you are looking at the precursor to that."

After a pause, she said with an expressive wave, "Our young people know they have the shitty end of the stick. So we do everything we can to keep their eyes on something else. Sports, many are very athletic. That and their connection with their culture and their lands. Because they have nothing else."

She faced me.

"Then they hear some settler from the city can just walk onto their land and squat."

Hal erupted. "You know damn well we don't see it that way!"

"Yes Mr. Pritchard, I know that, but they hear their parents talk about 150 years of injustice, and they do NOT know that. So they react."

Hal started to say something, but Nancy held up her small hand. "Just the same, we will stop it. We respect the courts and we will honor the ruling. Charles will take the matter in hand, and I can guarantee you will have no more problems before the Supreme Court hearing. You have our word on that."

She looked at me squarely and said, "I just wanted you to know how things are for us. Charles, will you take us back now please?"

Moral high ground can be a very narrow, rocky and isolated place, and tends to be exposed to winds from loftier places. The piece I was clinging to, that the cove was my home, and I meant no one any harm, was all I had.

But in the face of what I'd just seen, that grip seemed very tenuous.

THIRTY-EIGHT

Laketown
June 11th

I couldn't leave town with things still in the air with Libby.

At Otto's a couple folks were waiting for late lunch orders, while she worked behind the gleaming chrome and glass counter. Not knowing how she'd receive me, I tried to be unobtrusive, but she wasn't having any. Stripping off her throwaway plastic gloves, she came and took both my hands in hers, smelling of all the great things that go in sandwiches, and looking sexy as heck.

"I'm almost done. Would you wait while I finish up?"

"Sure."

We went to a small coffee-shop and ice-cream-parlor, that had 'Ma Maison' on a round decal beside the doorway, frilly half-curtains, polka dot wallpaper and little fabric-craft animals around the till. An attractive brunette barista, whom Libby introduced as Joan of the paint-stained sweats, made us tall lattes, and we went to the farthest booth. I said, "I'm so sorry about the other night."

"It's really fine, honestly." But her eyes had a contradicting shadow and after a few seconds she added, "It's just..."

"I scared you right?"

"No. Well, yes... but it wasn't the gun either. In deer season you hear that all the time. It was just the... whole situation."

She sat very still while I waited, then said, "I... It... It's..." The floodgates opened.

I got her tissues and covered her free hand with mine while she

152

dabbed.

"You see, I... well I was in an abusive relationship in Calgary."

My heart wrenched. "I'm so sorry."

"I know you're not like Gary. It's just..." Then she poured it all out. The churches of the Children of Menno are much more communities than congregations. As a teen she'd chafed at the enveloping nature of that. The restraints, and at times, the narrow judgments of some within. College had been her escape.

Initially she'd blossomed at U-Calgary, having secular roommates, and doing 'everything young college students do'. She let my imagination add meaning to that.

Then in her junior year she'd met Gary Alexander, a graduate student. Soon they were clandestinely living together. From there it was a short jump to marrying in secret and making excuses about why she couldn't come home more often. Inevitably, the community found out. There were family fireworks and a painful period of being shunned by people she'd known all her life. When Gary's career didn't take off as he'd expected, money worries meant she had to go out to work to help pay bills. That challenged his manhood. He became obsessive and domineering. She wasn't specific, but my imagination filled in the details and I wanted to strangle the bastard.

"So that's why you reacted on the hill that day, when I said I was too controlling to be an alcoholic?"

"Yes. Gary drank too." She wept disconsolately

I hung my head. I couldn't take the moment back and apologizing wouldn't change anything. Instead, I put my arm around her lower back and said nothing while the tears flowed. I didn't know if it was love, but it was something I'd never felt before. Not just the emotional power of it, but the feeling I'd put my life on the line for this person.

Eventually the tears did ease, and to change the mood she said overly brightly, "Oh gosh, what happened after I left? Did anything else happen?"

I told her about the RCMP visit and passing the gunshot test. And about Hal and meeting with the Nations' people.

"So what happens next?"

"Nothing until shortly before the Supreme Court case, then we have to get ready for that."

"What about the thing you mentioned in Seattle?"

I hadn't said much about the U.S. money until then, but I blurted the whole story out. She was aghast. "How can they think that? You were in the hospital!"

"They can think what they like. They have absolute power. There must be enough evidence to justify seizure warrants, but not enough to pinpoint who did what. Hal thinks they plan to bully everyone until someone cracks. If no-one does, it'll go on forever."

"Then you'll never get your money back. That's not fair!"

"It's not about fair. It's about power."

Then we talked about Bird for a minute, until she realized the time. "Oh heck, I've gotta get back to the shop. I have a thing Saturday morning, but I'll come Saturday night again if that's okay."

"Darling it's not just okay. I'll be counting the moments."

"It's a deal mister!"

Passing the hardware store on the way out of town, I remembered Bird and pulled in to buy a 20-pound bag of poultry-feed. As I wheeled the bag away from the checkout, I thought of Judd McCauley and his friendly fishing advice, and zigged.

He was at the counter working on some packages. I thought I saw his face blanch from a distance, but it had to be my imagination. I strolled up and put out my hand. "Hey Judd, how have you been?"

He kept his head lowered for a fraction of a second longer than was polite. When he looked up, he wasn't smiling. "Hello Mr. Adams. What can I do for you?"

Mr. Adams.

I let my hand drop away. "I just thought I'd stop by and say hello. Hey, how's the fishing been going?"

"It's good."

What have I done?

"Are you okay Judd?"

"Sure."

"Oh c'mon, must be something."

"No."

Mystified, I said, "Alright then. Sorry." As I turned away, his mouth was working as if he wanted to say something, so I turned back. "What's going on?"

His eyes flickered around the store while he massaged his neck a moment. "Well, thing is... I heard a rumor you have something going on with the Nations. Some kind of court case."

"That's right."

He grimaced. "A lot of my customers are Nations' people. Great folks. Look after their own."

"That's nice."

"Yeah well... you know how it is.

"No Judd. I don't."

"Yeah well they make good friends and ahh... not so good enemies."

"Surely what I have happening with the First Nations is my business. It shouldn't affect you. Come on!"

"You just don't know those people."

"Oh?"

"They're ah... famous for putting their money where, well, their friends are."

"That so?"

"Yeah and if we don't have their business in the winter when they're trapping and ice fishing, it's uh... that's bad for us. My boss finds out it's because of someone I know, I could lose my job."

"Are you saying the Nations would boycott you?"

"Yeah, they've done it before. They put Ken Smiley right out of business!"

"You're not serious."

"Yep."

A couple came into sight in hardware, a dozen steps away. They were oblivious to us but Judd flinched. It was just too much.

"Well Judd. I tell you what. This is chicken-shit and you know it. But you have a good one, okay?"

He mumbled, "You too."

Out at the truck I paced awhile until the urge to put my foot through the store's glass-frontage wore off. I'd been warned, but being confronted with it hurt. But Libby cared for me, and Hal was turning out a bulldog himself in tight situations. I'd draw to those two cards anytime.

THIRTY-NINE

Laketown
June 14th

"The problem is we're up against a huge stalling-machine," Hal said. "Water wears down rock faster than the U.S. justice system moves, unless it's made to."

We were in his office on a Thursday, talking about money. I was down to the last couple of hundred dollars of the cash John gave me. My Seattle First card was topped-out too: another thing weighing on my mind.

That left only the $3000 in the checking account and the small amount of rental money John still held, maybe $2000 or so. If I didn't get my money back from the Feds soon, I'd have to cash in my small 401K and IRA accounts and pay huge penalties. Even those might not be enough to cover Supreme Court-costs.

Hal obviously understood that too, because he'd asked me to come into his office to chat.

I said, "Surely the facts are on my side. I can prove I wasn't around when the company sold and had absolutely no knowledge of it. They kept everyone in the dark except the insiders."

"It doesn't matter. You're a major beneficiary. It's those insiders they want, and they know if they lock up all the money, people will have to come to them."

"That sucks."

That's big-government justice for you. Our best chance now is to distance you from the people they want, so it makes no sense to keep you in it. Particularly if you're also a royal pain-in-the-ass. I

156

can do the pain-in-the-ass part for you. How about you give me some ammunition? Tell me again about the players."

I said, "I think three are dirty. There may be collusion with some others, but I think they want Rick Cotton, Jim Burton and Graham Caldwell."

"Details. I need details. Anything you can think of."

"Cotton's kind of a slick guy, late thirties, good talker. But I'd say he's a follower, not a leader. Kind of... lacking in substance, you know?"

"Okay."

"Jim Burton's a bit older, came from the big software company on the east side like me, though I never knew him there. Clever man but always seemed, I don't know, maybe a bit too ambitious for the size of the company?"

"What about Caldwell?"

"He and Pete Prendergast started MagnaTECH. Pete writing the code and Jim running the business side. Before that I believe that he was a Seattle accountant. Serious guy in his mid-sixties. Moody, but sharp."

"What about your friend Langwell?"

I didn't know how to answer. Russ had gotten my stock options vested. He could have let them shaft me and I couldn't have done a thing about it. I owed him, particularly after my behavior at the hospital. "Russell was on the inside as far as the sale went, certainly. Someone had to do the demos to the buyers, show them all the new stuff. That could only have been him or me. But I don't believe he'd do something like this."

"Prendergast?"

"Pete's just a big kid and the company was his toy. He was just a figurehead though, after his original code was taken over by people like me. I don't think he'd be in this. I bet it broke his heart when his baby got sold."

Hal mused a minute. "Okay, try this out. Caldwell and Prendergast start the company but don't make a pile of money. Caldwell's getting on and wants a big win. He persuades Cotton and Burton to come on-board with promises of building the company up for sale and making a fortune. They don't have any money, so they make a deal to do it for illegally backdated options. Caldwell signs it off. Prendergast looks the other way. Your friend Langwell just does his job. He'd have had genuine options like you, anyway. Sound reasonable?"

"It does! I like Burton for it more than Cotton, though. But how does this help us?"

"A lot I hope, when I talk to the ADA's office about it. By the way, I'm going to need your U.S. bank statements. Can you drop those off next time you're in town?"

"Sure."

Then he looked at me kind of sideways. "Ben, I have a big favor to ask you. You won't like it much."

"No?"

"Yeah. I've been having some problems over the Nations' thing from a... family quarter, and I'd like your help with that."

"Okay."

"I need you to sit down with a couple of people."

"Sure. When?"

"Now is good."

Hal and I marched through the front doors of the District Council Offices shortly before 3:00 p.m. People looked up and some of them greeted him by name. We went up to the mezzanine where he knocked on one of the doors.

"Come in!"

It was a spacious conference room with an oblong table, overhead projector, and about 20 plush-upholstered, high-backed chairs. Three had asses in them. Hanrahan was in his trademark three-piece suit, fingers steepled, expressionless. The younger man opposite was ruddy, wide-faced and red-haired, balding early.

Hal sat next to the redhead. "Herm," he said, then, "Jim." Both said, "Hal," in chorus.

I took the seat beside Hal and we looked across the table at the other man in the room. I'd seen him at McGee's. Late 50s. Large and spreading. Thin hair combed back and tufty white sideburns. Though dressed for golf, his body language said he was the big-dog in the room.

Hal said, "Hello Grant."

"Well hello Harold," he said. "We appreciate your coming down. How's Jessica? The grandkids?"

"They're fine. Jeannie has her second teeth coming in."

"Let them know Mary and I are thinking of them."

He turned to me. "Mr. Adams I'm Grant Summers." He extended his hand. "Glad you could come see us. I don't think you've met Herman Peters, our District Manager? Can I call you Ben?"

"Sure. Anything but late for supper."

Not even a smile.

Summers said, "That's great, great. Ben we'd like to clarify the matter of your property."

"Seems clear enough to me now. That's why I'm taking legal action."

"I don't know if you're aware of the history, but ah…"

"I'm familiar enough I think."

"Then you can imagine we'd rather this hadn't come down to lawyers."

"I can understand that."

"So ah… we were wondering if there might be another way to smooth things over."

"I can't see how."

"Well it's a big district…"

Hanrahan exploded. "Wait a minute here Grant. Mr. Adams is under investigation for fraud in the U.S. and I don't think we should be making concessions to a criminal!"

I felt the hair on my forearms stand up. Hal leaned back out of the firing line. Summers rocked in his seat a little and started in with, "Now Jim…"

I turned square on to Hanrahan. "No, you wait a minute! Yes there's a fraud investigation going on in Seattle. I worked for the company and I'm caught up in it. But if you call me a criminal again, Sonny Jim, I will not only have this man," I indicated Hal, "sue your ass off, I will cram your teeth down your throat."

Hanrahan started to bluster but Summers said, "Here here, let's keep this professional, shall we?"

The banker settled back and I tried to calm down too for Hal's sake.

Summers said, "As I was saying, it's a large district and it's possible we could find ah… an alternative piece of land you could perhaps relocate to."

"As in move my cabin there?"

"Along those lines, yes. That's possible, you agree Herm?"

The ruddy guy said, "Yes, I think arrangements could be made Grant."

I said, "I have a question for you folks. My cabin has been right where it is for going on 30 years. It's been occupied, people coming and going, all that time. How come this is suddenly such a huge deal?"

"It's ah, been under the radar you could say. Around here we like to… live and let live."

"Somehow my wanting confirmed ownership, is some kind of challenge to the status quo?"

Summers did something halfway between a nod and a shrug.

I took a long breath. "Well I'll tell you gentlemen this. I'm sick to death of people trying to run me off. I like to live and let live too, and I like things professional as well. So I won't give this the two-word answer it deserves. But I'm going to stay where I am while I pursue this. And I'm going to pursue it just as far as I need to get justice. Good day gentlemen."

Summers called after us, "You gonna help him with this Harold? Over your own family and the town?"

Hal wheeled. "Yes, I am. If we can't work these things out by the rule of law, maybe we aren't much of a town."

Summers fixed his eyes on the table and shook his head slightly from side to side. "Jesus."

Out on the street, Hal said, grinning, "There goes Sunday family-dinners for a while."

"Sorry about that."

"Ahhh he's a self-important jerk. I didn't marry the family, just the daughter. Jessica and I are good."

"Sorry anyway."

"No problem. You did great. Thanks. It would've gone on and on if we hadn't done that. Hey, I'll be in touch, okay?"

As he walked off whistling down the street, I realized my respect for Hal grew every time I saw him. And I didn't know how many bridges I had left to burn, but I was certainly burning them in style.

FORTY

Laketown
June 14th

Libby heard me come into Otto's and beamed. She put her hand up on her heart as she walked close, went on tip-toes and kissed me. I saw the eyebrows of a plump woman at the counter elevate. "Hi you. I've missed you so much."

"It's mutual."

Her smile flickered as she picked up on my mood. "You okay?"

"Just a bad day is all."

"Come here then. I'll make it better." She went all out on the second kiss. "I'm looking forward to Saturday night."

"That's mutual too."

"You can cook for me. I like that."

"Alright, what would you like?"

"How about... fish?"

"Okay. How would you like it?"

"Surprise me. Now shoosh with you. I have customers."

At the food place on the way out of town, I got everything that goes with fish, including a bottle of the driest cooking wine I could find, except fish itself. It wouldn't stay fresh till Saturday. I had a better plan.

Life at the cabin over the next two days was a joy. The sun shone, the place sparkled, and the sky was a wonderful blue that deepened to indigo in the evenings. The scents of spring were fading as the foliage matured, but birds sang from the forest fringe, and the background sound of cicadas was incessant.

I had begun allowing Bird out of the cabin under my watchful eye, though not near the water in case it got out of reach. On the verge, it snapped up every green sprout it saw. It had more than doubled in size and was almost fully feathered.

But mostly I went out on the pier and fished. And completely unsuccessfully. Different lures and different retrieves; nothing worked. Even the damselflies, resting on the water from their constant circling, lived charmed lives. It wasn't for lack of fish. If I stared deep in the water off the end of the jetty, I could see schools finning quietly, among other larger shapes in the depths. Perhaps there was some kind of reef down there that attracted them. But whatever the circumstances, the fish weren't feeding.

Still I persevered, and on Saturday afternoon, with time getting short, I was changing back to the lure that caught my first fish, when a big bright-colored male salmon surfaced and circled beneath me. I perked up instantly. After quickly checking my work, I picked up the rod and cast. The lure plunked down and twinkled as it sank, but the salmon had dived. The lure weaved up through the water and clattered against the rod tip. The next time I let the lure sink right down. After only a couple of winds of the reel, the rod tip bowed down.

Who said perseverance doesn't pay off?

But the rod tip wasn't dancing, just bent down by a heavy weight. It wasn't the lake-bottom either, because the rod slowly straightened. Resignedly I winched in, and was surprised to see a cable maybe ten feet long, attached to a satellite modem identical to the one I'd bought from Kerry Hume. It hadn't been in the water long.

What on earth? What else is down there?

I shaded my eyes until the shapes on the bottom were as clear as I could make them. The angles were too regular for nature. Maybe junk that had been thrown out. Then I looked at the modem again.

Who'd throw a $400 item away?

But there was a more urgent problem to solve. Luckily, the food store on the corner had some plaice on ice at the seafood counter.

I stopped by Hal's office while I was in town and put the U.S. bank statements through his mail slot and still made it back to the cabin in plenty of time.

Libby waved as she drove up to the cabin not long after six on Saturday evening, straight from taking notes at a gathering of

Mennonite elders. I folded a corner of the page I'd been reading, collected up coffee cups, and came in from the deck. She was in the bedroom changing out of an unembellished ankle-length dress and loosening her hair down out of a bun.

We kissed deeply, and I said, "Mmmmm. Hi sweetie. How was your thing?"

"Really fun, but long. Got anything cold?"

Over fresh lemonade, she asked about my week, and when I shared about the district council and the confrontation with Judd McCauley, she was sad for me but not surprised. But we really didn't talk a lot; we needed time. For me to feel accepted again, and for her to remember I wasn't a maniac with a gun. I started on dinner.

I removed the heads and tails of the plaice, and the skin on the dark side, and was preparing a coating with flour, fennel, and salt-and-pepper, when she came and stood at my elbow. "You kept your promise!"

"Yep. Making Sole Meunière, or close enough."

"Men... what?"

"Meunière. It means the 'miller's wife' in French. That's why the flour. It's probably the essential French seafood-dish."

"I can't wait!"

"Well you have to. Give me a couple of minutes or I'll get flour all over you."

"Promises promises!"

I laid the flour-coated plaice in some shimmering-hot olive oil in my largest fry-pan, and while they sizzled, squeezed a big lemon and drained a jar of capers. Made a sauce out of it with some juices from the pan, and a big splash of the white wine. Poured it over the golden-brown fish and brought them to the table with some crisp garlic-bread and a green salad I'd made earlier. "Voila."

Libby said, "This is fabulous!"

"Did I promise you fish or did I promise you fish?"

"You've ruined me for McGee's. I'll always think I'm eating leftovers after this."

"Sorry about that. Eat it from the tail end first, like this."

"What's this piece?"

"That's the roe. It's one of the best parts."

It might have been the best thing I'd ever cooked.

As we were polishing our plates with the garlic bread, she said, "So you're doing your fishing at the supermarket now? Where are all those caveman skills?

"Absent I'm afraid. Caught that though." I nodded at the cable and the gray box. "Might make a stew out of it."

"Strange thing to catch."

"Yes, and there's a lot of other stuff down there too."

Libby made a face. "Darn dumpers! That's why the fines are so big for throwing things in lakes."

I was sure they were, but I was also thinking hard. After she popped the last of the garlic bread in her mouth, she read my mind.

"Didn't you say the guy who was renting this place left in a hurry?"

"Yeah."

"Maybe he was in more of a rush than you thought."

"Surely not that much. Those things cost beau-coup bucks. I bought one just like it from Kerry."

"Well, you found it in the lake."

"Yeah, I did."

After a few seconds she asked, "What other stuff?"

"Don't know. It looks boxy, though. The water's deep."

Seconds ticked by, then we both spoke at once. What if..."

Libby completed the thought. "...he didn't leave?"

I shook my head emphatically. "No that's just silly. John Campbell showed me a note."

"Anyone can write a note. Was it on letterhead or anything?"

"No, it was handwritten. Just a scrawl."

"Well there you go," she said, "Don't you think you should tell someone?"

"Maybe."

I scrubbed dishes, while she made hot drinks, and we enjoyed them in front of the fire. Soon dark thoughts of missing people faded as the anticipatory closeness grew between us. When eventually she leaned over and put a hand up high on my thigh, the thrill was electric.

We made it to the bedroom almost without breaking a kiss, shedding clothing along the way. Slipped beneath the covers and gave in to the hunger, but taking our time with hands and mouths until our arousal was unbearable.

We climaxed in an explosion of groaning and arching of backs. Complete again. Lay entwined and let sleep steal us away.

FORTY-ONE

Lake Kaldekut
June 18th

But those dark thoughts about the possible fate of Adrian Reeman had only retreated briefly. So on Monday morning I looked up the number for the RCMP station in Laketown. When they answered I gave my name and asked for Staff Sergeant McKinnon. On the line, he said, "Mr. Adams. You have something to tell me about the Jeep with the bullet damage?"

"No. I have a situation here and I don't know who else to call."

"Well, give me a try."

I explained it the way it had unfolded for me, and he was beyond skeptical.

"What you're telling me is someone rented that cabin and left in a hurry without settling things with the property manage? Major crime. And you've found a piece of garbage in the lake looks like it might have belonged to the guy?"

Put that way it sounded thin even to me. "I think there's more to it than that."

"People rent cabins up here all the time and move out on a whim. People throw their junk in the lakes as well. It's a big problem and we have bylaws against it. Don't stop everyone though."

"I think it should be looked into."

He was silent a few seconds. "I tell you what. Give me the spelling of the name again and I'll look him up, see if he's ever been in our sights."

I wrote it down, and asked if he'd talk to John Campbell to get his feel on it. "Right now, probably not. Give me your number as well, and if anything shows up suspicious I'll get back to you, okay?"

It was the best I was going to get, so we left it there.

And he didn't call back. He came out to the cabin around noon instead.

"Okay, I looked up the name Adrian Reeman, and a few variants, and didn't find anything. The only peculiar thing is he doesn't seem to have a Canadian driver's license. On-the-other-hand, he could be American but at least it's something odd. I spoke to Mr. Campbell in town as well."

"What does he think?"

"He doesn't share your concerns. He's had people skip on him before."

"When he owed THEM money?"

"Yeah well, we don't know the reason. Mr. Campbell did say the guy was strange. Just a bit too refined and well dressed for the neighborhood. Anyway, how about showing me this thing you found and where you found it?"

When I'd shown him the modem and explained its value, I walked him out to the jetty.

The day was still and without much glare on the water, and he had no trouble seeing the shapes in the depths. He walked back to the shore, working his jaw, and finally came down on my side. "Ah, I'll probably look stupid but I suppose we'd better check it out. Don't touch anything and I'll be back."

Late in the afternoon he showed up again, this time in an RCMP-pickup with a pile of large waterproof bags on the tray. And two lean, fit-looking men with military haircuts. I didn't catch the names, but I did hear "Regional Dive Team."

Soon they were in neoprene and at end of the jetty where they donned flippers and masks and slipped into the water. Free diving first, getting the lay of things, I guessed.

Within a minute, one popped up and then the other and they got out. Their body language said there was something interesting. McKinnon sidled over. "There's quite a collection down there. We'll have to rig-up to recover it."

I walked down from the deck and stood on the shore to watch. One of the bags contained a winch on spikes they drove into the ground at the water's edge. The divers donned tanks, ran a wire line out the 30-yards to where they wanted to work, threaded it through a buoy, and started the recovery. It was a clever technique. They pulled the line down to the bottom and hooked items onto it. McKinnon worked the winch and the buoy kept the items off the bottom, all the way into shore.

Soon they'd built up quite a pile; more cables and electrical items, parts of what appeared to be an impressive antique office desk but was just a screwed-together replica, also a chair even nicer than Hal's.

The weirdest thing was a wide projector-screen on legs, the kind you erect in a boardroom for presentations. But instead of being white it had a scene printed on it, the inside of business-office with views of skyscrapers in the background. The bulkiest item was a high-definition 50-inch video screen, the kind corporations use for teleconferencing. All of it was near-new before it went in the water. When the stack on-shore stopped growing, it was early evening.

McKinnon came over again. "I can't say what it all means, but you seem to be on to something."

"I see that."

"There's a pickup truck down there too,"

"Oh?"

"Yeah but it's old. Seventies-vintage, they think. Sitting upright over there." He indicated an area about halfway between the jetty and the beached log. "We're not going to recover it, just bring up the plates so we can trace it."

As he said that, one diver surfaced in that area. He had the plates in one gloved hand and some shiny tools in the other. On-shore he rubbed one of the plates on his thigh, and rinsed it to get the gunk off it. It was old-style, blue-on-white, with the characters AKB-467, between the words, 'Beautiful' and 'British Columbia.'

Just then I saw the last diver heading for the jetty in a hurry. McKinnon met him and leaned down to listen. When he turned and headed in my direction, his face was grim.

"What is it?"

"I need you to move back to your cabin now Mr. Adams."

"Pardon?"

"They've found a body."

FORTY-TWO

Lake Kaldekut
June 18th

The summer solstice was less than a week away, and it would be light until after eleven, but McKinnon and the divers packed up for the day not long after the gruesome discovery. They left the pile of recovered things by the lake for later collection. Or maybe they were my responsibility.

As they were leaving, a caretaker-shift of two officers arrived, erected a yellow tent with 'POLICE' on it where the access road came out of the trees, and hunkered down for the night. I couldn't imagine why. Whoever was down there wasn't going anywhere.

Though I'd been told to stay close to the cabin, I did the neighborly thing and walked across to the tent just as night was closing in, and asked if they need anything. They said thanks, but no; and went back to their sandwiches and hot-drinks.

I tried Libby's cell a couple times but the number didn't even ring, so I turned in for the night.

McKinnon, the dive team, and a support-contingent including a white medical van, arrived around nine the next morning. McKinnon came to see me, looking purposeful. "I'm waiting for a recovery vehicle. When it gets here, we're going to drag the old truck up on shore."

A mystery immediately unsolved itself. The remains had to be inside the truck, so it probably wasn't Adrian Reeman.

In due course a good-sized GMC tow-truck turned up, and

under the supervision of the divers, inched the truck backwards up on shore like a rusty mountain rising from the sea. It was an old International Scout, the pickup version. The tires were off the rims and the wheels didn't turn, so it tore twin gouges in the stones. The color was impossible to tell, but it was intact enough to spill quite a gush of water when an officer jimmied a door.

They photographed the interior, after which they brought the white van over to it, and a guy in a white coat and clear-plastic gloves started removing objects. Most were grayish-white and elongated, except for one that was larger and round. They laid the items on a gurney in a chillingly familiar kind of order. Tattered pieces of fabric and leather, they put into zip-lock plastic bags.

I got sick of watching and went inside and drink two glasses of milk to wash a sour taste from my mouth. When I came back out awhile later the van was gone, the Scout was on the flatbed of the truck along with the pile of junk from the lake, and they were packing to leave.

McKinnon paid me a morose final visit. "Doesn't seem to be anything else to find."

"I'd say you've done a thorough job."

"We don't know what the truck has to do with the other stuff we recovered, or who the occupant was, but we'll take it away and look into it. I'll be back in touch when we've reached our conclusions."

"Thank you Sergeant."

They departed in convoy.

The place seemed silent and empty after the invasion. but gradually the wildlife reappeared. Around dusk a flock of mallards made passes over the area before landing by the marsh. The grebe returned shortly afterward, and busied itself fishing, making up for lost time.

Bird had been ignored all day but seemed fine with it. I closed the cabin up and went to bed, hoping to sleep and get the macabre images out of my mind.

I slept long, though unfortunately not dreamlessly. When I'd showered, fed myself, and had some time out on the verge with a very-eager Bird, I thought of calling Hal to tell him about the RCMP and what they'd found. I didn't get the chance. He called me first, very upbeat. I told him anyway.

He said, "Well shit. But we can't worry about that now. I got a call from U.S. Justice. They're prepared to discuss options, but we have to go to Seattle."

"That guy Stoneman?"

"It was a conference call their end, but yeah he was leading the conversation."

"Did they say when they wanted us there?"

"Eleven o'clock the day after tomorrow."

"Thursday? That's tight!"

"Not if we fly. Meet me at the office at five-thirty in the morning. Plan for a couple of nights. One bag only and don't forget your passports."

My problem was what to do with Bird. I'd been thinking about a transition plan for when it could be outside, but for now it was dependent on me. Would it be okay alone for three or so days? Libby would be glad to watch over it, but she had the shop. I toyed with asking John and Marge but decided to take a chance. If I got hung up, I could always call someone then.

I put up the barricades again, covered the floor with a double-layer of newspaper, and put down bowls of water and a lot of dry food.

Sorry my little friend. No choice.

FORTY-THREE

Laketown
June 20ᵗʰ

Hal had me park the Explorer behind his building and climb into his Lexus GX. I thought we'd head to some airfield, but instead followed mist-wet streets and then open highway, north and west to Bouclier Lake.

After opening a padlocked gate on the left just before the lake-shore began, we bumped across open ground toward some buildings, startling several deer that raced away through a thinning mist and flowed gracefully over a boundary fence.

Hal parked beside a barn-sized shelter like half a giant corrugated-steel-tank lying on its side and unlocked a tilt-a-door in the rear wall. I followed him inside with our bags.

Tethered to piles where the shelter extended over the water, was a Cessna float-plane. White, with a long red stripe along the side. It had 'TU206 Super Skywagon' stenciled along the engine cowling.

Hal did his pre-flight checks. I'd had a couple of flying lessons a few years earlier at Snohomish Field east of Everett, so I knew at least enough to stay out of his way. He gave the fuselage a thorough going over, including antennae, the pontoon rudder, all struts and cables, and the travel of the flaps and trim tabs. After checking engine fluids, he drained some blue gasoline into a clear container to check clarity, before running out a hose from a white refueling-trailer marked 'BP AVGAS 110L,' and topping off both tanks.

Satisfied, he had me hand him his flight folder, stow our bags in the rear, and climb in the right front while he coiled his long frame into the pilot's seat.

Other Cessnas I'd been in had numerous round gages. This one had twin digital-displays. When Hal flicked on the avionics master-switch, they flickered to colorful life. In front of me was a GPS map. Hal's had the artificial horizon, and sliding-bar indicators for engine revs, airspeed, and temperatures. "Nifty eh?" he said, "Garmin 300 conversion. Sure makes managing the airplane easy!"

Hal set the propeller pitch, electrically built-up fuel pressure with a faint whine, and when everything was in the green, turned the ignition switch. The turbocharged engine roared into life with a momentary puff of blue smoke. He set beacons, transponders, and altimeter, then leaned out the fuel until the engine note was steady with revs at 1200.

Launching was a matter of Hal jumping down on a float, shedding lines and shoving off with one foot. It wasn't yet seven in the morning, but the mist had vanished, the water glassy, and the aircraft barely rocked as it drifted out. Another prop adjustment got us steadily underway out into the lake. Hal gave me a headset. The reception was so clear I could hear him breathe.

"Okay, we're going to take off to the west there." He indicated a stretch of water. "Once we're up, I'll clear us with NAV-Canada and we'll head sou'-sou'-west. I'll clear us again at Bella Coola-beacon, then we'll follow Queen Charlotte Sound to the ocean. Then south over Nanaimo, and land at Patricia Bay Seaplane Base near Victoria around oh... 10:45 a.m."

"You have the range for that?"

"Heck yes. It's 390 nautical, and this does 585 full. Anyway, we'll gas up at Pat Bay. Clearances for the States should take a couple of hours or so. Then it's less than another hour to Lake Union in Seattle. Sit back and enjoy!"

Hal lifted the rudder and smoothly advanced the throttle until the floats were barely skimming the water. At 60 knots, we broke contact and crossed the far shoreline at 200 feet and a steady rate of climb. While we flew a wide sweeping turn over a vast tapestry of hills and valleys, he raised NAV-Canada. A calm operator acknowledged our initial leg, and that we were flying under VFR.

The terrain became indistinct as we climbed higher, and I began relying on the screen in front of me unless Hal pointed something out. Passing over a lake so long I couldn't see the eastern or western ends, he said, "Francois. Longest and deepest in the country."

Beyond a fringe of settlement, along the big lake's southern shore, began the land-primeval. Canada of the tourist brochures; thickly forested, snow-capped and glacier-dotted, and unspoiled by man. "Tweedsmuir Park," said Hal, "Wild as Alaska."

I could make out large animals, probably elk, grazing the high meadows. Another rounded brown shape might have been a big bear, but it was behind us too soon to be sure.

But soon the landscape reverted to undulating coastal-lowland, and Hal pointed at a small clutter of civilization where a highway joined the head of a narrow fiord. "Bella Coola."

A different NAV operator confirmed us through to Nanaimo, before Hal banked the plane and we followed the fiord, which widened into Queen Charlotte Sound.

At the coast we turned south across a narrow strait, to the north-coast of Vancouver Island. The island, at first, seemed featureless, unbroken forest bounded by a rocky shore where surf pounded relentlessly. Then isolated areas of cultivation and tiny buildings began to appear and soon became hamlets and then towns. Around ten-thirty over the port City of Nanaimo, Hal cleared us once again to the seaplane base.

There was some back and forth about the route, because it was on the west side of the Saanich Peninsula, in the flight path of Victoria International Airport. We watched vigilantly, but the sky seemed empty as we settled down over the Strait of Georgia from north of Piers Island, and landed gently between the lane markers.

Hal taxied to a wharf lined with fuel-bowsers and killed the engine. We showed ID at a gate in a hurricane wire fence, and went through to a large building adorned with a big 'Pat Bay Air' sign, and a much smaller one that said 'U.S. Customs & Immigration This Way.'

We had burgers, while Hal used their Wi-Fi to check weather on his laptop and write a flight-plan he gave to an official with our customs-and-immigration forms. While they were processed, Hal gave the plane another look-over, and used a credit card to top up the tanks.

After about two-hours on the water, we made a slightly bumpy takeoff to the west into a still cloudless-sky. We kept that course while Hal reconfirmed his altitude and route into U.S. airspace, then climbed to 4500 feet on a heading over Bellingham and Camano Island.

Lake Union isn't really a lake but a bulge in a waterway connecting inland Lake Washington to Puget Sound via a series of locks. On the GPS it resembled an arrowhead aimed at the high-rises of downtown Seattle. We passed over Shoreline at 1000 feet, Green Lake at 500, Gas Works Park at 150, and touched down in the landing zone not much after 2:00 p.m.

Back in the cacophony of stress and bad traffic; my palms went clammy.

I wanted a beer so bad it hurt.

FORTY-FOUR

Seattle
June 20th

Hal had arranged rooms at a Courtyard Inn on Dickinson Avenue near the University District; the kind of place traveling-businessmen frequent, and where parents stay during U-Dub commencement. As we parted at the lifts, he asked me to be down in the bar at five-thirty. Uncharacteristically, he didn't say why.

The hotel room was spacious with more mod-cons than I'd seen in months. Though my hip was healed it still ached stubbornly if I was motionless too long. So, I ran a steaming bath, and emptied in those little containers of bath salts they give you. Then took a couple of bottles of water from the mini-bar, got in it with the Seattle Times; and soaked an hour. I was feeling much recovered when I exited downstairs and asked directions to the bar.

A sign at the door announced Happy Hour. Hal was in a booth with a little table in the middle of the U. Seated opposite was a very small and slim, red-frizzed guy about our age. The tail end of a power-tie trailed from the guy's tailored suit-coat. Both had tall frosty beers. Hal said, "Ben I'd like you to meet Frank McEachern. He's your new attorney."

"What?"

Hal grinned wider and the small guy joined in. "No, it's true," said Hal.

"What the hell..."

"Take a seat and I'll explain."

The cocktail waitress made a beeline. I waved her away. Hal's grin went a little rueful. "Yeah, I'm sorry. Just couldn't resist. I'm not U.S. bar-certified and we need someone who is for tomorrow's meeting. Frank is our man. We were at McGill together."

Frank chipped in, "We were both Redmen. I was a point guard when Hal was an all-Canada center."

I wasn't sure what a reference that was for legal work, but he did look a bit like ex-Huskie and Cavs-standout, Isaiah Thomas, apart from being white.

He added, "Did Hal tell you he was drafted by the Celtics?"

Hal looked really uncomfortable. "Yeah well, they were good times, but this is now. Ben, this short-assed Ontarian is in corporate law down here. Tomorrow I'll declare myself as your advocate and still do most of the talking, but Frank will handle any legal points."

I shook McEachern's hand, thinking about the extra cost. He had a good grip and confident eyes.

Hal said, "We sort of have a plan."

"What's that?"

"I'd rather not say."

"Why the hell not? I'm the one in the firing line here!" People looked over.

Hal sighed and said, "Let me point out a couple of things okay? You know by now that when it comes to playing mine's-bigger-than-yours, U.S. Justice always wins."

"So far."

"Yes, and they're used to it, and they have no reason to do you any favors. We'll have to trade."

"What do we have to trade? All I've got is my innocence!"

"We think we know, but we'd rather not rehearse it, so you behave normally if it comes up. It may not. It's a long shot."

I must have looked extremely unconvinced because Hal took hold of my arm.

"Look we can't seem too slick and prepared with these people okay? They'll swat us like flies if they think we're trying to sell them something. Two weeks ago, I asked you to stick with me, and you said you would. I'm asking you again. Will you do that?"

What could I say? I did trust him.

I said, "Okay."

The next morning the Feds kept us waiting long enough for TWO cream-and-silver monorails to go by the window.

Hal was sure there would be an entourage. They wouldn't want to be outnumbered. Frank added, "If you're asked a direct question and we approve your answering, give the shortest answer possible, okay?"

As I assented, they trooped into the room, Stoneman in the lead. The two men behind him were beefier. One probably mid-50s, long face and snub nose. The other older, balding and jowly. Stoneman put a recorder down on the table. Frank said, "We don't consent to this meeting being taped." Stoneman looked questioningly at the balding guy, who made an almost imperceptible head-movement. Stoneman put it aside.

At least we know the chain of command.

The oldest man said, "Some of you know Assistant DA Jason Stoneman, I believe." He nodded toward the snub-nosed guy. "This is Regional Counsel Bryce Matthews. I'm Chief Assistant DA Richard Curtin. And you all are?"

Hal explained his role as advocate and Frank's as counsel. The Feds shrugged and the baton passed to Stoneman, who said, "We understand you want to make a statement."

Hal said, "Actually the exact words used the other day were 'discuss options.'"

"And what do you feel those might be?"

Frank jumped in. "We feel that you think Mr. Adams should forgo his rights or you'll hold the property you've seized from him until he does."

Stoneman said imperiously, "Everything has been done in full accordance with the law."

Frank said, "Really? Can you guys do math?"

"What? What's your point?"

"You've seized a large sum of Mr. Adams' own money. More than the subpoena you had served on him calls for."

"He had adequate warning that we intended to investigate."

"What warning?"

"Written notification that we were questioning transactions related to MagnaTECH, and that all related funds were subject to restraint, unless the parties contacted us with proof otherwise. He didn't respond. We don't crack open piggy-banks and do, one-for-you, one-for-me. That was his concern, not ours."

Frank said, "You sent a target-letter?"

"Yes. On February 12th of this year." Stoneman gave the address on Crockett in Magnolia.

"Mr. Adams was in a rehabilitation center at that time. He never got such a letter."

They exchanged glances. "Very well, we'll check that out."

Frank said, "Not good enough. We want all monies released on the grounds Mr. Adams wasn't properly advised."

"We are not in a position to do that."

Frank said, "Would you rather we challenged the seizure warrant?"

"Can you prove Mr. Adams wasn't properly notified?"

"Can you prove he was?"

Matthews moved his elbows on the table to break up the impasse, and said, "Yeah, you can challenge it. But we'll only get another one. I don't think we'll have any trouble."

Hal said, "How about you free up the difference at least? What we can show is unrelated to the stock?"

I saw lips being pursed, eyebrows working. Curtin said, "Gentlemen will you excuse us a minute to talk this over?"

When they came back in the room Stoneman said cautiously, "We can see a way we might compromise here, if you could see a way to help in another area."

"We're listening."

"In one of your responses Mr. Pritchard, you postulated that if there was any illegal activity, then, one, Mr. Adams knew nothing about it and, two, such action could only have been taken by a small group of people. You claimed Mr. Adams had no association with those people outside normal work duties, except Mr. Russell Langwell, who was something of a friend."

"That's correct."

"Is he still a friend?"

I started to say something and Hal bumped me with his hip. "I don't think there's been recent contact, but I understand..."

I said, "Yes."

Stoneman looked straight at me. "Would you be prepared to talk to Mr. Langwell on our behalf?"

Before I could answer Hal asked, "Exactly what do you mean by 'on behalf'?"

"We're thinking a... candid conversation between Mr. Adams and Mr. Langwell might go a long way toward resolving things."

I said, "How could a private conversation between Russell and me about anything, be a help to you guys?"

Stoneman didn't answer, just looked at Hal and Hal looked at me.

Hal said, "He's talking about you wearing a wire Ben."

FORTY-FIVE

Seattle
June 21st

While the connotations of spying on a friend to get my money back sank in, Hal and Frank held a whispered sidebar. When they sat back down, Hal glared at me not to interrupt again.

Frank said, "Let's be sure what's on the table. You're offering to let go of any funds not specifically from the MagnaTECH deal, if my client will wear a recording device while talking to Mr. Langwell."

Stoneman said, "Correct. Transmission device to be exact. We'll do the recording at a different location."

"And this is win, lose, or break-even?"

"Yes, so long as we hear an honest attempt to draw Mr. Langwell out on the subject."

"We'd want details of all the transactions from the MagnaTECH sale."

"No. What matters to your client will be in his bank statements. The difference should be easy to work out."

Frank stared at Matthews. "You want us to add withholding evidence, to unjustified seizure and failing to notify? You're accusing these other people of criminal activity. How do we know Ben got what he was entitled to? If they stiffed the government as you allege, how can we be sure they didn't stiff him as well?"

The justice folks looked side to side at each other. Mathews conceded, "Alright we can give you a summary."

Frank said, "How long is your offer good for?"

179

"Today."

"Then we'll need a place to discuss, and I repeat, we do not agree to any part of our conversations being recorded."

A few minutes later we were in a matching meeting room on the other side of the foyer. Hal and I were holding lattes from the coffee kiosk downstairs, while Frank had his head down studying his printed copy of a spreadsheet.

"I didn't tell you yesterday," Hal allowed, "But Frank is corporate counsel with a venture-capital firm here in town. Berkalis and Partners. He looks at this stuff all day long."

The spreadsheet had been obviously pasted from a bigger workbook, because there was no page title. Just rows of information with headings, and some notes and totals at the bottom. After ten-minutes more, Frank said, "Ben I need you to confirm your end of it first."

The columns were people's and organization's names, their number of options, strike and sales prices, the tax withheld and how much was paid out. Mine confirmed what I'd already figured out at the Pines. I was the better off for the whole thing by a little under $530,000.

The founders had done well. 'Caldwell Venture Capital Equity' had invested $2.25M into MagnaTECH as a start-up. 'Prendergast Equity (Sweat),' valued Pete's original software-code at $2.5M. Since they each owned 125,000 shares and the company sold for $30M, those two had walked away with a little under $10M between them.

Then I saw that 'Venture Capital' was a company that LOANED Graham the 2.25M. They'd gotten $2.75M back on top of their investment, a return of 122.22%. I read that number out incredulously.

Franks said, "That's nothing. I regularly see 200% and 300% offered. Did you know three out of four start-ups fail? Anyway are your numbers right?"

"Yes."

He got my Seattle First bank-statements from his briefcase and did some math. "Alright you'll have a little over $28,675 coming back right away, if we do this deal."

"Why wouldn't I?"

"Maybe because I can see what they're looking at. See the three lines for Cotton, Burton, and Langwell? Did your friend Langwell join the company before or after you?"

"After by a couple weeks. Why?"

"Because strike prices go up with time and as a company does better, Ben, not down. Look at his."

Russell had 5,000 more options than me, which didn't seem out of line since he came in senior. But his strike price was an average of $1.25, which made no sense. Those for Cotton and Burton were the same. Those two had 45,000 options each. Both had pocketed over $800,000 after tax.

"No way it should've been that low, Ben. And certainly not identical. Looks fishy to me too."

I remember the nights on Russell's couch, his covering for me, standing by me. "I know Russell. I don't believe he's dirty."

Hal said, "Then that makes it easy. We'll take the deal. All they can get from a conversation between you, assuming one even happens, is evidence both of you are in the clear."

Back in the other conference room, we told them we accepted and got into specifics.

Stoneman said, "We can do the technical part in half an hour. It's all wireless and voice activated. Just a transmitter we tape to the small of your back and a mike sewn into a shirt sleeve. We recommend you keep a jacket on, but it's invisible either way."

"Any restrictions on where Ben can go?" asked Frank.

"Not technically. Long as the receiver, we'll have that in a van, is within a mile we're good. But the judge will want a rough location for the warrant. We'll need to get you and Mr. Langwell in touch first and then do the paperwork."

I said, "I have an old mobile number."

Stoneman said, "We have all that. The number you call from will need to be plausible though, because it'll show up on his caller-ID. I'd recommend your hotel."

Around 2:30 p.m., in my room, I dialed nine for a line, and the number they'd given me, and waited while it rang. Russell said, "Yeah yeah wait on. Russ Langwell hello?"

"Russ it's Ben."

"Christ Ben is that you? Where you been man? You just dropped off the map after The Pines. How's the leg?"

"I'm fine Russ. Sorry it's been so long. I got your note and wanted to thank you for everything you did."

"Oh man don't worry about it. Are you still in Seattle?"

"I've been away up north. Just here a few days."

"It would be great to see you. Hey, you feel like seeing a baseball game? I remember you like that stuff."

"Huh?"

"Yeah Mariners - Red Sox. Friday night. There'll be a group of us. We have a box now. Be awesome to catch up."

"Uh sure."

"Fine. 7:00 p.m. I'll leave a pass at the Center Field gate. See you then, man."

Conflicted feelings assailed me. "Great. See you then."

Hal, Frank and ADA Stoneman were sitting on the bed. I said, "Seven tomorrow night at a Mariners game at Safeco Field over in SoDo."

That's the South Seattle district that also houses the Seahawks' Century-Link Field.

"That'll work," said Stoneman.

FORTY-SIX

Seattle
June 22nd

The ushers at Safeco Field on Friday evening had dressed-up and stressed-down while I'd lived away from Seattle. The one who handed me my pass at the Center Field gate wore a Mariner's-themed outfit. And even smiled.

I tried to ignore the tape stretching and folding annoyingly across my back, as I went up to the luxury-box level. 'Bad to the Bone' was playing overhead, and there was a long line down the hallway, to a table where a famous 90s-era, shave-headed and goatee-bearded outfielder, was signing balls.

I knocked on the door of the box listed on the pass. A smiling Russell Langwell opened it and said, "Heyyyyy man, it's great to see you."

"Thanks Russ. Good to be here." I returned his high-five, and looked around at what could have been a classy lounge in a high-priced hotel. One table was loaded with beers, spirits, mixers and ice. Another had a great-looking buffet. There were pub-tables with stools distributed around the viewing-box, and a game-facing wall of glass.

As I stepped inside Russ put his arm around my shoulders. I tried not to flinch.

Down on the field, workers were raking running lanes and brushing off bases. From speakers above me, Rick Rizzs on KIRO 710 was announcing the line-ups.

He said, "Have you eaten?"

"Uh yes, I had something. Might snack, though. Looks terrific."

But I was disappointed. A dozen other people in the room boded badly for private conversation. Some were long-haired, geeky-looking, generation-Z kids at a beer-can-cluttered table, however, four were middle-aged men at a central table holding highball glasses, and one of those was Jim Burton, who showed no recognition. At the table nearest the door was Becky Watson, the girl-Friday from MagnaTECH, looking extremely sporty alongside a curvaceous, red-headed girl in a low-cut green dress.

Well what d'you know?

Russ said, "What can I get you?"

"Just a club soda thanks."

He pulled me up a fourth-stool at Becky's table before heading to the bar. The two girls smiled at me, the one in green very brightly. Becky said, "Hello Ben, how are you?"

"I'm good, Becky."

She indicated her friend, "Melanie, Ben Adams."

"Hello."

There was a fanfare as the Mariners' Wade LeBlanc jogged on deck and started his warm-ups. A journeyman, but a crafty one I had some time for. Russ put down the drinks and sat down beside Becky. She leaned against him. That didn't seem a good thing for his absent wife, Jill.

Russ said, "How's it going? Really."

"I'm better Russ. Hey, again, I appreciate you standing by me."

"Don't worry about it. Coding was killing you. I knew that. You were still the best. Just maybe using yourself up."

"Anyway, I'm sorry about how I was at Christmas."

"You shitting me? You were in a body cast man." He slugged half his drink. "Hey, I'm sorry I wasn't more in your vibe."

Rizzs said first up for Boston was Mookie Betts, everyone's next-big-thing batting .342.

I said, "Hey Russ, about the stuff with the company..."

The noise from the crowd surged as Betts got a straight-off single.

Russ said, "Later man, I need to check on these folks. Grab some food."

I got roast beef, shrimp, and coleslaw while he did his rounds, and when he'd settled again, I said, "How's Jill?"

He made a sour look. "Ahhhh we're having a few problems. Taking a break, actually."

"I'm sorry."

"Yeah she's down at her mother's in Pasadena with the kids.

We're working through it."

Then one of the men with Jim Burton called Russ over. Becky got up with him. They pulled up seats there and stayed.

Five runners had made it home for Boston in the top of the first, but Seattle came right back with a monster 3-run homer by Nelson Cruz and a loner by Ryon Healy. At the bottom of the third, LeBlanc was itching to pick off Dee 'Flash' Gordon on first and I was watching his back foot because it's usually a balk if it lifts, when Melanie moved to the seat beside me. She said, "You know I'm your prize."

"Oh you are?"

"Becky and Russell thought you might like me."

"You're very nice."

"Thank you. You're pretty cute yourself. You're here a few days?"

"Just the weekend."

"Well if you feel like company..."

I pretended I hadn't heard and concentrated on the game a little more than she liked. After a couple minutes she gave me a 'your-loss' kind of shrug and moved back to her original seat. I could only imagine the grins on the guys in the van outside.

The rest of the game was a slug-fest until Boston went ahead for good, 14-10, in the 7th, on some clumsy work by rookie-reliever Nick Rumbelow, and the stadium began to thin out.

Russ came over shaking his head and said, "I'd like to catch up, but this isn't the place. Are you up for dinner at my house tomorrow night?"

"Sure. You still in Ballard?"

"No uh I'm out on Whidbey Island now. Oak Harbor. You want me to send a car?"

"I can get there. What's the address?"

"I'll write it down."

At least I was in extra innings.

I'd need to do something about Bird.

About an hour later Stoneman leaned in from the front seat of a Dodge van in a nearly empty Safeco Field parking lot, to where Hal, Frank, and I were sharing the back with two technicians and their listening equipment. He growled, "You could have tried harder!"

I said, "Russ was right. It wasn't the place"

"Alright," he conceded gruffly. "We'll have to go with option B."

Frank said, "Hold on there. This was a onetime deal."

"Not for us. There had to be a genuine attempt to engage him about it. One question and getting put off doesn't qualify."

Hal said, "What do you think, Ben? You willing to go again?"

"Sure."

"Alright let's see that note."

It said '38 Hesperia, Oak Harbor. Six-thirty. Car ferry to Clinton and drive up is easiest. Look for the madrona trees. Don't bring a thing.'

I said, "I'll need a car."

FORTY-SEVEN

Whidbey Island, Washington
June 23rd

The island is one of a number within Puget Sound. It reminds a lot of people of Cape Cod, with that same rocky-shored, east-coast fishing-village feel to it around the southern ferry port of Clinton, and has filled in for the cape in movies like 'War of the Roses.' The terrain gets less stark the farther you drive up highway 525.

As I was. And uncomfortably. The transmitter at the small of my back chafed where it pressed against the seat. The Dodge surveillance van was in convoy. At least I was at ease about Bird. Libby was going to stop by the cove as soon as she could.

Eventually a wide bay came up on the right-side of the highway. The tide was out and groups of folks were probably hunting razor-clams. The madrona trees lined a sweeping highway-curve; fluttering powdery-green leaves contrasting with the rich crimson of their trunks.

The driveway was marked by impressive patchwork-stone pillars. A wrought-iron gate opened automatically. Halfway up the drive, an EA-18G Growler jet shrieked overhead toward the Navy's field at Coupeville. I imagined the neighbors shaking their fists.

Always gotta be one loose brick in paradise.

The house was Greek-pillared and huge. A couple of silver top-end Mercedes sedans, and an older yellow Porsche Cayman, occupied the crushed-shell, circular-driveway. I put the drab government-issue Chrysler 200 next to them and climbed a fan of steps to the towering front door. It was ajar. I followed music along a hallway with a vaulted ceiling, past a palatial lounge with a Beovision 85-inch TV that might have cost half the snazzy Porsche outside.

The party on the back patio wasn't quite black-tie, but I still felt under-dressed in my navy slacks, sport coat, and open-necked shirt. A white-attired server was circulating with finger food. Another staffed a full bar on a white-clothed table. It was a couples' soiree. The women's dresses I was sure were designer.

A large, swarthy and stiff-looking guy, stood out because he was smoking a cigar. The two other men were Jim Burton and Russell, with Becky of course, who came right over. "No problem finding the place?"

"None at all."

He nodded toward the bar. "Get what you want and come join us."

I'm totally out of my depth.

I used a tall soda as camouflage and did my best to follow discussion without intruding. I'd just gathered the cigar smoker was in venture-capital and there was some kind of business deal in the making, when Burton pulled me aside. "Ben it's good to see you up and around."

"Thanks Jim. I'm better than I was."

"What are you up to these days?"

"I'm in BC."

"Good to know. We should talk," he said, clapping me on the back, then went back to dominating a conversation.

A server announced dinner, and opened concertina-doors onto a dining room roughly the size of China. Seating was pre-assigned and Russ was at the other table, but he mouthed, "We'll get together later."

For all the ceremony the food was only average, and the discourse ranged over the economy, to the state of the IT industry, to politics with a decidedly Republican bias. I saw the women roll their eyes on occasion, and could almost hear the technicians in the van yawning.

Excuses began around nine o'clock, and soon just the Burtons, Russell and Becky, and I remained. We relocated to the lounge when the help began cleared away the dinner wreckage. Russ and Burton were probably on their third XO brandies, before Burton made another move. "So, are you working up north Ben?"

"No just settling some things with some property I have."

"Lot of opportunities about town at the moment if you decide to come back. Russell and I have one working right now. Be a place for you if you're interested."

"Good to hear Jim. Thanks."

"You'll know about this damn thing with the stock options."

"Yes, but I expect that's only temporary."

He lowered his drink level an inch or so and said, "You know this opportunity. Russell thinks it'd be great to have you involved."

"I don't know Jim. I'm not sure I want to get back into software. I appreciate you thinking of me though."

"You wouldn't be actually writing anything. Kind of an evaluation position. We could use someone knows how to look at what a company has, and ah, tell us how good it is."

"Russell knows how to do that too. I'm not sure what I could add."

"Russell says he's not you. If you were interested, we could probably help you with the stock problem, just as we've done for Russell. Tide you over you might say."

Paydirt. Maybe.

I said, "I appreciate the offer, but I expect that'll be cleared up soon. I mean, it's just a misunderstanding, right?"

"Sure sure." He drained his glass and lurched up to leave. "Just the same, you change your mind, you let us know."

"Thanks Jim, I'll think about it."

Becky came back in the room, yawning. "Russ I'm gonna go to bed I think. I'm sure you and Ben have a lot to talk about."

"Sure Pet. Night."

"Night Ben."

Russell was the worse for wear, but still bright and cheerful. He said "Hey you were a player once, weren't you?"

"Huh?"

"Yeah chess man, you know?" He waved toward a table with carved jade and onyx pieces on an oversized board.

"Oh no. Long time ago. I haven't played in forever."

"Oh c'mon, it's like fucking man. You never forget how. Gimme a game huh?"

He refilled his brandy and took white, and instead of the stock-standard Ruy Lopez, moved his knight in the Rèti opening. Challenging me to make a rash long-range attack. He'd been studying. As I started to assemble a French defense, he said, "I'm sorry about you and Eileen."

"Yeah it was coming though. We were in a steep dive a long time and just couldn't pull out. She's in Colorado with the kids."

"Yeah, I helped her pack up."
Really?
"Thanks for that."

We played some mid-game, each of us losing rooks. Then I traded him a pawn for a better position on the right. As he was putting it aside, he said, "You ought to think about Jim's offer."

"You said I should find another line of work."

"Yeah well this is different."

"It's still a job in the software business."

He waved expansively. "A job? C'mon man. Think I could afford this on a salary? The MagnaTECH deal was just the start!"

I put my knight in play and I'd have checkmate two ways if he screwed up, but he got out of it.

"With what Jim has planned that was chump change," Russell pressed.

I said, "MagnaTECH was all on the up-and-up right? The Feds don't really have anything do they?"

"No no no it'll all work out."

I hung a pawn out as bait, and went for the kill. Three moves later I'd taken his queen and had his king in a cross-fire. He reached out a finger, and tipped the piece on its side.

I guess there are some things you never forget.

"Alright Russ. Thanks. I'll think it over."

FORTY-EIGHT

Courtyard Inn, Seattle
June 24th

"C'mon Hal calm down," Frank said.

Stoneman was leaning back in the coffee-shop booth, gripping his mocha-grande in both hands, weathering the storm.

"The hell with calming down! You heard the damn tape! What the hell do you mean you don't have enough?"

Other customers were watching. At least there weren't that many of them. It wasn't even 10:00 a.m. yet, on Sunday morning. Still, we'd been hoping to have all this behind us and be in the air by now.

"What we heard was Burton offering Ben a job, and both he and Langwell denying there was anything crooked about the stock options. The job-offer sounded genuine. As I understand it, Ben has great credentials for anything in software development. And we already knew what their position was on the stocks."

I thought Hal was going to pop an artery.

"Did you hear their fucking voices? You don't think the denials were over the top? Did you hear Ben's voice? If he was involved in any of this stock garbage do you really believe he'd be asking those questions? Come on!"

"Yeah well, we kind of lean toward Ben being out of this too," said Stoneman. "But we just don't have enough to take to Legal for charges against these guys. And we can't release him off the case until we do. We'll stand by the initial deal, though. Give me your trust account number and we'll transfer the $28,000 or whatever tomorrow."

"Look, you're wrong on this," Hal said like he was sucking on a lemon. "Burton has something bigger going on and Langwell's involved. That was a $2M house for Christ's sake!"

"More like $3M," Frank chipped in. "Come on, Stoneman. This has nothing to do with Ben and you folks darn well know it. The fair thing is to let him out."

Stoneman didn't like being ganged-up-on, or hearing his name used that way. I wasn't that happy about being talked about in the third person either, but we both let it go.

"Yeah the house bothers us too," Stoneman said resignedly. "But the bottom line is we didn't get anything indisputable."

Hal looked at the wall and shook his head. "Ahhhh you fucking people."

With Frank and Stoneman gone on their way, I left Hal waiting for the courtesy van with our bags, and took a cab over to the shipping canal.

At the storage lot I crammed as much as I could into the one large box Hal had said we could carry, told the storage folks they could dispose of the rest, and still made it to the Kenmore Air Harbor Seaplane Base by noon.

We wasted no time boarding the Cessna. As he taxied from the dock, Hal talked about a different route home. Then we lifted into a strong localized-breeze that greatly improved our rate of climb, and turned north toward Canada under a sea-hazy sky.

This time around we closely followed the Washington coast and were back on the water at the seaplane terminal at Richmond near Vancouver International Airport, within an hour. Immigration and customs formalities were brief since we were Canadians coming home. Airplane flight-checked and gassed, we climbed straight to 2000 feet and followed the broad lower-stretches of the Fraser River, inland.

The sky flawless once we escaped the sea-haze, we cautiously skirted Abbotsford airport, overflew the town of Hope, and then followed the bends of the magnificent Fraser Canyon northeast. Though for fear of downdrafts; at a higher altitude than allowed good sightseeing.

Hal's next GPS-waypoint was the T-junction where the mountain route out of Lillooet joined the Cariboo Highway. From there it was a long steady drone into a slight headwind, over the broad inland, north of Carpenter Lake, south of Big Creek, and over Chezacut. I knew we were nearly home when we overflew bright-blue-and-sparkling Beauchamp Lake, before swooping in over Laketown a little before 4:30 p.m. and settling down perfectly on flat-calm Bouclier.

Stowing the plane took some time. Hal liked it ready whenever he needed it. The town was very quiet as we drove through it about 6:00 p.m. to Hal's office, where I transferred my box and bag to the Explorer and we went upstairs.

"Well it's at least progress," said Hal.

"They still have most of my money though."

"Yeah. But what we got back will cure a few evils. This trip used up the last of your retainer and put you a little in the hole. I'll need another $8000 to get you ready for the Supreme Court. We can talk about the actual trial-cost later. Frank will need $5000 to look after your interests down south. I'll take care of all that and put the rest in your bank account if you'll leave me the number."

I'll have probably $15,000 to survive on. I'll be good. For awhile.

"Okay and thanks. But what do we do about the rest of it they still have?"

"Nothing except wait for them to come back to us."

I said, "You're sure they will?"

"Oh hell yeah!"

The evening was golden when I came in sight of the cabin around 7:00 p.m. A fork-horned buck stood by the marsh with its big ears flared. On seeing the Explorer, it trotted nonchalantly the few yards into cover. Varied thrushes, the males with their orange breasts and black necklaces, flared in front as I crossed the verge and parked.

There was a white card with the RCMP logo, Staff Sergeant McKinnon's name, and 'Please call me' written on the reverse; in the door-jamb. I dropped it in a bag of the groceries I'd picked up and went inside.

Bird scampered out of its box with an excited squawk, and rubbed against my legs, flexing its short-feathered wings in excitement. I stepped around it and put down the groceries, prepared for the worst.

Sure, there was spills. And the place smelled like a chicken-coop. But that was nothing a good airing wouldn't fix, and apart from the corner the kitchen was surprisingly clean.

I stroked Bird's neck delightedly, murmuring pet words, and was surprised at how much it had grown. I guess I hadn't been paying attention. A perfectly formed, though still small, gray-and-black goose had emerged from its chrysalis. But it was looking for food more than attention. I refilled its bowl. It immediately buried its beak.

Libby had left a welcome-note weighted down with a row of Hershey's Kisses. She'd be with her congregation, so I'd have to wait till the morning, much as I longed to hear her voice.

The gloaming lasted long. I faded out with it and slept until noon Monday.

FORTY-NINE

Lake Kaldekut
June 25th

The sun was high when Bird woke me with some disapproving noises, wanting to be fed. I rolled over and stretched, then got up and did that, showered and ate.

Then I called Libby and explained that we'd made some small progress in Seattle, though it was still an ongoing-battle, and thanked her for watching over Bird. She said it was fun. We made plans to see each other during the coming Canada Day long weekend.

Next I called McKinnon, who was at a day symposium at district HQ, wherever that was, and his mobile went to voice-mail. I called his office back and left them my movements, so he could find me.

It was mid-afternoon by then. I tossed up whether to dash into town to the bank, or solve the very obvious problem with Bird. Bird won. I went out to see where I might build it a hutch.

I had plenty to work with, sheets of tin and plywood at the back of the woodshed, and timber off-cuts from the deck-installation. A big packing-case would have been perfect, but you couldn't have everything. For tools I had a bow saw, a small hatchet for a hammer, and the splitting-axe to drive things into the ground. Plus a Folger's-can of mixed nails I found under the wood-shed-eaves. There was room to add something to the back of the snowmobile-shelter, closing off the rear of it with the plywood, and then running out stringers to some uprights.

Design phase complete, I discovered the dirt was only a few

inches deep, and had to dig holes in the gravel for the uprights. It also took some time to trim a tin-roof down to size, using the axe-head as a guillotine, but by evening I'd knocked together something functional.

Bird pecked around my feet while I plucked dry grass for its bedding and entered happily when I threw in a handful of feed. As I pulled a leather-hinged doorway closed, it was scratching together a nest. A couple of minutes later I was on my knees scrubbing and disinfecting the kitchen floor, overjoyed to have it all to myself again.

In the morning I knew I'd overdone it. Every turn, bend or step sent a stab through my lower-left side. I took a handful of painkillers, the first in a long time, and decided to fall back on the walking stick for a while.

I was getting it out of the closet when McKinnon drove up in his red-white-and-blue. We sat out on the deck in the morning sun and he told me an interesting story about the submerged truck. It ended with, "It was sort of on your property, so we're obligated."

"Where was it stolen?"

"Can't say for sure. Our records don't go back that far. What little we have, came from an insurance claim that somehow got recorded in PRIME during old-data input. Just the plate number, the last known owner, that it was a theft, and the date in April '85. It's likely it was somewhere in the North Vancouver area though, because the owner's address was in Norgate."

"Are you allowed to talk about the body that was in it?"

"No problem there considering the time lapse. Regional Forensics say it was male, thirties, and the end was untimely."

"Really?"

"There'd been a through-and-through gunshot wound, shattered some ribs. Unlikely to be accidental or self-inflicted, since entry was in the back and there was no weapon or slug. Also, the victim was in no condition to drive and the truck had to get into the water somehow."

"So you'll investigate?'

"Probably not much more than we have, given the time that's passed. It's not the first unexplained cadaver dredged up in these parts. Just the same, you notice anything else, we'd appreciate you letting us know."

"Thanks Sergeant. I'll do that. Now what about the newer stuff you pulled out?"

"That big screen was bought in Toronto. Cash sale. Some

smaller items were paid for by check at Hume's here in town by your Mr. Reeman. Bank account still has a couple hundred bucks in it but hasn't been touched since April. The rest of it could be from anywhere, but we assume it's all linked. John Campbell says Mr. Reeman drove a black Yukon so he could have brought it with him."

He closed up his notepad. "In the end though it's not an extraditable offense to abandon stuff. If he shows up again in BC, we'll look at him on dumping charges, but in the meantime..."

"That's it?"

"Afraid so. At least you know your complaint has been noted, investigated, and we'll keep our eyes open. Do you want any of the stuff?"

After weeks in the water?

"No thanks."

He touched his lemon-squeezer hat at me. "Fine then we'll dispose of it. Thanks for your time."

"Thank you!"

The following morning, pre-emptively doped up, I got gingerly into the truck with my stick and headed toward town. Crossing the ford which was reduced to a trickle by several weeks without significant rain, though the yellow-clay banks were still soft because the place saw no sun; I noticed something disturbing and pulled up on the other side.

A vehicle had been stopping repeatedly. There were also boot marks from someone walking around. Regular vehicle tracks would have been understandable, considering the police operation and related comings and goings, but these were knobby, off-road tires.

Why stop halfway between the road and cabin?

It seemed ominous. I'd need to be watchful.

A smiling teller at the Canadian Merchant Bank gave me my new teller card and checks, also a statement that said I was $19,264.94 Canadian better off for the trip to Seattle. I'd forgotten about the favorable exchange rate. I used the card in their machine on the way out to confirm the pin number and took out a wad of cash.

I did chores like the gas station, feed store, and paying my hydro bill at the utility office. I also stopped by to see the Campbell's because it was long overdue, but their office was closed and there was a note on the door. 'Hello friends. Marge and I have taken advantage of the Canada Day break to have a few days off at her sister's in Smithers. If it's urgent give us a call on our cells. If it's not, we'll be back Tuesday July 3.'

Which only left the library.

I parked opposite the development-corporation's offices and headed up the alley between its enclosing concrete walls. I'd thought the gentle climb would be good exercise if I took it easy. I soon regretted it, but persevered anyway.

When I'd hobbled about a third of the way up, three slim figures in baggy jeans, bright shirts and ball caps, appeared at the top and started down. When they got nearer, they were young Nations' people. Two I remembered from my first visit to the offices. Then their faces turned truculent when they recognized me. I saw them draw closer together, lips moving.

As they passed on my right the tallest kid, who had long hair out through the back of his cap and down his back, shouldered me hard toward the wall. The bag of books went flying. I dropped the stick and broke my motion with both hands and turned on defense.

They'd spread out and were moving in from three sides. The one who hit me had watery eyes and I could smell stale beer. I was outnumbered by drunken belligerent kids on a day I was having trouble even walking. It was serious trouble.

The taller kid came in and kicked out at me. I blocked it with an arm, and he circled. I'm around 5-11 and 175. He had several inches on me but wouldn't have cracked 150. One at a time, I could probably hold my own, even hurting. Three was a real problem.

It proved a mistake to focus on the biggest one. One of his friends rushed in on my weak side and I couldn't turn fast enough. He caught me with a roundhouse above my right eye and dropped me to my knees, ears ringing. I saw their legs moving in and hoped I could block the kicks and get back on my feet. If I couldn't things were going to get very serious.

There was a roar of an engine followed by squealing tires. A blue double-cab pickup had charged up the alley and skidded to a halt opposite me. The driver's door burst open and a very large man in jeans and a black tee-shirt got out and moved to my side.

Prince Charles said something loud and the three kids visibly shrank in on themselves. He lifted me off my knees and moved me over so I could lean against the wall. Reached down again and handed me the stick, all the while glaring at the young people.

I was having trouble hearing, but he was firing questions without getting answers, so he shouted very loud one more time. The two smaller kids deferred to the taller boy, who was glaring back, not giving an inch. Like a cat pouncing, Charles grabbed his shirt and swung him with a thud against the wall. Held him there while he spoke to the others. They wilted further and walked away down the alley without looking back.

The right arm Charles was holding across the kid's chest had cord-like muscles. He asked a question, calling the boy Joseph, which rang a big bell for me. The boy didn't answer. Charles shook him like a rat and asked again. The boy gave a reluctant answer, eyes down at the ground. Charles spoke very slowly, giving the boy little shakes that elicited a few mumbled words and several nods, then released him. The boy backed away and followed his friends, who were on the street heading for the front door of the development corporation's offices.

The giant man walked to his truck and leaned against it with his back to the grille. Shook his head sorrowfully and said, "Are you alright?" His voice was very resonant.

"Yeah still hear bells but I'm okay I think." I was looking at the knobby tread of the wide tires on his truck, and at traces of yellow clay in the wheel-wells.

He sighed. "Yeah I'm sorry about this."

"You've been looking out for me. Haven't you? Out at my place."

He shrugged. "It's as much for those little jerks as you. That Elkpath kid's always been trouble. I seem to spend half my frikking time saving him from himself."

"Thanks anyway."

"You really don't get it do you," he said shaking his head. "This is the trouble you bring."

"I can understand that but this is my home too."

He laughed grimly. "You think?"

"I know."

"You got balls I give you that. You gonna press charges?"

"I think I'd rather just let it go." I moved away from the wall toward my scattered books. My head swam a little when I bent, but my hip was no worse.

"Probably wise," he said. "Here I'll give you a hand."

When I had my things, he nodded up the alley. "You going that way I'll drop you."

At the library entrance, we parted with a single nod at each other. I hoped his had a touch of respect to it. Mine certainly did.

FIFTY

Lake Kaldekut
June 26th

The next day, having not recovered enough to enjoy moving around much, I was browsing sports-scores while avoiding anything resembling a news-site, so as not to get depressed over the state of things back in the U.S., when I lapsed into deep thought. Trying to grasp the big picture.

When I was first learning to write computer-code, someone taught me if you're looking for something small within something big, don't look at the detail, look at the whole thing and figure out what's out of place. He was talking about software-bugs, but I'd learned it applied to life too. Don't look at the parts. Look at the whole. And never assume anything.

Applying this to my father, we came to the cove as a family that one summer, for maybe a week-and-a-half. What did he do? Either sat in the cabin like a smoldering stick of dynamite, or stalked the area studying the ground. I didn't see it achieve anything, but he certainly did a lot of it. Then we left, and it was as if this place stopped existing. Why?

It also seemed that window of time overlapped with his descent into the drunken violence that tormented and stunted me so badly. There had to be a connection, surely. My mind couldn't unchain itself from the blur of emotions and memories, but a realization took root he was searching for a THING. What was it? Did he find it or did he give up? Knowable? Or un-knowable?

But I wasn't so deep in thought I failed to notice Bird. It was nuzzling under pebbles for dragonfly larvae, amid the ripples raised by a cooling breeze across the blue water. From my angle it seemed, the wing on the side injured by the wolverine, hung lower. I called and made a finger-tapping motion on my thigh, it understood, and it came and rubbed against me.

I hadn't picked it up recently. It was surprisingly heavy, probably five or six pounds. When I parted feathers, the scars from the beast's teeth stood out. That side was definitely less developed. Still it was young and there was time before it had to use its wings for anything. I put it down and it walked briskly away.

But my father...

A spring was back in my step the following morning, but instead of a brisk walk, I turned to the laptop again for help.

During my worst times with Eileen, it was my livelihood, my comfort zone and refuge, and I'm not ashamed to say, at times my sexual relief. Now it was just a tool I happened to be skilled with. I needed to harness that and bring light to the black hole my father represented in my life.

His obsession with this place had peaked and ended, yet he hadn't sold it. It could be he didn't want to lose on the investment. It could also be, what he was looking for, was still here. And though he knew he'd never find it; he couldn't give it up either.

Two things dated from that time, besides my misery. The sunken truck and the body inside it. Why hadn't the RCMP come up with something more specific on those? They had the means. But then, officers changed stations. It was the nature of the job. And no doubt communications broke down in the process. Perhaps they just hadn't connected the dots. It's said you should never attribute to evil intentions, what can be explained by simple incompetence. Turning that around, why assume the powers-that-be knew everything, just because they had the power?

The RCMPs PRIME system had been around ten years, if that. McKinnon might have been in town two or three. Who knew the work-ethic, and diligence-level, of the people in his office? Had they considered every possibility? Unlikely.

Not being a related party to the truck owner, I couldn't just go to the vehicle bureau with the plate number. Besides, all they cared about were vehicles still on the road. The truck in the lake most certainly didn't qualify. I'd have to break into some systems. Where better to start than with PRIME? It was a government system like any other. The security might be weaker than in the States, but that was all relative. There are no easy systems to hack into.

My advantage was that when I was with the big software company on the east side of Seattle in the early '00s, I wrote a lot of the security code for those operating-systems. Me and others. It was common practice to put in our own 'back-door.' It's a rite of passage. The fun ones were called 'Easter eggs.' If you hold down the right combination of keys in a spreadsheet-program, for instance, you'll get to watch cartoon characters play with an abacus. Part hubris and arrogance, it was mostly convenience for testing. A back-door was what you went after, if you needed to break into a system.

But first I'd have to get through their external firewall. For that I'd need help from the hacker-community, which they were usually happy to provide if you knew where to go and how to ask. I opened a website called Gohackersyeah.crk. I couldn't browse to it, it had to be the exact address. After creating a chat account, calling myself 'Whizzit3469', I posted a question. I didn't expect an quick answer.

While I waited, Libby came to visit.

Libby came about 6:30 p.m. on Saturday evening, dressed summery in a light-cream skirt, pale-blue blouse and sandals, carrying a bottle of wine and a tall bottle of club-soda. She put it all down and kissed me.

All the doubts and fears I'd been holding onto, and my humiliation from being attacked, melted away. I was safe in the arms of someone I loved.

I made *Vitello Tonnato*: lightly-poached beef-rashers in a tuna and mayonnaise sauce. Libby helped with the salad, which had a lot of sliced tomatoes, chopped button-mushrooms, basil and olives. We ate outside in the pleasant evening, mopping our plates with crunchy pieces of homemade pita-bread, talking comfortably and lengthily about the police-search and what was found, and speculating about Adrian Reeman without any progress at all.

Later we lay naked on the bed with the last of the light fading and stars awakening in the cobalt sky. My hip still ached, and when our desires became needs, she made me squirm and groan as she brought me joy. Then I did the same until she shuddered. Then lay with my head on her hip while she stroked my hair, and we floated gently back down to earth.

I was content with what we had. I didn't like it that I occupied only part of her life, though a big part, or that we couldn't be together more. But she wasn't my possession, just a treasure to be enjoyed.

When she left early on Canada Day to do church stuff, I was happy and secure, and content enough to be left alone with my thoughts and the plan I had made.

FIFTY-ONE

Lake Kaldekut
July 2ⁿᵈ

While Libby's Honda was fading into the trees, I was already logging into my chat account at the hacker site. There was a promising message. The sender's avatar was lit up. I hit the 'Buzz' button by their name and they responded.

> Lowhanger432: Whazzup?
> Whizzit3469: U responded to my question about Canada.
> Lowhanger432: Yeah, like I said, not hard. They're weak on spoofing. Use a common name like 'John Smith' or 'Fred Brown.' U have to use their 1024-bit master-encryption key tho, but they only change that once in awhile.
> Whizzit3469: U know it?
> Lowhanger432: The lowhanger knows everything.
> Whizzit3469: What about the Canadian police system behind those firewalls?
> Lowhanger432: Shit PRIME? You fixing speeding tickets?
> Whizzit3469: Just doing research.
> Lowhanger432: Shuuuuuuuuuuuuuur. Very cool! Sure. Give me some time.

I turned off the power-save function, so the laptop stayed on all day, and in the evening he buzzed me and gave me the information. It included what I had to type on the address line in the browser. And what to do when I was prompted at several stages, in what turned out to be a lengthy process. But at the end of it, I was looking at a search screen inside PRIME.

Sometimes you gotta cut open the whole watermelon to get at the good parts, as they say in the software trade.

I started by typing in the plate from the truck, AKB-467. McKinnon had been straight with me. There was no important extra information. So I played around with the different fields and controls and found I could cross-reference records by any of several associated pieces of info. Good to know, but useless unless I had something to cross-refer, so I exited the interface knowing I could get back in at any time, and took a different approach.

What was going on in Laketown and its environs around that time? The newspapers would know, assuming they went back that far. The Laketown Bugle didn't, but the archives of the ones in Vanderhoof and Smithers, the two nearest main centers, went back to the '70s. I scanned through the years '82 to '86 and learned there was enormous development activity, a big boom in forestry and a substantial copper-strike inland from Smithers. But nothing else. I'd taken a dead-end route.

How about cross-referencing the people?

I logged back into PRIME and found the truck record. The owner had been a Chesterfield, James, 32 at the time. Thinking I was on to something, I tried anything associated with that name and got absolutely zip.

Idly, I started clicking through a list of major crimes by type and suspect in BC over the same period. Just testing the capabilities of the system really, because I was out of ideas. About the tenth name I clicked on under robbery was Vandervoort, Andrew. The 'Known Associates' field listed one Chesterfield, James. The crime they had in common was the armed-robbery of a Brinks truck in downtown Vancouver, Thursday, July 15, 1985.

Well now, looky there.

But oddly, there were no conviction details and no other activity for Andrew Vandervoort. Either he got off and went straight after that, or...

I looked again at Mr. Vandervoort's 'Status.' 'Deceased.'

After backing out of PRIME again in a hurry, I found the on-line archives of the Vancouver Sun and searched on the keyword 'Robbery,' for the few days either side of the Brinks event.

Multiple headlines for Friday, July 16, 1985 popped up on the screen. I clicked on the first one and got a digitized picture of a crumpled and burnt-out car wrapped around a pillar of a freeway overpass. The headline blared, 'Robbery Suspects Die in Flames Fleeing Police!!!!'

Well what DO you know?

A memory stirred of something I'd been told. I sat there, not touching the mouse or keys any more, thinking it through. When I'd done that enough, I had a new plan.

It was foggy along the unsealed road to the main-highway around 8:00 a.m. Tuesday morning, creating weird shadows in the diffused light of the dipped-headlights.

I was so inwardly focused I nearly hit a cow moose and its half-grown calf, while careering around a bend. But they galloped into the trees unscathed and I arrived in town wondering where to ask for what I needed.

The DIY store had equipment rentals, but not what I had in mind. The clerk said Smithers was more of a mining-supply town, and suggested McQuade's Equipment on Queen and Frontage, a block back from Main Street. I gassed up and drove the 80 miles along a winding and progressively more barren section of the Yellowhead Highway, parked in front of the store and went inside.

He was right. Whether you were a lone-prospector or a big construction-crew, they had everything you'd need, including several portable metal-detectors. Useful if I was sure I was looking for something made of metal. But right next-door was something better, a ground-penetrating radar system of the kind used by road-maintenance people to find power-cables and water-pipes.

Bright red and weighing about 25 pounds, it resembled a small lawn-mower. Where the blade would spin underneath were the electronics for sending a signal into the ground and receiving it back for analysis. In place of the engine was a battery like a motorcycle's, and a charging unit with a coiled lead to plug into a wall socket. Half-way up the handles was a foot-square display-screen and several up-and-down buttons for resolution-adjustment. It came with an instruction manual.

I rented it for a month.

Back at the cabin, I sat out on the deck and RTFM.

The device detected the density-difference between objects and surrounding matter underground, and displayed it on the screen. Range was about ten feet into normal soil, and though the book said it struggled with steel, seeing through concrete wasn't a problem. An alarm beeped when it hit anything significant so you didn't have to watch the screen constantly. A full battery charge lasted a few hours.

I got started right away.

To get a feel for the thing, I found where the water pickup for the pump in the basement exited, and tracked it to the lake's edge. It showed up clearly on the display, and I learned the ten-foot range-limit wouldn't be a problem. The soil over the underlying gravel only averaged about six inches deep.

Clear on what I was supposed to see, I spot-checked all the likely places around the cabin. Right up close to the foundations, and in the outbuildings, including inside Bird's hutch and the floor of the woodshed. The handles came loose with butterfly nuts to lay flat, so I also checked under the deck. I even took it downstairs and went over the concrete floor.

But by the end of the day, all I'd hit were a few pieces of tin and a discarded axe-head. I was beginning to doubt the signals I was getting, so I went back and mapped the water intake again. It worked perfectly.

The next morning, I went into the trees and did a careful scan for 20 yards either side of the track, from the ford to the forest-edge. Once I thought I was onto something and fetched a shovel, but it was just the way some tree-roots were tangled. I did learn the posts by the ford had large concrete-footings, and the buried hand-gun showed up as clear as day.

I had no doubt there was something to be found. A day-and-a-half of spot-looking had only eliminated the obvious areas. I'd have to be more systematic. I could imagine someone doing the 10-paces-this-way and 30-paces-that-way thing from old pirate stories, so I decided to search the entire verge, in a mow-the-lawn pattern.

But I didn't get the chance because that night Hal called me and asked me to come in and see him.

He'd heard from ADA Stoneman in Seattle, and there was a new offer.

FIFTY-TWO

Laketown
July 6th

Hal finished his summary of the new offer from the Feds with, "You understand they're saying there's some risk here? These are serious people."

"Yes, but it's the only way I can see to put myself in the clear. I don't have a choice."

"Alright make the call."

I looked at the paper Stoneman had given me at the inn in Seattle and dialed the number. Russell's voice came on the line. I said, "Hi Russ, it's Ben."

"Hey there. How are you buddy?"

"I'm good, Russ. Ah, I was wondering if that thing we discussed might still be open."

"Maybe working with us?"

"Yeah."

"Jim's here. Why don't I ask him?"

"That'd be great thanks."

Voices went back and forth and then Russell said, "Uh, yeah. He's still interested. When will you be around?"

Hal stuck a hastily written note in front of me. 'Weather lousy 4 flying all this week.'

"How about early next week?"

There were garbled voices again, then, "Sure thing. How about you come into the office at 9:00 a.m. next Tuesday morning? That's uh... the 10th."

"Okay."

Russell gave an address on Pike Street a few blocks up from the market. A trendy area of restored warehouses I remembered being popular with public-relations and advertising companies. He signed off with, "See you then man!"

Hal was right about the weather. The mini-drought broke and four solid days of downpours marched across the region. I couldn't continue my search, so I slept, read, worked hard on my fitness; and spent time with Bird, which loved the rain.

Libby came and stayed Saturday night, and very early Sunday morning I followed her Honda to Hal's office, where she jumped out and gave me a final kiss. As I retrieved my bag, I heard her ask him to look after me.

The coastal mountains were still clouded in so we took the inland route, refueled at Richmond, and splashed down at Lake Union seaplane base around 3:15 p.m.

U.S. Justice put us in a plush suite at the Pike Street Marriott, but not from generosity. It was in line of sight of the building I was going to.

They had their surveillance equipment in the lounge. It included something resembling a small eight-track recording-system, and a couple of devices like oversized ray guns out of Star Wars.

The tech operating them said they could pick up conversations inside a room by the vibrations of the window glass. I gathered there was some frustration due to the building layout.

Monday was a blizzard of meetings and coaching sessions, some of which Frank attended. When I was surprised to see him, Hal said quietly, "Trust but verify, my friend, trust but verify."

Words to live by, when you're at the whim of the most powerful law enforcement machine on the planet.

Stoneman and his two technicians came into the lounge of the suite at the Marriott a little before 8:00 a.m. on D-Day. One tech took his seat among the black-boxes, ray-guns and surface-run cabling. The other put down a suit carry-bag, opened his bag of tricks and got ready to wire me up.

The ADA held up a bundle of photographs and said, "I'd like us to look at these before Ben goes across the road." Frank groaned and Hal's shoulders slumped. Stoneman said, "Humor me!" and plopped the photographs on the coffee table. "All from the last 24 hours."

One showed the inside of the office, and I saw again why they needed me. It was the whole first-floor, except for an entranceway for lifts and stairs, and the inside was wide open with trendy raw-brick walls and polished-wood floors. The meeting rooms were in the rear, as highlighted in black marker. There was no way their long-distance voice-detection equipment would work, not to mention the place must be hell to work in with the clatter of high-heels.

"I'm going to say it all again," he said, as he separated out a picture of a couple of brutal-faced men in ill-fitting suits, filmed getting in or out of a cab. "We still don't know who these guys are. ICE doesn't have anything. They're Eastern European, though. Possibly Uzbekistani judging by the odd phrase we've picked up."

Another familiar figure had been captured on a cross-walk. "The large guy you saw at the party on Whidbey is Jacob Wickmeyer. He doesn't have a sheet but was a big venture capital player in Silicon Valley in the '90s. We think he's just come back in the game."

He covered the rest quickly. "Burton and Langwell you know well, also this guy Richard Cotton."

I just wanted it over with, but Stoneman looked at me directly and said, "Main thing is Ben, that you're sure of what you can and can't say. If it gets thrown out for entrapment, the deal is off."

Frank said, "He's not going to screw up. Just as long as there's no doubt he's free and clear afterward."

"No question. We're case building now. If he does this right, Ben's out of it."

Hal said, "Let's do it!"

They molded the transmitter to my lower back with putty, so it was undetectable under a specially tailored, charcoal suit-coat unless someone touched it. The microphones were in the coat-cuffs.

"Try to keep your arms out straight on the table," the tech said as he knotted the tie. "If you can point them at whoever's speaking it's even better."

I was sweating as I crossed the street, feeling trussed-up like a turkey. And not just because Seattle was in the midst of a 90-degree plus heat-wave. The front of the building was reflective glass and something like a movie was playing across the lower part of it as I walked up. I didn't realize it was cars going by on the street behind me until I grasped the chrome door handle and pulled.

A brunette with a spectacular figure and vacuous smile greeted me by name at the front desk. Distracted or not, I got a kick from watching her ass wiggle in front of me all the way to the back. Russ was already in a meeting room, in probably a $1000-suit, open-neck lime-green shirt that looked fitted, and $500 shoes without socks. "Heyyyyy," he said, pumping my hand.

The meeting room had a glass-topped, chrome-framed table surrounded by black leather director's chairs. As I took the seat next to Russell, another-well designed woman brought in a tray of coffee cups, an espresso machine, and all the things that went with it.

Before I could ask Russ anything, the others shambled in.

FIFTY-THREE

Seattle
July 10th

The new arrivals were as expensively dressed as Russ, but no-one but I wore a tie. Jim Burton nodded courteously. Wickmeyer looked just as stiff as he was at the party, in contrast to Rick Cotton who clasped my hand enthusiastically. When the two hulking and expressionless Europeans entered, the room darkened somehow. I wondered how it was possible to spend so much money on suits and still look like bar-bouncers.

"Ben, it's great you called," Burton said. "We're at a crucial point in this deal. I'll tell you right up front it's a leveraged buyout of Xenith Systems."

I was mildly stunned.

When the Dot.com era went in the toilet in the mid '90s, Xenith was one of the last withered software-behemoths standing. I interviewed there once, when I was looking to leave the east side company, but it was so well known they were struggling I didn't pursue it.

Takeovers and mergers have always driven the software industry. It's a giant monopoly-game for the big players, but with real money. Microsoft has won a lot of rounds, picking off start-ups with products compatible with their Office suite. Likewise, the German company SAP with the small databases. No one had wanted Xenith at any price. They were a hollowed-out shadow of themselves, trying to survive off the dwindling customer-base for their outdated technology.

Burton launched into a spiel about diamonds-in-the-rough, down deep in the product line, that could be brought sparkling to the surface with minimal tidying up, thus triggering a company resurgence. The longer I listened, the more my scepticism grew. It might have been entertaining to everyone else, but it was total fantasy to me. And Russell too I would have expected.

There's an old Irish joke about two Catholic matrons sitting in Mass on a Sunday, hearing the Priest extol the joys of motherhood. One turns to the other and says, "Faith Mary, I wish I still knew as little about it as he does." I was with her. The company was the ultimate dog. I looked at Russell and he did a very subtle full-body shrug.

"May be right Jim," I said when he paused, "But all their revenue's based on legacy stuff. They haven't had a new release in... I can't remember."

"Yeah well that's not really the focus. We think the company has market-presence. Name recognition."

That was true, at least. Most people would know the name. "Okay, but where do I come in?"

The two Europeans stared like sphinxes. Wickmeyer had his head at an angle, lips pursed, appearing to think things through. Cotton looked bored. Burton smiled like a shark contemplating breakfast. "Evaluation skills Ben. We'd like you to find those diamonds in the rough for us."

"And if there aren't any?"

"Then be creative."

Vaporware. He wants me to just make it all up.

"Let me get this straight. You want me to evaluate their code, which is all likely to be lousy, since they still have storage-applications based on OS/2 for heck's sake. And put my reputation on the line that it's all bleeding-edge? Or invent some new version in the works that is?"

"That's reasonably accurate."

"What would be in it for me?" I even said it with a straight face.

"For a start, if you join us it won't be today, it will be a few months back. We'll want you to sign some backdated paperwork, but I think you'll appreciate the salary we've been paying you. Call it a signing bonus. Plus, I think you'll like the options package. You'll have had them quite some time."

"Don't options need a stock price that goes up?"

"You're smart. Yeah, usually. But all that really matters is the price when you sell and what you have to pay for them. We think with the right PR we can engineer a good dead-cat-bounce based on your, ah... creative analysis of the product line. Jacob here is bringing in the budget for that. And that's only the first bite of the cherry."

"Isn't this illegal?"

"Who gets hurt?" He did an open-hands, palm-up thing at me and smiled wider. "No one cares. It's just another stock that bumps a few points and dives again. Happens every day of the year."

"This is how you did things at MagnaTECH?"

"That was a dress rehearsal. This is the big time. Know what a market cap is?"

Jackpot!

"Roughly," I said, "Total number of shares of a company at a given time."

"Trade-able shares actually. MagnaTECH had a cap of 30 million. Xenith is close to 50 times that. Your share, not counting the salary, would be proportionate to what you got with MagnaTECH. Plus, the same on the second deal."

Fifty times is $1.5B. On that scale my MagnaTECH options would have been over $26M.

"Second deal?"

"Correct. When the stock dives again we'll de-list it from NASDAQ and re-register the name and assets, as an over-the-counter-stock company, controlled by our friends here in Eastern Europe. They have an excellent promotional-mill."

Twice the deal I had at MagnaTECH? No wonder Russell is living in a $3M mansion and watching an $85,000 TV. Just on an advance!

"You're talking a pump-and-dump operation with what's left of the company?"

"We'll strip it first. They have a few patents with awhile to run. So, are you interested?"

"I uh, don't know. It's all a bit much."

I felt Russell move beside me, and in his Californian touchy-feely way, he put his right arm around my shoulders. "Ah this is quite a bit to take in. It took me awhile, remember? Maybe Ben and I should talk it over?"

Burton's eyes went hard and cold. "Just remember you guaranteed him Russ. Don't forget that."

"Yeah yeah I did. Ben's cool. I stake myself on it."

"No doubt about that."

The threat hung there a second or two. Russell let his hand slip down my back. Right on the transmitter. He went rigid. He let the hand drop away, and after a second said, way too cheerfully,

"Hey, let's take a break for a bit, get some Java, have a breather. What do you say guys?"

Burton, frowning, said, "There's coffee here we haven't even touched."

"Oh no. Let's just stretch our legs, okay?"

"Five minutes."

Russell got up and looked hard at me, then inclined his head. We went across the room to a coffee nook with no-one nearby. He turned and hissed-out, "Is that what I think it is? Tell me I'm wrong Ben!"

"You're not wrong."

"You're recording this? For yourself or..."

"The Feds have the whole thing Russ. I'm sorry."

I saw his whole life crumble behind his eyes.

"You're fucking sorry? Man you have no fucking idea who these people are! You have no fucking clue!"

"I said I'm sorry."

"Fuck your sorry. I stood up for you, man. I stood up for you!"

"I didn't ask you to do that."

"Jesus. What happens now?"

"I honestly don't know. I..."

A door banged towards the front of the building and I heard stomping feet. People in cubicles turned and watched as Stoneman elbowed past the bewildered receptionist. A half-dozen grim and bulky individuals in blue tactical-vests with 'U.S. Marshal' in yellow block letters, were right behind him. Each had a black weapons-belt and a hand on the Beretta 92 on their hip.

"Oh fuck. What have you done?" Russell said.

Stoneman announced, "Everyone in this room is under arrest for violations of U.S. Code of Justice sections 78FF and 10B-5. Breaches of and conspiracy to breach, security exchange regulations for the control of stock trading."

He located Russell and me, made eye contact with a guy who seemed senior among the marshals and said, "Please take Mr. Langwell into custody also."

"Russ listen to me man," I said very quickly. "I swear I didn't believe you were involved. I was trying to clear both of us. I swear it. Honest to God."

Russell choked out, "You asshole. I trusted you. You absolute asshole."

"They're what?" asked Frank in disbelief.

"Russian Mafia or a version of it," repeated Stoneman wearily.

We were back in the Marriott a couple hours later, having been asked to attend this debrief and given up on getting airborne that day. Stoneman had his hands together on the table, looking no place in particular. It was his screw-up. He'd been in charge. He knew it and we knew it.

I'd gone from heartsick over what I'd done to Russell, no matter what my intentions were or how much he might deserve it; to stunned and quite scared. Hal looked shocked.

Stoneman continued, "Interpol only advised us when we were processing them at the Federal facility. Indications are they ring-bolted in on a freighter. Facial-recognition is completely blank on them at any airport. Their international-sheet has them down for money-laundering and extortion."

"You put Ben in there with those guys?" asked Frank quietly.

"We warned you these were dangerous people. Yeah, so this is at the top of that scale. But the only difference it would have made is we'd have warned you better. We still needed that conversation on tape. By the way, Ben you did a great job."

Whoop dee fucking doo. I've just pissed off a bunch of people famous for eliminating their business problems permanently. Saying I've done it well, fails the feel-good test.

"Look guys, if Ben was living here we'd probably look at some protection. So, what do you want to do?"

I said, "I just want to go home." I needed this to be over.

No-one looked comfortable with that.

Stoneman said, "You sure? We can put you some place while this dies down, at least."

"Yes."

He sighed. "Alright we'll get the other stuff in motion."

"Other stuff?"

"We need a court order to take you off the case. It'll take a few days. And a release of this-much money requires AG approval. After that we'll start preparing for your testimony."

This is never-ending.

"Yeah, the tape's no good without it!" He got up. "Enjoy your trip home. We'll be in touch with Frank about the hearing."

FIFTY-FOUR

Seattle
July 11th

We lifted off Lake Union into a gusty wind. When the western horizon came in view, it was roiled with billows of cloud extending north. They promised relief from the heat-wave but poor flying conditions. We'd expected it. Hal had called in a last-minute flight-plan change to the canyon-route, from a pay-phone in the seaplane terminal.

Still, the weather improved the closer we got to Richmond. And then again as we turned east along the Fraser at the start of our second leg. Competing air traffic was also light, except around Pitt Meadows airfield right beside the river, which was abuzz with small aircraft.

One was a dark blue helicopter. I recognized it by its distinctive streamlined-shape and enclosed tail-rotor, as an Airbus Eurocopter EC135. It stood out clearly as it rose from the bare end of the runway, because it had no identifying numbers. I thought all aircraft had to have those, but what did I know? It tagged along, perhaps 500 feet below, for quite a distance before vanishing.

The sky over the canyon quickly extinguished all dark thoughts of taciturn thugs. Cumulonimbus-towers constantly morphed from one fantastic shape to another, like living things. Shafts of gold slashed down through rifts, lighting up the jagged-rock faces below.

Yeats would have written 'An Irish Airman Foresees his Fate' on just such a day.

217

We kept a prudent clearance above the rim, while enjoying every enthralling twist-and-turn, and we'd just swept around the big s-bend south of Yale, when I felt a slight flutter in the airframe. The airplane dipped. Hal frowned, adjusted the trim, and it steadied. But immediately shuddered again and sank 50 feet. Worse, it struggled to recover.

Hal eased on more power, but it barely helped. The engine-note had also changed, from a steady-roar to a two-tone sound with an overlaying flutter. Hal looked at me in horror and jabbed a finger upwards. I understood in a horrible instant. Something was there, stealing our lift and forcing us inexorably downward.

"Jeez hold on!" he yelled and shoved the controls forward. We picked up airspeed. When we leveled out the plane was smooth again, but we'd lost half our safety-margin.

Hal jinked left as much as he dared without losing more altitude, and I crammed my face against the plexiglass to see what threatened us. It was the Eurocopter. And it was coming down fast after us.

I shouted, but Hal didn't answer. The shuddering had started again. We dipped sickeningly and when Hal stabilized us, we were barely above the canyon's maw. We'd started to buck-and-heave also. Downdrafts snatching at us as the water-cooled air from the river-rapids sucked down the sun-heated air above.

Hal didn't need to speak. We had to get out of this before we lost all lift and plunged to our destruction. He judged which side was closer, extended the landing flaps to give us more wing-area, then poured on power and banked hard to port. We lost another few precious feet, but it got us into clean air. The helicopter overshot but turned tenaciously to follow.

We were rushing toward a sheer cliff-face, close enough I could see individual ice-cracks in the stone. Hal had the yoke back as far as he dared without risking a stall. Gradually we rose until I could just see over the top. There was summer-browned pasture and a fence. We were going to just clear it.

Hallelujah!

But the Eurocopter was fast and agile. It didn't need smooth air like the 206 with its massive pontoons. It was on us again and we sank sickeningly. Hal hammered the power lever against its stop and screamed, "Brace! Brace!" The canyon edge and fence beyond it were so close, I could count three wires. Suddenly we broke free of the suction and the plane jumped a few precious feet. We cleared the rim by inches.

We'll hit the fence. We'll flip and die.

Then faster than the mind could process the fact, we were beyond the fence and swooping upwards at serious risk of stalling. Hal eased in the yoke and we settled into a slower climb. Adrenaline tingles rippled all over my body.

Hal and I stared at each other. I had never imagined a human being could be so pale. But we were alive. Sweet Lord, we were alive.

The Eurocopter had gone as if it had never existed.

Hal leveled us off and retracted the flaps with a corresponding surge in airspeed. He said tersely, "Water. Big water. I need to get down. Where?"

I looked at my display. "Inkawthia Lake! Straight ahead!" But he'd already seen it, a strip of water aligned roughly northeast.

He did one circuit looking for obstructions and then put us down in a fast, jolting landing that threw big splashes of spray sideways from the pontoons. He didn't taxi, just let all the speed bleed off. Turned us into the wind, killed everything and slumped over the yoke with his head on his fore-arms.

We didn't sit and recover long because we were in a small reedy bay and the breeze threatened to blow the plane out into the deep. Hal restarted briefly and taxied to where we could both jump down into the shallows.

The aircraft drew only a foot or so of water, but I was soon soaked to the waist, holding it against the wind while Hal did his inspection. The only visible problem was some cable-stays that helped link the floats to the fuselage were sagging. Greater danger lay back the way we'd come, however, so Hal elected to go on. The rest of the flight was uncomfortable as my clothes dried on me, but at least uneventful. We said little.

At the hangar on Bouclier Lake, Hal skipped his usual after-flight inspection, intending to call a mechanic to come fix and re-certify the aircraft. We were back at his office in Laketown a little after 4:00 p.m. with the first specks of an incoming storm pattering at the window.

Hal said, "So think that was the Russians, or whoever the fuck they are?"

"Had to be." I said. "But how would they know it was us?"

"Plenty of people in that terminal could have overheard me calling in the changes to the flight plan. I had to repeat the tail number a couple of times, remember? If they had us followed..."

"Jeez they nearly killed us!"

"Yeah got my pucker-factor up where you wouldn't believe, but I'm guessing if we'd crashed, it would have been a bonus for them. More likely harassment. Warning you not to testify. Better watch your step man."

No doubt.

FIFTY-FIVE

Laketown
July 11th

Persistent-drizzle had strengthening to drenching-rain when, after stopping for supplies, I turned south from the junction about a half-hour later.

There was a green sign with yellow-lettering on a stake by the side of the road. It could have been a political hoarding, except there was no election I knew of. Then there was another one. I saw a BC Fish and Wildlife logo and pulled over.

WARNING! Please report any BEAR SIGHTINGS to the local Fish and Wildlife Officer. DO NOT EXIT YOUR VEHICLE but LEAVE THE AREA and REPORT THE SIGHTING IMMEDIATELY.

Jacques DeLeon's name and mobile number were written below in indelible-marker.

An odd business.

Even more oddly, there had been major traffic on my access road in my absence, including the tracks of a pack of dogs. Recently, too. The downpour had barely smudged the sign.

Horrible thoughts about Bird and dogs flashed in my mind. I accelerated through the trees and across the verge and skidded to a halt by the cabin. Bird's hutch was empty, and the big bowl of food I'd left was empty and tipped on its side. I turned frantically to look through the rain, past the jetty and along the beach.

Bird was a few yards out from shore, treading water nervously, in the company of two wild geese. They immediately decided I was trouble and heaved skyward with plaintive honks. My feathered friend paddled straight to shore and ran to me for protection. I scratched its head, which now reached well above my knee, with a heavy sigh of relief.

With Bird in its pen until I could feed it, I collected the stuff from the Explorer and walked to the back door. Another card was in the jamb. This one from DeLeon. It said, "Please phone me urgently!" But I didn't get the chance because the phone was already jangling insistently. It was John Campbell, sounding very concerned.

"Have you been away?"

"Yes, in Seattle."

"Ahhhhh I didn't know. Look we got a bad bear situation!"

"I saw some signs and got a note from Mr. DeLeon."

"Ben this is very bad. Fatality."

"You're kidding me!"

"Nope. Up at the road-kill dump Sunday night. Some Nations' kids went up there with a .22 plinking-rifle, looking for rats or some damn thing, and stumbled on a grizzly over a carcass. One kid put some shots in it when it came at them. It killed him, and the two others only got away because it stopped to savage the body. They made it to their Cherokee truck and got the doors closed, thank God. But then they had to wait a couple hours to report it because the keys were on the mauled kid. Can you imagine that?"

Three Nations' kids. Reckless behavior. Jeep Cherokee truck.

"No."

"Anyway, the beast was long gone by the time Jack got up there with his dogs. But we know it headed south-east. That's your direction, Ben."

"Oh God."

"Tell me about it! In this one case? Forget everything I told you about grizzlies always being on the move. This is likely the same one that took the moose in late May. It's stayed."

"What's been done?"

"We've scoured the area for three days. Found nothing. The kid with the best view of things is sure it got hit in the face a couple of times, so wherever it is, it's sore and mean. Look, do you want to come into town and stay with Marge and me while this gets sorted out? We don't know if it's anywhere near you, but... just to be safe, okay? What do you say?"

I thought about Bird and the rented equipment in the basement

I was busting to get back to.

"John, I'm really grateful for the offer. Can I take a rain check until I've talked to DeLeon?"

"No problem. Just let me know soon, okay?"

Fortunately, the wildlife officer painted a rosier picture. He had a lot of faith in his tracking-dogs and was fairly sure the beast had just kept going. Its gait said if it was wounded, it was slight. Probably only enough of a sting to chase it out of the area in a hurry.

"One thing to watch for though Ben, if you're out and about, is any droppings."

"Okay, what do I look for?"

"Black bears leave lumps the size of ping pong balls, with a lot of berry seeds and often squirrel fur in it. What a grizzly leaves, is twice as big and has a strong stink of pepper. Don't get out and smell it if there's cover real close, but just so you know what to look for."

More information than I wanted, but my concerns were mostly eased. "Thanks, I'll keep my eyes open."

I called John back to thank him and let him know I was staying put. Later after getting settled, I called Libby's cell number twice without success. The second time I left a loving message. While I was taking Bird a big bowl of feed, I checked the garbage-drum lid again.

You certainly never do know.

At last I could let the gentle hiss of the rain on the deck lull me away into an exhausted and surprisingly dreamless sleep.

A watery sun glowed through thinning overcast as I looked out the next morning. I hoped the storm might restore some greenness to the parched 75-yards of verge between the lake and trees.

I went straight into town to see Libby, watching for evidence of bears in every clearing, needless to say. Otto's was quiet. Libby hugged me warmly. We stole some of the slow-period before the noon-rush, to hold hands at Ma Maison. I told her what had happened in Seattle and before she went back to the shop, we made plans for the weekend.

John wasn't at the realty office, but I found him in the driveway of his house with his heavy-caliber rifle leaning against the siding, and a hose in his hand. The sides of his Ford pickup were mud-encrusted, and the bed of it a carpet of dog-tracked slush. He'd been out since dawn and finally agreed with DeLeon that the danger had most likely passed.

After declining lunch, I headed home, stopping only to gas-up. When I emerged from the trees into the cove, it was shaping into a better afternoon. I went down right away to get the radar unit from the basement and got to work.

I'd already covered the likely places. If whatever I was seeking had been taken back in the hills and hidden deep, it would never be found. All I could do was eliminate every other possibility, and hope that would satisfy me and banish the shadow that had hung over me for most of my life. Perhaps you could say I was ghost-hunting.

I set the machine so it threw out a signal about a yard wide and began my grid search. To keep on course, I put two sticks in the ground about six feet apart on both sides of the verge. By aiming at the first one in one direction, and the second on the return, the strips overlapped like mowing a lawn. Moving the stakes progressively covered the area. I must admit to a few glances at the trees as I went, but this was dog-with-a-bone time and I wasn't letting anything deter me.

Half-an-hour later, I hit something and excitedly uncovered what showed up as a wide patch on the screen. But it was just a strip of roofing iron, which I excavated anyway to make sure it wasn't covering anything, but found only stones beneath. It took the rest of the day to cover from the edge of the marsh to where the broken ground and brush got too difficult, twenty-plus yards past the woodshed. Only to find utterly zero.

Later, while cooking dinner, I reflected on the effort I'd made. It was frustrating, but the fact was I'd completely misread my father's behavior. But then, who really knew why anyone did anything? Certainly I hadn't understood him at the time. Whatever made me think I could figure him out in retrospect?

In truth, he was just a brutal drunk, and I needed to sever the last link to that pain. It had been a good hunch and if I'd been right it would have explained everything. But I'd examined every horizontal surface and found absolutely nothing. I would have to let it go.

I decided to return the equipment the next day, before Libby came over Friday evening. Then, as I leaned over to thicken the casserole I was making, I stopped in mid-motion.

Horizontal. Every horizontal surface.

FIFTY-SIX

Lake Kaldekut
July 12ʰ

Turning off the stove and abandoning the casserole, I wiped flour from my hands with a dish-towel. Lifted the trapdoor in the pantry, went downstairs and unplugged the GPR-unit, and took off its push-handles.

One side-wall was blocked by propane tanks. Stairs covered most of the other. The back wall had the water pump, electrical panel and bolted down backup generator blocking it. Only the long wall running the width of the cabin under the lounge, lined with sheets of very-old plywood joined by vertical wood-strips, was bare. I picked the detector up by the battery-bracket, and pressed it to the plywood to see what was behind it, working my way along.

At the end nearest the stairs, I found a cavity.

I fetched a screwdriver, removed the strip holding the wall panel in place, and pried back the ply. I was looking at one end of a wooden box with a metal carry handle. It was jammed in by some collapsed gravel, which I scraped out, and with some twisting-and-tilting it eventually crashed to the concrete at my feet.

Reinforced by rusty metal bands, it was about two-feet by three-feet by eighteen-inches tall. Brushed the dust off stenciled red letters on the side. They spelled out 'Keebler Mining Ltd.' The hasp that once held the lid closed had been busted loose. I lifted the lid and looked inside.

It took a while for my excitement to die-down enough to begin carrying the contents carefully upstairs.

One item required some effort. Though small, it weighed close to 25 pounds. The last item, though the box had kept it dry, was thin and light and fragile. I sat down with that last thing at the kitchen table and studied it. Then found McKinnon's card and called his mobile. It was shortly after 7:00 p.m. and he answered from his car. I told him what I'd found and done. He said he'd come right out. I heard his siren start to whoop before the phone clicked off.

I caught Hal at the dinner-table with his family. He too said he'd be right over. While I waited, I played with the fragments of new knowledge in my head like a Rubik's cube, trying every combination, until things lined up.

McKinnon still had his roof lights going when he stopped outside. I added some additional details. He didn't press me on my source-of-information. While we waited on Hal, the RCMP officer spent the time talking on my phone. At one point he asked if he could call Ottawa, and I told him it worked over the internet and to do whatever he wanted.

By the time the three of us were finally seated together looking at what was on the floor, McKinnon had put it together the same way I had. Hal was still catching up. He asked me, "Where's the rest?"

"I'm sure the ledger explains that."

"Yeah, I'm sure it will," said McKinnon, nodding in agreement. "An assay report with the robbery record, says there were eight of what they call 'good delivery' bars. 3,200 troy ounces. Keebler had their own smelter and liked to ship it out as ingots. That's around 100 kilos with the box. A lot for three guys to lift, especially in a hurry."

"Wasn't one of them wounded?" I asked, thinking of the body in the lake.

"Yes, but that was afterward when they were climbing in the getaway-vehicles. We'll look into him again, but will probably never know his name unless there's a DNA-hit on those bones. Anyway, they got it all and what you've recovered looks like one, and almost a half-bar. I'd say that rusty hacksaw was used to cut the rest into small pieces."

"What was it worth back then?"

"Value for insurance purposes, whole shipment, $2.32M."

Hal whistled long and loud. "That's a crime-of-the-century in these parts! How come it's not famous?"

"They didn't publicize in case of copycats," McKinnon said.

I pointed at the two dusty yellow chunks of metal. "More important, what's that worth?"

"I asked for an estimate on that as well. They say it's hard to say with the cut bar but at today's prices and supposing it's a half, and the whole one is 400, you've got about 600 troy ounces there. Gold's down at the moment, but still fetching US$1,245 an ounce. That would make it ah... U.S. three-quarters of a mil. More or less."

"That small volume?" exclaimed Hal.

"You bet," said McKinnon, then put his hand on the ledger book and looked sadly at me. "Your father was a metals-dealer?"

I nodded, and he nodded back.

"Figures. I guess there's no guilt by association, but it looks like he was fencing it for them, at maybe an eighth-bar a week or something to start with."

He opened the ledger carefully and pointed at entries on a page.

"At the beginning he was giving them 80-cents on the dollar. See that? Then over here it looks like he begins paying them every penny it's worth. My guess is they were blackmailing him by then and he couldn't get out of it.

McKinnon glanced around the cabin. "I think they planned all along to use this place as a hideout. Probably bought it with proceeds of some other crime through a front-person. They snuck the gold out of the area gradually and made a deal with your father. When he realized what was happening, probably because of the amount, he tried to back out." He held up the tattered booklet. "So they took this and held it over him. Then this other thing happened, and they died, and well..."

We sat in silence until Hal asked, "Finders keepers?"

McKinnon snorted. "You wish. Insurance company owns it now. Imagine there's a reward though."

Hal smiled. "I can get the insurance-company name from your station, right?"

"Sure thing."

Hal insisted on an itemized receipt before we helped McKinnon put everything including the strongbox in his car. He left us with a warning not to talk about any of it, an unwritten rule around gold robberies, apparently.

Soon Hal went also, back to his cold dinner, and left me with the hole in my basement wall, and an ache in my heart for what it must have been like to be my father when he was being blackmailed. The shame of it, the risk to his reputation and his family if found out. How that would eat at a man.

After a long sad while sitting in the dark, tears came. Terrible wracking sobs, for my father's anguish and mine, and for the frightened lonely boy I had always been.

FIFTY-SEVEN

Laketown
July 13th

The 180-mile round trip to Smithers to return the GPR-unit, got me back into Laketown in the middle of a warm-and-sunny Friday afternoon.

The businesses along Main Street should have been bustling with end-of-week trade. And more than a few tourists. Instead downtown was unusually still and quiet. Much of the curbside paraphernalia had been put away, and there were even 'CLOSED' signs in some windows.

Vehicle-traffic however, was heavy, including a couple of heavyset, plain-leather-jacketed bikers riding Moto Guzzi touring bikes, all chrome and black. Perhaps making the end-of-summer run down from Telegraph Creek I'd read about.

The traffic backed up at the bend just east of the Laketown Inn. A Mountie with white gloves was directing a funeral procession into the Memorial Gardens. Aaron Elkpath was laying his son Joseph to rest.

I felt sad. And excluded somehow. Though I highly doubted my presence would have been welcome, had I even known. Still, what did any problems I had matter, compared with a tragedy like that?

Black Friday, indeed.

Libby arrived that evening dressed church-style. When she was comfortable, I drank orange juice, and she sipped wine, while dinner cooked. We ate more than we should have, mostly one handed because I had her other one in mine.

We talked about what I found downstairs, and the circumstances around that. It was difficult to express my changed feelings about my father. Not that I held back, but it had been a polar-shift and many were still unresolved. Later we relaxed in the lounge.

Libby was unusually quiet. I first thought my unburdening had triggered it, but gradually understood it was something more profound. There'd been other times when she'd been down in the dumps, but it had usually passed quicker.

"Want to talk about it?" I asked quietly.

"What?" She lifted her hands and dropped them back down. "Oh it's... nothing."

"No it isn't."

I maneuvered around and lay my head down in her lap, moving my hand gently on her thigh. Some seconds passed before she sniffed loudly and her upper body moved like she was wiping away tears. "Remember I told you about Gary?"

"Sure. He was abusive."

"Yes, but I didn't really say how."

"I thought you'd get to that in your own time." Which wasn't really true. I thought I already understood.

She sniffed again. "I suppose when I got to Calgary I was ready."

"For?"

"Anything I suppose. Little sheltered girl. I'd only dated twice. Badly. I guess I just let loose."

"Sounds fairly normal considering," I observed.

"Well for me, arriving in Calgary was like being totally free. All the judgments and rules were gone. I didn't go home for over a year until my Aunt Janice died. By then I was... I suppose, well..., running wild."

"That's not a crime sweetheart."

"Maybe not, but I took it to extremes. I'd read some things, like Germaine Greer, and Erica Jong, and I thought I could act like a guy and it wouldn't touch me."

"Maybe you needed it out of your system."

"Probably. I did back off a lot in my junior year. I had to, or I'd have crashed out of school and I wouldn't do that to my dad."

"Okay."

"Then I met Gary, it was just a casual thing at first. I was seeing someone else. He didn't seem to mind. In fact was interested in the things we... did. I didn't think much of it at the time. We started living together almost by accident. One of those times the cherries all line up on the slot machine. My friends and I were losing our apartment. His roomie moved out. I guess I was probably head-over-heels by then. He was smart, good looking, all that stuff. I would have done anything for him." She paused. "And I did."

"You mean physically, sexually?"

I felt her nodding above me. "It started with his ex-room-mate, who came around for something or other. And I kind of enjoyed it too."

"You didn't think it was wrong?"

"Not then, no. But it ruined Gary and I, even though we married a month or so later. After that, it was all he was interested in. Getting me into bed and other... situations with men so he could... I suppose watch and direct."

Then she sobbed heart-brokenly.

"It got awful. Then he was interviewing and not getting offers, and he began to drink... God just all the time! And after graduation, I found a job to help out, and that just made it worse. He couldn't stand it when I had friends he didn't know. It made him... it was so awful." Her voice dropped to a whisper. "And I couldn't tell a soul. Who would have understood?"

"So how did you get out of it?" I asked when her breathing was more even.

"I basically ran away. Said I was going to the store or something, and I had my bag with a few things in the stairwell and just drove."

She cried a minute or two. I got up off her lap and swept her hair aside and pressed my face tenderly to hers and held it there. When I eased back the look on her face broke my heart. "You'll hate me now. You'll think I'm a slut."

"No, I think you really cared about him and wanted to make him happy."

"I... suppose that's true. That's why I've needed the church. I couldn't tell you before. I hoped it would all just shrink into the past and not have happened, but that's not life. Is it?"

"No. It's not."

She looked like a bereft child. Another sob wracked her body.

And suddenly I was no longer the center of my own universe. We were. This wonderful woman-child I hoped to spend the rest of my life with, and I. And it would take more than words to prove I truly did accept her. I took her hand. "Come."

By the bed, I undressed her and kissed every part I uncovered. She stood still at first and then began to sway, biting her lip as I kissed down her breasts and around her nipples. She helped me get my top off and clung to me as I took off the rest. We took two steps together and collapsed on the bed and I parted her hair from her wet face and kissed her lips gently.

"I love you, Liberty Mueller. All of you, past, present and future."

Her face came up hungrily and sought mine. Then we truly made love, with our hearts and minds as well as our bodies, each of us fully open to the other, and holding nothing back until we could barely move.

Then we lay, arms entwined and moisture drying, with our hearts bonded, until sleep soothed away every remaining care.

FIFTY-EIGHT

Lake Kaldekut
July 14th

My Saturday couldn't possibly have started any better.

A luxurious sun beamed down from an eggshell-blue sky onto the most beautiful place on earth. Songbirds trilled and the wafting air smelled of pine-trees and wildflowers. I made us breakfast. We ate in bed. Then lay back in each other's arms wishing we'd never have to get up.

But we did. The phone rang, and it was Hal. He told me about the Elkpath funeral, which had been poignant, and also cathartic in bringing together divided factions of the community.

"I wish I'd gone."

"No need. The town knows how things were. I offered your condolences."

"Thanks."

"Now Ben, a couple things. The money from Seattle hit my trust-fund yesterday."

He gave a number much higher than I expected, and I whistled.

"Yeah some interest. I'll transfer it to your account Monday."

"Thanks."

"Also, I haven't nailed down the insurance company yet, but that gold's been valued. A little more than we thought. Other settlements have been in the ten percent bracket, so I think you can count on another seventy-five grand or so, coming your way."

I was about speechless.

"You have a great weekend now and I'll see you next week."

"Hal I..."

"Yeah, I know. It's been entirely my pleasure. Well... apart from that thing with the helicopter."

We laughed, and he clicked off.

It was raining cash; I was with the woman I loved, and the world was my abalone, or some wonderful kind of shellfish.

Libby joined me at the deck-railing and we thought about how to spend this glorious day. Perhaps another magical walk in the forest. There wouldn't be many more such days before fall descended, which she said could last as long as 30-seconds before the wham of winter. At which point I chased her around the kitchen in a determined quest to verify she was ticklish until we were weak and aching from mirth.

Instead, we did ordinary domestic stuff. Laundry, dusting, bathroom duties, fixing holes in basement walls. All the things I hoped to share with her forever once I could confirm my divorce and pop the question.

But I didn't get much more than the hole-in-the-wall fixed, before there was a growing rumble coming from the trees. I first thought it was a helicopter, but it wasn't whoof-whoofy enough. It was the two Moto Guzzis. They crossed the verge and went up on stands by the side of the cabin. I went down to investigate.

The two riders had removed their helmets. They were road-weathered men, and probably mid-to-late-40s, with beards like ZZ Top in their heyday. One had a leather patch on the seat of his jeans. The other nicotine-stains around his mouth. Both had pot bellies but muscular shoulders and necks that suggested indulgent living more than lack of fitness. They nodded at me and I said, "Hello there."

The one with the patched pants stepped away from his bike and gandered about the place. The yellow-bearded man stripped off his heavy riding gloves and put on lighter ones. I guessed cold hands were a constant problem when you were on the road. Yellow-beard said, "Doing some looking around. Only you here?"

"And my lady."

Patched-rear-end walked a few steps toward the outbuildings, looked around the side of the cabin and said, "Great place you have. What's down this way?"

Huh? What you see is what there is.

Before I could answer, Libby came out on the deck, wiping her hands. Patched-ass said, "Hello little lady." It came out wolfish. She'd been doing bathroom duties, wearing that old paint-stained outfit. She'd never looked better.

Yellow-beard had his jacket off and was putting it in a saddlebag. As Libby came to me, I thought I saw him put something behind his back. Patched-ass stepped purposefully around behind Libby. In an ugly instant, I realized we were being cornered.

Yellow-beard said in a flat voice, "Step that way please." He was motioning toward the open area with a sawed-off twin-barreled shotgun. Patched-ass shoved Libby in the back. She stumbled past me and turned to face them, eyes going back-and-forth in horror. "Back, back," grated Yellow-beard. We'd no choice but to obey.

My mind raced. Patched-ass was the shepherd. Yellow-beard the executioner. They were driving us where there'd be less mess to clean up. We'd simply disappear.

Is this what happened to Reeman?

Yellow-beard steadied the gun at me. Brought his left hand up to grip the fore-end. Libby shrieked and her hands flew up to her face. Yellow-beard instinctively switched-aim and fired. I screamed as the blast flung her backward.

With a cacophony of hisses and squawks and flapping of wings, Bird stormed out of its pen. It went straight between Patched-ass' legs and between me and Yellow-beard, heading for water and safety. Yellow-beard reared back in surprise and his arm shot up. The shotgun fired.

Two barrels. It's empty.

I broke and ran for the trees, ignoring the flare of pain in my hip, past Patched-ass who was frantically reaching for something in his pants, maybe a handgun. I heard a clack as Yellow-beard ejected the empty cartridges and imagined him reaching for replacements.

My mind was screaming about Libby, but stopping and getting killed wouldn't help either of us. If she was alive and I could keep them distracted, I was giving her the best chance possible. But if Patched-ass did have a handgun, and knew how to use it, I was dead-meat either way.

I listened for the shotgun closing. Then zigged hard left. There was a roar, then a hiss of buckshot going by on my right. I was half way to the trees. He'd need luck to get me. And he got some.

Simultaneous with the second roar was a thump like I'd been kicked in the back of my knee, but I didn't go down. It didn't hurt particularly, but there was an instant numbness I ignored in my headlong-flight for cover. In the last seconds before I reached the trees, a handgun came into play. Crack-crack-crack. Bark flew, in front of me.

Then I was in safety behind a thick trunk, temporarily anyway. My leg was starting to sting and felt weak. There was a bubbling mass of blood, but at least it still worked. There was no time to worry about it. I knew where I needed to get to.

I eased my head around the tree. The two men were back at their bikes, agitated. Patched-ass was getting something from his saddlebags. Then they wheeled and came after me in a pincer movement, Yellow-beard in my direction, Patched-ass heading left. He had a sawed-off too.

Pushing off the tree-trunk in the direction of the stream, I kicked right through a big pile of something soft and pungent. The impact hurt my leg. I cussed but didn't slow down. The men were walking quickly. I probably only had a minute before they reached the trees.

I made it to the barrier by the ford in half-that-time, dived straight to my knees by one post and dug desperately, hand-over-hand, thanking God for the recent rain. How deep was it? I couldn't remember. My fingernails tore on small rocks. Then I felt plastic and pulled the muddy bundle free. My fingers couldn't penetrate the layers of plastic. I ripped a hole with my teeth and enlarged it. Everything spilled.

Snatching up the handgun, I found a full magazine and jammed it home. Started to rack the slide. A large hand closed over mine.

I've been too slow. I've failed Libby and I'm dead!

I swiveled to look into the eyes of who-ever was going to kill me and stared disbelievingly at the massive black-clad form of Prince Charles.

After checking my wound, and binding my shirt around my thigh, he dragged me behind cover, got the gun ready, and we settled in to wait.

And wait we did because they took their time arriving. Eventually Charles hunched a little, and I followed his line-of-sight and saw Yellow-beard cross between two trees to our center-right, perhaps 20 yards away.

Where is the other guy?

A shadow moved uphill on the right, where the trees were thickest. Then there was a movement to the left. It was Patched-ass creeping furtively.

Where did this third guy on the right come from? Did they leave a lookout?

They had us in a vice.

Then from out of the thicket came a 'whuff.' I'd heard something like it before, but this was infinitely more menacing. Something was moving downhill.

A giant hump-backed bear as tall at the shoulder as a man, and with the bulk of a small car, bounded into the open and straight at Yellow-beard, who was frozen in an open gap, staring in horror. The grizzly reached him in seconds. White fanged jaws gaped, then closed on his shoulder. The beast swept its head left-and-right, flailing Yellow-beard about like a terrier with a rat. The jaws tore out of the body and it flew through the air, glanced off a tree, and landed out of sight from me.

The bear turned its great head and saw Patched-ass. Roared and went for him. Patched-ass let go both barrels, one-two, into the body-mass. The charging beast reared and screamed, pivoted in the air and dropped on all fours, and galloped out of sight into the thick cover.

Patched-ass had his shotgun cracked open and was grabbing for shells. Charles got up from his crouch and brought up the Smith and Wesson in the combat stance. "Hey motherfucker!"

The biker turned his head and his face contorted. He had two red cartridges between his fingers that he dropped into the shotgun's chambers. He flexed his wrist to snap the barrels closed and started to swing. Charles fired twice, a double tap. A red cloud erupted around the biker's head and went over backwards.

Running forward in a crouch, gun still extended, Charles went by the man he shot with hardly a glance, and stooped where I last saw Yellow Beard. He came up holding a weapon by the barrels, pulled it apart and threw down the pieces, then came back toward me.

Pain flooded my right leg like a dam had broken. I cried out. Charles sped up. Helped me up on my good leg. "Other one's alive, though his shoulder's hanging off. He can wait. We gotta get you some help."

The image of Libby being smashed backwards in that unspeakable instant flooded my mind. I had to get back to her.

Charles had my weight. I tried to use my good leg to help us move, but it was useless. He swung me effortlessly up into a fireman's lift, and took off at a fast lope, through the trees into the open, then across the verge towards the cabin.

As we approached, I twisted and struggled to see ahead. He tried to stop me but I wailed and pleaded with him to put me down. He hesitated, then did so.

I fell beside Libby.

Her eyes were open and fixed. I reached out and touched her face. It was cool and limp and unresponsive. I nestled mine against hers, howling from unbearable anguish.

FIFTY-NINE

Lake Kaldekut
Eight months later

It had been snowing all day. Huge fluffy flakes that settled silently atop winter's accumulation. I'd been standing at the kitchen window watching. And reflecting on what had happened since I'd lost the love of my life those many months before.

Prince Charles had left me draped over Libby's body and used my phone to call the RCMP, who sent cars, and an ambulance from the nearest trauma hospital at Burns Lake. Then he went back in the forest and stabilized the surviving biker. Somehow also learning useful information that later helped put it all together.

The ambulance rushed me to surgery. I'd lost a lot of blood, but Charles had saved my life with his Special-Forces medic-skills. There was nothing anyone could have done for Libby. She'd been struck in the heart and wouldn't have felt a thing.

Yellow-beard's name was Raymond Cheswick, President of the 'Runners,' short for 'Freedom Runners.' A biker-club in Fairview near the Port of Vancouver. Patched-ass Clinton Casbury was their master-at-arms. They were the major muscle on the Vancouver docks, into extortion, drug trafficking and people smuggling, as well as this foray into contract-murder. Cheswick pleaded out, hoping for leniency when faced with the information he'd shared with Charles. He should have been starting his 17-year stretch at the Supermax in Edmonton about then, assuming the Mounties had finished bleeding information out of him.

The Runners knew the Karamov brothers, whose brooding

company I'd endured in Seattle, through their people smuggling side. An enterprise the brothers ran in Vancouver's eastern-suburbs, owned a blue Eurocopter EC135. Or they did until the whole rotten nest was swept up about a month after Libby's passing.

I never did testify in Seattle. Russell agreed to give evidence for the Feds. The others in the Pike Street offices that day, all pleaded 'guilty.' Jim Burton got eight years. Cotton and Wickmeyer, four. Russell, a suspended sentence and probation. I heard he's back living in Ballard, but without the trappings from Oak Harbor, or Becky.

John later told me Jacques DeLeon's dogs found the grizzly bear dead in the heavy brush beside my gravel road, bled out from shotgun wounds. Several small lead bullets lodged along its swollen jaw must have been driving it crazy.

I was in the hospital four days. The Campbells came daily to try to lift my shattered spirits. Charles came once, and I thanked him. He said it didn't make us friends, but he left his mobile number and said if there was ever anything he could do personally, he'd listen. Hal transported me home and got me settled and became my driver during the inevitable aftermath.

Libby's funeral was at the Pillars of Faith Mennonite Church, on Bouclier Lake, the day after I was discharged. All of Laketown attended. Hal was with his family. His wife Jessica was very kind. John Campbell hovered but said nothing. He knew there were no words that could possibly help. Marge leaned down and hugged me a long time and mingled her tears with mine. Nancy Robitaille and a contingent from the Nations took seats just as Libby's father started the service. Charles filled the place with his presence and stared straight ahead. One time I looked over and his cheeks were wet, but there wasn't a quiver to his huge frame. When Otto Mueller finished the eulogy, austerely dressed members of the congregation came to my wheelchair and laid hands on me and prayed, while Otto wept unashamedly in the pulpit. The memory of that will stay with me always.

And I thought that was the end of my life.

I went back to the cabin and stared at the wall for weeks, just Bird and me. John Campbell brought food and carried wood inside, but had the patience to leave me to my misery, except for telling me I stank and needed to wash and shave more.

McKinnon and Hal visited also. They provided very different kinds of support.

McKinnon said, in a roundabout manner, that he knew I'd been in possession of an illegal pistol and had fired it when the kids visited. But since Charles was now the owner and a war hero, and had every class of firearm-license known to man, it was never going to be an issue. He also said the GMC Yukon Adrian Reeman had been driving in Laketown, was found off the side of a mountain road near Banff, Alberta. It showed signs of being rammed and had traces of blood on the seats. He didn't doubt the man came to a sticky end, but exactly how and why would have to remain one of life's impenetrable mysteries, like who killed Kurt Cobain.

Hal waited until I could walk again, then confronted me. If I hadn't grudgingly done what he asked, I swear he'd have seized me by the scruff of the neck. We went out to the Explorer, and he climbed in with me and told me to start it up and do two circuits of the verge. When I shut it off, he said, "So now you can fucking drive! So get yourself together and pull yourself out of this self-pitying shit. Because you're my fucking friend and it's breaking my fucking heart!" Then he got out and left.

That night I took a very long shower and shaved off the beard. I cooked a decent meal. Tore the stinking sheets off the bed and slept under a couple of sleeping bags. When I got up, I walked out on the deck and stepped shakily into the *shui kai do,* the crouch before the stretch that begins each Kami no Michi routine, and began to get well.

A week or so later Hal called and said gruffly, "I'm at the lake. I could use your help. Come or not. Please yourself."

As I got into my truck, it was full-blown fall with a bitter squally wind, and sleet sticking to the exposed trunks of trees.

Hal's airplane was hanging by chains from the center beam of the shelter, and he and a mechanic were replacing the floats with struts and wheels. I fetched them tools for the rest of the day, constantly aware of Hal's watchful gaze.

When the job was done, we pushed the plane out into the open. Hal motioned me aboard, and we took off across the bumpy ground in the fading light, and flew for less than three minutes to a bleak airfield with a single huge hangar and a cluster of refueling-facilities. Hal parked inside the hangar, and on the way back to the lake, he said only two sentences. "I'm going to teach you to fly, you miserable son of a bitch. Then I won't just be your fucking cab driver."

No more beautiful words were ever said between friends.

But in fact, Hal couldn't turn me into a pilot. He could show me how, but he wasn't qualified to certify me.

Over the next few weeks, he had me fly innumerable circuits and stops-and-go's, until handling the 206 was second-nature. Then he handed me off to a lanky, angular man named George Western, at Vanderhoof Field, for my private-license check-ride.

George was a stickler with the paperwork on the ground and a jovial overseer in the air. "Hey, how hard can it be?" he said. "There's only left, right, up and down. You'll be fine!"

And I was. I drove home a qualified pilot, subject to the paperwork and a medical-check.

Bird, on the other hand, couldn't fly at all.

I didn't understand that at first. I thought its frantic flaps along the top of the water were practice, and it was just a matter of time. Meanwhile, vast flocks of waterfowl teemed south overhead, and some landed in the cove. Bird would mingle excitedly, but after rest they always launched up into the next leg of their journey to the San Marino marshes, Salton Sea or Gulf of Mexico; leaving Bird abandoned and bereft on the broken water.

In late September the glassy-edging that formed on the rocky shore each evening and melted away each day, suddenly stayed. The cove's open-water shrank to a pool a hundred-yards across, on which Bird paddled forlornly and cried plaintively.

I paced the shore in heavy clothes and thick gloves, willing it to go free. Finally, with the temperature hovering below freezing, I admitted defeat and called to it. It came reluctantly, straining against the call-of-the-wild.

We shared the warmth of the cabin that night. The next day I had a carpenter come out from town and build a proper enclosure, over a heating pad powered by an underground cable from the cabin, and lined with fluffy wood-shavings like a horse-stable.

I can't say Bird was happy about it, but it was safe and warm, and two out of three would just have to do.

Hal also sent two men with theodolites, out to do a survey, after calling me first to tell me they were 'friendlies,' and not to shoot anybody. They parked their van on the verge in a light snowstorm, making Bird bark and cackle nervously, and traipsed around for most of a day, lining up angles and recorded findings. It sent me into an emotional nosedive. What did it matter without Libby? But that passed. The cove was my home.

December came and I had Christmas brunch with John and Marge and family, which was warm and companionable except that Howard had visibly hollowed out. He listened excitedly to the outcome of the gold- robbery as if it completed something for him.

Christmas supper with Hal and his family was raucous, with small girls dashing about exhausting every possible use of toys and posing saucily in gifts of big city clothes. I drank sparkling grape-juice and got to know Jessica, who was gloriously pregnant and just as smart and sensitive as I'd observed at Libby's funeral.

Winter began easing in February and despite today's brief snowstorm, had been in steady retreat ever since.

I began leaving Bird's hutch open, so it could exercise when it pleased. It took less than a week to become airborne. Soon it could circle the cove effortlessly, though it always came back to me. For how long, I didn't know.

But I'd run out of time, and had to turn away from the kitchen window, and go back to packing. The next day Hal and I were flying to Victoria.

The court case to decide ownership of the cove would begin in two days.

For Bird, I could only hope for the best.

SIXTY

Victoria, Vancouver Island
March 18th, 2019

The Supreme Courthouse was on Burdett Avenue, a hundred yards up from our hotel, off the main Blanchard Street thoroughfare that spears into the heart of the Harbor District. Remnants of a hailstorm littered the lawns, as we lined up for security-checks from brisk, courteous folks in semi-military tunics, before being directed to the lifts.

The floors were color-coded. Our hearing was scheduled for two-days in room 506 on the green floor, starting at 10:00 a.m., and we were early. The room was already bustling.

Hal, like Alfred Longfellow and his several assistants, wore a robe and white forked-tie. They had designated positions in front of the massive judge's bench, from which to make their respective cases. The only other table was for clerks, so Nancy Robitaille, the unpleasant Coral, and myself; were relegated to the gallery. I sat down and studied the attendees.

The people holding notepads and small recorders, had to be reporters. There were others of indeterminable interest or purpose, but two stood out. Thirties, thin-lipped, close-cropped dark hair, and white shirts with plain dark ties.

Door-to door missionaries?

But I didn't get to wonder about them long. The judge entered, and his clerk made his announcement right on time.

"Judge Hiram J. Volman's Court is in session. Today we will hear opening statements in the case of the First Nations of the

Stokely-Wa'anedot District v. Benyamin Adams. The plaintiff is seeking a judgment regarding right of possession. Tomorrow we will hear evidence and closing arguments, after which the judge will make his ruling."

Longfellow took the floor.

After bowing he said, "If it pleases the court, the words, 'a judgment regarding right of possession' seem simple. But what do they really mean? I submit that what is being asked for here, Your Honour, cannot be understood except in historical terms.

The Nations' economy in British Columbia initially thrived back in 1843 when James Douglas opened a Hudson's Bay Company trading post at Fort Victoria. Then it all went terribly wrong as decade-after-decade of exploitation and betrayal commenced."

Volman, a thin-faced, bespectacled man, shifted in his seat as if he was going to say something, but he was still again.

Longfellow continued obliviously, "There's no doubt the First Nations would always have struggled for equality with the British, but the profound breakdown of relations that I submit contributed to us being here today, was as much because of the way things were done, as what was done.

The Nations were systematically dispossessed of their foundation, their lands, often without even realizing it. Since then, Nations' grievances have always been viewed as 'land claims', which I attest is exactly why we are here today.

The British Colonial Office could have headed off the current mess in 1861, if they'd been willing to spend the tiny sum of £3,000 on treaties. Instead it was left to those bent on land-acquisition-at-any-cost, to sort out.

In 1864 an American, Joseph Trutch, was made the first BC Chief Commissioner of Lands and Works, and later became Lieutenant Governor. Trutch was convinced that reserves were already too generous. From then forward, the Nations were always on what the English call, 'a hiding to nothing,' Your Honour."

Judge Volman glared at Longfellow over his glasses. Longfellow did a slight 'ahem.'

"Forgive my immoderate speech, Your Honour, but that was just the beginning. In 1877, national fears of an Indian uprising brought a gunboat to Fort Simpson, to settle a dispute between the Metlakatla Nation and the Church Missionary Society. That Nation's heinous crime, Your Honour? Constructing a building outside their reserve, on land they had inhabited for millennia!"

He sipped water.

"But, Your Honour, anyone thinking the Federal Government

has been any fairer, would be wrong. In 1884 they declared their ignorance and intolerance by banning Potlatches, an important festival, and an integral part of native culture and governance. The Salish and Cowichan Nations twice appealed to the English Queen about it. 1906 and 1909. Entirely without avail. And what about the duplicity of the McKenna-McBride Commission of 1916? And the years of stalling of the United-Council-of-Chiefs' Privy Council petition of 1922-27? The list, Your Honour, goes on and on.

And those were just the economic injustices. What about the decimation of the Tsimshian, the Haida and the Stikine, by the smallpox-epidemic of 1862, in the so-called 'secure and supported communities' they were forced into?

What about the long history of that other gift from the settler, for which you will find no gratitude? Alcohol. Or the arrogance of the church missions. in forcing Nations' young-people into residential-schools to... civilize them.

And if you think this is all just ancient history now, Your Honour, what about the lip service paid by Prime-Minister Lester Pearson and his Indian-Affairs-Minister Arthur Laing, to the 1960 petition by George Manuel and the Shuswap?

Or perhaps you think I'm talking about other parts of this country now. Not at all. How about the squabbles as recently as 1973, between BC-Premier Dave Barrett and Federal-Minister of Indian-Affairs, Jean Chretien, who at least desired that some degree of fairness should apply?"

Judge Volman ahem'd a couple of times, while his inscrutable gaze was very steady on Longfellow, who continued quickly.

"Your Honour, please allow me one more example. Homesteading. Anyone could do it. It was the law. Up to 320 acres of land could be settled per family, so long as it had never been officially incorporated by a municipal, provincial or Federal authority.

What do you think happened when the Nations tried to exercise that right? A law was quickly passed requiring the Governor's approval for all non-white allotments. How often do you think that might have been granted, Your Honour?

But please forgive my indignation and digression. We are here today to discuss a small piece of land with enormous significance to my clients. I only ask that it pleases the court, when hearing the arguments for and against, to take into account the context I have stated. I defer to my learned colleague, Mr. Pritchard, at this time, Your Honour."

Oh. My. Lord.

Hal spent the lunch-recess. pacing the hall looking at his notes. I spent it thinking about Longfellow's words. Despite being, it seemed, one of those liars, exploiters and betrayers, I'd been moved. I couldn't help but respect the man's knowledge and passion.

When our turn to open came, Hal paid his respects and said, "Your Honour, as my respected colleague Mr. Longfellow has alluded, this case concerns only a tiny part of our country's land mass, but involves an enormous part of its heart.

Today, Your Honour, we confront an issue which challenges the right of every Canadian, to live in peace and security on whatever piece of this wonderful country they call their own. That issue is the conflict between a nation's responsibility to treat every citizen equally under law, and the harsh reality that no nation can easily apply that rule without risking the collapse of its social order.

Generations of leaders of both this province and this country have tried to find that point of balance. As Mr. Longfellow has accurately pointed out, far too often they have failed.

In a perfect world, our Judicia might be able to examine both the intent and spirit of every documented interaction between the European arrivals and the First people. And establish perfect ownership-divisions based solely on those historic moments-in-time. In our world, that cannot be done without taking into account accumulated history. Decisions must be made case-by-case, taking into account things-as-they-are.

My client wishes no harm to anyone. He seeks only a fair judgment, based on the facts-as-they-are, regarding one small piece-of-land and a cabin, bequeathed to him in good faith.

May it please the court."

I liked what I heard, but was expecting more because of the length of Longfellow's opening. So was the judge, it seemed. He looked around as if there were other parties involved, then asked if there were any final statements for the day.

Longfellow stood and said his clients were owed. Actually, that natural justice and the long overdue benevolence of a compassionate province and dominion, required that his clients receive the benefit of the doubt in all matters involving land boundaries.

I felt a slight headache coming on.

Hal stated that this was a simple case of ownership.

Determining it and acting on that determination.

I felt we'd gotten spanked on the moral front, but how much it mattered, I had no idea.

Court adjourned for the day. The ice had vanished as Hal and I went down the exit-steps on to Blanchard Street, intending to cross the road and walk to our lodgings at the Quality Inn.

A Lincoln Town Car with tinted windows stopped in front of us. Both front doors opened and the cookie-cutter guys from the court got out. I noticed the Lincoln had Canadian Federal Government plates.

"Mr. Adams, a chat if we may," said the nearest of the two. "Not you sir," he said crisply to Hal.

Hal made an offhand motion toward the rear number-plate and shrugged his shoulders. I stood there, uncertain.

"Aww come on," said the man. "We don't bite. Much."

Hal picked a gap in traffic and crossed without looking back. I got reluctantly in the back seat and we headed the opposite way along Blanchard to the corner of Broughton, where we turned the wrong way down a one-way street, and into a courtyard.

A branch of the Victoria Public Library overlooked the courtyard, but it wasn't our destination. Tweedle-Dum and Tweedle-Dee let me out of the vehicle and steered me towards a building with a tinted brown-glass frontage, red maple-leaf flag, and 'Department of Internal Affairs,' in raised-metal lettering.

They sat me down in a sparsely furnished room on the third floor. Stepped back outside and flanked the doorway, hands clasped in front. After a short while a small harried-looking man in a brown suit, white shirt, and plain tie, and sat down opposite me. Put his elbows on the table. He said, "Mr. Adams," without inflection.

"Yes."

"I'm glad we could have this talk."

"And you are?"

He did a thing with his hands in front of him like he was describing a fish he'd caught. "A guardian of the nation, shall we say."

"Am I under arrest?"

He did the thing with his hands again, then he rubbed them together, leaned forward and said, "This thing you're doing. It's troubling."

"Really?"

"Yes. We've had difficulty with it before. It has caused...

agitation."

"And you would like?"

"An equitable solution."

"Meaning we pack up our tents and go away?"

I hadn't thought anyone could smile that wide without the slightest warmth, but he managed. "That would be very nice."

He had me talking like him by then, except for the snake-like hiss to some of his consonants. "And if we don't choose to comply?"

He looked at me predatorily. "This early in the election-cycle, a fuss about inference with the judiciary wouldn't be the end of the world."

Gee-zus.

"Or," he said, "Perhaps we'll just make it ALL go away."

The silence was menacingly palpable.

He means me. Well fuck you! If I can deal with bikers with shotguns, you don't scare me you little prick!

"Then I'd say you need to do what you need to do."

He rubbed his chin with his fist a moment or two, before appearing to make a decision. He stared at me again. "Perhaps not."

He levered himself to his feet. The whole event had lasted all of three minutes, not counting travel and waiting time. He'd said absolutely nothing, and I hadn't the slightest idea who these people were.

He paused in the doorway and said, "They'll drop you back to your hotel, but Mr. Adams?"

"Yes?"

"We'll be keeping a close eye."

SIXTY-ONE

Victoria
March 19th

Hal began our second day by calling to the witness stand, a thin, spinsterish woman named Adele Whitcomb. Playing nervously with a reading glasses hanging by a cord from her neck, she confirmed she was the Curator of Historic Records for the Provincial Library of British Columbia. He read from her prior-affidavit, ending with, "So Mrs. Whitcomb, there are no records in existence that define the boundary of the We'tutahe reserve on the northeast shore of Lake Kaldekut."

"That is correct. The boundary appears to be customary in nature, but there is no way to be sure without documentation."

Hal held up what looked like color photo-copies of yellowed, hand-written letters. "Do you recognize these?"

"Yes. That is the only documentation of ANY kind. It's the correspondence between Surveyor-Sergeant William McColl of the Royal Engineers, and the offices of Governor Sir James Douglas, in 1864. He proposes reserves and settler-allotments in that district, but Governor Douglass was leaving office at the time. If any were ever formalized, the records were lost in a fire in Laketown in 1991."

"So, you can therefore certify unequivocally, that no documentation presently exists showing where the We'tutahe Nation's reserve actually begins and ends."

"Yes, that is correct."

During Longfellow's cross, he asked, "Can you say for sure that the piece of land in question is NOT on the We'tutahe reserve?"

"Oh no," she said. "It may well be. There's just no way to know."

Hal grimaced, and Ms. Whitcomb stood down.

Hal then called Justin Avery. The muscular and fit-looking man who'd traipsed around my back-yard with a companion, clipboard, and theodolite quite recently. He also distributed copies of drawings and a map.

Avery said he was a registered surveyor from Burns Lake and gave his license number. He described the surveying process, including the challenges of working in several inches of wet snow, and took us through his findings.

He'd come up with a larger area than stated in the will: 5.341 hectares or 13.19 acres. That was from the stream west of the outbuildings, down to the lake, along the shore past the cabin and jetty to the marsh, then up the stream to the starting point.

"And those are the logical boundaries?"

"Yes sir. These are the natural features any original-surveyor would have followed."

Longfellow stood and said, "Isn't it true, Mr. Avery, that these documents are entirely fictitious?"

"Uh no, I..."

"Oh I have no doubt you did the work. But your results have no foundation in reality. There's nothing to prove that there was ever an allotment. The previous witness testified to that."

"I treated the land as if it had been allotted and established the logical boundaries."

"I'm sure you did, but it's meaningless isn't it?"

"I stand by my work sir," said Avery a trifle pompously.

Longfellow then called a middle-aged, florid man from the Westminster office of the LTSA. The man suggested that given enough time, further land documents might be found. Hal in turn, questioned the feasibility of searching the LTSAs archives hand-to-hand, for something misplaced.

The man admitted, "I said it was possible, but whether it's practical is above my pay grade."

Longfellow asked the judge for a pause to consider the matter. Volman refused, stating sternly that the case would not be delayed.

The last witness was a man from the Nations with a lined face, and long white hair. Longfellow introduced him as a We'tutahe elder. There was a sidebar to decide whether he could provide his recollections of land dealings. Judge Volman questioned him and having receiving only vague replies, ruled it out as hearsay.

We recessed for lunch, with closing statements to begin immediately afterward.

Hal waved me away so he could concentrate. I used the time to take a long walk, and to think things through. It had snowed overnight, and my mood was as bleak as the streets.

I trudged, coat pulled up around my neck, past parks where not even a squirrel braved the cold. Sightseeing boats where people huddled against a biting breeze. The BC legislature, with its broad lawns all in white, was solemn and stately. The modern-looking museum, massive, and the ivy-clad Empress Hotel, magnificent. Tourist carriages drawn by horses with steaming nostrils, added character.

We seemed so far behind we weren't even on the map. The stark fact was, we'd accomplished nothing except to establish that nothing could be established. How could that possibly be a defense?

If Hal had another plan, he hadn't shared it with me. Except for a few words over room-service about my meeting with the people Hal believed to be the Canadian Security Intelligence Service, we'd barely spoken. Still, I knew he'd stayed up well into the night, and if anyone could pull something out of his bag, it was Hal.

When I walked back into the courtroom, I wouldn't have been surprised if Hal had called for a conference to try to get us out of it gracefully. But he didn't and proceedings got back under way.

Closing arguments were in reverse order, so Hal rose first.

"May it please the court, as my learned colleague Mr. Longfellow has rightfully raised, our country has an at-times, shameful history of bullying the weak.

Thankfully, though he didn't mention it, in the almost 152 years since Dominion, much more often it has acted with respect, fairness, and compassion. Just the same, rights cannot unmake wrongs. As citizens, we can only hope that over time, the good will assuage the bad.

In my opening-words, I said my client desires only that the facts be heard, and that wise judgment be made in the light of those facts.

It is a fact that Mr. Adams inherited his property. It is a fact that there is no deception here, and Mr. Adams has no agenda. He came to that place, with what he believed was factual legal-proof of his right to do so, in his hand. Wanting only to live in peace in his own quiet corner. Bothering no-one. In harmony with his neighbors under the framework of law."

I squirmed in my seat. He was only stating the truth, but I felt for a moment the weight of my entire life was on my shoulders. Which it was, I suppose.

This is all about me. ME.

Hal gestured in my direction, which only made me cringe lower.

"Mr. Adams is no-one's enemy. In the course of recent events he has suffered greatly due to circumstances outside the purview of this court. He wants no pity. He asks no favors. Only the natural justice due any man who acts in good faith to all.

Our First-Nation friends here today, have also suffered wrongs and endured enormous pain. They have every right to feel aggrieved. If I could, I would personally make up for that. And I will leave this court today a wiser man as a result of what I have heard.

However, Your Honour, this is not the place to redress those wrongs. Nor should they be redressed at Mr. Adams' sole expense. Mr. Adams is simply a good man trying to live peacefully on his own piece of land. As anyone would. Please allow him to do that, by setting the example that a Canadian is a Canadian, regardless of inherited ethnicity.

It's been shown that it is impossible to factually identify the boundaries. Therefore, justice must rightly be placed in your hands, Your Honour. Please find for Mr. Adams and allow him to live peacefully and permanently on his small property, as a good neighbor to all.

We thank the court, and Your Honour, for your indulgence."

SIXTY-TWO

Victoria
March 20th

There was a long silence in the court, before the shuffling of papers resumed as Longfellow prepared for his turn.

He lifted his large body from his seat and hooked his thumbs into his robe. "May it please the court, I ask you today, Your Honour, not to perpetuate the injustices I have outlined." He gestured expansively toward Hal. "And that my kind colleague Mr. Pritchard has acknowledged. Or to take any action that could further undermine the vestiges of trust, the indigenous people of this country clings to. Because, Your Honour, the wounds accumulated over decades are very deep and that trust is extremely frayed."

Judge Volman glared down at Longfellow. "Are you threatening this court, sir?"

There was a stir among the crowd, and I saw reporters writing furiously. Longfellow gulped, but he recovered quickly.

"I am most certainly not Your Honour. Please forgive my poor choice of words. However, Mr. Pritchard can speak as eloquently as he likes, about tolerance and desiring to live in harmony. We thank him for his kind wishes. But it flies in the face of nearly two centuries of harsh reality, where only power has mattered."

I looked at Hal. He shook his head almost imperceptibly.

"Your Honour, of course no-one believes two wrongs make a right. And we are not asking you to base your ruling on that. But throughout history many nations have experienced wide swings, between benevolence and perfidy, justice and injustice, and taken steps to remedy those. For my clients, this is such a time.

Mr. Pritchard claims his client has acted in good faith, so have mine. Just as Mr. Adams may feel he has right on his side, my clients have resided on their lands for generations believing in theirs. And have had those rights confirmed by numerous court decisions.

We ask that my clients receive the benefit of the doubt and be permitted to make their own determination as to the boundaries of the We'tutahe reserve. We thank the court."

Judge Volman consulted with his clerk before asking the Nations' people if they had anything more. Longfellow rose and said, "No, Your Honour."

"And has the respondent anything to add?"

Hal stood and said, "Your Honour we rest our case." As the judge was making some notes before his next instruction to the clerk, Hal flashed me a cheeky grin and mouthed, "I always wanted to say that."

I smiled for the first time in days. The man was irrepressible.

The clerk said, "There will be a half-hour recess before his Honour delivers his decision."

It was approaching 4:00 p.m. when we exited the lifts to return to the hearing room. There was a queue at the pay-phone, and people were pacing about talking on mobiles.

Inside the courtroom the gallery was packed, with an overflow standing along the back. Tweedle's Dum and Dee and the harried guy were front and center.

Judge Volman took his time organizing his notes before looking up.

"In the matter of the First Nations of the Stokely-Wa'anedot District versus Benyamin Adams I have three rulings. The first is that the survey conducted by the respondent, is accepted as an accurate and binding record, of the logical boundaries of the piece of land occupied by Mr. Adams, to be recorded as 'The Land.'."

That can't be anything but good for us.

I looked at Hal, but he didn't look back.

"The second is I accept that no records exist to prove or disprove, whether the land is within the boundaries of the We'tutahe Nation's reserve, or any incorporated area."

Good too, surely.

"My last ruling has a number of parts.

One, that since the land is declared unincorporated, the Dominion Lands Act of 1872, also known as the Homestead Law, shall apply, subject to conditions appended by the Province of British Columbia, stating that land can only be claimed by a male head of household who has resided continuously on the land for two calendar years.

Two, that the land' is awarded to the person who most recently meets those criteria, or to someone to whom they personally sign over their right of claim.

Three, that should no such qualified person come forward, the land shall become provincial property with a strong recommendation that the boundaries of the We'tutahe reserve be confirmed, and it be included."

There was stunned silence. Hal and I stared at each other in disbelief.

Judge Volman had delivered a judgment worthy of Solomon. No one owned the land. Only one person met his criteria for claiming it: Adrian Reeman. And Adrian Reeman was dead. Did our opposition know that?

I looked across the gallery and my heart sank. Jubilation. If the hearing had been a sports event, Nancy and Coral would have been giving each other high-fives.

The clerk called the court to order, and Judge Volman said, "Of course if the plaintiff or defendant disagrees, they are quite entitled to take the matter up with the Supreme Court of Canada."

Longfellow got up quickly. "Oh no Your Honour. We gladly accept your wise-judgment. In fact, we're prepared to waive our right of appeal, on condition that this ruling takes prompt affect."

Judge Volman adjusted his glasses and brought up a desk-calendar. "Very well, I have in mind a time-frame of 30 calendar days. Does the respondent wish to comment?"

Hal eased up slowly. "We would accept that too, Your Honour."

I was horrified.

"Then so ruled. Any legally entitled person has until close of business at 5:00 p.m., 30 days from now, Thursday the 18th of April, to present a homestead claim at this court. If he is not that claimant, Mr. Adams must also vacate the land on that date. Court is adjourned."

Pandemonium ensued.

SIXTY-THREE

Lake Kaldekut
April 17th

"It would have made no difference Ben. We had just spent days proving we had nothing to go on." Hal had said. "I'm so very sorry."

That was during the sad flight home from Victoria. His not appealing immediately had been hanging in the air between us.

"No, I suppose not," I'd replied. "Thank you for what you did for me. No one could have done more."

Now it was almost 29 days later. I'd just arrived back at the cove from a storage unit John Campbell had arranged for me in town and simply pulled up in the middle of the verge.

One more day. One more day left.

I had arrived here lost and broken, cast up on shore like that broken-log after the storm. I'd learned to love here; with my whole being. And to let myself be loved. I'd recovered my physical strength, and for perhaps the first time in my life, been surrounded by true friends who respected me. With their help and Bird's company to keep me sane during the dark unbearable-time, I hoped I'd become worthy of their respect.

Leaving seemed unimaginable.

Yet I was.

That's not to say I was taking it well. I'd mostly been a bundle of negative emotions since the hearing, and at times, downright bitter. If it weren't for Alfred Longfellow's words, I think I'd have heaved gasoline around the cabin and burned it to the ground. But he'd taught me there'd already been far too much churlish behavior around Nations' reserves.

Looking around now, I was struck with wonder at the place all over again. Sure, sleet ice speckled the verge but signs of spring were there also. Green buds studded the alders by the marsh. The pool of open water had grown to almost occupy the cove. And yet another flock of wild geese, dozens this time, had come down from on-high and landed on it in my absence. The great spring migration to the northern-steppes was well under way.

I got moving again, and as the truck rocked and rolled across the open-ground, the wild birds erupted. They jockeyed for position as they gained height, then swept away across the main lake and shrank into the distance. One bird remained. It hurried ashore as I parked the truck and waited for a head-scratch and some food treats I always had in my pocket.

John had offered me numerous places to lease, both in town and on various lake shores, but if I'd learned anything at all, it was that life was not about places, it was about home. There was nowhere else for me like the cove. I'd been redeemed here. So, since I had no idea what I would do, I was storing everything I wanted to keep and giving away the rest. If redemption was all I took away with me, it would have to be enough.

Meanwhile, in its own way, Bird had also been preparing to leave. It had been luring down passing flocks with excited honks and deep mutterings of companionship. When they left again, and again, it would mournfully circle the cove, before settling and calling some more, often well into the dark. I knew it was a matter of time.

As I stood with Bird by my leg, more geese arrived, skimming to rest 50 yards from the end of the jetty. Bird ran to the shore and paddled out to greet them, talking up a storm. Afternoon was darkening quickly, and I had a lot to do in the next 24 hours, but I stayed to watch, hands jammed in pockets, shoulders hunched against the cold, wondering if this would be the moment.

Soon the geese lifted off with great scoops of their broad wings and turned toward the center of the lake. It wasn't unusual for Bird to follow a short distance, but this time it flew farther.

And farther.

At last it peeled off from the flock and came back to me and swooped over my head, wings waggling, calling mournfully. Then it turned away again. I mouthed a silent goodbye. It rejoined the formation, which steadily faded into the limitless sky.

Tears streaming, I trudged away toward the back door, to finish removing the auxiliary generator I had promised to John.

Later, walking out to the Explorer to put tools away, I glanced up at the satellite-dish on the roof. Did I really want to climb up there and take it down? I still had the computer and phone set up inside as well. So much to do. I'd need a box for those also, and to cancel the billing, which reminded me of the expensive electronics Adrian Reeman had dumped.

The one thing the divers had brought up that I'd never understood was the projector screen with the high-rise-office photo-printed on it. Sure, the cabin had been awful bare when I arrived, but if he'd wanted decor, why not western paintings like the ones that looked so good on the Campbell's walls? Or Chagall prints or MC Escher sketches? Why a picture of an office?

Back inside I started to make a hot drink. Looking for a teaspoon I noticed the collection of cards and things in a drawer. On a whim, I fished out McKinnon's business card and dialed his number. After pleasantries he said, "Hey I'm sorry about how your property case worked out."

"Thanks Scott, it wasn't real great."

While pouring water in a mug I said, "Uh, I remember you saying the police in Banff cleared up that thing with Mr. Reeman. Did you hear anything more?"

"They sent us an updated report. But unless he pops up in relation to something else, that's probably it."

A cold hand touched my heart. "Pops up? I thought he was dead!"

"No that was a miscommunication."

"I thought they found blood."

"Yeah, they did but on testing it was female. Likely from a minor injury in the accident."

"Accident? The truck wasn't rammed?"

"No, they changed their minds on that too. The rookie who wrote the original report wasn't used to what mountain roads can do. Seems the driver lost it on a corner and collected a tree with the rear end. Then they got out and abandoned it."

My mind raced "Well, thanks for the update."

"Don't mention it, Ben. Hey, I hear you're leaving?"

"Not sure yet. If I do though I'll definitely stop in and see you before I go."

"Please do that. Bye now."

I was kicking myself. Not that this late news took me anywhere new. I'd had a year to wonder about Adrian Reeman and didn't even know what he looked like. The judge's decision made him important, but only theoretically. Since I had no chance of finding him, he might just as well be dead.

While swallowing some coffee, I looked across at the desk with the laptop on it. I'd found the Vandervoort gang and solved the mystery about my father, hadn't I? But of course I had something to work with there: the truck. This time I had nothing. Or... did I?

When the computer came to life, I opened a search window. The realistic picture on the projector-screen had to be a clue. But in what context?

A search on 'Crime Screen Picture of Office' brought up links to crimes, and movies, and all the cheap office furniture I could wish for. Just nothing linking a picture-on-a-screen to a crime. I'd need to think laterally.

It followed that if a crime had occurred, and an office was involved, it had to be white collar. Maybe the picture was some kind of backdrop for a video setup. Fraud was the most common white-collar crime, so I tried 'Fraud Fake Office.' And got a four-year-old hit from the Boston Globe.

A con-man had been soliciting on-line stockholders, to invest in volatile penny-stocks through publicly advertised video-conferences. All from a remarkably convincing replica of a New York City brokerage-office, constructed in a house in suburban Waltham, Massachusetts.

This was a classic 'pump and dump' scam, where even a small amount of trading activity could make a cheap stock jump a large value-percentage. Say, 500,000 shares at 20-cents going to 30, before buyer's remorse sent it diving again. With automated options to both buy and sell, the scammer made money in both directions of the price movement. The real trick, was hiding the location long enough to spirit away the $50,000 or so in proceeds before it could be frozen by the SEC, or SCE up here.

Clever!

Two-or-three of those a month would have added up to real money, if he hadn't been interrupted. Which happened purely by accident when some kids looked in a window and saw the equipment. One boy's father was a cop, who thought from the son's description it was a porn-studio. The scammer apparently saw the police-raid coming, abandoned everything and hadn't been seen since.

All very interesting. But I was deflated again a few moments later. The police had found counterfeit ID, including an MA driver's license. The man, who went by the name Andruw (like the Atlanta

Braves slugger) Runyon, looked the kind of trustworthy man in his 40s you might see in a TV sitcom. But he couldn't be Reeman. He was African-American.

Still, I thought I might be on to something with the modus operandi, so I kept trying different word combinations along the same lines. Half an hour later I got another hit a year newer, from, of all places, Calgary, Alberta.

Someone had been soliciting financial-investments around retirement-villages without a license. The story had only registered in the search-engine because the suspect used fake ID. That gave grounds to search an address where an interesting video-setup had been discovered.

I skimmed the rest of the article and was about to try another search, when a comment near the bottom stood out. This particular person was apparently 'not known in the local African-Canadian business community.'

I felt my pulse accelerate. I looked at my watch. Then reached for the phone.

SIXTY-FOUR

Lake Kaldekut
April 17th

It was after 7:00 p.m. so I'd called the Campbell's home number. John answered with a cheerful, "Hey there Ben. How's the storage unit working out?"

"It's fine, thanks. Uh, that little Honda generator, I'm going to drop it off in your driveway tomorrow."

"That's terrific. I'll give it a good home. You mind putting it up on the porch with all this rain due?"

I had no idea where he got his weather-tips. Maybe he had a knee that ached or something. "Sure thing. Hey, I was talking to Sergeant McKinnon about Mr. Reeman today."

"That guy? I'd have thought he was the least of your interests right now."

"Yeah, well I was wondering what he looked like."

"Oh, you know, early to mid-40s, prominent forehead, medium-length usual-color hair. Kept in shape like one of those retired players you see doing round-ball commentary on ESPN."

"You're saying he was African-American?"

"Yeah didn't I mention?"

"No, ah..."

He read it totally wrong. "What damn difference does that make? You think we're a bunch of rednecks up here? Jeez, I never picked you for someone cared about that!"

Goddamn! I'll have to put that right another time.

"No no no John I'm not. I don't. Look, I'll explain when I see you

262

okay? I gotta go. Thanks. Thanks a lot."

I needed to get into PRIME in a hurry. I found my notes and broke in through the firewalls. And hit a dead end. The master-encryption key had been changed. I was stranded on the outside, looking in.

Quickly logging on to the hacker's site, I left a message asking my friend Lowhanger432 for the new key and to buzz me urgently. Then I got up and stretched and went to get a TV meal from the freezer. I couldn't decide between chicken and meatloaf. I took both.

Why not live it up?

While microwaving, I realized I needed sleep as well. The day had been a roller-coaster. I lay my head down on my arms for a moment.

Next thing I knew, a harsh 'buzz' from the computer speakers jerked me back awake.

Lowhanger432: Yeah I can get U that. When U need it?
Whizzit3469: Can't thank you enough. 2nite if you can.
Lowhanger432: Keep Ur speakers on.

It was after 11:00 p.m. before the computer woke me again. In a few minutes, I was back in a search-screen in PRIME trying different combinations of words, and having no luck whatsoever.

'Adrian' for first-name, and 'Reeman' for last, found nothing new, of course. McKinnon had already told me that. Nor did 'Andruw' and 'Runyon', but I'd guessed those were fictitious. I kept at it for over an hour before I realized that, once again, I wasn't seeing the big picture. I sat back and ran through it all in my head.

Three things jumped out. The initials 'A' and 'R.' He seemed to like those. Perhaps he had monogrammed clothing or something. Also, he was into white collar crime, not involving violence. Finally; his ethnicity. He wouldn't be able to hide that.

So, I selected 'African-American,' sorted first-name on 'A' and last name on 'R', and for the next hour punched in every conceivable type of non-violent crime. When I got to 'Money Laundering', the name 'Archibald Ross' moved to the top of the results. Fingers crossed, I clicked in the link. The frowning face of a middle-aged man appeared.

Frantically I found the first article from the Boston Globe, and compared the driver's-license picture with the mug shots. They were similar.

Back in PRIME I clicked on Mr. Ross' most recent details and read '...arrested November 23rd, Port of Vancouver, departing Canada by freighter with forged documentation, in possession of mixed un-declared American and Canadian currency to the sum of $817,000. Pleaded guilty to federal currency violations. Serving a two-year sentence at...'

I rubbed my eyes. Read it again. Compared pictures again. There was only one way to be sure.

It was 1:10 a.m. I decided it was better to ask for forgiveness than permission and pressed 'redial'. When a machine picked up, I waited 30 seconds then redialed again. The third time, John's sleepy voice said, "Damn Ben. What are you doing? It's the middle of the night!"

"I'm really sorry, but I need your help. Can you please start up your home computer and go on-line for me? Please?"

He grumbled in the background but I heard him doing it. When he came back on the phone, he said, "Alright where do you want me to go?"

I told him word-for-word and heard him typing, then there was a silence longer than I liked.

"John is it working? Do you get anything? If you do, look at the bottom picture. John?"

He said quietly, "Hello Mr. Reeman. Long time no see."

But what could I do about it?

I instantly banished any doubts. I couldn't possibly have found Reeman this late in the piece, for no reason. The fates couldn't be that cruel. But I only had about 16 hours to act, and only one person who could help. I still worried I was imposing, as I made the call. To my relief, Hal sounded wide awake. "Uh just up doing some paperwork. What's new?"

I explained what I'd found and what I needed. His pauses got longer and his "hmmm's" more thoughtful. When I paused for a response he said, "I'm sorry that's just flat out of the question."

"What? Why?"

"Because the 206 is up in the air at the lake with the struts and wheels hanging off it. I'm halfway through converting it back to a float-plane for the summer. I'm really sorry. I'd have got you involved, but I knew you were packing."

"Oh."

"Anyway, the weather wouldn't have worked. The whole lower province is under a layer of cloud from this front moving in. The 206 isn't certified for instrument flight rules, and nor are you."

I couldn't believe the door was being slammed shut again. But before I could argue, he made it worse. "Actually, this time of year there are thousands of reasons why it's a bad idea at the altitudes the 206 flies at."

"Shit shit shit!"

"But that doesn't mean we can't go."

"What?"

"Just not in the 206. I can work something out. Be at the hangar at nine in the morning. Don't be late. We won't have much time."

"But you said..."

"Not that one. Over at Laketown Field."

9:00 a.m. seemed awfully late. "We can't make it earlier?"

"No. I have to talk to some people first. See you at nine. Not a minute later."

SIXTY-FIVE

Laketown Aerodrome
April 18th, early morning

The inside floodlights were ablaze when I parked by the side-door of the hangar at 8:50 a.m. When I walked inside, it was obvious Hal had been there awhile. He'd used a forklift to pull a piece of machinery out into the wide-open area just inside the main roller-door.

The piece of machinery was a twin-engine airplane with a disproportionately large tail-fin. The plane was all white except for a red side-stripe with the words 'Cessna 421C Golden Eagle.' A decal beside the fold-out stairs said 'Crag Mountain Mining Ltd'. Hal came down the stairs from inside.

I said, "Wow. How d'you get hold of this?"

"Local flying club rents it out when it's not in company use. She's an oldie but a goodie. Don't ask what it's costing you, but it'll do the job. Now throw your gear inside and make yourself useful."

The big plane had the same turbocharged Lycoming engines as the 206. I was used to checking those and the avgas in the tanks. I also took charge of the structural examination.

The pre-flight, though, had multiple printed check-sheets. The internal systems were blindingly complex, and the plane was pressurized, with dual hydraulic systems. There was a host of additional electronics, including both weather-detection and ground-avoidance radar. I left that to Hal and took a look inside.

The passenger-cabin had three rows of twin seats, and porthole windows along each side. An alcove just back of the

266

cockpit, housed a tiny galley where Hal had connected his laptop up to a printer/scanner/fax machine and rigged his android phone as an internet-modem.

The cockpit had dual controls, duplicate gages, and twin screens for the radar systems. Making sure everything was healthy, took a maddeningly long time, but couldn't be rushed. Attention to detail was what made the tall man, well, Hal.

At last, shortly before 11:00 a.m., Hal said he was satisfied. We moved her out clear of the building and started her up. With everything in the green, he said, "We'll taxi a short way then set the brakes. I'll ease the RPMs up to 2200, pop them off and we'll go."

The sanded runway, edged by snow-banks, swirled with white powder in a sharp crosswind, under a leaden overcast. The engine roar was quieter than the 206, and even with the crosswind, she tracked straight and true down the centerline and lifted easily as the airspeed needle passed 115.

With the undercarriage retracted, she became silky smooth. Hal gave NAV Canada the familiar Bella Coola-route at FL120, 12,000 feet, well above any bad weather. A second or two later we were in solid cloud with little sense of motion, just an eerie ghostliness. We topped out and rocketed comfortably along above the whiteness at 200 knots on 190 degrees.

Hal set the autopilot and visibly relaxed. I was feeling good too until I realized it was 11:45 a.m. and we were racing toward... what?

As if reading my mind, Hal said, "So what's your plan when we get there?"

"I thought I'd go in and talk to him."

"That's it? You'll just go in there and persuade him to give up his rights because you're a nice guy?"

I couldn't blame him for the scepticism. I also couldn't explain my certainty it would work.

"Yes."

"Jeez. Have you even asked if they'll let you in?"

"No. I only found him this morning."

"Well, you better get back there on my laptop and get their number, while we still have some phone-coverage!"

Nanaimo Medium-Security Federal Correctional Center had a website with a map of the location and a phone number. The friendly woman who answered said it shouldn't be a problem. Visiting hours were flexible between ten and three. I felt encouraged when I returned to my seat in the cockpit.

Hal watched me sit down before bursting my bubble again. "Then what?"

"Sorry?"

"So, you get in and see him. You'll need to have him sign something, right? You haven't thought about that?"

"I had a kind of long night."

"Okay, I'll rattle something up. Keep an eye on things here, please. We should be coming up on Bella Coola in about... 22 minutes."

I watched the needles remain perfectly steady and the unchanging snowy carpet flow by beneath us.

"What name's he using?" Hal called out at one point.

"Archibald Ross."

The printer rattled, then Hal returned with two pieces of paper. One was a printout of the judgment. The second acknowledged the facts on the first, transferred all homestead rights to me, and had a place for signatures. Except I was having trouble concentrating. Lack of sleep, I supposed.

Then Hal frowned, leaned forward and tapped at a gauge. Pushed a press-switch a couple times. "Shit cabin pressure's not holding. We'll have to go down."

Throwing off his headset, he produced some oxygen masks. He hit a knob marked 'O2.' There was a hiss around my face and the fog in my head cleared.

Shaking the yoke disconnected the autopilot. The airplane wobbled slightly. Hal made some trim and prop adjustments and pushed it in again gently. The horizon indicator line elevated, the altitude needle began to unwind, and the cloud surface rose up and engulfed us.

When Hal leveled off again at 6,000 in murky cloud, he pulled off his oxygen mask and motioned me to do the same. "This couldn't be worse, Ben. Just couldn't be worse."

"We'll be okay won't we, at this altitude?"

He shook his head emphatically. "We can't keep this heading. Too much tall terrain. We have to get to the coast, goddammit! That means getting under this shit."

Hal gave a NAV operator his tail number, with two souls aboard. "Uh we need to change our flight plan due to altitude limitations. We're currently at GPS..." He rattled off a string of numbers. "Bella Coola beacon."

"Are you declaring an emergency?"

"Negative."

"Low altitude flight in the vicinity of the Georgia Strait is not recommended at this time."

"Understood. We have terrain and weather radar."

"Acknowledged. Reconfirm at Namu. And good luck."

Luck?

"Will do." He flicked the microphone back to intercom. "Hang on to your seat Ben. This could get very hairy."

We followed the southern shore of Queen Charlotte sound on the terrain radar, for nearly 20 minutes before Hal began inching the plane lower with small trim adjustments. His focus never left the radar displays.

The cloud thinned at around 3,000 feet. We began seeing breaks in it at around 2800. Glimpses of a wrinkled sea began appearing at 2500.

Suddenly we were in clear air and Hal cried out, "Oh fuck hold on!" and lurched the plane into a steep left bank and slight dive. Tiny blobs of white cloud were skidding by around us. Then the plane leveled, and it wasn't cloud. They were geese, white snow-geese stretched out in a long line northbound.

A goose saved my sanity, and now geese are trying to kill me! How ironic is that?

The skein scattering awkwardly on wildly beating wings. Hal turned inland away from them, white-faced and shaking his head. My heart pounded. An improvement. It had seemed to stop for a moment back there.

"Pacific waterfowl migration flight-line. Understand now?"

I nodded. Speech was beyond me.

The remaining 50-minute flight to the island and along its north-eastern coast to Nanaimo was much less eventful. Anything short of kamikaze attacks would have been.

Hal cleared us well in advance for Nanaimo Airport, because unlike the 206 which had two or three knobs, levers and switches to adjust before setting down, the 421C had a whole sheet of activities.

We needed only one go-around, to stay clear of an arriving Jazz Airways turboprop. Then came in from the south, touched down around 1:15 p.m. on the large runway, and taxied leisurely to the commuter-end of the terminal.

SIXTY-SIX

Nanaimo, Vancouver Island
April 18th, early afternoon

The prison took some getting to. Though only a 10-minute drive up Nanaimo Parkway, we had to arrange parking and refueling for the aircraft. And a car.

A Budget agent raised eyebrows when we said we only needed it for a couple hours, but rented me a small Ford.

It was almost 2:00 p.m. when we arrived at a tall hurricane-wire fence with an inward razor-wire overhang. The visitor's section of parking was empty. I stuffed the paperwork in my pocket, and we walked to the gate.

Two very hard and fit-looking men in federal-correction uniforms manned the check-point. The one in charge looked particularly powerful and had black hair cropped military-style. When I said I'd made phone-arrangements to visit Archibald Ross, he shook his head. "My apologies, sir, no can do."

My world came crashing down.

"I'm sorry? They said visiting hours were until 3:00 p.m."

"Shorter hours today sir. We have a lock-down in one section. You'll need to come back tomorrow."

"Can you please make an exception? I've come from Laketown. It's very important."

"I'm sorry sir, I can't let you in. You'll need to come back tomorrow."

It was clear he considered the conversation over. I had to find a way to persuade him. "Is Mr. Ross in the locked down section?"

"Archie? No, he's a lowbie. But it doesn't matter. We're not letting anyone in. I'm sorry!"

It seemed hopeless. Then I saw something across the parking lot. I looked back at the officer and his short haircut. "Thanks anyway officer."

"You're welcome sir. Sorry I couldn't help."

I walked a few yards back toward the rental car, then grabbed Hal by the arm. "Did you bring your mobile phone? Please tell me you did!"

"Sure. Why?"

"Give it to me. Please."

I fumbled out my wallet to find a piece of paper. Punched in a number I'd never called.

"This is Charles."

"Charles, its Ben Adams."

"Ben. Hello."

"You told me I could call if I needed your personal help."

"Sure. Long as there's no conflict. What can I do for you?"

My spirits dived, but I had to try. I looked again at the vehicle in the staff parking area. "Do you happen to know anyone drives a white SUV, with Canadian Special Forces stickers in the back window, and a vanity plate that means maybe, bandy-legged or something like that?"

There were a couple seconds of silence. He asked suspiciously, "Why do you want to know?"

"Charles please! Do you know him or not?"

"Sure I do. David Banderas. Bandy's his nickname. Used to be a Warrant-Officer in my unit at Petawawa. He's not in the military any more though. I heard he's joined the Prison Service. Why are you asking?"

"Big strong guy very short hair?"

"That's him." His voice deepened. "What's going on?"

"I'm looking at him, and I need a huge favor from you. I need you to ask him to let me in to see a prisoner at Nanaimo."

"Who's the prisoner?"

"Adrian Reeman."

"Oh man! Do you realize what you are asking? You want me to go against my own people? How can you ask me that?"

"Charles I really need your help. Is this all about winning? Or about doing the right thing?"

"Damn you! The right thing is taking care of my people! How can you do this?"

"Is that what you fought for? Countryman against countryman?

271

I'm talking about my home. Isn't that supposed to mean something too?"

"Damn you. God damn you!" There was a very long silence. He finally growled resignedly, "Ah put him on."

I walked back to the booth. The officer with the haircut looked at me, slightly annoyed.

"Officer Banderas?"

"Yes. How d'you know that?"

"Someone would like to speak to you."

Five minutes later I was sitting in one of 20-or-so partitioned cubicles in an otherwise very stark visiting-room.

I watched over a chin-high divider as a slightly graying, distinguished-looking African-American man, was led in by a guard and sat down on the opposite side of the divider. He wore a bright orange jumpsuit with 'PRISONER' stenciled in black across the chest.

The guard stepped back a few feet, and stood with his arms folded, appearing disinterested. Reeman and I studied each other for a few moments. Then he said, in a cultured voice that caressed as much as enunciated each syllable, "And you, sir, would be?"

"My name is Ben Adams. I live in the cabin you leased in Laketown."

"Oh yes." He bowed his head in acknowledgment. Smiled. "From the Scottish couple. Lovely people."

"Yes, they are. But from me actually."

"Oh." He raised an eyebrow. "And you would be here because...?"

I explained and he listened courteously. When I mentioned the judgment, and that I had a summary with me he asked to see it. The guard saw me digging and stepped close. "You can't pass anything directly, sir. Show me what you have."

"Oh sorry." I handed the guard the two sheets, but held onto the pen. He scanned them, shrugged, handed them to Reeman and stood back again.

Reeman read carefully for two or three minutes.

Then he looked up and said, "So that I understand this Mr. Adams, you have come here this day to try to obtain a signature, forfeiting my rights to an extremely beautiful and probably quite valuable property, by appealing to my what... good nature?"

"Yes."

"Since you have found me, and believe me I am something of an expert at not being found, you probably know a lot about me.

You should therefore be aware that I do not have one."

"Everyone has their good side."

He snorted derisively. "Au contraire. And you are offering me not a single thing in return?"

"No."

"Mr. Adams, I don't know if you if you are crazy or naïve or both." Reeman gestured around him. "I'm in prison. Why in the world would I do such a thing?"

"It's my home. It's all I have. I hoped you would do it because it's the right thing."

He snorted again.

The guard said, "We're making a special case here mister. Fifteen minutes is all I can give you. You need to finish up."

I was heartsick. I'd expended all this effort for nothing. How could I have been so sure? Reeman was right. I was a naive fool.

But he wasn't done.

He leaned forward so his eyes looked right into mine over the divider. "So, if I sign this paper you will be able to provide it to the court and they will give you this piece of land, to which you feel such attachment, completely freehold?"

"Yes."

The guard uncrossed his arms. It was over. I started to get up.

Reeman said, "Did you bring a pen?"

"Huh?"

"A man cannot be an asshole every single moment of his life. Give the guard the pen so I can sign. And make sure he does too."

"What?"

"You need a witness, correct?"

Hal and I wore grins that just wouldn't quit all the way back to the airport. I clutched the signed document to my chest, knowing all I had to do was get it to the courthouse in Victoria.

Rental car returned, we strolled jubilantly back to where the plane was being serviced. The maintenance supervisor gave us the airport's Wi-Fi details, and by 3:15 p.m. I was online getting the contact details for the court.

Ten minutes after faxing the signed release, I called to confirm they'd received it. I was transferred to a professional-sounding voice belonging to Margaret Whitaker, Chief Clerk of the Court. Savoring the moment, I pressed the 'speaker' button so Hal could listen in.

She said, "Congratulations Mr. Adams. We've received your paperwork and spoken to Judge Volman's office in clarification, also to the Warden up at Nanaimo. It's not on the right form, but we're not going to make a fuss about that. We're prepared to accept it in fulfillment of the court order, subject to a few formalities like affidavits of residency to be provided at a later time."

"Thank you. That's great news." I give Hal a high-five, in his case very high. My face ached with joy.

Ms. Whitaker said, "Now all we need is you."

"Excuse me?"

"Yes, Judge Volman's ruling seemed quite clear but we checked to be sure. I paraphrase. 'The legally entitled person has until close of business at five pee-em on the eighteen of April, to present a homestead claim at this court.' That means in person, Mr. Adams."

"You're joking."

"Not at all. I trust we will see you some time in the next... 95 minutes then?"

"I dearly hope so."

"I'll look forward to it. My office is by the payment windows on the orange floor. Goodbye now."

I looked at Hal in horror. "Can we make it?"

He rubbed his chin with his thumb. "I honestly don't know."

SIXTY-SEVEN

Nanaimo International Airport
3:25 p.m.

We squandered precious minutes considering alternatives.

The maintenance supervisor confirmed there was no helicopter-and-pilot we could rent. Google maps said the center of Victoria was only a hundred kilometers by road, but with weekday rush-hour traffic that wasn't an option.

Hal estimated it would take a half-hour to fly to the small-plane side of Victoria International Airport on the Saanich Peninsula, not counting any delay getting takeoff and landing clearance. Finding a car and driving to Victoria would take about another forty-minutes at that time-of-day. It would be very close. Fortunately, the plane was ready to go.

We caught a break when the tower let us to taxi out immediately, but lost time holding while a Horizon Air flight landed. We were wheels-up at 3:49.

Our flight plan was simple. Straight down the coast as fast-and-low as we were allowed, directly in over the Saanich Inlet with a tight turn for an easterly-landing. And to hope like hell other air-traffic didn't hold us up.

But of-course it did. For several exasperating circuits. Just the same we were on the ground at 4:18, 16 and some miles from central Victoria.

We taxied at the maximum-allowable speed by the shortest-possible route to the commuter parking area.

Then we ran like fiends.

I'd been working the phone all the way down the coast.

Avis had promised to have a Volvo waiting by their counter for a quick pickup. We lost a minute or so showing Hal's credit card and license and squealed out of the parking garage at 4:27.

We ran an orange light turning on to Patricia Bay Parkway. My Google printout said PBP became Blanchard and took us right to the courthouse. Traffic was light and Hal hammered the SUV hard along the divided-highway. Then vehicle-stoplights started to come on ahead. Our speed dropped through 90, 80, 70, 60 kilometers, until we were at a standstill with Hal banging on the steering wheel in frustration. Some distance ahead, workers in orange fluorescent-vests and white hard-hats were clustered around some road re-construction.

4:38. We have to get around this somehow.

Hal's jaw tightened. He wrenched the wheel right, squeezed the SUV out of line, and began driving in the emergency lane. Cars flickered by on our left. Then 50-yards before the road-works, I saw a red-white-and-blue Crown Victoria with rooflights, in line. Before I could warn Hal, we were past it and he was looking for a way around the yellow tape.

Behind us came a short blast from a siren and roof-lights came on. Hal swung right into a side road, cut across traffic, and rejoined the now wide-open parkway; accelerating furiously. I prayed the RCMP cruiser had stayed stuck in traffic. But within three miles it raced up alongside us, lights flashing.

There were two Mounties aboard. As we all rolled to a stop Hal's head was on his hands, high on the steering wheel. The passenger got out, put on his hat, came to the driver's window and asked Hal for his license.

4:44. We'll never make it. We're beaten.

But I had one last piece on the board left to play. I might be besieged by rooks and knights and bishops but I still had that one piece and I decided to play it, right or wrong.

I pulled out my wallet and Hal's phone and found the card. A calm authoritative voice answered, and I interrupted and blurted out the situation in 30-seconds of breathless un-punctuated-monologue. When I stopped talking the voice said, "Just tell me the number off the back of the cruiser. Now!" I did, and the call cut off.

4:46.

The trooper with Hal's license was writing on a small clipboard. I saw the one in the cruiser pick up a microphone and have a short conversation. Then he climbed quickly out of the vehicle and called to his partner. They converged on my window. I lowered it. The one from the car said, "Sir, if your name is Adams, you're under arrest. Would you step out of the vehicle, please?"

"What? What for?"

"Attempting to influence an RCMP officer in the line of his duties. Get out of the vehicle now. Sir!"

They hustled me to the cruiser and shoved me in the back seat where I slumped. The door closed like a tomb being sealed. The troopers leapt in and the cruiser screeched away down the highway with blazing roof-lights reflecting off every vehicle we passed.

They're sure in a damn hurry to lock me up.

The traffic parted like the red sea before Moses, but quickly became heavier. At each major intersection they blipped the siren, edged across and then floored it, most times on the wrong side on the road.

The court building I'd been trying so hard to reach appeared ahead, taunting me. I felt like I'd swallowed razor-blades.

How can I have come so close and still failed?

Then, before we passed it by, the cruiser swerved and screeched across traffic into Burdett Avenue. The driver killed the overhead-lights as we rolled to a halt on the wrong side of the road outside the courtroom security-entrance. The passenger-side Mountie jumped out and opened the back door. "Do you know where you're going?"

In that instant I understood.

I looked down at my watch. 4:57. At the same moment the Mountie hoisted me bodily out of my seat and growled in my ear, "You'd better run. We'll wait here."

I sprinted up the steps. Two security guards tried to block the door. The Mountie shouted, "Let him through!" They stepped aside and I was inside by the lifts.

No time for those.

I dashed to the stairs and raced up two-at-a-time. When I stumbled out onto the orange floor, panting, side aching, I saw metal screens coming down over the payment windows. I forced my legs to move. Stumbled toward them.

Ten yards. Five.

A door opened and a red-haired woman stepped out. I looked at her imploringly.

She smiled.

"Mr. Adams? I'm Margaret. This way please."

SIXTY-EIGHT

Redemption Cove, British Columbia
Sometime later

Nancy Robitaille came to see me in the summer. We took seats on the deck and she sat with her tiny hands clasped. She gazed across the lake in silence. I wasn't sure what to say, so I waited. She said wistfully, "I remember walking here when I was a little girl."

"Oh?"

"Yes, with my brothers. They had a trap-line and I would go with them. It was beautiful then too."

"I'm sure it was."

She turned to me and said, "Mr. Adams I came by to say we have no hard feelings at your success."

"Thank you."

"May I call you Ben?"

"Of course."

"I sometimes wonder what you think of us."

"Well, I sometimes wonder why there's not more anger."

"We do have that element of-course. Resentment has poisoned some of our families."

"I have some first-hand knowledge of that."

She nodded. "I was an angry activist myself when I wasn't much older than those boys. It wasn't that long ago I came to realize how counterproductive bitterness can be. I hope they'll come to that realization themselves, one day. In the mean-time Charles is working with them. It's a matter of providing alternatives."

I recalled stories of sweat-lodge ceremonies. "Re-establishing traditions?"

"Jobs, Ben."

"What happened to being close to the land? Hearing it sing?"

"You're entitled to be cynical. Lawyers say what they choose and courts are naturally adversarial."

"So, you'll expand your tourist interests? Perhaps a chain of model Indian-settlements showing the history of your people?"

"You've been watching too many westerns on television. We were putting in a casino right here. Chinese finance. Since the decision, the architects have been working on a design closer to the main highway. You'll see activity there soon."

"I wish you well."

"As I do you. You know, if this were the old days, you would have been considered a warrior."

"I'm honored."

She nodded again and got up and smiled at me. "Goodbye for now Ben. I hope we will be good neighbors for a long time."

I took her hand in mine, a simple short clasp. Then she walked, serene and dignified, to her Grand Cherokee and drove away.

That was on a gorgeous evening just like this one, with a warm pine-scented breeze flicking at the tufts of grass along the verge.

But I don't stay full-time here at Redemption Cove any more. Marge's father Howard passed from cancer and they moved to Lucy's larger house to take care of her. I live in theirs with an option to buy because it's closer to my work. John has me hooked on ice fishing now. Last winter I caught a 16-kilo Lake-Char on Beauchamp Lake, though I don't want to brag.

The work part I mentioned came about when Bertrand Latour approached me to become Chef at McGee's. I'm not worthy of that title yet, but I'm trying hard. And getting plenty of practice since business is booming with the increased tourism from the Nations' venture. I see Chief Charles is getting a good-deal of national media-attention as a progressive First Nation' leader.

If that didn't keep me busy enough, Otto Mueller sold Bertrand and me the store, and that's going extremely well too.

Sergeant Major McKinnon's career survived the reprimand he received for misuse-of-resources on the day of the mad-dash to the courthouse. He's the head of special-tactics in Smithers now, though I still see him on occasion.

Hal got his instructors' license and taught to fly the 206 as a floater, and multi-engine aircraft, as well as under instrument-rules. We still get up as often as we can, though it's been harder since Grant Summers resigned over the scandal that saw James Hanrahan and Herman Peters jailed for bank-embezzlement and civic-fraud, and Hal became Mayor. I'm proud as hell to be godfather of Hal and Jessica's first son, Anthony Benyamin Pritchard.

Speaking of young people, I've been twice to Colorado in the 421C. I can't say we're close yet, but the situation seems to be improving. I have a lot of ground to make up.

Each spring and fall I watch the geese fly across the smoky sky and remember the friend that came and saved my life and flew away.

And I regularly tend a small plot at the memorial gardens, and think about a time and a love that was not for always, just forever.

~~~~

ACKNOWLEDGMENTS

I owe too much to too many people in writing this novel to name them all here, but would like to thank a few in particular. My dear friend Jan Wilcox for her invaluable help with early versions of the manuscript, and her caring and support in all things. Dawa Rowley, my wonderful editor - you're the best! My beta readers - Pauline Schiappa, Joel Niemeyer and Ian Howard. Audrea and Harald Wulf for their kindness, hospitality, wine, and marvelous tales of life in the far northwest, Staff Sergeant Mike Kisters of the RCMP for his invaluable advice on northwest policing. Robert Exell for his most informative treatise 'History of Indian Land Claims in B.C.' Last but never least, my family to whom I owe everything.

For my successes I am beholden to the people who have assisted me. My mistakes are all my own.

www.ingramcontent.com/pod-product-compliance
Lightning Source LLC
Chambersburg PA
CBHW021414110726
47901CB00008B/2169